TWISTED ECHOES

Also by David Sale

Come to Mother
The Love Bite

TWISTED ECHOES

David Sale

HEADLINE

First published in 1993
by HEADLINE BOOK PUBLISHING PLC

10 9 8 7 6 5 4 3 2 1

Grateful acknowledgement is made for permission to
quote from the following lyrics: 'Tenderly', Warner
Chappell Music Ltd/International Music Publications.
'Everything I Have Is Yours', Lyric by Harold Adamson.
Copyright © 1933 (renewed 1961) Metro-Goldwyn-Mayer
Inc. c/o EMI ROBBINS CATALOG INC. Worldwide
Reprint Rights granted by CPP/BELWIN, INC., Miami,
Florida 33014 USA. All rights reserved. Lyrics reproduced
by permission of the Copyright Owners.

British Library Cataloguing in Publication Data

Sale, David
Twisted Echoes
I. Title
823.914 [F]

ISBN 0–7472–0746–1

Phototypeset by Intype, London
Printed and bound in Great Britain by
Clays Ltd, St Ives PLC

HEADLINE BOOK PUBLISHING PLC
Headline House
79 Great Titchfield Street
London W1P 7FN

To

ROB LOVELL

ACKNOWLEDGEMENTS

For generously sharing their knowledge with me, my heartfelt thanks go to Lorrae Desmond; Dr Bruce Benjamin; two of the recording industry's good guys – Rod Tamlyn and Leon Gaer; and, of course, to all the kids who shall remain nameless.

PART I

'By 1990, no Australian child will live in poverty'

R. J. L. HAWKE,
Prime Minister of Australia, 1987

1

Somewhere between seven-thirty and eight o'clock on an otherwise ordinary Tuesday evening there came a moment which shattered Allan Steinbeck's life, resulted in five violent deaths and irrevocably changed the lives of at least four other people.

As usual the television was on, the sound turned up high in a vain attempt to drown out the baby's fractious cries.

Allan swirled the remains of his third scotch around in the glass, impatiently. Tonight's edition of *Upfront*, a current affairs program which followed the evening news bulletin, was proving a bore. A dull item backgrounding yet another move to legalise the use of marijuana had been succeeded by an equally tedious account of a faded stage star's successful heart transplant.

And now came more commercials.

The living room could have doubled for a sauna. Allan felt hot and hungry and sick to death of the baby's noise. He glanced across to where his wife was rocking their baby back and forth to little effect.

'When can we expect to eat?'

Joan Steinbeck was wiping dribble from the baby's chin with a wad of Kleenex, dabbing it from side to side and sometimes missing the target as the baby jerked its head perversely to avoid her ministrations. She replied without looking up.

'I can't do everything. His chest's playing up again.'

As if to substantiate her words, the baby's screams gave way to a violent outburst of coughing; harsh, hacking coughs which forced their way up the tiny respiratory tract, causing frothy gobs of saliva to well from the tortured rosebud of a mouth. Joan grabbed a handful of fresh tissues from the box.

'You see?'

Her voice had an accusing tone as if the coughing had been deliberately triggered off by Allan's question.

Allan bit back a retort. That was the way rows started these days.

3

He looked at her and saw the lacklustre hair scraped back into an untidy knot, the pallid face and the untidy, stained maternity smock, an unnecessary and unsuitable leftover from the palmy days of pregnancy. He wondered where she'd gone, the attractive young advertising executive, the one who fourteen months before had announced she was taking a year off to have this baby, then it would be back to business as usual.

And why did she have to appear so careworn and badly done by? God knows, she had enough help. There was a cleaning woman for the housework, and someone else to do the washing and ironing. The trouble was that she was enormously unconcerned about everything except her child.

Her child.

Not *their* child.

She had no time for herself, her husband, nor interests of any other kind. No north, south, east, west. No far horizons. Just a tunnel view of the kid and all its clamorous, disgusting functions and malfunctions.

Allan sighed. Perhaps it would pass. Maybe it was natural. He would just have to bear it for as long as it took and get by as best he could. There were always compensations of one kind or another he had found, even in the most difficult of situations. One door closed, another opened.

He heaved himself up from his armchair just as the commercial break ended. Might as well have another drink. At this rate, dinner could end up being a midnight snack. He walked across to the sideboard where the liquor was assembled on a silver tray, courtesy of Doris Lytton-Scott, and heard the anchor man introducing another (probably just as boring) item.

'. . . and what's more, the statistics are awesome. Frightening. Fifty thousand homeless youngsters in Australia. Awesome because of their numbers. Frightening because most of them actually *choose* to be homeless, they actually *choose* a life of hazardous vagrancy on the streets in preference to domestic violence and parents who are uncaring or cruel or both.'

Allan splashed a good two inches of whisky into his glass. In this heat, he could use some more ice. He started for the kitchen, glancing back at the screen.

There had been a vision mix from the anchor man to film. One of the program's regular reporters, a classy-looking blonde, was speaking to camera against a background of garish neon signs which plugged bars, fast food outlets and strip joints.

'I'm Sharon Pettifer and this is Kings Cross or, as it's affectionately known "the Cross" – an apt name, considering that this is
where we crucify our children.

'Ninety percent of Sydney's runaways head straight for this place
like flies to a honey pot. But the Cross is no honey pot. It's a
web, a spider's web of drugs and disease, pushers and prostitution,
starvation and suicide.

'Then why do they come here?' She paused and permitted a
wry smile. 'We've had enough theorising from the do-gooders, the
psychologists, the social workers. This time around, we asked those
who really know the scene – the kids themselves. To seek them
out, we went underground. We filmed them on the beats, in the
squats, along the back alleys, amongst the garbage . . .'

Allan paused in the kitchen doorway. This sounded as though it
could be interesting.

Joan's voice cut across the reporter's commentary.

'If you're going to the kitchen, would you bring the baby's linctus
and a teaspoon? It's a small brown bottle in the cupboard where I
keep all the baby food and stuff. And if it's not there, it'll be on
the shelf over the sink.'

The baby's coughing fit had subsided, but its breathing was
laboured and rasping. Allan looked back at the screen. Now, the
cameraman was shooting from a slowly moving vehicle, cruising
along Darlinghurst Road.

'At first sight,' came the reporter's voice-over, 'this seems like a
glittering road to adventure. Too late, kids find it's a one-way street
with no going back. For many, it's a dead end in more ways than
one . . .'

'Allan!'

Joan's voice whined insistently.

Allan went to the kitchen. The TV report had caught his interest
and now he was keen to get back and see the rest of it. Quickly,
he went over to the fridge and took out a tray of ice cubes. He
twisted the tray this way and that, but they refused to budge. He
wrestled with it some more, then gave up in exasperation and
slammed the tray against the inside of the sink. Ice cubes went
everywhere. He scooped three or four into his glass, then picked
up three or four more from the floor and threw them into the sink
with the rest. He took a quick swallow of the drink on the way
over to the cutlery drawer and grimaced because, despite the ice
cubes, the scotch was still warm from the bottle. Having grabbed
a teaspoon from the drawer, he slammed it shut and looked for the

bottle of linctus in the cupboard Joan had stipulated. It wasn't there. It wasn't on the shelf over the sink either, so he went back to the cupboard and stood there letting his eyes sweep over the contents, shelf by shelf.

It drifted into the kitchen on the sultry air like a half-remembered aroma. But it wasn't an aroma, it was a sound.

The sound of a voice.

It teased at his subconscious for several seconds before he became fully aware of it. At first, as his mind groped towards recognition, he assumed that it must be Joan speaking softly to the baby. And then he realised that for all its softly persuasive modulation, the voice was much deeper than his wife's and had a metallic edge achieved only by recording techniques.

And yet it was so familiar to him.

A strangled cry, almost a yelp, came from the living room. That was most certainly Joan. Was she annoyed, impatient for the linctus? No. The cry conveyed a sense of surprise . . . shock, an exclamation mark not at the end but in the middle of a sentence being spoken by the voice.

The voice.

And then full recognition hit him with the crushing intensity of an avalanche. Dropping the teaspoon, slopping his drink over the sides of the glass, he hurried to the door and out into the living room.

Joan was standing there, clutching the now silent baby to her bosom. Her eyes were riveted to the television screen. In the kitchen doorway, Allan stood and felt all the heat drain out of him leaving him as cold and clammy as a corpse.

She spoke, over the sound from the TV, her voice now shrill and staccato.

'It's you, isn't it? I mean, it *is*, isn't it? Look! It's you, Allan, it's you!'

And on the screen he saw the spurting puffball of the El Alamein fountain. In the foreground was the boy. And himself, head close to the boy, talking persuasively. Oh yes, anyone could see it was him. The eyes, the light catching the cheekbones, the tilt of his nose, the generous full-lipped curve of his mouth, even the sandy colour of his hair.

Then the image was gone and the camera was inspecting the interior of a filthy squat, its eye lingering on battered inner springs and rubbish-tip decor.

Joan literally ripped her startled gaze from the screen and turned to face him accusingly. She still held the baby tightly against herself as if surgery would be the only means of dividing them into separate entities. Her face crumpled with anguish and disgust.

'You. With that – that boy. And . . . oh, my God, the things you were saying to him . . .'

Her voice choked into silence.

The baby coughed twice, gurgled and became quiet.

Allan stood there. Silent. Unmoving. There was nothing to say. He had been there on the screen in vision and sound and he had no defence.

Joan had seen him.

And the terrible reality came to him that others would have seen him, too. And recognised him.

Joan gulped in air as if preparing to say something more. But she was incapable of speech. She gathered the baby even closer, turned and ran out of the room. He heard the bedroom door slam behind her.

On the screen, a girl in her early teens with the face of a fifty-year-old was saying:

'Generally, when you've got nowhere to go, you can get a feed out of a bin. Maybe somebody's old fish and chips . . .'

2

The fragment of crack gleamed with a mysterious opalescence as if it were precious quartz dug out of a rich vein in some forgotten mine, instead of a lump of synthetic shit.

Andy, front man of Zapperama, shoved his sweaty palm closer to the boy.

'Go on. Take it, mate. It's on the house.'

Kenneth Mitchell didn't move. To take one step backwards would be akin to giving in. He let his head flop on one side and tried to look Andy straight in the eye, which was difficult because the man's protuberant eyeballs had a habit of moving independently of one another. An oculist's dream was the tactician's nightmare. Kenneth tried not to let it faze him.

'I don't use the stuff, Andy. I told you – I'm straight.'

There, it happened again. Andy glanced up the avenue of wall-to-wall video games to make sure no one was watching and his eyeballs swivelled in different directions. Then they united in a single gaze, to focus on the screen of 'Rodor Skyfire' behind Kenneth.

'A hundred and fifty-eight thousand four hundred,' he mused, reading the score Kenneth had reached in his last game, 'that's still the record, eh? You're still the champ.'

'Nobody can top me on "Ninja Warriors" and "Vindicators" either,' Kenneth was quick to point out.

Andy shook his head solemnly. 'Thing is, you'll never better them scores, will you? You need something to sharpen your wits, something to get the cogs moving and them fingers jabbing even faster.' He looked down at the crack he was cradling in his hand. 'This'd do it.'

'I bet they say that to athletes on steroids, too. And everything's excellent till their balls drop off. No thanks, Andy.'

'You've been listening to too much bad-mouthing from too many stitched-up holy rollers, you have. They don't want no one having any fun.'

'I haven't just been listening, I've seen it happen. To practically every kid I know. Remember Chris who brought me in here when I first came to the Cross?'

Andy tried to cast his mind back, but couldn't go beyond the week before. He scratched his patchy grey crew cut and took a punt on what he liked to think was one of the positive scenarios awaiting his young regulars.

'Didn't he split? Isn't he shacked up with some filthy-rich archi-tect in Vaucluse?'

Kenneth shook his head. 'I just heard he carked it. He busted out of a methadone program and OD'd.'

Now Kenneth's head jutted forward belligerently.

'He showed me the ropes when I was new up here. And he told me things. Like how he got on to heroin because all his mates were using. They told him it was better than dope and made you feel good and you wouldn't worry about nothing. So he tried it and felt good and all his hassles were gone, and he told me he just liked the way heroin felt, sort of, and getting high was good.

'But then he started to get sick and that, and he wanted more and more, just to make himself feel better, except he never did. So I know what happens, and I know it's happening to almost every kid around here. Every kid except me.'

Andy shifted his bulk uneasily. This one rattled on too much. Usually, a kid wouldn't put more than two words together, and even when they did they just grunted like a zombie.

'You'd better be careful what you say, son. Otherwise you might not be welcome in here.'

Now it was Kenneth's turn to feel uneasy. They were like a brotherhood, kind of, all the kids that played the videos. And Zapperama was somewhere to go, off the streets. You could forget everything when your eyes were glued to the screen and your mind was on the game. You could forget about being scared because you had nowhere to stay, or because some rock spider might beat you up for not doing what he wanted you to do, or because some hoons on the town of a Saturday night might bash you just for kicks, or because you hadn't eaten anything for a few days, or because you didn't have any money and no prospects other than thieving or a quick trick.

He had to cool it, get in good with Andy again. Andy wasn't

9

really the boss at Zapperama, but he was the one who counted.

The real owner, so the word had got around, was a highly respectable and respected bigwig in the banking world who had a mansion up the North Shore, a hobby farm around Gosford way, a wife who was forever grinning at you from the society pages and two sons at Cranbrook. And he didn't just own Zapperama, he owned the whole block and that meant the Chinese takeaway on one side, the cheap flophouse – now boarded up since a fire had crisped three backpackers – on the other, a brothel, a Thai restaurant, the Purple Orchid bar and strip show, a bottle shop, and half a dozen terraces coverted into offices.

But at Zapperama, Andy was king and Kenneth's survival instincts told him he'd gone too far. Maybe he should have just accepted the crack, pretended to use it, then faked the effects. Maybe he should have just used it. After all, it wouldn't have been the first time, despite all that crap about Chris. Now it was too late. The 'gift' had been knocked back.

Gift.

Free the first time, then you never stopped paying once you were hooked. The same, tired old story. The prospect of having some big money soon had made him resent being pushed around, being forced deeper into the pit he was desperate to get out of. But he shouldn't have showed it.

'You owe me, you know,' Andy was saying. 'Handouts so's you can play the games when you're broke. Using this place as a pick-up joint. Somewhere to get rid of the stuff you pinch.'

Owe you? Kenneth wanted to yell. The big fat pig had just listed the very reasons for Zapperama's existence, plus its being a marketplace for the bigwig's thriving drug syndicate. He swallowed.

'Aw, Andy. Give us a go. You know me, I'll be in anything. It's just . . . tonight I feel crook. Sick in my stomach.'

He put on his forlorn look and stretched out a hand to touch the man's fat arm.

His plaintive act plus the slight physical contact seemed to work. Andy rolled his eyes to the two rotating electric fans at ceiling height, one eyeball to a fan, or so it seemed.

'Yeah, it's stinkin' hot in here, too, that doesn't help any. I keep on askin' for air conditioning, but it's like talking to a brick wall.'

Just then, Lulu arrived from the Mandarin's Kitchen next door with Andy's evening meal order in four foil containers. When she'd gone, Andy gave Kenneth a suggestive wink.

'How about coming in the back? Half the food for a bit of fun.'

The sickening prospect of that lent a convincing realism to Kenneth's act. He shook his head wistfully.

'Aw gee,' he said with regret. 'If only I didn't feel so crook. Besides, I've got to go soon.'

Andy shrugged and carried his food into the back room, trailing an odour of rancid cooking oil.

Kenneth turned back to 'Rodor Skyfire'. The harsh fluorescent lights overhead made his reflection in the game's screen a sharp study in black and white. He saw dark hair, shaved short at the sides, a tousled mass on top. There were two cavernous holes where his eyes should have been, and his cheekbones crowned sooty hollows. His mouth was a depressingly downward smear. He realised he needn't try consciously for a forlorn look any more.

It was there all the time.

3

The traffic along William Street was as sluggish as blood in a thickened artery. Half of Sydney seemed to be making its way to Kings Cross, belts unbuckled, flies unzipped, inhibitions left at home with the greasy dishes. This wasn't the half that regarded the Cross as sleazy and overrated and utterly undeserving of a romanticised reputation founded on fables of naughty sex and good-natured sin. This was the half conned by the legends.

On this Tuesday night there seemed to be a Saturday night bottleneck of vehicles, all crawling as if not anxious to get anywhere. Perhaps it was the heat. The air was heavy with it, hanging like damp drapes. It enervated and seemed even to drain the automatic efficiency of the traffic lights which clicked to red and stayed there.

Allan Steinbeck stared at the red light, willing it to change to green. The air conditioning had packed up in the car but it didn't matter, he remained cold.

It seemed strange.

All the passions, every emotion he had suffered in the past hour – shock, fury, frustration, despair – were those that generated heat. They had surged through him in a holding pattern, one agonisingly succeeding the other, round and around. But not one of them could banish the iciness of the fear which had gripped him initially, the awful horror of having his most subterranean self revealed.

In the meantime his mind, his bruised and reeling mind, had managed to sculpt the formless mass of what had happened into a shape that could be comprehended.

It had been a set-up, of course. A trap. And he had walked right into it. The boy had been the bait, a decoy wired for sound, a decoy who had manoeuvred him into the range of a hidden camera for all to see.

Allan glanced to the car on his right. The driver was leaning towards him, making signs for him to wind down his window.

Allan shivered and felt sick. Had it started already? Had the man recognised him?

He forced himself to look straight ahead. There was no way the man could get at him.

Out of the corner of his eye he could see the man was still making signs. On an impulse, he wound down the window and looked inquiringly at his neighbour.

'Just heard it on the radio, mate,' the man said. 'There's been a three car collision up ahead, right across the entrance to the Kings Cross Tunnel. That's what's causing this bloody bank-up. Just thought you'd like to know.'

'Wondered what it was,' Allan replied. Relieved, he forced a smile and nodded. 'Thanks.'

At that moment, the lights turned green and the cars in front edged forward. Allan's car barely made it over the intersection before there was another halt. He shrugged it off. Delays didn't matter any more. He'd get there sooner or later and there was one sure thing about the Cross – it never closed.

The iciness of his body temperature hadn't changed, but the reasons for it had. Now, the chill of fear was the cold-blooded anticipation of retribution. There would be a certain relief in carrying it out. A cleansing. The grim satisfaction of an eye for an eye.

Idly, his gaze drifted to the pavement on his left. Up ahead, a couple of transvestites, arm in arm and dressed in the style of movie stars of the nineteen-forties, brought hoots and yells from a carload of young men and wiggled their bottoms even more feverishly as they turned down a side street. A drunk collided with a parking meter and hung on to it, talking to it like a buddy. A group of yuppie types passed him, smiling as if the drunk were a busker, doing his stuff for their enjoyment. They were still smiling as they walked into the Boulevard Hotel.

The whores were out in force like beetles coaxed out of their nests by the warmth of the evening, moving in a desultory saraband from corner to doorway to kerb. The heels were stilt-high, the minis crotch-high and the minds drug-high.

One of them caught him staring and started to move towards the car. He turned to face front immediately.

'I wasn't looking at you, I was admiring the Mercedes Benz in the showroom window,' he would say if she tapped on his window with her claw-clone orange fingernails.

No, that would sound weak and apologetic and she'd just stand there and jeer at him, making a scene. 'Piss off' would get rid of her more satisfactorily. But it didn't come to that. The line of traffic started to move again and this time he had a-clear run through to the top of William Street. He took a left turn, veered into Victoria Street and was lucky enough to find a parking space by the kerb halfway down.

As he locked the car door, he detected the acrid smell of woodsmoke. He remembered that at least four major bushfires had been blazing out of control in the Blue Mountains since yesterday. And now there was misty rain in the air, not falling, just suspended like airborne dew.

The moisture and the windsmoke seemed to intensify the suffocating heat. Allan pushed off down Victoria Street. His stride was purposeful. The devious little bastard could be in any one of half a dozen places. He intended to check out them all.

4

Kenneth was getting twitchy.

Andy would have finished stuffing Chinese chow into his gut by now and any minute he'd reappear burping and farting, all ready to start leaning on him again. Kenneth had already conned a couple of coins from Dino who was high on speed and playing 'Double Dragon' down near the door. He'd used the money on two more 'Skyfire' games and not even got close to his champion scores. That showed how edgy he was. He couldn't just stand there, leaning against the machine all night. He'd have to go. But where?

He didn't want to go back to the squat. He could handle the filth and the rats, but he couldn't handle Donna. Sometimes she got violent and cut up her wrists with broken glass or tin-can lids. Once, she'd crawled back after being beaten up and wouldn't even let him touch her, when all he wanted to do was try and ease the pain. Another time, he'd found her screaming after some guys had butted out their smokes on her tits. There was always something new, and it was always something more shocking.

The heat-sodden air carried in all the fried-rice smells from next door like it was a magic carpet someone had vomited on. Muted explosions, gunshots and the stretched-out whine of lasers came from the machines as men, monsters and missiles were pulverised electronically. All good clean fun.

More kids drifted in.

Apart from Dino, Kenneth didn't recognise any of them. A new batch, fresh from the suburbs. Baked to rebellious perfection in the parent-controlled pressure cookers of the family torture chambers.

They seemed to get younger all the time.

Some of them didn't look more than eight or nine, swaggering around with a kind of desperate bravado, loudly trying to drown out their insecurities. And because they were small and undeveloped and their unravaged choirboy faces hadn't yet acquired the rat-like sly look or the living dead visage or otherwise gone through

15

the fast-forward aging process of the streets, they appeared as vulnerable midget clowns, romping briefly into the arena. They would either disappear unaccountably in an instant, or take further bows in rapidly changing, increasingly less attractive disguises. And then you'd hear they'd been found dead in an alley with needle marks peppering their arms and that final lethal cocktail flooding their still-innocent veins. Or that they'd hung themselves. Or that they'd been physically beaten to the consistency of mashed potatoes. Or that they were sliding down the rotting helter-skelter of AIDS.

Kenneth turned back and took another quick look at his reflection.

What did *he* really look like?

Vanity had never come into it before. The mere fact of being young was passport enough in the Cross. It seemed an eternity since he had taken a good, long, hard look at himself in a mirror. There were reasons. Squats didn't come with furnished bathrooms. And the mirrors in public toilets were usually flyblown and stained and enabled you to see just enough to make sure that your hair was back off your face and that you were at least one or two neat steps up from a derelict. Besides which, you made any such pampering brief and you got out of public toilets quick, if you were young and in Kings Cross and had other things to do besides get molested.

Somebody stumbled against him and he turned around.

It was a kid called Matthew whose pale blonde hair, bloodless complexion and skinny build gave him the look of an albino ferret.

'Hey man, I just scored,' he said, and from the vacant look in his eyes Kenneth knew he wasn't referring to one of the games. Rumoured to have rich, influential parents who found him an embarrassment, Matthew's life was a constant quest for oblivion, a state he was achieving with alarming regularity and for longer periods each time.

'You oughta find somewhere to crash,' Kenneth told him. 'How much have you had?'

'Enough, man. Just enough,' replied Matthew, swaying. He elongated the 'just' into an arc of dreamy content. Then, sensing Kenneth's concern, he smiled emptily.

'It's only a drug. It's not gonna kill me. I can beat it any time I want to.'

It was Chris all over again, Kenneth thought wearily, not that it really mattered because there'd always be a Chris and there'd always be a Matthew.

Then Dino, up near the entrance, yelled that somebody outside wanted to see him. Not a cop, no risk, just a bloke.

Kenneth propped Matthew up between two of the games and immediately the boy slid down to the floor. Kenneth let him lie there and started towards the entrance and suddenly he was filled with an agonised longing for some kind of home, some kind of security, some kind of peace. He didn't give a thought as to who could be wanting to see him. At least it gave him a reason to leave Zapperama before Andy reappeared.

Outside, there was a fine mist of rain. Within a moment his skin, his T-shirt and his jeans were glistening with moisture.

Kenneth looked from side to side. The usual types were hanging around but nobody approached him. The spruiker outside the Purple Orchid was huddled under the canopy over the club's entrance and half-heartedly urging passers-by to come in and see the greatest sex show on earth. Maritza, a fortune teller as old as the Cross itself, was hastily folding up her card table, caught by the rain and making ready to scurry for cover. You'd think she'd know in advance, wouldn't you? Kenneth thought as he looked the other way up the street.

Someone was hurrying towards him, but it turned out to be a man holding his head at an angle so that the rain might wash the blood off his face. The man blundered across the road brushing with death at least twice as cars swerved to avoid him, then disappeared on the other side.

Kenneth stood there at a loss. Was Dino having him on? No. Jokes weren't Dino's scene, or any other kid's for that matter. He walked a few steps to the left across the front of the Mandarin's Kitchen, keeping an eye out for someone he might recognise. Then he turned back and, keeping close to the buildings to avoid the rain, passed the entrance to Zapperama.

Just as he had almost passed the burnt-out flophouse, he was grabbed from behind and dragged back into the darkened doorway. A strong arm went across his neck, almost choking him. His left arm was grasped at the wrist and bent upwards, his fingers almost touching his neck.

Unable to breathe and with his arm excruciatingly bent to breaking point, he was pulled further back into the dark.

5

Allan Steinbeck held the boy there, crushingly, gaining a special satisfaction from the hoarse gasping for breath, the thudding of heartbeats accelerated by fear and the painful arching of the thin body as he forced the arm even higher.

They stayed there in the gloom of the doorway, Allan with his back pressed against the boards which had been hammered across the hotel's entrance, two figures carved from a single piece of stone, forever locked together by the art of a sadistic sculptor.

And then it came to Allan that in his planning, this was as far as cold fury had led him. The fervour of revenge had spurred him on, even when his search had seemed destined to fail, when the drizzling rain had soaked him to the skin and had cleared the streets and the notorious beats. It was only now, with the stinking little betrayer literally in his clutches, that Allan realised this was as far as he'd thought ahead. Beyond was just a satisfying but confused blur of fists hitting flesh, bruising and drawing blood; the snap and crunch of broken bones and the thumping and kicking and twisting and tearing of an ecstasy of violence against the one who had inflicted upon him the ultimate in humiliation.

It was most unusual for Allan not to have thought out his plans every step of the way. On other occasions, he had gone into action with each detail carefully considered. But on other occasions he'd had the time to formulate his strategy, whereas this evening's events had happened too quickly, catching him off guard. He had no doubt that he was still a brilliant strategist, given the opportunity. But there was no getting away from it, he hadn't ventured on to this plain of self-survival for a long, long time. He was a little rusty. He'd grown complacent over the years, perhaps *too* complacent—

The boy wriggled and Allan held him even tighter, jabbing the arm up further and intensifying the lock he had against the boy's windpipe. He couldn't do any of the things he wanted to do here in this doorway. Anything he did there would have to be quick, whereas he wanted the retribution to be long and lingering. He had practically cut off the boy's breathing, squashing the Adam's apple back into the throat. The strangled gasps were coming more slowly and the heartbeat he felt through the boy's back was fluttering wildly. He'd have to think of something quickly, otherwise he'd have a corpse on his hands.

There was only one way, and the realisation of it brought home to him that his approach had been all wrong. He should have greeted the boy like a friend and on some persuasive pretext or other got him back to the car, knocked him senseless with a swift belt to the jaw, bundled him into the car, then driven to one of several isolated spots which came to mind.

But no. He couldn't blame himself for not thinking more clearly, not after the shock he'd had, not with the blind fury building up inside him.

He could still get the boy back to the car by force. It would be risky, but he could do it. He *had* to do it.

6

Kenneth was just about to lapse into unconsciousness when the pressure on his throat was relaxed. He coughed and gulped air into his lungs while the stars which had faded as he became weaker now burst explosively in front of his eyes again. The man's arm had slipped down across his chest, still holding him firmly. It was just as well. Kenneth felt his legs folding and needed the support.

The man spoke into his ear.

'I don't want any trouble from you. At the first sign, I'll break your arm, and that'll be just for starters.'

Kenneth found himself surprised at the threat to break his arm. From the pain, he'd assumed it was broken already.

There was a pause. The man breathed hotly into his ear. He wasn't some western suburbs hoon, that was for sure. His accent had been polished by education and his voice, even as a hoarse whisper, had none of the roughness of a Kings Cross desperado. And it was because of these qualities that his threat held more menace. Kenneth reckoned he'd heard the voice somewhere, but before he had time to consider where and when the man was speaking again.

'This is what we're going to do. We're going to cross to the other side of the street and go on from there. We'll be sticking close together and I don't want any trouble, understand?'

Kenneth tried to twist his head around to look up at the man's face, but couldn't. As the jumble in his mind started to sort itself out, it came through loud and clear that there had to be a reason for this. It wasn't a casual mugging for gain or kicks. He had been conned into leaving Zapperama for a purpose.

Him. Not just any kid. Kenneth. Asked for by name, and then set upon with a violence that was almost fatal.

And still it wasn't over. He tried to speak between the gasps for breath.

'Why . . . ?'

20

'Shut up!'

The tone was vicious, the instruction final.

Keeping Kenneth's arm firmly and painfully pinned up his back, the man relaxed his hold across the boy's chest. He gave Kenneth a push out of the doorway, then put his arm protectively – or what would appear so to the casual observer – around his captive's shoulder. At Kenneth's side, but slightly behind to mask the hold he had on the twisted arm, the man was in complete control.

He guided Kenneth quickly across the pavement, then over the roadway on to the other side of the street. To anyone who happened to look, they were two people, man and boy, huddled protectively together and hurrying through the rain. And raining it was, no longer a misty drizzle but a heavy fall.

The cool splashes on his face helped revive Kenneth, but his legs were still weak and he would have fallen but for the man's grip around his shoulders.

'Slow down a bit . . . slow down,' he gasped, and because they had turned abruptly into an alley where there was no one else in sight the man did so, but only a fraction.

On one side of the alley was the blank, high wall of an old apartment block. On the other side, a row of dilapidated cottages waited like bad teeth for the developer/dentist to come and yank them out.

Kenneth felt completely powerless. To yell out for help would be useless. By the time anyone came – and in the Cross, where yells and screams were as familiar as birdsong in a country lane, that was extremely unlikely – he could be lying dead in the gutter. Besides, his throat was so dry and painful, a cry for help that would carry any distance at all just wasn't on.

Coming to a corner, the man dragged him to the left into a slightly wider street. Kenneth had lost all sense of direction, even though he had often boasted that he knew Kings Cross better than a Gregory's. He was still dizzy from lack of oxygen and the rain had transformed the smooth stone panels of pavement into distorting mirrors which reflected light and shadows with hallucinatory effect. Again, he tried to sneak a look at his captor but the man's face, being above and slightly behind him, was out of his range of vision particularly when even the slightest twist of his neck sent pain darting up and down his throat.

Now, he was being forced across the roadway. The rain had sent people scurrying for cover, and whereas the Cross always came alive at night, all the life this evening was going on indoors. A passer-by might, just might have responded if Kenneth had attempted to make a fuss, and the man would hardly start to beat him up in front of a witness. But there were no passers-by.

They turned into a narrow passageway and the man forced him to put on speed. Kenneth's mind raced likewise. He had given up trying to find a reason for all this and was now concentrating on the only important issue. Survival. In combat, he'd be no match for the man. But to do anything more than hurry him through the streets the man would have to relax his hold and it was that moment Kenneth was waiting for.

If it ever came.

At the end of the passageway they emerged into what Kenneth immediately recognised as Victoria Street. His breathing was more or less normal by now and it was the man who was panting. Huge spreading trees towered gloomily along the kerb weeping tears of rain.

Suddenly, the man pulled him to a stop beside a white Volvo 740 GLE, the kind that – given a straightened-out wire coat-hanger – Kenneth could be into in less than thirty seconds. At last his left arm was released and he straightened it out gingerly, moaning as he experienced even more pain than when it had been shoved up to his collar bone.

The man's grip around his shoulder strengthened with vice-like pressure. Despite the pain, Kenneth figured out that the man must be feeling for his car keys. And then he was pulled sideways as the man leaned inwards to unlock the car door. Darting a sideways glance, he saw the car door open, and then the hand gripping his shoulder wrenched him around so that he was facing his attacker.

In the split second which followed, Kenneth registered two things. One was the man's face, the other was an upraised fist.

He ducked instantly and butted the man backwards into the car. Off balance, Kenneth almost fell in, too. The man's flailing hands clutched at him, but the rain had made Kenneth's bare arms slippery. He wriggled free and was off down the street. Glancing back, he saw the man clawing his way out of the car.

Victoria Street seemed to stretch endlessly. Kenneth ran past the passageway from which they'd emerged a minute or so before. The open thoroughfare appealed more than a claustrophobic alley.

Up ahead, he saw the lights of a corner delicatessen. Sanctuary? Forget it. The man only had to race in after him and concoct a 'Stop Thief!' yarn and the shopkeeper wouldn't give a damn. Few did, where street kids were concerned.

A trail bike had zoomed up and was being parked in the shelter of a tree at the kerb in front of the shop. Its rider put the engine into neutral, kicked the stand down, jumped off and ran across the pavement into the shop.

Kenneth veered off the pavement and headed straight for the bike. It was a gift from heaven, his salvation. He could hardly believe his luck. As he got closer, he saw it was a Suzuki ER 185, a gleaming red and black charger, throbbing and ready to go. Expecting any second to be grabbed from behind by his pursuer and pulled off, he scrambled astride the big leather seat, kicked the stand, knocked off the brake handle, twisted the accelerator and gunned off with a roar.

His relief, his exhilaration at having escaped, was short-lived.

He failed to allow for the weakness of his left arm, the one pinned up his back for the last six minutes. As well as still being sore, there was no strength in the limb and he found it impossible to hold the bike on a steady, upright course. After only a few seconds, his right-hand grip failed to stop the front wheel from veering left. Automatically, he put his left leg down and the machine slid from under him. He staggered back and overbalanced as the bike tipped on its side and stalled, wheels spinning.

As he pushed himself up from the road, Kenneth glanced back. The rain had eased so he had a clear view of what was happening. The bike's owner, alerted by the zoom of the engine, had come out of the delicatessen and was now running towards him. Further back, headlights swept in an arc as the white Volvo pulled out from the kerb.

Kenneth ran over to the bike. He wasn't hurt, but he clenched his left fist and moved the arm back and forth and yelled out at the pain in his shoulder. By the time he was lifting the bike the pain had been replaced by the pins and needles of restored circulation.

With the bike upright, he jumped back in the saddle and prayed as he tried to start the engine. It spluttered to life immediately. He looked back over his shoulder. The trail bike's owner was less than twenty yards away, howling obscenities and silhouetted by the lights of the Volvo which was speeding up fast behind him.

Kenneth turned up front. He twisted the accelerator desperately and zoomed forward with a thrust that almost threw him off. This time, he leaned heavily to his right to compensate for the weak left arm. And above the roar of the engine, he heard the tortured squeal of tyres and a trio of bangs. Hopefully, the Volvo had got itself into trouble.

7

Yes, he thought as he cruised along the New South Head Road away from the menace of the Cross and up towards Edgecliff, that's what had happened. The Man had swerved to avoid hitting the owner of the trial bike and side-swiped two or three of the cars parked along the kerb. And it served him bloody well right, too.

Kenneth knew who he was, now. Once seen, never forgotten. The glimpse of the face above the clenched fist had solved the mystery of why he was being abducted. Or part of it. There was still the puzzle of why he'd been left in ignorance. She said she'd give him plenty of warning.

Devious bitch.

She was just like all the rest. Not to be trusted. And that meant he could forget about the bread she'd promised him.

Shit!

But at least he was out of it. At least he was out of danger.

A warm wind, free of rain, whipped at his face, blowing away his troubles. He felt as if he could ride like this forever and would do, too, provided the cops didn't stop him for not wearing a safety helmet.

A warning bell sounded in his mind. That was an important consideration, his lack of a safety helmet. Another consideration was that if he were stopped, he was at a slight disadvantage. He was on a stolen bike.

On the other hand, maybe that would be for the best. He'd done it before, purposely got himself arrested. It meant you had a bed for the night, access to a shower, and a couple of meals. And most of all, it meant you were safe because you were inside. But not this time. The minute he walked out, The Man would be waiting for him and it would be back to square one. No, this time there was no easy way out. He had to split. He had to split quickly, and he had to stay split.

He stopped for the lights at the Edgecliff intersection. He had no idea where he was heading but it didn't matter. It was like the future. If you left behind the pain and the pressures it couldn't be anything else but an improvement. Watson's Bay or the year 2001, they were both uncharted territory as far as he was concerned and there was always a slim chance, a very slim chance that they might be better than what had gone before.

The lights seemed forever red. A car pulled beside him in the lane on his right. Kenneth glanced at it.

Something deep down in his gut turned into a claw that wrenched at his innards. The white Volvo had been trashed all along its side. From the driver's seat, The Man glared at him with a simmering fury.

Kenneth didn't hesitate. He zoomed off across the intersection against the lights. A car coming from the right squealed to a halt to avoid hitting him as he streaked across its path. The car stalled in front of the Volvo, just as the lights changed. Now, The Man had the right of way, but the stalled car prevented him from going forward. Viciously, he slammed into reverse, backed, changed lanes and charged across the intersection, missing the stalled car by inches.

Kenneth had the advantage of a head start, but as he sped down the hill and through the Double Bay shopping centre he knew it wouldn't last long.

Again he encountered a red light where Cross Street and Bellevue Road intersected at the end of the shopping centre and again he went through it, thankful that there wasn't much traffic around. He glanced at the rear vision mirror and saw the lights of the Volvo coming down the hill behind him. He knew he would never shake The Man off on a major road like this. He was too easy a mark.

The road was still shiny from the rain, as if coated with an oil slick. If he made a turn into one of the streets leading off New South Head Road, he would have to slow down or risk a damaging skid. Knowing that he would lose his precious lead the moment he reduced his speed, he gritted his teeth and started to apply the brake, his eyes searching up ahead.

At that moment, he saw the sign 'To Point Piper' pointing up a road to the left. He had just negotiated a bend and the headlights of his pursuer were not yet visible behind him. Because of its decreased speed the bike took the turn into the side road easily. Once done, he accelerated immediately.

Then he realised his mistake.

On the main road, the bike's engine hadn't sounded all that loud to him. Now, in this narrower road with smart houses and apartment blocks crowding in on either side, the engine noise became deafening. It was a dead giveaway. All The Man had to do was follow the noise.

The road climbed, curled a bit and curved to the left, where it widened. Kenneth knew he would have to ditch the bike quickly and continue on foot. But the problem was where?

Fate, in the form of a large possum, decided that for him. The animal was crouched on the roadway, right in his path, hypnotised into immobility by the approaching headlight, mirroring its brightness in unearthly luminous orbs. He swerved to avoid it, and for the second time that night he felt the wheels slipping from underneath him.

This time he was unable to jump clear and the bike came down heavily on his right leg. He extricated himself from under the machine quickly, wincing at the daggers in his leg. The engine spluttered and died. He switched off the headlight. Grasping the handles, he hauled the bike off the road and into the shadows of a tree growing at the kerb.

Kenneth looked around desperately. His leg was really hurting and he knew he couldn't go far on it.

The street was bordered by imposing houses, some hardly visible because of high brick walls, ornamental iron fences or dense vegetation. He started to limp away from the bike and along the street as fast as he could. This was alien territory to him. A few street lights provided illumination he could well do without, but they enabled him to see that the entrances set in walls and fences seemed very secure, with pinpoints of light indicating the panels of intercoms. Few windows were lit in the houses, but that was normal because by now he reckoned it must be towards midnight.

And that time of night meant that security alarms would probably be on. There seemed to be nothing he could do but push on and hope that—

He stopped, inclining his head. Listening.

All was quiet except for the distant revving of a car's engine as it made its way up the slope in the narrow road which bent and curled and eventually widened into this one.

It had to be the Volvo.

He felt sick. There was no way he could climb over one of the walls or fences. Not with his injured leg. And for the same reason, he couldn't make a run for it.

He had nowhere to hide. Any moment the car would come

around the bend and he would be caught in the glare of its headlights, as defenceless as the possum which caused his accident.

He limped on a few paces and it was then that he saw the gates,
big wrought iron ones, gleaming black and apparently secured only
by a large ornamental latch. He reached through and pulled the
handle down. The latch went up at the other end. He pushed the
gate open, slipped inside, then pushed it shut. The latch engaged
with a subdued clang. Quickly, he limped over to the shelter of a
group of large tree ferns at the edge of the drive. The gigantic
fronds, still dripping from the recent rain, enfolded him.

From this sheltered vantage point, Kenneth could see through
the gates and out into the street. Almost immediately the approaching car turned the bend and its headlights beamed along the roadway. He held his breath and felt his heart thudding rapidly.

The Volvo crawled past slowly, so slowly that Kenneth was able
to see the white blur of The Man's face inside, turning this way
and that as he scanned both sides of the street.

The car passed on.

Kenneth drew back further against the fibrous body of the closest
tree fern, the stumps of dead fronds digging into his spine like an
upright bed of nails. He didn't mind that or the nagging soreness
of his leg. He'd put up with anything, just as long as he could
escape from The Man.

He heard the car make a turn and again it crawled past in the
other direction. Just as it passed out of his field of vision, he heard
it stop. The engine was still running, but he heard the car door
open then shut.

The Man had found the bike. He'd know now that he was on
the right track. And that meant a closer inspection of the street on
foot.

Kenneth had to move away from the gates and get as far away
from the street as possible. He turned and groped his way through
to the other side of the tree ferns, going slowly and quietly. The
fact that there were no locks on the gates and no lighting in the
grounds *could* mean guard dogs. He'd have to take that chance.
He could see the the surfaced drive to one side, still gleaming wet,
but he kept to the undergrowth. The grounds inclined gently up
towards the house, which appeared even more of an impressive
bulk because of its elevated position. Only one upper floor window
was lit. Bedtime. That was good. Less chance of being detected.

He limped from one clump of trees to another, traversed some
flower beds, and followed the perimeter of lawns which had the

27

flowing spaciousness of a golf course. He avoided the front terraces and made for the side of the house. Halfway along, he encountered a high brushwood fence in which was set a securely locked door which prevented access to the rear of the premises. And he knew that in all probability there would be a twin on the other side of the house.

Ordinarily, Kenneth would have scaled over it with the agility of a monkey. But ordinarily, he didn't have a leg that felt like it was being ripped to shreds. And ordinarily, his energy hadn't been sapped to the point of exhaustion. And on that subject he was aware that if he didn't rest soon, he'd just pass out.

Standing there in the gloom, he became aware that there was a small open verandah nearby on the side of the house. He climbed three steps and found it was furnished, as far as he could make out, with two large cane chairs and a divan.

This would have to do. It was sheltered, it was comfortable, and he could be away at first light.

He lowered himself on to the divan. The cushions were big but unwelcoming, being covered in a waterproof plastic material. Still, it was the best kip he'd had in months, he decided as he hitched up his injured leg. He could feel that his jeans had been shredded where it hurt most and there was an unpleasant dampness, but whether it was blood or just a legacy of the rain he had no way of knowing. He lay back gratefully, and was asleep almost immediately.

He could have been unconscious for five minutes or fifty, but either way it seemed only an instant before he was struggling awake with a blinding light hurting his eyes.

He knew immediately that he was cornered.

8

Kenneth never slept long or deeply, not since he'd been on the streets. He always felt as if he were asleep and awake at the same time because his brain was forever on the alert. At the slightest noise, his eyes would snap open and his muscles would tense. Too many people had their throats slit while they were asleep, and not only kids. Derelicts, drunks, nobody who wasn't a hundred percent on the ball was safe.

And yet here he was, imprisoned in a circle of light and he hadn't even heard the warning signals, the telltale sounds of someone approaching. It said a lot about how much the events of the evening had taken out of him. Even getting to this stage of cognition had taken a great deal of groping out of a deep, dark pit.

Instant impressions and conclusions computerised in his head. This couldn't be The Man, this amorphous form behind the glare. He was a creature of the shadows, too much a victim of his own desires to want to be recognized. Unwanted exposure was what had churned him up into tonight's one-man posse of vengeance to begin with. *He* wouldn't be flashing lights. Given a victim who was asleep, he would have crept up and done his dirty work in the dark, however cruel, disgusting or fatal that work was, and Kenneth was aware of that because after three years on his own he was tuned into desperate people and knew how their minds worked. The very fact that nothing had been said or done since he had blinked awake in the glare of the flashlight told him that here was someone more cautious than aggressive, more curious than lethal. He squinted and brought up an arm to try and shade his eyes.

'Jesus Christ! Look what the cat dragged in. Thank God I settled for vinyl!'

The voice was that of a woman. The accent was American.

'Well?'

The tone became more aggressive. That was to be expected, once she'd established he wasn't a great hulking hoon with rape on his mind.

Still he didn't speak. Or couldn't. But that was working in his favour because the longer he remained silent, the more she'd give away about herself.

The source of the light moved up and down, then from side to side. If this were a jungle, she would have been circling him, a wary beast inspecting its prey. Instead, she was moving backwards and forwards, left and right, because circling was out of the question with him in a corner, stretched out on a divan, not only hazy from exhaustion but aware of pain rushing in to take advantage of this return to consciousness.

She continued to survey him.

'You're hurt. Well? For God's sake, *say* something!'

He could stand the glare no longer.

'Put the light out,' he grunted. 'Put it out.'

'If I do that, we'll be in pitch darkness. Every light in the place is out. The goddamn electrician installed some kind of overload trigger, said it was a safety precaution. Safe? I'm likely to go downstairs ass over tits in one of these blackouts.'

The torchlight moved from his face to the wall over his head.

'There's a red button in the fuse box up there. It has to be pushed in.'

Kenneth wasn't sure whether she meant for him to do it or not, but decided to show willing. He stood up on the divan, wincing from the soreness in his leg, and pulled open the fuse box door.

'Hey!'

The beam of light moved to his dirty sneakers on the already soiled cushions.

'Oh, what the hell. I'll have to hose 'em down, anyway.'

The beam came back to the box. Kenneth located the red button and pushed it in. Instantly, the verandah was illuminated by light coming through open French doors the woman had obviously used to get out here. He turned around and painfully lowered himself to the floor.

The woman backed, holding the torch defensively as if its beam were the blade of a sword.

'Now don't try anything. I can take care of myself, and you're in no shape to pull any funny business.'

Kenneth nodded towards the torch. 'You're wasting the battery.'

She snapped it off impatiently, as if resenting level-headedness from a culprit caught trespassing. He saw that she was a woman well into middle age, but what he'd heard called very well preserved. She was in a bright-blue satin kimono, knotted around the waist so tightly that it was a lumpy betrayal of a tendency to overweight. A sort of knitted cap covered most of her hair except for a bunch of improbable reddish-gold curls frothing out at the front. Her round, slightly chubby face gleamed with a sheen of night-cream. Apart from some puffiness under rather prominent blue eyes and the suspicion of a double chin, she seemed to carry her years lightly.

Kenneth frowned and put his head on one side, inquiringly.

'You said every light in the place went out. I saw one lit upstairs.'

'That was candlelight. The overload happened an hour ago. It took me all that time to get up enough courage to come down here, and then when I did – look what I found! You wouldn't have got much past the front gates had the power been on. Electronic eyes pick up any sizable movement, floodlight the grounds and start the alarm.'

'That's why you're getting an overload. It should be on a separate circuit.'

'Oh, get the expert!' Her voice was heavy with sarcasm. 'Well if you're such a mister smarty-pants, how come you're in such a mess?'

He'd had enough. Her manner irritated him and he was too weary to spar with her any longer. She wouldn't call the cops. She was too ready to talk, almost relishing the opportunity for conversation even in this uneasy situation. With any luck, The Man would have given up by now and gone away.

'I'm pushing off,' he said quietly and made a move towards the steps.

'You're not going to get far on that leg,' she observed. 'Besides, you go out there and all hell'll break loose. The security system's on now, you know.'

Kenneth hesitated. He could sense her reluctance to be rid of him and he was puzzled as to her motives. Surely no one could be *that* desperate for company? Maybe he should take advantage of her attitude. Already he knew the best way of drawing her out was to keep silent.

Sure enough, when he showed no signs of replying, she spoke again.

'That little guy in the story. Yeah, Oliver Twist. That's who you remind me of. All screwed up by the cruel ole world.'

Her tough sarcasm belied any sympathy. Despite himself, Kenneth had to speak.

'Look lady, I didn't mean you any harm, coming in here. I didn't intend to break in or pinch anything, I just wanted to rest. So now you've had your fun, let me go.'

To his surprise, she dropped the tough act.

'The way I see it,' she said quietly, 'is you need to get cleaned up, you need some attention to that leg, and you need some food.'

She regarded him queryingly.

'Well, buster? What d'you say?'

9

She took a bowl out of the microwave oven and placed it in front of him on the kitchen table. It was a kind of beef stew, lumps of meat and bits of vegetable. It was steaming and it smelled good.

It tasted fantastic.

'Did you make this?' he asked between mouthfuls.

She nodded.

'I do two things exceptionally well. I vocalise and I cook. No, I do *three* things exceptionally well, but the third is none of your business.'

She took a gulp of the generous drink she had fixed herself and watched him eat with great intensity. Everything she had done for him, everything about her had a 'take it or leave it' quality, except the way she was watching him eat, noting any signs of enjoyment, ready to pounce if he left one spoonful. He guessed this drink she was throwing down wasn't exactly her first of the evening, which accounted for her erratic behaviour, the overdone sarcasm, the sudden changes of mood.

He had accepted meekly her invitation into the house, even though she laced the invitation with plenty of warnings to behave yourself, buster, or else! He didn't really fancy going back into the street and chancing his luck on whether The Man had gone or was still hanging around. He didn't feel too crash-hot either, and it would be a long walk back to the Cross.

It was the largest house he'd ever been in, and certainly the most luxurious he'd seen outside of the movies. She had led him through innumerable rooms and although he had no standards of quality with which to assess them, they overwhelmed him with their grandeur and elegance.

As he limped along, weak from fatigue and the aching soreness of his leg, their progress became a blur of soaring ceilings, leadlight windows, wide skirting boards, marble fireplaces and sculpted columns, friezes and archways. Finally, they arrived at the kitchen,

33

lofty and huge with a cumulous cloud of burnished copper cooking utensils overhead. The benches and cupboards, table and chairs were polished cedar, all set in what seemed like an acre of black and white tiles.

The woman had marched straight across to a door and opened it to reveal a modest bedsitting room. It was in humble contrast to the rest of the house and was obviously intended for live-in help. She stood aside and gestured for him to go in. She followed him and then went over to another door and opened it.

'See? It's a bathroom. In you go. Take off your clothes, and I mean the lot – shoes, T-shirt, jeans and underpants, if you're wearing any! – then throw them out the door.'

He did as he was told. As he threw out his clothes, she threw in a towel with more instructions.

'Take a shower, as hot as you can bear it, and let the water run over that gash in your leg. Don't rush it, take as long as you like.'

She was being bossy and enjoying it. Kenneth responded without question. It was weird the way she was taking over, and it was new to him, having this kind of attention.

He took a long time under the shower, and emerged from the bathroom feeling clean and refreshed. His clothes were gone, so he wound the towel around his middle and went through to the kitchen.

She'd been waiting there with a bowl of warm water laced with antiseptic, a tube of ointment, cotton wool and a roll of bandage.

'Sit down and put your foot up on this stool.'

She regarded the purplish swelling which extended from just below his knee three-quarters of the way down the front of his leg with the split in the skin now washed clean of blood. She grunted dubiously.

'I don't think it can be a fracture. You wouldn't be able to walk on it. So speaketh the Flo Nightingale of the Twilight Zone!'

She shrugged, then proceeded to bathe the wound, apply the ointment and wrap it tightly with the bandage. She also attempted to pump him.

'How'd this happen?'

'I fell over.'

'Is that how your throat got all red, too?'

Kenneth closed up.

'I don't want any third degree.'

She stopped dabbing the wound and looked at him with elaborately feigned indignation.

34

'Oh, excuse me for living! Here I am, putting myself out for you, and you clam up like—'

'I didn't plead to come in here. I didn't beg you to look after me.'

It was a reaction natural to him. He just blurted it out and left it at that. But it shut her up.

He hated questions. They really spun him out. He couldn't handle probing because whatever came out would always go against him. However, by the time she was winding the bandage around his throbbing wound, he felt calmer and relented. She might as well know.

'A trail bike fell on me. It skidded.'

'Had you stolen it?'

'Yeh.'

'And that's it? That's supposed to explain everything? Okay, already.'

She tore the end of the bandage into two strips and tied a knot.

'Put your finger on this.'

He did, and she doubled the knot. The throbbing in his leg was bad, but not as bad as before.

'I didn't steal it 'cos I'm a thief, if that's what you're thinking,' he said abruptly. 'I had to get away from this guy who was going to trash me.'

And as the woman cleared away, he found himself telling her the reasons. The deal with the TV bird, the set-up, her assurance that he'd be told in advance when the program was going to be shown so's he could split with the five hundred bucks he'd been promised. And tonight, the betrayal.

'You've probably helped ruin that guy's life, you realise that,' she said as she got a bowl from the refrigerator.

'So what? He's a pederast,' Kenneth flung at her belligerently. 'He's like all the adults. They're the ones who do things to us kids. They're the ones who need the counselling and putting away, not us!'

'Am I included in that indictment?' she asked archly, as she put the bowl in the microwave oven. 'If not, I'm flattered. If so, why do I bother?'

He knew why she bothered, but he was smart enough not to tell her. She was actually enjoying this diversion. She needed somebody around. Shit, she must be hard up.

And now he was eating her food. He grabbed another chunk of French bread to mop up the gravy and clean the bowl. She was still watching him like it was feeding time at the zoo. He didn't care. This was the first decent meal he'd had since . . . He tried to cast his mind back. You got so accustomed to not eating, meal times no longer provided a framework for the day and hunger just joined the rest of the familiar discomforts as something else to be endured.

Sunday night. More than forty-eight hours ago. That was when he'd had his last decent feed. That was when he'd had the Big Mac.

He shoved the empty bowl away and slumped back in his chair, replete with an unusual sense of well-being.

'What's your name, kiddo?'

'Kenneth.'

'Well listen, Ken, I—'

'I don't like it shortened.'

'I'm not crazy about it either way, but if that's the way you want it . . .'

She poured milk into a glass and put it in front of him. He picked it up immediately and drank.

'How old are you, Kenneth?'

He drained the glass then looked at her.

'Fifteen. How old are you?'

She gave an outraged laugh, more amused than annoyed.

'Oh – fresh! You come out of your shell pretty darn quick with a bit of TLC, huh?'

She regarded him intently, her eyes squeezed almost shut with concentration.

'My God . . . fifteen. Was anybody in this world *ever* fifteen? You look so much younger than that, and yet . . . older, too.' She raised her glass to her lips only to find it empty. 'Come into the drawing room while I fix me another drink.'

He got up, adjusting the towel.

'Don't trust me, do you?'

She smiled at him, beguilingly.

'Kind, caring and compassionate I may be. Stupid, I'm not. Come on.'

He followed her out, through the panelled dining room with a heavy table that looked like it could seat twenty people, and into the spacious living room. Drawing room, she'd called it, but there wasn't a pencil and paper in sight. He stood with all his weight on his good leg while she poured herself a vodka and tonic, not game to sit on any of the expensive furniture. He had felt more comfortable in the kitchen.

She perched on the arm of a king-size scarlet leather armchair, sampled her drink with satisfaction, then motioned him to sit down in an identical armchair across from her.

He remained standing. She shrugged and held up her glass.

'This is my last one before bed. I'm not going to turn you out, so you'd better get used to the idea that you're staying the night.'

'No!'

He uttered the word vehemently. That was the last straw. He was getting to feel too vulnerable, too dependent. That was the way you got hurt.

'What are you afraid of?' she asked.

He paused for a moment, then tried to hedge the question.

'Where I'll be next year. Whether I'll be alive or whether I'll be dead. Whether I'll be a junkie or whether I'll still be straight. Wondering why I was put on the earth . . .'

He could have gone on and on because it was all true.

'I'm not asking for a lifetime commitment,' she broke in, 'I just suggested you stay the night. There's no need to worry,' she added lightly, 'I won't rape you.'

'That's not funny!' he flung back at her. 'It happens, you know. That – and worse!'

'I'm sorry,' she said quietly and sipped at her drink. A suffocating silence enveloped them like smog over a city. But not for long.

An ear-shattering clamour exploded outside the house. Simultaneously, every window in the room became alive with bright light. Because he was closest to a window, Kenneth looked outside.

The drawing room was at the front of the house and consequently overlooked the terrace and lawns. He saw that they were totally floodlit by the glare of countless arc lights, every blade of grass, every branch of every tree, every leaf of every bush, every petal of every flower being illuminated in harsh detail.

As was The Man, who was standing halfway up the drive.

Kenneth flung himself to one side of the window, back pressed against the wall.

'It's him, the guy who's after me!' he yelled over the noise.

'Did he see you?' the woman asked urgently. 'Well? Did he?'

Kenneth shook his head.

'He was looking around at the lights. Blinded.'

'Check,' she said. She hurried over to another window, slopping vodka and tonic over the sides of her glass. She pushed aside the heavy drapes to reveal a digital panel, which she prodded with her index finger four times. The terrible clamour stopped, but the floodlights stayed on. She turned to Kenneth.

37

'Stay there. Or if you want to come and listen, get down on all fours if you're able with that leg.'

He saw that her cheeks were flushed. Her eyes sparkled with excitement and seemed bluer than ever. She put down her drink and marched out through a grand archway. He dropped to his knees and winced at the griping jabs which augmented the throbbing in his leg. By the time he had crawled across the floor to the archway, she was across the circular entrance foyer and was pulling the double front doors majestically open.

She strode out on to the stone terrace which ran along the front of the house, and stared down imperiously at the figure in the drive.

'You must realise by now that you're trespassing. Who are you and what do you want?'

'I – I was looking for someone.'

Allan Steinbeck's voice barely made it to the terrace.

'And waking up half of Point Piper in the process, I'd say. Members of my staff are probably on their way down from the servant's wing right now. They're good at finding people. They can assist you. Until the police arrive. That alarm also registers at the local police station. And *nobody's* better at finding people than the police.'

Allan's face glistened with sweat. He took a step back.

'I must have made a mistake.'

'I believe you have. Nobody you're looking for could possibly be on this property. Certainly not as a guest. And if they were un-invited, the alarm would have gone off, but this is the first time tonight.'

'I'm sorry . . . I'm sorry!'

The repeat of his apology was shouted as he backed down the drive.

'Please close the gate behind you,' she called after him. 'I'll be turning the alarm back on the minute you're out.'

And with that, she turned and re-entered the house, closing the doors behind her.

Kenneth looked up at her from the floor.

'Hey, that was top.'

And he meant it. He realised now that the tough act she'd put on for his benefit until now wasn't all surface. She could stand up for herself, no risk. She'd just shown it by sending The Man into retreat.

She looked down at him, flushed even more by his compliment.

'Oh, I know, I know. Sweet Jesus, I should have been an actress.

I mean, I *am* an actress . . . I just never had the chance to prove it.'

And she swept past him, back into the drawing room.

When Kenneth got there, she had reprogrammed the alarm system and was already on the telephone.

'Hello? This is Adele Ventura Hatherley of "Horizons", Boniface Road. False alarm, guys. Sorry. Better luck next time, huh?'

She hung up and looked at him.

'The cops. They're so on the ball, they hadn't even left yet. Never mind, what with one thing and another, your boyfriend's probably crapping in his pants all the way down to the main road by now.'

'Thanks to you,' he said, shifting his weight uneasily from one foot to the other. Crawling around hadn't done his leg any good.

She picked up the remains of her drink and finished it, noting his discomfort.

'I don't think we need any more argument about whether you stay the night, huh?'

Back at the door of the room off the kitchen, he turned to her.

'Where are my clothes?'

'You don't need clothes for bed. Besides, we wouldn't want anyone disappearing with the family silver before morning, would we?'

She gave him a knowing wink and before he could do anything, she tweaked the towel from around his waist. He dived into the room, slamming the door, and he could hear her laughing as she went out of the kitchen.

He snuggled down between the smooth, cool sheets and tried to remember when he last slept in a bed, but names soon crowded thoughts of the past out of his head.

Adele Ventura Hatherley.

'Horizons'.

The names seemed strangely suited to this enchanted world of wealth and power that until now had been beyond his comprehension. Oh, he'd always known there were the 'haves' as opposed to the 'have nots', and had resented them and stolen from them because it was the natural thing to do. But until now he'd had no way of assessing the limitless gratification that 'having' could bring to a person's being. And now, briefly, he'd become a part of that privileged world, the immense house creaking nocturnal lullabies all around him and sheltering him as if he were one of its own.

Adele Ventura Hatherley.

He'd never met anyone quite like her. And as she'd said, she was not stupid. Even her precaution of depriving him of his clothes was not enough. As he drifted into sleep, the last thing he heard was a key turning in the lock of the door.

He didn't mind a bit.

10

Jim Abrahams knew there'd be trouble, so it came as no surprise when his secretary gave him a look and told him Sharon Pettifer was on the warpath. He sighed as he riffled through the morning's mail.

'Get me a black coffee and tell her I'm here – in that order,' he said and walked into his office. He was a heavily built man in his late thirties, barrel-chested and with the beginnings of a paunch. You didn't get to be executive producer of a show like *Upfront* by spending long hours in a gymnasium.

His secretary brought in his coffee.

'I didn't see her in the office – where is she?' he asked.

'The viewing room, watching the rushes from Newcastle.'

'No she's not,' Jim said, looking over her shoulder. Sharon came in, blue-grey eyes flashing. She waited until the secretary had gone out.

'You bastard!' she said.

Jim gulped down the black coffee. These days, he felt exhausted before he even started work. Nothing like television to suck a man dry, except maybe a vampire.

He guessed he was lucky it was merely sapping his energy. The first thing to go in most people was the soul. But then, they were the ones who didn't have anything worthwhile but their soul to trade in the first place. They were the 'stars', who only came to life on camera or in public, and for the rest of the time slept in the coffins of their private lives. And the company men, the walking talking fax machines whose reaction to success either past or present was 'Copy it!' And they were the ones who survived because they never initiated, only duplicated and therefore could never be blamed, rarely be fired, and could be distinguished from human beings only by the hunted look in their eyes.

He held up his cup.

'Want some?'

'What I want,' Sharon grated, 'is an explanation.'

Her naturally flaxen hair was pulled back casually and secured by a black ribbon into a fall. She was wearing a peasant-style white cotton dress which, though cinched in at the waist, covered her loosely to mid-calf and helped disguise the angular frame of her body. Her leanness didn't matter on camera. The camera's magic (or curse) fleshed out people an extra fifteen pounds. On Sharon, that looked good. Her face had the advantage of visible bone structure and though almost gaunt in real life, it became utterly photogenic and therefore appealing when the camera looked at her with the eye of a doting parent. Her nose was aquiline, balanced by eyebrows several shades darker than her hair and generously arched.

Jim took another gulp of coffee. Sharon was going through the business of sitting down, gathering the voluminous skirt up and wafting it out front with both of her hands.

'I know what you're on about,' he said, seeking to stave off further onslaughts before they came. 'We shoved "Street Kids" on last night.'

Having got it out into the open, he waited for the outburst. It didn't come. Her eyes crackled like they were plugged into Frankenstein's laboratory, but the traditional rearing up of the angry monster with hands outstretched and clasping for the throat didn't happen.

He felt a little easier. He drained the last of the coffee from the cup, then switched his voice to a more rational mode.

'We had to fill in at the last minute, love. You know how these things are. Remember the panic last month when we had to ditch the Aboriginal Rights story and shove in shit? It was the same situation all over again. The legal bods suddenly got the trembles about the Treasury scam. We had to can it, and that meant the strength of the show was gone. And that was at four o'clock.'

Sharon's body in the moulded plastic chair was as unyielding as the chair itself.

'You didn't try to ring me till six.'

Jim slumped back in his chair. The discomfort in his chest was there again. It was supposed to be indigestion, but who got indigestion from corn flakes?

'It took us till that time to work out the new format. Availability of material, running times, balance. All we had left in the show was a transplant tear-jerker. We hauled a marijuana beat-up from

42

the stockpile, but it wasn't enough. I had to give the show some substance, some bite.'

'I was in Newscastle, Jim, not . . . Nepal. I was back at the motel at four. You could've got Sally, or even one of the typists to ring me. I made a deal with the boy in that feature. I told him I'd tip him off before it went to air, so that he could get the hell out of the Cross if he felt there were going to be repercussions.'

'How would you have got in touch with him from Newcastle at that late stage? Bush telegraph?'

Sharon shook her head vigorously.

'I couldn't have done. But at least I would have had the opportunity to try and dissuade you from using the piece because of the principles involved.'

'Talking of principles, are you aware we could be charged with inciting a minor to prostitution with that set-up?'

'He didn't go all the way, for God's sake! He knew what to do. He begged off before it got too nasty. You know that. You saw the rushes, you approved the final cut. And you knew I needed notice before it went to air, yet you deliberately—'

Jim sighed and thrust fingers through crinkly black hair in desperation.

'I didn't *deliberately* do anything. Being responsible for the show, I had to make a decision for the good of the show, and if that upset your private little applecart, then too bad and I'm sorry. Where were you at six, anyway?'

'We worked through the lunch hour: it was the only time the mayor could fit in the interview. The crew was hungry. We decided to go out for an early dinner. By the time I got back, it was too late.'

She got up and went over to the window, her movements stiff with tension.

'Those kids. They have no security, no escape. That boy could be intimidated for what he did. By the man he conned, by others who might see it as treachery. What must he think of me? And if anything happens to him, it'll be my responsibility. Your fault – my responsibility.'

Jim lifted the coffee cup to his lips and realised it was empty. Cold and empty, like whatever he'd once had with Sharon. There was a production meeting in half an hour, and before that he had to examine the day's news feature possibilities and go over several assignment schedules. And then there was Grant Olsen and his demands for a new set, a means of flexing his power after the ratings had put him several points ahead of the opposition.

Jim glanced across at Sharon, still with her back to him, and for the fiftieth time that week tried to reject the glaring evidence that it was over between them.

No.

This was just a professional bone of contention. Once it had blown over . . .

Once it had blown over, he still had to face the fact that she'd been making excuses about seeing him away from the office for over a month.

He remembered when working with her was stimulating. Fun. She'd joined the network after working through her cadetship with a chain of suburban weeklies and stints with various country town 'Chronicles', 'Advertisers' and 'Clarions' in three States. She had found the switch from print to television journalism petrifying, but she'd had the guts to tell him so. He made few concessions in assigning her difficult, sometimes arduous subjects to cover, but had helped her all he could. With more experience, her confidence had increased and a dynamic enjoyment soon began to characterise her approach to work. She came up with fresh angles on old themes; she had the ability to dig up obscure facts that led to new stories; she had persistence and she had professionalism, and in her eyes it was her professionalism that was at stake here, he knew that. The failure to keep a promise, the letting of someone down.

'Look,' he said, 'it happened and I'm sorry it's put you in a spot with the kid, okay? But there's no point in turning it into a mini series. We have to accept it was unavoidable and we have to go on.'

He waited for a moment, but there was no response.

Sharon stared out of the window, not seeing a thing, biting her lip and remembering another kid, her young brother Terry who was not unlike Kenneth Mitchell in looks. She had let Terry down too, and had carried the guilt of it ever since. She was not going to let that happen again.

Jim tired of waiting for her to speak. 'Now about this Newcastle stuff you shot yesterday. There's a report on architectural safety factors for buildings in earthquake territory being released on Friday. I thought we could tie it in with what you've got on Newcastle's rebuilding program.'

Sharon still appeared to be mesmerised by the view from his window, which was odd because all it overlooked was the studio car park and a couple of loading bays.

'How about we look at the rushes together?' Jim asked, making an attempt to be vigorous and positive. 'Shall we say half-past ten?'

Sharon turned, shaking her head. Her voice was impersonal.

'It'll have to wait until after lunch,' she said. 'I need to take a couple of hours off.'

She walked out before he could reply.

11

Kenneth awoke with the terrifying fear that the squat was on fire. It was a constant dread of his, surmounting all other dangers in the minefield of his existence. With all the garbage strewn around, the old newspapers and the rotting woodwork, it only needed a smouldering joint, a carelessly dropped match or the deliberate act of malefic vandals and most squats would be infernos in seconds, as several had been in the recent past.

The events of the previous night crowded in on him and he realised where he was. The ominous stench of burning became the aroma of freshly percolating coffee. There was no clock in the room but he felt he had slept long and deeply.

Now his rush of fear had subsided he was inclined to languish, to stretch out and enjoy the softness of the bed, to luxuriate in the kind of comfort he might not experience again for weeks, months, if ever. But the coffee aroma was tempting and there were other tantalising smells of cooking and he realised he was hungry. Usually, hunger was not enough motivation for him to start the day, but hunger that could be satisfied instantly was a different matter.

He scrambled from under the sheet and saw his clothes on a nearby chair. Everything appeared to have been washed, the T-shirt, the jeans and his underpants ironed and neatly folded. Even the mud and scuffmarks had been scrubbed from his sneakers.

He started to dress, taking an inventory of his physical condition. His throat was rough, like he was getting the flu, but that was probably the bruising. The muscles in his left shoulder and arm still ached. His injured leg felt tight and sore but provided he favoured it, there was little pain when he put his full weight on it. Pulling on his jeans, he noticed the tear had been mended.

Somebody had been busy.

Did she have servants to do all this, Abi – no, Adele Ventura Hatherly? Apart from all the shit she'd hurled at The Man, which wasn't to be believed anyway, there had been no mention of staff. He'd got the impression she was alone in the house, yet that seemed unlikely. If you were loaded – and she obviously was – then you wallowed in it, and that meant being waited on hand and foot. It was strange. He felt *he* was the one being waited on hand and foot. Fed, tended and protected last night, his clothes washed and mended and now the prospect of a cooked breakfast . . .

He pulled the cover over the bed, smoothing out the creases, then went over to the door. He remembered his last waking memory, the turning of the key in the lock. But the woman had been in the room to return his clothes, so it came as no surprise when the door opened easily.

It was as though she had been waiting in the wings, fully rehearsed and impatiently ready to give a performance. His emergence from the room into the kitchen was the equivalent of the curtain going up. Sitting over a cup of coffee at the table, she rose immediately.

'Well, that's certainly an improvement on last night. How's your leg?'

She went over to the refrigerator and took out a glass of orange juice, not waiting for him to reply to her question.

'Here's your juice. I fixed some hotcakes. There's butter and whipped cream and there's corn syrup in the jug. I didn't do any bacon or sausage to go with them because you Aussies seem to get kind of queasy if there's *too* much of a mixture, though in my book a nation of people hooked on Vegemite should be able to stomach anything!'

She paused and stared at him.

'Well? What are you waiting for? Siddown, siddown!'

This morning, she had worked on her face with the dedication of a graffiti artist confronted with a blank wall. A couple of pounds of make-up had given her a doll-like prettiness which Kenneth thought aged her more than no make-up at all. Her hair was a confusion of carrot-coloured curls and she wore a voluminous housecoat with yellow and purple sunflowers crawling all over it. Her manner was belligerent, as if daring him to refuse her hospitality.

He sat down obediently. While he drank his orange juice, she poured him a mug of coffee then picked up her own cup and left.

He was glad she hadn't hung around to watch him eat like she'd done the night before. He couldn't hack that kind of probing attention. Her defensiveness, too, made him nervous. He could recognise it, excuse it even, because he put up his own barricades as well, but two sets of barricades meant no man's land in between.

Her timing was perfect. Either that or she had the kitchen bugged. The minute he washed down the last of the hotcakes with his last mouthful of coffee, she reappeared in the doorway. She put her empty cup down on the table.

'I liked the way you fixed that overload trigger last night without being asked. You showed willing.'

She walked over to the small room in which he had spent the night. She opened the door and glanced inside, then she looked back at him, not smiling but with a slight nod of approval.

'Made your bed, too. Another Brownie point.'

She moved back closer to the table, taking a pack of cigarettes from the pocket of her housecoat. She got one out for herself, then almost as an afterthought she offered the packet to Kenneth. He shook his head.

'Go on,' she said, waving the pack. 'I know about you kids. Drugs, booze, cigarettes . . .'

Kenneth swallowed. He was beginning to feel nauseous. He wasn't used to food so soon after waking up, particularly the kind of rich breakfast he'd just polished off.

'I don't do drugs,' he muttered. 'I haven't been charged up – drunk – for months, and I gave up smoking when I was thirteen.'

She snapped open an expensive lighter, lit her cigarette and inhaled.

'My, my,' she commented, clothing her words in smoke. 'Quite the little angel, huh?'

'No,' he replied matter-of-factly. 'I've done plenty of things I'm not proud of, and I reckon I'll do plenty more. But I've seen too many of my mates wreck themselves, and I'm not gonna go the same way.'

'Determined, too.'

Her tone was bantering and it was beginning to irritate him.

'I'd better be off,' he said, rising.

'There's a little something you could do for me. If you wouldn't mind?'

She motioned him to follow her. They went out through the panelled dining room and crossed the drawing room. Everything seemed even bigger in daylight. In the foyer, she turned and followed the graceful curve of the staircase to the rear of the house.

'This is my favourite. The morning room.'

Again, it was enormous. Kenneth was conscious of overstuffed chairs and sofas covered in chintz, display cabinets filled with oriental porcelain and curios, and bookcases taking up an entire wall.

But it was the view which immediately claimed his attention, the view from the many large windows opposite the door. Kenneth gasped and took several steps forward. It was like looking at outer space, this vast expanse of Sydney Harbour, stretching away to the Heads and on into infinity. No matter it was an oppressively grey and humid day. No matter that there was no sunshine, none of the vivid colours referred to in tourist brochures and nothing to justify the clichés churned out by travel writers, no azure sky nor glistening water, no breezes to fill the sails of fleets of yachts, not even many yachts to speak of being a weekday morning. The sky was a dome of dirty grey. The harbour water was a metallic sheet incapable of reflecting the tankers trudging seawards or the ferries which scuttered like water beetles across its surface. But to Kenneth, after the overcrowded confinement of Kings Cross, the sheer openness of it all was overwhelming.

She saw he was impressed and seemed to take it as a personal compliment.

'I tore down the drapes and left the windows bare. I mean, no amount of swagged brocade could compete with that, huh?'

'It's fantastic,' he managed to say.

'Rotten day to see it,' she went on, 'but that's Sydney. Every summer people complain about the weather, as if it's ever been any different. We're subtropical. Thunderstorms, humidity, days like this, that's what summer's all about here. The schmucks. They want sunshine, they should wait till fall. That's autumn,' she added for Kenneth's benefit.

She indicated a small side window of the sash type.

'That would be great for breezes, if I could get it open. I thought maybe you could try.'

He went over and opened the catch. He pushed the bottom frame upwards but nothing happened. He inspected the edges.

'It's dried paint,' he said finally. 'They painted it shut.'

The cream paint was faded and cracking in places. The window must have been stuck like this for years. Either she didn't have anyone to fix it in all that time, which didn't seem likely, or it wasn't really important until now when it had become a means of giving him something to do. What did it matter? Nobody got anything for nothing. She'd given him shelter for the night, now she wanted something back.

'I need a thin blade, a knife or something, to cut through the paint,' he said.

She went over to a small writing desk and brought back a paper-knife. Then she rummaged in the pocket of her housecoat and produced a steel nail file.

'If those won't do, there's a whole bunch of stuff I can get from the kitchen,' she offered, but he told her he thought he could manage with what she had given him.

He worked slowly and carefully, as he always did, easing the blade of the paper knife between the window frame and the inside edge of the surround, then using the nail file to dig down deeper once he'd cut through the surface paint. Now and again, he would try to move the window upwards, but though it was rattling more freely now, it still wouldn't budge. So then he would start again from the beginning.

'You certainly have a lot of patience,' he heard her murmur.

He just grunted. He'd been taught by experts. You didn't break and enter by bulldozing in, and those who did usually got hurt or caught. He'd done jobs where he'd been so quiet and painstaking, the people were at home watching the telly and didn't even know he was in the house.

Finally, he pushed and pulled and the bottom frame slid squeakily up. He jerked it up and down a few times, then asked her for some soap. While she was gone, he realised that all the standing on his leg had brought back the throbbing. Still, he'd almost finished now and he'd try to have a bit of a sit down before he left. He might even con her into giving him the money for a taxi if she was pleased with the job.

She came back with a tablet of soap and he rubbed it vigorously up and down the inside surfaces of the frame. Now when he applied pressure to the window it slid smoothly.

'Oh, that's great,' she said, practically applauding. 'The place is air conditioned but I hardly ever use it. Plays hell with my sinuses.'

The throbbing was worse. He limped to a nearby chair and sat down, stretching the leg out straight.

'Are you all right?' she asked. She was looking at him strangely.

The nausea was back, too. It must have been all the bending over. He knew with a deadly certainty that he was going to throw up. That was why she was staring at him. His face must be green. He struggled out of the chair, gulping.

'Where's the . . . I'm going to be sick.'

She grabbed him and part ushered, part dragged him across the

room and out into the foyer and shoved him into a small guest
bathroom under the staircase. He sank to his knees and retched
into the bowl. He stayed there, frightened to move, long after he
had finished. He felt so weak he knew that if he moved he would
fall over or faint or both.

Presently, a cold, damp towel was placed around his head. He
heard the toilet flushing and he was helped up.

They went back into the morning room and he had to lean on
her for support.

'My God, I thought you looked thin, but you're just skin and
bone,' she was muttering. 'What have you been living on that you
can't keep decent food down?'

He wanted to tell her. The odd hamburger or pizza. Chips.
Sometimes even a sit-down feed. But never two meals in a row.
And never rich stuff like beef stew last thing at night and then . . .
and— He stopped right there. If he started thinking about what
he'd had for breakfast, he'd be vomiting again.

She helped him lie on one of the overstuffed sofas facing the
windows.

'There,' she said, taking the towel away and propping his head
up with a cushion. 'Concentrate on the view, since you like it so
much. And get some rest.'

'Just for a bit,' he managed to say. 'Then I gotta go.'

'Where? Where do you have to go? Do you have a home?
Friends? Folks who are going to worry about you if you don't turn
up?'

Kenneth shook his head.

'Check. All you have out there is that pervert waiting to beat
the crap out of you. So listen, kiddo – you ain't going anyplace.'

12

The Dainty Dry Cleaners was just a hole in the wall shaded by a tilted metal blind which at night could be pulled down over the opening like an eyelid. A girl, Marieta, slumped on a high stool behind the counter. Behind her were racks of chemically sanitised clothing, each article on its own wire hanger and quarantined from its neighbours by a plastic shroud.

'Aren't you on the telly?'

Having the girl squint at her like that made Sharon far more self-conscious than the camera and a whole battery of arc lamps.

'Yes, I am,' she replied, hoping that would dispose of it.

Marieta had a tousled mass of lustrous black hair, white unblemished skin except for the yellow and charcoal half-moons under her eyes, and a massively impressive bust. With a bit of time and effort, Sharon thought, she could be stunning. As it was – and like many who lived or worked in Kings Cross, Marieta's inner concerns seemed to override any interest in her outward appearance – she presented herself as a listless sloven.

'I was asking about Kenneth,' Sharon reminded her, forcing a smile. 'He nicknamed you his Post Office Box. He told me I could leave a message with you, or anything else for that matter.'

'Yair, that'd be right,' Marieta agreed. 'Nice kid.'

She remembered the time she had mentioned her dad's birthday and he'd given her a tool kit, no questions asked, and wouldn't take a cent for it, either.

'Passes by almost every day. I think he lives in a squat down in MacFarlane Place. Him and a weirdo called Donna.'

'Where is it?' Sharon asked eagerly. 'I *could* leave a message with you, but you see I'd really like to see him straight away.'

Marieta eyed her warily.

'You're not going to get him in trouble, are you?'

'No, no . . . oh God, no,' Sharon protested with humour she didn't feel. 'I'm a friend.'

She walked down Macleay Street repeating in her mind the directions given to her by the girl. She wanted to hurry, but the sultry oppressiveness of the morning was making her sluggish. She was already perspiring under the loose white cotton of her dress and the fingers that clasped the leather strap of her shoulder bag felt tight and swollen.

Someone was moving out of the solid art deco splendour of the Macleay Regis. Sharon was almost grateful for the rest when she had to stop to allow the removal men passage across the pavement with a heavy studded leather settee. Like the other furniture she saw ready for loading near the removalist's truck, it was faded and slightly worse for wear. She wondered about the owners, how long they'd lived there, the changes they'd witnessed.

Kings Cross – and the name often blanketed its neighbouring environs of Darlinghurst, Wooloomooloo and Potts Point – had always been an area of change, but rarely for the better. In the early days of the colony, the area had been a domain of the elite, the rich and the powerful who built elegant residences in spacious grounds.

By the 1920s it had deteriorated into a densely populated haunt of criminals, the razor gangs and the sly-groggers and the evil trinity of Kate Leigh, Tilly Devine and Nellie Cameron, Macbeth's three witches metamorphosed into female Godfathers, Women's Libbers with the sanction of the Devil.

The underworld still called the Cross 'home' in the thirties, but so did the influx of artists, actors and writers whose raffish creativity did much to soften its image into one of a semi-respectable Bohemia. World War Two brought further changes – thousands of American servicemen, and the underworld established new outlets to cater for them. Black markets, brothels and booze.

The Cross had staggered through the sixties, seventies and eighties reeling from yet more invasions. A new generation of American servicemen on R & R from Vietnam crashed in. And then came the devastating advance of the developers with their jackhammers.

The pavement was clear and Sharon forced herself to move on. It occurred to her that the Cross had always been as much a casualty as the people it attracted, except it was no longer just a venue for the struggle of dog eat dog. Now, it was where lambs were slaughtered.

MacFarlane Place was a lonely blitz site where rubble and discarded hypodermic needles scrunched underfoot and neighbouring buildings turned blank walls as if to ignore the destruction. Just as Marieta had said, only one crumbling terrace house had been inexplicably spared. It stood there, a doomed Miss Havisham of a dwelling, awaiting the inevitable.

Sharon stepped carefully towards it. At that moment, the sun appeared through a gap in the cloud. It was just past noon and the sudden heat was searing. She quickened her step. The prospect of forcing her way into the ruin had seemed grim. Now, any shade would be a blessing.

Stout planks had been nailed firmly across the front door, but the window beside it gaped open. Sharon cleared broken glass and as much dirt as possible off the sill, then gingerly sat down on it and swung her legs inside. She stood up, vainly brushing at her backside. The room was a nightmare of rotting linoleum, stained and pitted walls and dried clusters of faeces. A filthy pile of rags in one corner obviously served as a bed. Several broken bottles littered the place and the air was tainted with the smell of stale urine.

A shaft of sunlight penetrated the room, shaped by the window behind her. She found herself in a column of iridescent dust. The door hung drunkenly on its hinges and was decorated with a mutilated poster advertising the Sydney Dance Company's *Some Rooms*.

Some rooms, Sharon thought. They ought to see *this* room. She stood there, uncertain as to what she should do next.

An almost indiscernible creak came from another part of the house.

Quickly, she crossed the room and edged herself around the door without touching it for fear it might fall on her if she dislodged it. On the other side was a long hall running the length of the house.

'Kenneth? Kenneth, are you there? It's me – Sharon. Remember?'

Her voice sounded oddly muffled and there was a tremor in it which betrayed her uncertainty. She waited for a reply, not moving.

All was quiet and still. No sunlight penetrated the gloom of this hall, but she was still hot. A bead of sweat crawled down her back to be intercepted at the waist by the tight belt.

'Kenneth?'

She could have sworn she'd heard a noise, but then in an old place like this on the verge of tumbling down, that wouldn't be unusual. The best thing to do, she decided, was to make doubly sure the boy wasn't here hiding, trying to avoid her because he thought she'd let him down, and then get out as fast as possible.

She began to walk down the hall, glancing into the shadowy rooms that led off it and becoming more and more distressed at the thought of the youngsters forced to seek shelter here.

She stopped.

Another noise. But whether it was inside or out, she couldn't be certain. She continued on, almost to the end of the hall, and saw that it led to one more room.

She went in.

It was the kitchen, or had been once upon a time before the taps had been ripped out, before the sink had become encrusted with grease and filth and before the cupboards had been torn down or smashed in. Fingers of light, bent arthritically by the gaps between slats nailed unevenly across the window, enabled her to see it was a good-sized room, an old-fashioned family-size kitchen with a walk-in pantry leading off it. There was a broken wheel-back chair on its side, a rickety-looking table near the pantry door, and the usual putrid debris scattered over the floor.

It was only then that Sharon saw the girl.

Half-hidden by the rusting hulk of an ancient gas stove, she lay pitifully crumpled like a puppet which had been tossed aside. Despite a mounting dread, Sharon moved closer.

The girl's upturned face was blotched with bruises and streaked with blood. It was a child's face, coarsened by experience and drugs. The hair was bleached white-blonde, crew-cut and spiked with gel. A green tuft sprouted from her forehead like a virulent weed. But the red patch extending from the left temple and over her ear, glistening like crushed mulberries, owed nothing to the art of hairdressing. Sharon now saw more bruising and bleeding on the girl's bare arms and legs.

The girl had been beaten to death. The eyes, the open, staring eyes, were a testimony of terror.

Sharon took two steps closer and squatted down, reaching to touch the girl's outflung arm. The flesh was still very warm. And she noticed that blood was still trickling from the head wound.

It had only just happened.

The girl had been dead only minutes.

Sharon rocked back on her heels. The noises she had heard—

Her heel was catching on something and automatically she reached back, her mind still on the fact that she was at the scene of a crime and the murderer might still be around. Her hand closed on something and as she straightened up she brought it around to the front.

It was the leg of a chair with the blood still wet on it.

Even that was not enough to claim her complete attention.

Out of the corner of her eye, and now as she shifted her gaze sideways, she could see the pantry door shifting almost imperceptibly, moving open ever so slowly, ever so slyly, being pushed by the merest whisper of an effort, fraction by fraction, and if she waited until the hinges creaked then the game of stealth would be over and someone, something, would leap out at her and she would end up like the girl on the floor.

Every childhood fear of the monster in the closet flooded back. But into the flood was released the adrenalin of survival.

She flung herself at the edge of the table and shoved it with all the force she could muster against the door of the pantry. The door slammed shut.

It could have been pushed open immediately, even allowing for the weight of the table. The door had no catch, no lock, and the hammering from inside erupted with an unbridled fury. Sharon had one factor in her favour. A rotted floorboard gave way under the two front legs at the narrow end of the table and they dropped down below floor level to their thickest circumference, jamming the table against the door.

Sharon turned and ran out of the kitchen.

In her panic, she blundered through the shadows of the hallway, on course but out of kilter. She found herself bumping against the walls, pushing crazily away from the traps of open doorways, her fingernails scrabbling and tearing, her heels catching along the obstacle course of decay.

Sobbing, and with screams fighting the sobs in her throat, she fell against the half-open door to the front room. The hinges gave way and the door fell flat on the floor with an ear-splitting crash. Choking in clouds of dust, she ran almost blindly over to the window and clambered out, losing a shoe in the process.

At the same moment, Allan Steinbeck pushed his way out of the pantry when the sheer force of his efforts snapped off the submerged legs where they joined the tabletop. He ran up the hallway to where a dusty fog welled from the front room. He went in and carefully peered around the side of the window, just in time to see Sharon Pettifer staggering and stumbling over the moonscape that was MacFarlane Place. He waited until she had disappeared, then quickly made his move.

PART II

'Being another character is more interesting than being yourself.'

Sir John Gielgud

1

The woman left Kenneth alone in the morning room for the rest of the day. She may have looked in now and again, but he had no way of knowing because he lay facing the windows. He dozed off several times, too, and she could have checked him out while he was asleep. But basically, he had this relaxed feeling of not being intruded upon.

The nausea had gone. Rest soothed his throbbing leg and time seemed to float by, its passage silky smooth and charted only by the changing pattern of the day's weather.

It was a completely unfamiliar experience for him, this placid drifting of the mind coupled with physical wellbeing, and he felt a stranger to himself and the exigencies of his past. It was curious but pleasant. Very pleasant.

At first, he was hypnotised by the monochrome shadings of the view, a harbour bled of its colour by the absence of sunshine. It was like a line drawing waiting for crayons to fill it with life and it reminded him of the colouring books he'd had when he was young.

Stories came to mind, simplistic yarns about Old Sydney. The harbour became a gigantic amphitheatre in which his imagination placed frigates bristling with weapons making ready to conquer the savages of the South Seas. Cargo ships rode at anchor while their holds were loaded with wool bales. He heard echoes of squeeze-boxes and shanties as diggers from the goldfields caroused with jolly Jack Tars and squandered their earnings on grog and women.

He had never indulged in fantasising, not for years.

It wasn't important.

It was a waste of time when you had to be thinking always of the main chance.

It was stupid.

But because of all those reasons, there was a mischievous enjoyment about it, a comforting regression to an innocence long gone.

Later, he became aware that the sun had made an appearance.

The harbour regained its vivid, glittering splendour and distracted him from his dreams.

He knew he should be making plans to leave. There was no place for him here. He didn't fit in. And caring though the woman seemed to be, the novelty would soon wear off. It always did.

Oddly, none of this seemed to matter. Odder still, he had no urge to see what he could pocket before she gave him the boot. And no way in the world did he feel inclined to dwell on what awaited him outside, or how he would avoid the menace of The Man. As long as he kept reality at bay, nothing bad would happen.

It must have been late afternoon when she made a grand entrance because she was brandishing a full crystal tumbler, clinking with ice cubes.

'Cocktail time! But for you, bouillon!'

And she held up a large mug in her other hand. Noting his questioning look, she hastened to explain.

'Bouillon. Clear broth. Good for what ails you. Come on, sit up.'

He pushed himself up and started to sip the broth, warily at first, then with more relish as he found how tasty it was.

'If you keep that down, we can try something a little more substantial later on. But no more hotcakes and corn syrup for a while, huh?'

She smiled at him vivaciously and raised her glass in mock salute. Kenneth reckoned she'd had more than a couple already. Her effervescence rankled him. It wasn't just that she'd broken into his space. He wasn't used to people being this cheerful. There wasn't any reason for it, ever, and if people thought there was then they were kidding themselves. Or if they *did* have a reason for happiness, then it made them one up on him, it made them superior, and that made him nervous.

He scowled at her. Suddenly, she was a whole bad scene.

'Why are you doing this?' he challenged.

Her eyes popped. She regarded him with amusement, and that irritated him even more.

'Why *not*? Is there any law that says a person can't help another person, particularly when that other person happens to be in big trouble?'

'You don't even know me,' he countered.

Then she really let out a big laugh.

'Oh, I know you. I know you so well. You're a matching set, all you street kids, like cutlery. We hear about you, we read about you. I'm not trying to diminish your problems, though. I think it's terrible there are so many of you with identical reasons for taking the same path.'

Kenneth was getting angry.

'How do *you* know about it? What do you know about anything?'

'I've been around the block a couple of times, buster. This isn't Mary Poppins you're talking to, you know, so don't get crappy with me!'

It was as if he'd pressed a button. The humour was gone, the toughness was back.

'To do what you did, con a man into propositioning you with a mike taped to your chest and a hidden camera trained on you means you're not exactly straight from the monastery.'

Her polished red mouth twitched, the humour not entirely gone.

'Or from what I've heard about monasteries, maybe you are.'

'I'm not queer!' he blurted out.

'Praise the Lord,' she chanted drily and demolished her drink. 'Not that I have anything against gays,' she said, choking on a sliver of ice. She coughed, then recovered. 'I'd say you were a runaway, like all the others, and you had valid *reasons* for being a runaway. I'd also say you'd been forced to survive by any means that offered, like not living by accepted rules and not recognising accepted standards.'

She was so spot on, he couldn't come up with anything to say. He wasn't used to conversation, anyway. Particularly conversation which escalated into the numbing regions of discussion. To cover up the way he felt, he finished what was left of the broth and considered throwing the empty mug at her to shut her up.

She would have made a difficult target. She was pacing the room as if looking for hidden words in the corners. For the first time he noticed what she was wearing, probably because it hadn't hit him in the eye immediately like the rest of her stuff. She had on fawn pants and a loose top of soft browns and greens. The make-up job and the hairdo hadn't changed, but the overall effect was flattering.

She came back and sat on the edge of the settee and he noticed how carefully she did it to avoid nudging his sore leg. She caught his eyes with her own and held on to them, her voice softer.

'I know you're hostile. You're unsure of all this,' she gestured with her empty glass, 'and you've probably never met anyone like me, either.'

She leaned closer.

'But try to imagine how *I* feel. I'm trying to give you some kind of support, and all the time I have a sneaking suspicion I might be bopped on the head while you take off with the family jewels. Why am I persisting? I don't know. Maybe I do. You're not a deadbeat. You're intelligent. And I guess . . . yeah, that's it . . . I guess I like you.'

Kenneth winced. Next minute she'd expect him to hop into bed with her. Yuk! To his surprise, she cloned his very thoughts into words.

'Don't take that as sexual!'

She rose from the settee and started pacing again. Behind her, the vista of the harbour was darkening. Lights had started to twinkle along the suburban foreshores. Headlands of green bush were metamorphasising into impenetrable jungles, lazy bays into secretive hollows.

She was talking again.

'I'm not into toy boys, particularly toy boys who look like they just posed for a Famine Relief poster. I like men. M – E – N.'

She spelled it out proudly as if it were some prize she was awarding herself. And then she was back on the settee, not crowding him, keeping her distance, as if she knew.

'Deal time, okay? You stay on. A few days, till you're feeling better. You can make yourself useful. I saw how you handled that window. There are other things I need doing around here. But no tricks, understand? You step out of line and you've had it.'

He had to get at her. She was undermining his defences.

'Threats, huh?' he grunted disparagingly. 'Some friend.'

'Yeah. It's the only way, kiddo.' There was a sadness about the way she said it. 'It's for your own good – take it or leave it.'

That was the way it had been with her from the start and it hadn't done him any harm, so he decided to take it.

2

Two or three drinks later, she suggested he take a shower.

First, she led him to the kitchen and unbandaged his leg. The bruising still looked an angry purple, but the wound was clean. When he'd showered, she redressed the leg, then asked him if he were hungry.

He nodded.

She heated another mug of broth in the microwave and gave it to him to drink while she made thick ham sandwiches. She ate one, he had three.

A silence had settled between them, but it was not the awkward silence of strangers. Kenneth concentrated on the food and left the talking to her. Except, for once she didn't seem inclined to talk. When he'd almost finished, he looked up and saw a frown on her face. She took a sip of her drink then put it down.

'A kid was found dead in Kings Cross, a young girl. There was a newsflash on the radio this afternoon.'

Kenneth shrugged.

'It happens. One in seven kids commit suicide in Australia, did you know that? I've had four mates kill themselves lately. And they keep coming up with new ways. I heard two kids deliberately infected themselves with AIDS.'

'Oh, Jesus Christ!' She shook her head, her voice a whisper. 'But this girl wasn't a suicide. She was battered to death. Murdered.'

Kenneth shrugged again. He didn't want to know about it. Kids who ran away to the Cross these days knew about the dangers. There was no way they didn't, but they still poured in looking for freedom. And they got it. For the first few hours. After that, they were in too deep and there was no way out.

The woman was still looking miserable. He knew she wanted to go on talking about it, but he wasn't having any. He changed the subject.

'How does a Yank like you come to be in Australia?'

She smiled and looked into the depths of her glass.

'Now there is a story and a half.'

'Well?' he ventured encouragingly.

'Oh no. Not tonight. Some other time, maybe, when I know you a little better. Besides, I don't think you need a bedtime story to put you to sleep.'

She had caught him stifling a yawn. He did feel tired again. It was as if he was making up for all the sleepless nights of the past. The winter nights when there was no shelter except for a doorway or an industrial waste bin in an alley. The nights when he stayed up till all hours, thieving from cars and selling the parts for peanuts so's he could eat the next day. The nights in the squat when Donna's demented moaning made sleep impossible.

He undressed in the small bedroom off the kitchen, and this time she didn't ask him for his clothes.

She still didn't trust him, however.

Again, he heard the key quietly turn in the lock just before he drifted off into sleep.

3

The next morning, she gave him the Grand Tour.

He was by now quite familiar with several of the rooms on the ground floor; the kitchen and the servant's room he was using; the dining room with folding double doors, usually kept open, leading into the living room – or drawing room as she called it; the morning room with its spectacular views.

But there were other rooms on the ground floor, reached by a door on the other side of the foyer, and each with a specific purpose. The sewing room was small and stuffy, with two high-backed chairs and floor-to-ceiling linen cupboards. The music room boasted a Steinway grand piano and a rickety stool Kenneth knew he could fix with a bit of glue. There was a study, booklined and musty, and several small bedsitting rooms tucked away at the side of the house, for use as either guest or servants' quarters. Adele conducted him around offhandedly, but her pride of ownership was obvious.

In the drawing room, she pointed out the large fireplace with its elaborate cedar mantelpiece atop richly moulded side columns. In passing, she let her hand caress a highly-polished surface here, a deeply carved embellishment there. She drew his attention to fluted archways and delicate friezes of plaster wreaths.

The formal rooms at the front of the house opened out on to the stone terrace through French doors. At the rear, because the ground dropped away sharply, the morning room and its neighbours overlooked a similar terrace running across the back of the house, which could only be reached by going out of a door in the kitchen and walking around the side of the house.

From the entrance foyer, the gracefully curved staircase wound up to a wide hall off which opened two enormous bedrooms on the rear side of the house, both facing the harbour, and three smaller ones overlooking the front grounds. Kenneth noticed that every bedroom had its own bathroom and dressing room.

She briefly allowed him to see her bedroom, dominated by a

magnificent four-poster, but waved him airily past the closed door of the one next to it to the end of the hall, where a couple of steps led to several smaller bedrooms and a back staircase down to the kitchen.

As they returned to the ground floor, a telephone rang. Adele hurried off into the living room and spoke haltingly for ten or fifteen minutes, as if she were finding it difficult to break in on what the person at the other end was saying. Kenneth squatted down on the stairs. His leg was bad, there was no doubt about it. It was aching, throbbing, just from walking around the house. He continued the inventory to pass the time. His shoulder muscles, wrenched by The Man's hold on his arm, had benefited from rest and made their presence felt only by bearable twinges now and then. His throat, though tight, had ceased to be painful.

She returned, waving her hands in exasperation, leaning on the balustrade of the staircase as if exhausted, but for exhaustion he read boredom and he was right.

'You should have heard that conversation! Then you'd know why I choose to live in this mausoleum alone.' She waved her arms some more. 'No! It's not a mausoleum, I love it to death. But, of course one would prefer company.'

'I've tried everything,' she continued. 'Live-in staff, for instance. I found myself spending evenings, not watching television or relaxing with records, but listening to their fights. So then I tried the "paid companion" bit, the so-called secretary who's supposed to put the cover on her typewriter and then become a friend.'

She shivered dramatically.

'For paid companion, read "misfit". So then I made the worst mistake of having so-called friends to stay. Disaster.'

She shucked her shoulder in the direction of the telephone in the drawing room.

'That was Holly Zimmerman, the last of them. She just moved out a couple of weeks ago. I used to think she was fun, cute as a button.' Her eyes went to heaven. 'Lemme tell you something. You have to live with someone to know them. That woman had every ailment known to man and a few that still have to be scientifically recognised. And yet she wants to be taken for the perennial teenager. Her whole life is dedicated to preserving looks which weren't great to begin with. I mean, we all try to make the best of what we've got, but she's ridiculous. For Holly, read "Gidgit Goes Geriatric!" '

Donning an outsize pair of sunglasses rimmed with gold, she

banished the subject of Holly Zimmerman and took him outside, naming hydrangeas, roses, fig trees, flowering gums and crepe myrtle with professional panache. A towering camphor laurel dwarfed them with its immensity. Sparrows, blue wrens and cheeky wagtails squabbled amongst the shiny leaves of a giant magnolia, its great white blooms as big as dinner plates, their overpowering perfume beguiling swarms of buzzing insects.

As they walked back across the lawns, Kenneth got his first good look at the house in broad daylight. Built of large blocks of sandstone, it was a blossoming of stone, solid as a rock.

'Late eighteen hundreds,' she said, seeing his interest. 'Built in an era when they built forever. From what I've heard, there were only about twenty houses on Point Piper when this one was constructed.'

At the back of the house below the terrace was a large rectangular swimming pool. In contrast to the neatness of the rest of the grounds, the water was murky and its surface a carpet of leaves.

'Don't you swim, then?'

She gave a little shudder. 'No way! Jorge doesn't have time to attend to it, and Mr Fitzgibbon – who's as temperamental as a chef – doesn't regard it as part of his duties. He's so imperious! I practically have to get his written permission to pick a flower!'

Kenneth learned that Jorge and his wife Rina were a young refugee couple from El Salvador who came three days a week to clean, launder and generally take care of the house. Mr Fitzgibbon, the gardener, also came three times a week. Kenneth gathered he was inclined to be surly, was omnipotent in his realm and was to be avoided.

'Come over here. I'm going to show you something more interesting than that crappy old pool.'

He joined her further down the slope where a rocky outcrop pushed out of the soil, providing an anchorage for a confusion of jasmine and hibiscus. She clawed at a tangle of branches.

'God, this stuff grows. It's the sandy soil.'

Eventually, she uncovered what she was looking for and, keeping the foliage well pulled back with one hand, she stood aside.

'There. It's an old aboriginal carving. It must be literally hundreds of years old.'

Kenneth craned forward to see, and was rather disappointed. Instead of something flamboyantly primitive, the carving was little more than a couple of elongated curved scratches with a dot between them at one end.

'See?' she said excitedly. 'It's a fish. That shows they must have fished a lot around here before the white man came.'

Kenneth's leg was hurting more, so he sat down on the grass, leaning back on his elbows.

She looked down at him.

'You know, I'm already getting very bored with that ratty old T-shirt and the jeans. How about we go get you some decent clothes?'

'No – I don't want to go out!'

It came to him suddenly, the fear, without prior warning or consideration. Only hours ago, he'd been all set to leave. Now, the feeling of being safe and protected overwhelmed him. Outside, he would be defenceless. The spell would be broken.

'Okay,' she replied easily, seeing the idea had upset him. 'I have to meet friends for lunch, so I'll just go shopping for you myself after that. You can use the rest, anyway.'

When they got back to the house, Jorge and Rina had arrived and were busy with the housework. The woman introduced him as the son of friends of hers who was boarding with her while his parents were overseas. Jorge had the golden moonface of a Mayan warrior, with shiny black hair and flashing white teeth. Rina was petite and darkly attractive. Both of them were taking lessons in English and seemed intelligent and friendly.

Rina was sent off to the sewing room for a tape measure and Jorge carried the vacuum cleaner out of the kitchen. The woman got a scribble pad and pen.

Kenneth looked at her.

'They call you Mrs Hatherley.'

'Hatherley was the schmuck I married. Before that I was Adele Ventura, a name I much prefer, let it be known.'

'What do I call you, then?'

She considered the question.

'What do you think of me as?'

'The Woman,' he replied.

'Charming.'

'Like I think of *him*, the one who's after me, as The Man.'

She threw up her hands. 'Oh, sweet Jesus, it gets worse. Call me Adele and be done with it.'

'Yeh. All right.'

'Say it,' she ordered.

'Adele.'

And then Rina returned with the tape measure, and Adele looped it around his middle and screamed with a mixture of envy and chagrin when his waist measurement turned out to be only twenty-four inches.

'Nobody's *that* blessed!' she wailed.

'But I am only twenty-two inches, Mrs Hatherley,' said Rina innocently.

'You mind your business, Carmen Miranda!' Adele roared at her. Rina giggled and ran off. 'Actually,' said Adele, turning to Kenneth, 'you're far too thin so I'll buy larger because, kiddo, I intend to fatten you up!'

4

She installed him on a reclining chair under an umbrella on the back terrace with sandwiches and milk and then left for her luncheon and the shopping.

He soon became fidgety.

He had welcomed relaxation when it was a fleeting experience, to be indulged in before he resumed his day-to-day existence in the outside world. Now, the knowledge that he could have as much of it as he wanted made him uneasy. He had always found inactivity a strain. If nothing else, playing the video games exercised his mind and reflexes and gave him something challenging to do. There were no video games here. And two nights of uninterrupted sleep plus one day of complete rest had replenished his energy.

The one thing he could see that needed attention was the neglected swimming pool. There must be some kind of shed nearby to house the filtration pump and pool equipment. He got up and went down the steps.

After a few minutes, he found what he was looking for screened by bushes below one end of the terrace. Fixed behind the door was a sheet of instructions: 'The Trouble Shooter's Guide to Pool Problems and Maintenance.' It was in basic, easy-to-follow language and Kenneth read it through.

He found a pool scoop on a long pole and within half an hour he had the surface of the water almost clear of leaves, which he dumped behind bushes. Then he located the filler box and brought out handfuls of the leaves that were clogging the basket inside.

Back in the shed, he saw that the filtration unit had been disconnected from the power needed to run it, merely by having its plug pulled out of the electric socket. He replaced the plug in the socket, and switched it on. The filter burped and coughed to life, and for a few anxious moments Kenneth thought it was going to explode. Then the motor settled down into a steady, uninterrupted hum.

He consulted the guide again, then found the chemicals it referred to, the liquid chlorine, syneric and hydrochloric acids, the clarifier and the sanitiser, all stored in clearly labelled plastic containers and bottles.

No amounts were mentioned in 'The Trouble Shooter's Guide', so he just carried each container out, one by one, and generously slurped the contents into the pool, on the assumption that none of them had been added all summer. Then he exchanged the net on the end of the long pole for a brush, which he used to dislodge the algae clinging to the tiled lining of the pool.

By this time, his leg was aching again and he was tired from the unaccustomed physical activity, but he had a satisfying sense of having done something useful. This enabled him to lie back and take it easy for the rest of the afternoon.

He had moved his chair around a little so that he could observe Adele's reaction to his labours on her return. When she finally made her appearance, walking down from the house with arms full of packages, he glanced back at the pool and noted happily that the water was already several shades lighter than its original murky green.

He could tell by the jauntiness of her step that she was well pleased with the results of her outing, and she began talking long before she reached him.

'Just you wait till you see what I've got for *you*, kiddo! If you don't make this year's Best Dressed list, then I'll—'

She stopped, freezing almost in mid-stride. Her eyes were concealed by the blacked-out portholes of her sunglasses, but he could see that her gaze had gone past him and was resting on the cleaned-up pool. She stood there, immobile, her face an impassive mask.

Kenneth waited for his reward, the exclamation of surprise, perhaps even a mild scolding for not resting as instructed, but at least an observation on the improvement he'd achieved.

He waited in vain. Without a word, Adele turned around and stalked back to the house and he didn't see her again until an hour later when he'd summoned up enough incentive to follow her indoors.

5

By the time he joined her in the kitchen, she had whipped up a lethal-looking concoction in the blender and was drinking it from a large V-shaped glass on a stem. The incident by the pool appeared to have been forgotten and she was bubbling with enthusiasm about the clothes she had selected for him.

The packages had been strewn over the furniture in the drawing room. She attacked them with enthusiasm, ripping off the wrapping paper, producing and displaying the contents with all the showmanship of an illusionist pulling a rabbit from a top hat and all the while carrying on a running commentary about where and why she bought this particular thing, inviting his opinion on colours and materials, and relating how she had 'kidnapped' a boy of Kenneth's build in the menswear department of one store and had him model her selections just to make sure.

It was as well she was doing all the talking. The situation was way beyond Kenneth's comprehension.

Here was this woman who had given him food and shelter. She had protected him when he was at his most vulnerable. She had tended his injuries and given him more caring and friendship than he'd had in years.

And now she was buying him clothes.

Warning bells were ringing all over the place. It was all so unbelievable, and therefore open to suspicion. Nobody was *this* benevolent, not for nothing, not without reason. He wasn't much of a talker at the best of times, but his amazement at the number and variety of garments she'd purchased coupled with the conflict of his doubts and half-formed suspicions left him speechless.

Fortunately, Adele seemed to attribute his silence to grateful acceptance, and happily rattled on while holding garments against him to assess size and suitability. There were at least four pairs of jeans, summer trousers in cream linen and pastel cotton, and shirts ranging from the traditional styles in pale colours to more avant garde designs in bold, imaginative patterns. He tried on two jackets, one in denim, the other leather. And there were underpants and socks, pyjamas, several T-shirts and two pairs of sneakers with obscure brand names.

'I didn't get you Reeboks or Nikes,' she said. 'I've heard about those Colour Gangs, and I don't want you mugged just for your footwear. You'll find the pants a little big around the middle, but I expect you to fatten up with regular meals. Now take everything into your room,' she instructed, piling things into his arms, 'and put them away carefully. Hang up the pants. Put the shirts and underwear into the dresser drawers, and—'

Hands finally free, she picked up her glass and drained it, then pulled a face.

'Oh, shit! Why do I bother? Yuckky, not to mention fattening!'

He finally found himself able to speak. He asked her what she'd been drinking and found out they were called Brandy Alexanders.

'Try everything on, just to make sure and pick out something sensational to wear for dinner,' she yelled after him as he went through the kitchen to his room.

He followed her instructions and found she'd got most of the sizes right. Some of the things were too straight and boring but after all, she was an oldie and wouldn't know.

It occurred to him she'd expect him to have a shower, so he did. Afterwards, it was pleasant pulling on the smooth, white jockettes and socks. It was an experience he'd almost forgotten. There were no lingering stinks that even washing wouldn't take out, and no stubborn stains either.

He sat down on the bed and debated what he should wear, since she had made such a big thing about it. It was unusual, having to think about it. That was something you didn't have to do when you had no choice. Eventually, he decided on the cream linen pants and a black T-shirt with muddy splotches all over it.

When he emerged into the kitchen, she was pulling the cork from a bottle of white wine. She looked over at him.

'Well,' she commented, 'it's different, I'll give you that. But try to remember, kiddo, T-shirts for daytime, regular shirts for the evening. Don't worry about it now, that's just for the future. Besides, I guess in a looney-tunes sort of way, we match.'

She was in light-coloured pants and a black top, too. She wrapped a white napkin around the wine bottle and gave it to him.

'Take this into the dining room and put it into the bucket of ice you'll find there.'

He carried it into the dining room and was surprised to find the heavily carved table set for two at one end. The folding panelled doors had been pulled together, closing off the drawing room, and the place was given a further intimacy by candlelight. He slid the white napkin up around the neck of the bottle and pushed the bottle down into the ice-filled bucket which stood on a place mat next to a crystal bowl of tossed salad.

Adele swept in.

'It may look as though I've gone to a lot of trouble, but not so. No cooking tonight, we're dining very al fresco.'

She placed a large platter of seafood between the two set places. It was piled high with unshelled King prawns, cracked crab claws and lobster tails, with quartered segments of lemon scattered between them.

'I usually have everything delivered, but I passed a seafood shop this afternoon and just couldn't resist all of this stuff.'

She took her place at the head of the table and indicated the place set to her right.

'Okay. What are we waiting for?' She sat down and stared at Kenneth. 'You may pour the wine. In fact, you may pour a glass for yourself, too. Wine in moderation is healthful and beneficial, and a cold Riesling like that one is a perfect accompaniment for seafood.'

He went blank. He couldn't hack all this. It wasn't him and it wasn't anything he was used to. It was a lot of pretentious shit and he wanted to tell her so. What was she trying to turn him into? Some kind of poofter flunkey? A human Barbie doll?

'Kenneth? Are you all right?'

She was staring at him with concern in her eyes. Genuine concern. You couldn't fake something like that.

He thought: Accept it, she just wants you to be happy. And he took the bottle from the bucket and splashed wine into her heavy crystal glass and then some into his own.

'That's better,' she said. 'You know, sometimes you worry me. You're off in a world of your own.'

He wanted to yell 'Yeh, and you fuckin' worry *me*, too, like when you saw the pool and turned yourself off, you ungrateful bitch!' Then he thought: What did it matter? It was over, in the past, and to dwell on it would spoil the festive atmosphere which seemed to prevail this evening.

He tried his wine and found it icily refreshing. He had some

more. Adele was shovelling seafood on to his plate and soon he
realised he'd been wrong. There was nothing pretentious about the
meal. It was like a picnic. Knives and forks weren't necessary except
for the salad. Just fingers, to peel the cellophane skins from the
prawns, to hold the crab claws while you sucked the meat out, and
to forge deep into the crevasses of lobster for its sweet flesh.

They tucked in like ravenous urchins, wolfing down the feast
without a thought for good manners, wiping their lips with the
backs of their hands and licking their fingers.

Adele's enthusiasm and bubbling good humour were infectious.
She seemed to drop years and the tough banter that usually charac-
terised her manner of talking to him gave way to a youthful genial-
ity. There was nothing awkward about it. She wasn't making an
attempt to patronise him by trying to impersonate a teenager. This
was more an unconscious lowering of defences, allowing a peep
under the tent of her personality. Kenneth's earlier misgivings slid
away like thawing snow down a mountainside.

Adele allowed him a second glass of wine, then finished the rest
of the bottle herself. Appetite satisfied, she asked Kenneth if he
wanted milk, tea or coffee. He shook his head and burped. She
laughed and went out of the room. He capitulated to greed and
reached for the last King Prawn on the platter. While he was peeling
it, he became aware of music. He looked around, but decided the
speakers must be hidden behind the panelling. The music was lush
and orchestral, softly romantic and old fashioned. It wasn't his style
at all, but somehow it seemed to suit the afterglow of a good meal.

Adele returned, cradling a brandy balloon, a third full of the
amber liquid.

'Sure you've had enough? There's plenty more salad,' she said
nodding to the bowl as she sat down.

Kenneth shook his head. Adele cupped her hand around the
glass, swishing the brandy around reflectively. There were four
candles in the silver candelabra on the table. Their light cast a
flickering radiance which made Adele look softer, almost girlish.

Kenneth leaned back in his chair. He never knew what to say in
periods of silence like this but with her, he was beginning to realise,
it didn't matter. She didn't expect brilliant conversation from him
and was quite content with the rare pauses she allowed when she
herself wasn't speaking.

She began to hum to the music, imperceptibly at first then more
distinctly. Gradually, words crept in here and there as if being

retrieved from her memory bank. And then she was singing, softly enriching the flow of the lyrics with the warm huskiness of her voice.

'The evening breeze
Caressed the trees
Tenderly

The trembling trees
Embraced the breeze
Tenderly . . .'

She continued on for a while, as if in a trance, and like the evening breeze and trembling trees her voice embraced and caressed the words of the song as if they were the limbs of a lover. She swayed slightly in her chair, raised her chin, used her eyelids like veils and leaned slightly forward, each movement a deft but unobtrusive punctuation.

She raised her eyes and broke off, and Kenneth was aware that a moment of the most fragile intimacy was over.

She gave him a sad little smile. 'Ooops! Haven't performed for an audience in years.'

'It was really excellent.'

He meant it and she could see he meant it. She bowed her head politely.

'Thank you. I take that as a rare compliment.'

She raised the brandy balloon to her lips and took several reflective sips.

Kenneth cleared his throat. He had thought of something to say.

'Did you sing . . . er . . . like, as a job, then?'

'Professionally? Oh yes,' she replied, her eyes twinkling as if she found humour in the very fact that he had asked the question. She took another sip of brandy. And another. And looked at him as if considering whether or not he was ready to be confided in, and assessing, perhaps, whether or not she was ready to confide in him. She hummed along with the music a little more, then began to speak as if from a great distance.

'I can't believe it all started over forty years ago. I was so very young . . .'

Her eyes darted to him and she tapped the top of his hand with a long vermilion fingernail to emphasise the point.

'. . . *very* young. Girl singers were a dime a dozen around Los

Angeles and I was a complete unknown, so when I got a chance to strut my stuff at a little place in the Valley, I grabbed it. What the joint was, if you want to know the truth, was a gay bar. But in those days everyone was in the closet, so it sort of masqueraded as a jazz club.'

She took a swig of brandy.

'One night I was spotted by the head of production at one of the big motion picture studios. My big break!'

Kenneth leaned forward. 'You mean he made you into a movie star?'

'Ha!' The derisive laugh shot out like a bullet. She waved the brandy balloon. Kenneth jumped to his feet, ready to get her a refill. She gave him the glass, but stopped him when he made for the kitchen.

'No, kiddo. The drawing room.'

She got to her feet and went to the folding doors. She pulled them apart, but instead of going through and switching on the lights, she walked back to the table and picked up the candelabra. Then she led the way into the drawing room, the candlelight creating hugely distorted shadows which stretched and shrunk as she passed by, the flickering illumination not even reaching the furthest corners of the room. Reaching a small rosewood table, she turned to him indicating one of several crystal decanters clustered on its surface.

'Be generous,' she said, and crossed to one of the red leather armchairs. She placed the candelabra on a side table nearby, gathered up several cushions and threw them on the floor, then settled into the armchair lighting a cigarette. Kenneth splashed a large helping of brandy into the glass and took it over to her. As she accepted it, she pointed to the cushions at her feet.

'Make yourself comfortable.'

Kenneth squatted down, aware that he was being manipulated as an audience and wondering whether she had done all this before. She took a drink, then waved her cigarette vaguely.

'Where was I?'

But of course, she knew exactly where she was.

'Oh yeah. My big break. But there was no hyped-up debut on the silver screen like there'd been for Doris Day a few years before, no way, not for me. Didn't matter at the time. I was ambitious and ready for anything. That's why I agreed to dub the singing voice of this new girl they had under contract.' She paused significantly. 'Her name was . . . Kelly Green.'

Adele's eyes popped at Kenneth, who was staring at her blankly.

'Well? Doesn't the name mean anything to you? Sure, she was dead before you were born, but so was Queen Victoria and you've heard of *her*, haven't you?'

As far as Kenneth was concerned, Queen Victoria was a shopping arcade in the city. But Kelly Green? Yes, he'd heard of her. He'd even seen some of her pictures and he knew she'd been a top super-star in her day, a sex symbol with her perpetually tousled mane of red hair and her sinuous body with the firm, upstanding tits and the long, long legs. But although she pouted and growled a lot, she always seemed nice with it, as if it were all a bit of a joke.

'I know who you mean,' he replied. 'I've seen her in old movies. She didn't do her own singing, then?'

He said it casually, as if it didn't matter. And of course it *didn't* matter, to him. But obviously it did to Adele, who continued in hushed and secretive tones as if she were telling him how to make a neutron bomb.

'They swore me to secrecy. It was in my contract. Nobody knew. Ever!'

Incredibly, she had already finished the brandy he had given her. She jumped up and made for the decanter, so involved with the intrigue of her story she had forgotten it was no longer necessary for her to pour her own drinks. Kenneth noted this but stayed where he was, while she upended the decanter over her glass and kept talking.

'Musical numbers have always been prerecorded and mimed in movies, and that made it easier to fake. Oh, Kelly would go through the motions and record the vocals with the studio orchestra, then mime to the playbacks when the the numbers were shot. But after-wards – and strictly undercover – I'd dub in the lyrics and bingo! Another Kelly Green soundtrack.'

Kenneth was perplexed. 'Why all the secrecy?'

Adele returned to her chair and swallowed about half the brandy she had poured herself in one gulp. She gave a bitter smile.

'Kelly's singing voice was as flat as a pancake, but they kept putting her into splashy musicals because the colour and the costumes showed off her looks. Plus the fact that musicals of that era didn't require much acting ability.

'There was a lot of voice-dubbing for actresses who couldn't sing in those days, and a girl called Marni Nixon did most of it. She dubbed Deborah Kerr in *The King and I* . . . Natalie Wood in *West Side Story* . . . Audrey Hepburn in *My Fair Lady*. But you see, it didn't matter if the fans knew *they* didn't use their own singing voices, because all those ladies had something else going for them. They were damn fine actresses. But despite the fact that Kelly had ability too, the studio bosses didn't think she had anything going for her but her body. In their opinion she was the triple threat. Couldn't sing, couldn't dance, couldn't act. They thought she was shit. A box office bonanza, but still shit.'

'And was she?'

Adele shook her head vehemently. 'She had this amazing presence on film. It didn't matter who else was in the scene – and believe me, she worked with some of the best – you only looked at her. She had something indefinable that reached out and grabbed an audience by the balls and by the heart.'

'But when she died . . . wasn't that the finish for you, too?' Kenneth asked.

Adele leaned forward intently.

'When Kelly was killed in that plane crash in Arizona, a whole new industry sprang up. Reissues of her movies and records . . . books, calendars, posters . . . you name it. And all without the bother of the little lady herself around to screw things up! And naturally, they didn't want *me* around, either. I might blow it, you know? That it was me singing and not her? So my contract was terminated with a nice, fat settlement fee and it was quietly but firmly suggested that I should get lost. Permanently. One hundred thousand bucks. That was a lot of money in the early sixties, but what they had at stake was a billion dollar industry and they didn't want anything or anybody lousing it up.'

'So what did you do?'

She shrugged. 'I call that period my empty years. I tried breaking back into the music business as myself, but it had been too long, and besides, the Beatles and all that kind of music were in – not my scene at all. Eventually, I took myself off to Mexico, and it was there I got lucky. I met this big-time investment broker, name of Joe. Joseph Zampini. And if you want the truth, him and the Mafia weren't exactly strangers.

'I lived with Joe for seven years in Acapulco, the seven happiest years of my life. God, he was good to me.' Her voice wavered and she drank a little more brandy. 'Then his ticker gave out in the pool one day and it was all over.'

Gotcha! Kenneth thought. That explained her aversion to swimming pools.

She was on the verge of being maudlin, but managed to swallow her emotion with the remains of the brandy.

'I'd trusted him enough to let him invest my capital. Soon after his death, I found out that thanks to him, the original investments had grown into millions. Besides that, he'd left me a sizable chunk of his own fortune. So, I picked myself up, dusted myself off, and started all over again. It wasn't easy without Joe, but I did it. I guess you could call me a survivor.'

Adele was showing the effects of the evening's drinking. The words were coming more slowly, her pronunciation slurred. But apparently, there was still more to tell.

'There's a little place called Puerto Vallerta in Mexico. It was a tiny fishing village of no more than a few hundred people before Richard Burton made *Night of the Iguana* there in sixty-five. Liz Taylor went along to make sure he behaved himself, and they both fell in love with the place. They bought a house there, and pretty soon Puerto Vallerta was right on top of everybody's must-see list.

'I bought a hotel there, a wreck of a place. Did it over, built on extensions, added a pool, landscaping, kept on with the improvements until it was an entire resort in itself. A regular playground for the well-to-do. Then I sold it. Did the same with a restaurant in Miami. Put in a dinner theatre, used some contacts of Joe's to get top drawcards for the shows, did a little singing myself just to keep the vocal cords from getting rusty. Sold that, too, after a while. But always for profit. Always the sure thing. Joe taught me, and I'd learned pretty good.'

She smiled vacantly, looking way over Kenneth's head.

'Funny. What do they say? The rich get richer?' She nodded. 'You'd better believe it, kiddo. I was a regular gypsy. I'd buy a place, do it up, sell it, move on. The only constants in my life were a flair for business and a taste for the tropics. Then, four or five years ago I was in Tahiti and I bumped into this Aussie guy, Lambert Hatherley. He was what you'd call a real gentleman. All the best schools, good manners, Savile Row suits, loads of charm . . . and flat broke! Still, I had more than enough for two, so when he suggested we come back to his old home town, I thought why not? We got married in a cute little church in Papeete, and came here for the honeymoon. We were just in time to rescue this place from the auctioneers.'

She gestured around, waving her arms limply. The empty glass dropped from her hand and landed softly on the thick carpet without breaking.

'Yeah, kiddo. This was the old family home. The Hatherleys had been real big in this town. Heard of their shipping line – Hatherley

International Steamship and Transport? No, before your time. That was their trouble. They didn't move with the times. They stayed with the steamships when they should have been talking diesel and airplanes. So, the company ran out of business, the family ran out of money and started dying off, and "Horizons" was about to go when l'il ole' Adele stepped in waving her trusty ole' cheque-book.'

Kenneth was almost afraid to speak. She was fading fast.

'What happened to—?'

'Lambert? The light of my life, or so I thought? He ran out on me. Can you believe that? Ran out on me a coupla years back.' She threshed around fitfully in the chair. 'Why does everyone important to me either run out or die? Kelly. Joe. Lambert. Lambert . . .'

Her voice tapered off and she slept, slumped in the chair, chin down on her chest cushioned by a fold of surplus flesh.

Kenneth stayed where he was.

Ghosts moved in the dark corners of the room, the wraiths of long-gone movie queens and mafia hoods stirring restlessly, churning the shadows into cataracts of discontent.

One of the candles guttered, pointing a finger of acrid smoke at the ceiling.

Kenneth was back on the outskirts of that faraway world she had shown him, back in the dismal no man's land that lay on the wrong side of highly coloured reminiscences. The visions of exotic places and untold wealth were disintegrating. The shadows were still again. And then there was nothing. He was just a kid in a murky house with a passed-out drunk for company.

A ship's siren boomed distantly from the Harbour like an animal in pain. Kenneth got up and fumbled under the shade of a nearby lamp until he found the switch to turn it on. The sudden light had no effect on Adele. She didn't stir. Kenneth looked around. He saw a Spanish shawl draped over a carved wooden screen and decided that would have to do. It was large and silky with a heavy fringe. As gently as he could, he used it like a blanket to cover Adele.

He blew out the remaining three candles and switched off the lamp. He stood there for a few minutes while his eyes adjusted to the darkness, then carefully made his way through the dining room and the kitchen and into his room.

This was one night she wouldn't be locking him in, but it didn't matter. As she'd said very early in the piece, he wasn't going anywhere.

6

The door of the Conference Room had hardly closed behind them when Jim Abrahams swung Sharon around, cupped her face in his hands and kissed her. She put her palms flat against his chest and ever so gently pushed him away.

'Don't make it harder for me,' she pleaded softly.

Jim smiled. 'It couldn't be any harder. One kiss and it stands to attention.'

He came in close and tried to kiss her again. This time her push was more forceful.

'No, Jim. No fooling around and no bad jokes. This isn't the reason I wanted privacy. We're fighting a lot lately, and usually in your office. Somebody overhears us and then it's all round the newsroom.'

'You're anticipating a fight then, are you?'

'Not necessarily. I just want to do my job.'

The stale stench of tobacco still clung to the room, even though nobody on the staff smoked any more. Sharon wrinkled her nose with distaste and walked past him. She pulled out a chair from the long polished maple conference table, turned it slightly outwards and sat down.

Jim stood his ground, only his eyes following her.

'Well?'

Sharon rubbed at an imaginary smudge on the tabletop with her fingertips.

'Jim, you know it wasn't working out between us.'

'It was fine with me.'

'Well, it wasn't with me, and you know it,' she snapped back.

Jim still hadn't moved. 'I know it as a fact, but I still don't know why.'

Sharon jumped up. 'This isn't what I asked you here to discuss!'

'But since the subject's been raised—'

'All right!'

Her voice had been getting loud. Now she made a conscious effort to bring it down, choosing her words carefully.

'With time, I came around to thinking it wasn't necessarily a good idea to be sleeping with my immediate superior.'

'It's not necessarily a bad idea, is it?'

'It is if you're the one who's two or three rungs down the ladder. People tend to put the worst interpretation on it. I don't want that, not at this stage of my career. I want to do it on my own.'

'You mean masturbate?'

She glared at him, angry again. 'Oh, very funny. You know what I mean.' She swallowed, then continued, trying to contain her temper. 'Jim, I'm not saying everything's over. I just need some space. Nobody could have been kinder, sweeter than you when I first came to work here, and what happened between us seemed a natural progression. But I started to feel confined. Everything started to overlap. We'd go to bed and your idea of foreplay was to go over the following day's shooting schedule.'

He laughed in spite of himself and nodded. 'I can't deny that. I reckon I was so long without anyone, I got married to *Upfront* and didn't even know it.'

Sharon sat down again. She hoped it would signal a change of subject. She looked at him, her body leaning forward eagerly.

'Jim? I want to do a follow-up on that girl Donna's murder. Background it, show the kind of life she was leading, maybe even get a few pointers as to who did it.'

Jim's body seemed to slump. He shook his head slowly and gave a sigh which came from somewhere midway between weariness and exasperation.

'Sharon, we're not doing one of those "Most Wanted" shows, and that would be the only reason to resurrect the story.'

'Resurrect? Her body's hardly cold.'

'But the story is. Every angle was covered in our news bulletins. Look love, you discovered the body, and it's natural you have an intense personal interest in the case. But you dealt with that scene fully in your street kids story.'

'There could be a link, don't you see that? The missing boy, Kenneth. He shared that squat. He still hasn't turned up. What if someone tried to force his whereabouts out of the girl?'

Jim went over, pulled out the chair next to her and sat in it facing her. 'I take it you told the police all this?'

'Of course I did.'

'And?'

Sharon shrugged, putting a hand to her forehead and massaging the skin as if to soothe away a headache.

'They placed no importance on it. Which is a sad commentary on the plight of these kids. Which is the fresh approach I'd like to use. One street kid murdered, another missing and nobody gives a damn.'

The hand came away from her forehead, made a helpless gesture in the air and flopped into her lap. In her mind she saw Kenneth's face and without too much of a metamorphosis it became the face of her brother Terry. Terry, dead from sniffing glue. She heard her mother's anguished screeching. 'He idolised you, but you were never here for him! You were too busy with your rotten career. You would have seen the signs, you could have saved him!'

Jim reached out for her hand and held it between both of his. 'Sharon, look at it realistically. That girl had a history of assaults. She was a masochist. She invited violence.'

Sharon wrenched herself back to the present and shook her head dismissively. 'She was fourteen years old. An addict. She didn't know what was going on half the time.'

'But it *was* going on, and just that once, somebody went too far. You can't make more of it than that. As for the boy, runaways come and go; they're gypsies. You just feel bad about him because you let him down.'

She looked him directly in the eye for the first time since they came into the room. Her tone was dispirited.

'Then I take it I don't have your approval to go ahead with the story.'

Jim was trying hard to be reasonable.

'It's not really a question of my approval. This is not what *Upfront* is all about, milking a subject till it's dry. Your own experience should tell you that. You've already shown the plight of these kids and you're getting a lot of kudos for the sympathetic, down-to-earth way you handled the subject. Being on the spot at a murder scene won't do you any harm, either. You had a lot of exposure in the newscasts, and you can't buy that sort of publicity.'

Sharon sat bolt upright, pulling her hand from his grasp.

'Publicity? Is that supposed to make me feel good? Will publicity bring that pathetic girl to life again?'

She stood up, looking down at him with disdain.

'You see? It's that kind of paternalistic attitude of yours that makes me mad. You started out being a father figure to me and you've never bucked that image or even tried to, not even when we were lovers! In your eyes, I'm still teacher's pet, someone to be controlled and appeased and patted on the head.' She turned away, not willing to face him for the rest. 'So if you wanted some more reasons why things have changed between us, there's another little variation on the theme to add to your list.'

Jim got to his feet slowly. It seemed the longer they talked, the more he got hurt. He patted his pockets, automatically feeling for the cigarettes he had given up three years before. It must be the latent stink in here, he thought. Either that or you never really kicked the habit and all it took was something infinitessimal like a punch in the gut from the girl you loved, to bring back the craving.

Sharon turned back to him with a wry smile.

'I suppose I'll never be anchor-person of *Upfront* now.'

He pushed aside dreams of inhaling fragrant, scorching smoke down his parched throat.

'Maybe. When you're more experienced. You don't have the live on-camera technique, yet. Or the background.'

'And I'm a woman,' she said flatly.

That got him mad. He could handle her high-powered, almost neurotic approach to her work. Better that, than some bimbo who never said 'Boo!' except to her hairdresser, and was happy doing stories about dolphins and rock stars and gift suggestions. He could try to accept – and probably would, given time – her accusations about his attitude towards her, because he knew they had some foundation. But her last remark was the match that sent up the fireworks.

'That's bloody rubbish!' he burst out. 'The media is full of highly respected women in positions of great importance which they've earned on their merit as professionals. What makes me sick is the rest – the failures who give interviews and whinge about missing out on jobs and blame it on being a woman, when it was their own inadequacies that got in the way. Losers, that's what they are, looking for a way to get out from under. Don't become one of them. You don't have to, with your ability.'

'If that's the case, what does Grant Olsen have that I haven't got, besides a penis?' asked Sharon, turning her back.

'He has likeability, which at this moment and from where I'm standing, you lack most profoundly!'

And just after he'd said that, hurling it with force at Sharon's back he was surprised to see her turn. The antagonism had gone from her face. There was even a crinkle of humour around her transparently blue eyes.

'Jim, that was probably the most honest observation you've made yet, seeing I've been a bit of a bitch about everything. It gives me hope. What else does this paragon have that I should aspire to?'

He treated the question seriously, calming down.

'Grant's not even close to middle age, but he has a certain maturity of style. He has credibility. Charm. He generates trust, and he's dependable.'

'His hair transplant's not dependable,' Sharon observed. 'Lately, it looks like it should have "Welcome" printed across it.'

Jim had to smile in spite of himself. He heaved himself up and decided to push her to the limit. At least then he'd know if he still had a chance.

'If you don't think you're getting a fair go here, you can always leave. Any of the other networks would grab you.'

'Oh no. I'm not running away.' Sharon put her arm through his and walked him towards the door. 'I still think you're wrong about not doing a story on the girl, but you're the boss.'

It sounded as if she was capitulating, but that was just to keep the peace. It was not going to be Terry all over again, and she was determined not to let the matter drop.

7

Kenneth had left the swimming pool filter running all night and the next morning he saw a great improvement in the quality of the water. It still wasn't exactly sparkling, but the algae had gone and with it the stagnant green look.

He found a test kit and read the instructions. Trying it out, the readings showed a chlorine level far higher than what it should be, while the total alkalinity was down. Apart from pouring in another quantity of Pool Clarifier because the label said it 'produces clear, sparkling water', he decided to leave everything as it was for a couple of days before he checked the balance again.

Returning the test kit to the shed, he found an inflatable rubber ring still in its unopened plastic cover, stashed in a corner. He almost did in his lungs blowing it up, but once he'd stripped down to his underpants and was floating around in it, legs and arms trailing in the cool but not cold water, the sunlight pricking his skin, he reckoned it was worth it.

Earlier, he had reheated some coffee left in the percolator from the day before and taken a cup of it into the drawing room where Adele was still sleeping. He prodded her a couple of times and she stirred noisily awake, spitting out strands of Spanish shawl, looking at it and growling: 'No wonder I dreamed I was being screwed by a bullfighter.'

Kenneth handed over the coffee, which she accepted with trembling hands, and left without a word. He knew enough to know when not to stick around. Later, when he went back, the armchair was empty and the shawl thrown carelessly on the floor. He picked it up and rearranged it over the carved screen as best he could.

Now, as the ring floated him around so that he was facing the house, he saw Adele march out on to the terrace, swathed from top to toe in terry-towelling with a turban to match, and settle herself with a great deal of fussing around on one of the reclining chairs in the shade of the umbrella.

He saw the sun glint on the gigantic sunglasses as she glanced his way, but she didn't wave or give any sign that she had seen him. He wiggled his right hand like an oar, so that he floated around in a full circle to face the Harbour, and similarly allowed his thoughts to drift.

It must have been more than half an hour later, close to noon, when he became aware that the sun was almost directly overhead and burning with a disturbing intensity on his skin. He rolled out of the ring, dog-paddled lazily to the steps, then made his way up to the terrace.

Adele reached into the large beach bag she had brought out with her and produced a towel which she threw at him.

'Here.'

Then she took out a tube of sunscreen. 'And when you've dried off, you'd better slap on some of this, if it's not too late to save you from melanoma already.'

Her head tilted down and the sunglasses focussed on his underpants.

'Swimming togs. They'll have to go on the shopping list, since you seem determined to become the next Esther Williams.'

She settled back in her chair.

'Why don't you come down by the pool?' he asked.

She reacted as if he'd made a crass remark, pulling the overlap of her robe up around her throat.

'Out of the shade? You're kidding! With *my* colouring, I have to be extremely careful.'

Kenneth thought if she was so worried about her colouring she could just put it all back in the bottles, because that was where it all seemed to come from, her hair and complexion, right down to her red toenails. He sat down on the other chair and started using the cream.

'And another thing,' she continued, 'you shouldn't be in the water with an open wound.'

'I checked before I went in. It's closed up.' Then he added: 'Thanks to you.'

That seemed to mollify her. She nodded towards the pool. 'Quite the little expert, aren't you?'

'Just followed the instructions,' he said. 'I catch on quick.'

Now the sunglasses were trained on his face, unmoving.

'You certainly do. You're actually rather bright, that comes through loud and clear. When did you stop going to school?'

He thought. 'Must be over two years ago. Longer. Not since . . .'
His voice trailed off.

'Not since what?' she asked quickly.

He shrugged. 'Nothing.'

She didn't pursue the question. Trespassing would get her
nowhere. Instead, she diverged optimistically. 'You should find it
easy to catch up, once you decide what to do. There are all sorts
of extracurricular avenues of learning. Night school, technical col-
leges, lots of different courses I should imagine.'

Her talking about the future bothered Kenneth even more than
the questions about his past. He had to change the subject.

While he was floating around in the pool, he'd been going over
what she'd told him the night before, and trying to relate it to all
the Kelly Green movies he'd seen. And he had seen more than
most kids of his age. That's what came from being shacked up with
a fanatical devotee of ancient movies for a couple of months at a
time when he was really desperate. Felix Fulton was his name, and
he had an older sister he only ever referred to as 'Treasure' and
treated like a servant. She went along with it, pandering to his
every whim, even to her brother's fascination with boys. However,
she seemed to draw the line at one being introduced permanently
to the household.

'Let's give Treasure time to get used to it,' Felix would whisper
conspiratorially as he munched on salami. He had once owned a
chain of smallgoods shops, the kind that sold nothing more exotic
than jellied trotters and devon before European migrants brought
the true meaning of 'delicatessen' to Australia. When all the new
products overwhelmed him, he sold out to an Austrian couple and
now lived comfortably in a world of endless cold cuts and wall-to-
wall nostalgia. He smelled of garlic sausage, was as small and fleshy
as a liver dumpling, and an ill-fitting hairpiece of rusty brown waves
sat incongruously on his natural rim of pepper and salt grey.

As far as Kenneth was concerned, Treasure could take all the
time she wanted. While she continued to baulk at the arrangement
there was no funny business going on, apart from a surreptitious
squeeze of his knee now and again. He had his own bedroom and
Felix kept to his and their only indulgence was watching scratchy
movies thrown by a rackety projector on to a cotton sheet morning,
noon and night.

Finally, when Treasure got around to accepting the inevitable,
and Felix became more demanding, Kenneth split, taking with him

nothing but a better-than-average knowledge of Hollywood's output during the thirties, forties and fifties.

Now, this all came back as he sat there, head on one side, looking at Adele and seeking to change the subject.

'Kelly Green. Nothing against you, but I never thought her singing was much good.'

He was taking a risk and when she snapped back impatiently at him he wasn't surprised. But it was better than her telling him what she thought he should do.

'Of course it wasn't all that good. I take that as a compliment. It wasn't *meant* to be perfect. If I'd sung in my natural voice, nobody would have believed it came out of Kelly. But the way I did it fitted with the rest of her. And the singing, combined with that fabulous face and figure, all came together in a kind of sublime perfection.'

Adele settled back, her voice becoming more reflective.

'Oh my God, she was certainly something, but there was so much of her wasted. They wanted a sex symbol, nothing else.'

She fell silent and remained morose for hours.

Apparently, it was her custom to check on the efficiency of Jorge and Rina every now and again, in parts of the house she rarely used. After the two cleaners had gone late that afternoon, and fortified by her first drink of the day, Adele decided to make one of her tours of inspection. She insisted that Kenneth accompany her, and he was so glad she seemed to have cheered up again that he agreed readily.

He thought it would give him the opportunity to catch up on what he'd missed before, namely the big bedroom adjoining hers, which she had patently ignored the first time she'd shown him around. She checked the other bedrooms first, and while she ran her index finger over polished surfaces and looked under the beds for telltale balls of fluff, Kenneth took in the opulence of the furnishings, the mirrored sliding doors of massive built-in wardrobes, the richly textured bedspreads, the marble and chrome of the bathrooms.

As they emerged into the hall, Kenneth went and tried the door of the only bedroom he hadn't seen. It was locked.

'What about this one?' he asked.

Adele dismissed the subject with a wave of her hand.

'That was Lambert's. I rarely go in there, and if you've a shred of understanding then I don't have to tell you why.'

Having found nothing to displease her, Adele's mood became

more expansive. It was only when she stopped halfway down the curling staircase and gestured grandly over the entrance foyer that Kenneth realised she was still dwelling in the past.

'I like to fantasise,' she confided wistfully, 'to make believe that I really made it big in Hollywood and became a great big movie star . . . and that this is my great big movie star home in Beverly Hills, California. Somewhere along Summit Drive, maybe. Right up there next to Pickfair.'

'But you *did* make it,' he found himself assuring her. 'What about all this? What about all the money?'

Adele laughed derisively. 'You think the only reward for making it is money?'

'It'd do me,' he said.

'You'll learn. Making it means having power. Gaining the respect – or the envy – of your peers.' She considered for a moment, and then continued, her voice becoming an awed whisper. 'And . . . yes. It means a kind of immortality. *She* has it. Kelly. And Monroe too. It's what keeps them alive.'

'Immortality? You mean . . . living forever?'

'In a way.'

'Who'd want to live forever in *this* rotten world?' he snorted. 'That's dumb!'

She turned her face to him and he got a shock. Her eyes were wide with the innocence of a child, her smile sweet and full of compassion.

'Whether it's a rotten world or not, you're clinging on to life right now, aren't you? Just as I am. In fact we're probably using each other to strengthen our grip.'

And while he was working that one out, she swept down the staircase leaving him standing there like a gook.

8

Just as afflicted believers journey to Lourdes in the hope of a cure, so Sharon trudged to Kings Cross yet again in the hope that some way, somehow, she could find Kenneth and set her mind at rest. It was plaguing her beyond belief that she had made a promise she had not fulfilled, particularly to a kid who had a jaundiced view of adult reliability in the first place.

The fact that she'd had a personal note from the head of the network that morning commending her work on the street kids story heightened rather than assuaged her guilt feelings, almost as if she had achieved success by default. Her devotion to her career had already cost Terry his life. Her mother had been right. Time and time again she had promised 'I'll be home next week for a few days,' and then some story had caused her to cancel an interstate flight. Meanwhile, Terry had been sneaking off for God knows what reasons and inhaling toxic fumes. She blamed her mother, but she also blamed herself.

As far as Kenneth was concerned, he didn't know things had got out of her control but she couldn't rest until she had explained to him that she had not let him down. There was also the matter of the $500 owed to him for his participation. She had always hated loose ends and there were several here she wanted tied up, for her own peace of mind.

As she walked along Macleay Street towards the hole in the wall presided over by the dreaded Marieta, her thoughts switched to Jim Abrahams. Another loose end that required very tight and careful knotting. All of the reasons she had given him for not continuing their relationship had been truthful and, to her mind, valid. She had been honest right down the line except for one other factor she couldn't possibly mention. Jim had started to bore her. His fatherly, guiding influence had been so comforting early on, and there was a similar cosiness about their transition to lovers. But comfort and cosiness couldn't make up for the excitement and

92

passion she needed in a sex partner. And for all his sweetness and kindness, or perhaps because of it, she found Jim Abrahams a dull lover. She hoped their confrontation had helped put the situation into a sensible perspective.

There was a queue of three people carrying trousers, skirts and jackets waiting to be served at the Dainty Dry Cleaners. Sharon sought the shade of a plane tree at the kerb, and hung around while Marieta dealt with her customers.

She wondered what Jim would think if he knew she was here. Obsessed might be a word he'd use, and he would probably be right. But there was nothing odd about an obsession to right a wrong. And when the shoot with the Minister for Tourism at Darling Harbour had ended early, it seemed logical to put the unexpected free time in town to good use. She had refused the politician's invitation to coffee, told the camera crew she would make her own way back to the studio, and here she was hanging around like one of the hookers she had passed on Darlinghurst Road.

A group of Japanese tourists approached, three young couples who were probably on one of the packaged honeymoon junkets which crammed so much sightseeing into five days it was possible that many of the marriages were not consummated until the newly-weds got back home. Inevitably, and with much delicate courtesy, they handed her an Asahi Pentax and automatically arranged themselves into a symmetrical pattern while she took their photograph. She handed the camera back and after more smiles and bows they continued on their way.

Sharon glanced at the Dry Cleaners. Now, only one person remained to be served. She leaned back against the tree and watched the retreating Japanese, immaculately groomed in assembly line fashion, the girls diminutively pretty, the boys much more tall and muscular than Japanese men used to be. It must be something to do with their Westernised diet, she thought idly.

She summoned a smile for Marieta as she moved across the pavement to front up at the now empty counter. But the smile went for nothing. The girl stared out of her hole in the wall like a scared hermit crab.

'It was you that found her, wasn't it?' It was less a question than an accusing statement of fact. 'After you'd been here, wasn't it? I told you she was a weirdo.'

Sharon was prepared for morbid fascination and coped as best she could until the right moment came for her to ask about Kenneth.

The girl shook her head.

'Funny. He used to pass here every day, but there's not been a sign of him, not since it happened.' Her eyes narrowed. ''Ey – you don't think he did it, do you?'

Now it was Sharon's turn to shake her head. 'According to what the police found – footprints and other indications – it wasn't Kenneth in the pantry. It was a fully-grown adult, and he was ready to kill me, too.'

'Ooo-a!' The girl shivered.

'Is there anywhere you know of that Kenneth might be? Where did he hang out in the Cross?'

'Well, he was too young for the pubs. There's the coffee shops,' Marieta said uncertainly, 'but there's so many of them, I wouldn't know which ones.' She thought again. 'There's Zapperama,' she volunteered with more enthusiasm. 'He was mad on video games.'

And so, apparently, was every other kid in Kings Cross. Sharon had to push her way through an untidy avenue of undernourished, jostling bodies to get to the overweight hulk she presumed was the proprietor.

Andy looked in her direction with eyeballs that floated like buoys in a heavy sea and waved a hambone of an arm.

'See for yourself. He's not here. Hasn't been in for days.'

Sharon found herself caught in a headwind of fetid breath. To her, he was the unsavoury embodiment of the Three P's – Pimp, Pusher and Pervert, and fifty times worse than the yobbos in sweat-stained singlets sucking on tinnies who had yelled good-natured obscenities at her on the way over. She moved to one side, and was mesmerised when only one of his eyes followed her.

'You're a relative of his, then, are you?' Andy asked. He knew well enough who she was, he'd seen her on the telly dozens of times not to mention in the reports of the murder, but his God-given slyness cautioned him to play dumb.

Sharon shook her head. 'Just a friend.'

'We get 'em here all the time, relatives looking for missing kids. Never find 'em, usually. Heartbreaking, it is. The youngsters are too smart, you see. Never stay in one place for long. Here for one minute, gone the next.' He stuck an exploratory finger up one of his nostrils, but fortunately for Sharon's already queasy stomach he drew a blank.

One final question occurred to her.

'Has anybody else been asking about Kenneth?'

'Nah.' He transferred his finger to the other nostril, hoping for better luck. He wasn't going to tell her about the sandy-haired bloke, the nervy one who'd come in the morning of the murder and slipped him fifty bucks for any information on Kenneth's whereabouts. Andy had told him about the squat and had no doubt now that the bloke was the one who'd trashed the girl, but that was the last thing he'd blab about. He didn't want the cops sniffing around Zapperama, no way. And after all, fifty bucks was fifty bucks.

It was dusk when Sharon stepped over the empty beer cans, styrofoam beakers and discarded takeaway containers that were overflowing from the Tidy Bins and clogging the gutters of Darlinghurst Road. She got into a taxi and was so immersed in her own sense of failure, she didn't even notice the white Volvo with the battered side which pulled in behind as they left.

9

Allan Steinbeck settled into his favourite armchair with a large scotch and soda. It was the middle of the night and all was silent. An aura of peace had settled over the house ever since Joan had departed with the baby, but only now was he beginning to appreciate it.

The silence enabled him to think, to review the events of the past few days without the panic and depression, without the desolation which had engulfed him with a crippling intensity in the hours following the airing of the *Upfront* feature. Even another evening of prowling the Cross in vain hadn't fazed him.

Now, he knew for certain what had to be done and he was determined to do it. It gave him a steely calmness unlike that first evening when he'd thirsted for revenge but had felt cold and clammy and disoriented and panic-stricken. That was why even if he had been successful in abducting the boy, his vengeance would have been flawed. He would have kicked and clawed and pummeled and maimed, but he mightn't have made fully sure of killing the boy.

Not any more. What he felt was no longer just anger and lust for revenge at being exposed, at having his lifestyle wrecked. The boy had to be killed because while he lived, Allan felt his very existence was threatened.

The TV documentary had spawned a series of sensational feature articles in the daily newspapers calling for action against the men who preyed on child prostitutes. The articles suggested that the victims be made weapons of retribution in identifying the ones who had preyed upon them. Heady, over-the-top stuff, perhaps, but ominous no less, particularly as the newspapers indicated that from now on, investigative reporters would be following this angle, looking for fresh leads. And that very day, he himself had seen the blonde bitch from television climbing into a taxi with a face like a wet Sunday. Obviously, she was still searching for the boy, too, but it was also obvious from her expression that she had so far

96

drawn a blank. Perhaps she was planning a sequel to her documentary, again featuring the boy if she could find him. So, as long as the boy was alive, no matter what Allan did to salvage the rest of his life from the existing wreckage, there was always the chance that the little swine could appear out of nowhere backed by media hype to point a finger at him. It was an ongoing threat, one which wouldn't go away until Allan *made* it go away. Forever.

He drained the glass and felt the burning, not of the liquor but of the twin consuming passions of utter revenge and future salvation. Positive action to wipe the slate clean. Waiting passively for the whole affair to blow over was no longer an option. Oh, he'd been thrown into panic at first, but that's what came from stagnating in marriage and a steady job, cushioned from adversity by the money which had come to Joan from her father's generous bequest. Earlier in his life, this had not been the case. Anybody who crossed him, who disturbed his well-being, had been dealt with swiftly and effectively. And now he was back in control of his destiny and prepared to act accordingly. He got up and poured himself another drink.

When he had returned from the chase that night, soaking wet and exhausted, it was to an empty house. Joan and the baby had gone. He knew where, of course. To her mother's. That was where she had fled once before when her constant whining about the curses of pregnancy had intruded on his concentration at a time when he needed all his mental capacity to cope with staff problems at the office.

All the confident assurances that she wasn't going to allow having a baby to alter her lifestyle and interfere with her career had diminished in contrasting ratio to the size of her stomach and the imagined extent of her purgatory. He hadn't really *hit* her on that occasion, he had merely pushed her out of the living room and it was her misfortune that she had slipped on the tiled floor of the kitchen.

She had returned to him from her mother's house after three days.

The current reason for her flight into the night, of course, was much more serious than a shove and a skid. But because of his exhaustion, he had collapsed on to the bed without giving it a thought, not even stripping off his damp clothes before he slept.

Rotten as he felt the next morning, he had made the obligatory phone call. Not unexpectedly, Doris Lytton-Scott had informed him coldly that her daughter did not wish to speak to him, not now or ever, and that he would be hearing from their solicitors. Even though her attitude was not a surprise, the words brought on a fit of shaking. He had always been aware the woman had never liked him, considering him an unworthy match for her precious Joan. Now – in her eyes – all of her misgivings about him had been confirmed. The fact that he had worked damned hard to make up for the absence of God-given advantages in his life had never meant very much to Doris Lytton-Scott. She was not impressed by his Bachelor of Arts with the major in Psychology, nor with his position as Personnel Manager with Horne-Maynard Plastics. Despite Joan's pride in him, her mother had almost sneered when he had added to his skills by completing the computer course in a class of young people almost half his age. And squeezing into his already-gruelling schedule the evening TAFE language courses in Greek and Italian to improve employer communications with the many ethnics who worked in the factory had further alienated the woman. She had taken this as evidence that he was neglecting her daughter even more, and in this she was quite correct. But Joan had her career too, and the marriage was functioning in ways that fulfilled them both.

That is, until they decided to start a family. Or rather, until *Joan* decided to start a family. She wanted it all – marriage, career, children – and she wanted to show her mother she could have it all and cope in an adult and efficient manner. But she couldn't. And mother, gratified to find she still had a weak, dependent daughter, was always there with a devouring compassion when things went wrong.

And now had come her ultimate triumph. The Hallelujah Chorus of 'I told you so's' was swelling in the background, the self-righteous armour was in place and she was ready to do battle on her daughter's behalf to purge this degenerate outsider from their lives once and for all.

'It's not something I do all the time!' Allan yelled into the phone. 'It happened at school, yes, but it's like that with a lot of boys! There were a couple more times before I met Joan, but they were always willing, I never forced it on them, kids get very sexy and some of them will try anything for kicks!'

At some point, possibly immediately she had said her piece, Doris Lytton-Scott had hung up. He realised he'd been yelling at the bleeps of a disengaged line, but somehow it didn't matter.

'It never happened after I married Joan, never, I swear it! Not until she started giving all her attention to the baby and nothing to me. I had to have *some* release, I had to!'

The receiver dropped from his quivering fingers and he fell to his knees with great shuddering sobs, not at the prospect of losing Joan and the baby, but at the unfairness of what was happening to him.

He let the sobs come out until there seemed no more emotion left inside him. Then, somehow he had pulled himself together. He forced himself to shower, then he put on a white shirt and his best grey suit and teamed them with a blue and green Paisley patterned tie. He made some instant coffee, black and strong, and drank two cups.

There was a determination growing in him which he had experienced only on the two other occasions in his life when he'd felt horribly threatened. It wasn't as powerful yet, but it was coming and already it was enabling him to plan his cunning strategies.

It was imperative that he brazen it out. He must not be absent from work this morning, he must not even be late. They couldn't be absolutely certain beyond a shadow of doubt that it had been him on television the previous evening, therefore he must not betray in any way that there was anything wrong. There might be whispered conjectures, but he had to show them by his smart appearance and calm demeanour that he was entirely oblivious of this unknown man who just happened to bear a slight resemblance to him.

'Well, they say everyone in this world has a double, don't they? Pity mine has to be such a bent bastard!' he imagined himself saying.

He had left the car parked in the drive, too exhausted to bother putting it into the garage. He winced at the deep dents and scratches along the side, but decided there was no point in worrying about the damage. Of more concern was the fact that he'd left a window down. Obviously, there had been more rain during the night and the driver's seat was wet. One of the baby's blankets had been tossed in the back seat, so he folded that to sit on. The wet had soaked through it by the time he eased the car into his reserved parking space at Horne-Maynard's head office in the city. The seat of his pants was uncomfortably damp. Good. He would use that discomfort as a constant reminder to keep his face pleasant and his manner brisk and businesslike.

He knew immediately by the sideways glances he got that there had been talk. There was an imperceptible forced quality about the usual 'good-morning's', and that old cow Sybil Barnaby in Accounts had actually turned her back on him as he passed down the corridor.

No matter.

They couldn't prove a thing. If he went about his business normally, they'd realise their mistake. No man shown trying to pick up a boy on television could ever face the world so blamelessly the following day, therefore it had to be someone who *looked* like Allan Steinbeck, not Steinbeck himself.

Peg Ward, his secretary, was a sparrow of a woman with sharp eyes who took pleasure in her own efficiency. Either she had not heard the gossip or chose to ignore it, because she was her usual friendly self. As always, she had made it her first duty to type that day's commitments on a sheet of paper which was centrally placed on his desktop. She also indicated several pages of re-scaled employee benefits which she knew he would want to transfer to his personal computer.

By the time he had added the list of benefits to his document file, mapped out a display ad for an executive vacancy in salary administration and studied and arranged in order of preference a dozen written applications and resumes from candidates seeking the post of supervisor in the company's factory canteen, he was feeling decidedly optimistic. An eleven o'clock appointment with Barry Overton, Head of Accounts, concerning a disputed superannuation payment had been cancelled abruptly, but Allan saw nothing strange in that. Overton kept an erratic schedule and was always running backwards and forwards to the factory in Homebush.

When lunchtime arrived, he was fully confident that his plan to carry on as usual had worked out. It gave him a pleasant feeling of superiority to know he had them all fooled, and this led him to tell Peg Ward that he was meeting his wife for lunch (would a child molester take his wife to lunch?) and that he would be back in an hour.

When he returned, Peg looked at him, her small black eyes bright with anticipation.

'Well? Have a nice time?' she asked.

'Oh yes,' he smiled back, and wanted to add: 'I went out and killed a girl. Doesn't it show?'

He would have given anything to fill her in on how clever he had been. It had taken him only five or six minutes of brisk walking to get from the Horne-Maynard offices to Kings Cross. Another two or three minutes and he was slipping a fifty dollar note to the pop-eyed retarded ape who ran Zapperama. The information about the squat had been more than he expected from the man. It had been a disappointment to find only the girl there, but he had been convinced she could tell him where the boy Kenneth was hiding out.

Then came the setback, the first of a day that had otherwise been going brilliantly in his favour. The girl was so full of drugs she could hardly speak and she seemed to think that all he wanted was sex.

Allan smiled grimly at the recollection.

Sex? With that pathetic slut? She was probably riddled with AIDS, apart from anything else.

He thought a few slaps might snap her out of it and convince her to talk but they only seemed to make her more confused so he tried thumping her, and then her condition ceased to matter because if she really didn't know where her little mate was, she had become redundant. By now, he'd picked up the chair leg and was smashing her head in and at least it had helped him overcome his disappointment.

Such a pity he hadn't been able to inflict the same punishment on the bitch from television, particularly as it now occurred to him that she was probably the brains behind the boy's treachery. Even so, her escape hadn't really bothered him.

She'd keep.

His main concern from then on had been to leave the squat unseen and get back to the office. This he did with ten minutes of his lunch hour to spare. He'd used the time to clean up in one of the downstairs washrooms and to examine his clothing for any telltale stains. Apart from a couple of smudges which he sponged out quickly with wet paper towels, only his shoes showed evidence of where he had been. More wet paper towels brought off the dust and dirt of MacFarlane Place and lots of buffing with a wad of dry toilet roll restored them almost to their former lustre. Then he needed to wash his hands again. He ran a comb through his hair, straightened his tie, took another long look at himself in the mirror, and left.

He became aware that Peg was still standing there, waiting for details about the luncheon with his wife. How could he deal with that? He had walked out an ordinary man and returned a killer, full of the dynamic power that came from an ability to rule over life and death.

Allan was making a great effort to switch his thoughts from the unrepeatable truth to the boring fable of a fictitious meal, when the intercom on Peg's desk buzzed. She went to answer it, giving Allan the respite he needed.

'Yes, he's just this minute come back from lunch. Yes. Very well.' She replaced the receiver and turned around. 'Ringwald wants to see you right away.'

Hugh Ringwald was General Manager of Horne-Maynard Plastics. Had the summons come first thing that morning, Allan would have been extremely worried. Now, he saw it for what it was. There were a number of unresolved matters they had to discuss, in fact he himself had requested a meeting earlier in the week.

Consequently, he was perfectly at ease as he made his way to Ringwald's office. He noticed no sly glances now, no embarrassed turning away by the colleagues he passed, just the usual nods of acknowledgement. He must have imagined them when he first arrived at work that morning. The realisation added to the warm afterglow of murder.

Hugh Ringwald's face was unusually grave. He was not exactly a cheerful man at the best of times, but he could be relied on to manage a brief smile before getting down to business. Not so on this occasion. He motioned Allan to a chair, then began speaking at once as if to get the encounter over and done with.

'Steinbeck, it's been brought to my notice . . .'

His voice trailed off. His hands attacked one another on the tooled leather surface of his desk.

'Yes?' Allan looked at him alertly.

'Well.' Another pause. A clearing of the throat. Then a rush of words.

'My God, man, far be it from me to be judge and jury on anyone's private life, but there are some things—'

Realisation hit Allan immediately, and he was in there fighting with the rueful smile and the half-suppressed laughter he had rehearsed.

'Oh. You mean that TV thing last night? I didn't see it, but hell did I hear about it! Just a resemblance, that's all. An *unfortunate* resemblance, that's all it was, and apart from the roasting I've had from my mates, I'll just have to live with it until they've all had their fun—'

Ringwald shouted him down, shaking his head hopelessly.

'It's no use, Steinbeck, it's no use! According to colleagues whose judgement I trust—'

'And whose envy of me no doubt influenced their wild fantasies—'

'Confirmation!' Ringwald's voice brandished the word firmly like a battle flag. 'Confirmation came from an unimpeachable source outside this organisation!'

'Who? Where? I demand to know. It's my *right* to know!' Allan had now replaced ruefulness with righteous anger. The battle was on and he had the power to win.

Ringwald lowered his voice. He looked at Allan with a kind of questioning pity in his eyes.

'Homosexuality we could cope with. We move with the times and are not unenlightened. But this . . . this monstrous behaviour is untenable. This preying on youngsters discarded by society . . .' He shook his head, his eyes never leaving Allan's face. 'My God. Why, man, why?'

'Who is this unimpeachable source? Who is it?' Allan demanded. But he knew who it was.

Hugh Ringwald again ignored the question.

'We – the directors and I – cannot allow you to continue as a high profile representative of this company. You've served us well in the past, but even if there were some excuse for your behaviour, there are still too many risks involved. Your reputation becomes the company's reputation and we can't have that.' Ringwald stood up and squared his shoulders as if readying himself for a punch-up. 'If you don't resign, we'll fire you,' he said. 'The choice is yours.'

Allan had made his choice swiftly and with dignity. He walked out of Ringwald's office with his head held high. He scribbled a brief note of resignation, not bothering to embroider it with reasons or regret, and delivered it back to Ringwald's secretary.

Then he had left Horne-Maynard Plastics forever. He had worked there for twelve years, climbing with determined application from junior to assistant, from associate to executive. And suddenly it didn't matter, not any of it. Nor did it matter, not really, that when he arrived home and was checking the mailbox by the front gate, an old woman from down the street spat at him. She had literally stopped, pursed her lips, propelled a gob of spit at him, wiped her mouth and shuffled on her way as if it were something she did every day on her way back from the supermarket. Most of the spit had landed on the envelopes he was holding. He squatted down and wiped it off on the lawn. But he couldn't wipe away the look in her eyes, not right away, not until he was able to file it with the rest of his former existence under 'Unimportant'.

So.

He could overcome minor setbacks and the spits and stones of geriatric adversaries. It was easy, now that the power he had acquired was nourishing him with optimism and exhilaration.

Somewhere, in some trashy satanic literature, he had read that the life force of a murder victim passed on to the killer. At the time, he had regarded it as so much superstitious mumbo-jumbo, and even now it didn't make much sense. Life force? That drugged, disease-ridden scrap of dung hadn't the life force of an amoeba. And yet, despite the bravado with which he'd managed to face that 'morning after' at Horne-Maynard's, the real invigoration had not come until he'd beaten her to a pulp during his lunch hour.

It had not proved a transitory stimulation. The tonic effect had remained with him in the days that followed and even the futile searching around the Cross each evening had not diminished his resolve to ensure a cast-iron safe future for himself.

He went for another refill, deciding it would be his last for the night. He must keep a clear head. He still had to find the boy and dispense with him and settle a few other important scores, too. Then he would be safe. Possibly out of guilt, Horne-Maynard's had given him a sizable chunk of severance pay. Then there was his superannuation, plus the rest that had come to him through Joan. Financially, he was sound. And when he had finished what he had set himself to do, he would be free to go forward to a brand-new life, unencumbered by threats from the past.

But only, he reminded himself as he splashed the remains of the scotch into his glass, after the debris had been cleared away.

10

Adele tossed a blond wig at Kenneth and said: 'There. Try that on for size.'

He looked at it dubiously. It was a brassy yellow and reminded him of a dead animal.

'I got it one time when I had this crazy idea of building a nightclub act around impersonations of the stars,' Adele explained. 'Kelly Green . . . Zsa Zsa . . . Marilyn . . . Mae West. Then sweet reason stepped in, praise the Lord, and I never went ahead with it.' She looked at him, blue eyes wide and popping. 'Well? What're you waiting for? Try it on, try it on!'

He returned her look suspiciously. 'Why?'

She lit a cigarette with exasperation.

'Oh, for God's sake, do I have to spell it out? You're scared shitless of going out, but surely it must have occurred to you that you can't spend the rest of your life holed up in here.' She had left the cigarette dangling from her lips where it wobbled as she spoke. Then, she squinted at him through the smoke, remembering all the times she had unsuccessfully tried to convince him that it was safe to go out.

'This guy isn't going to spend twenty-four hours a day looking for you,' she had argued. '*Or* the rest of his life. That just isn't logical.'

Kenneth had glared at her. 'What's this logic crap? D'you think that applies to him? I saw the crazy look in his eyes. He's mad. Off his rocker. And mad bastards don't act like we do. He's got things going on in his brain we'd never know about. Sure, I exposed him. But by now he might have fifty other reasons for snuffing me out!' He swallowed, never taking his eyes off her. 'Mad bastards. I've seen 'em on the loose, roaming the streets, looking for blood. They can be cops, they can be drag queens. But if they've got a bee in their bonnet, watch out mate, because they're never gonna give up till they do what their fucked-up brains tell 'em they have to!'

He'd stormed out of the room, leaving Adele to shiver and ponder on the delicate balance of the human mental condition. Could revenge or fear make someone that blindly obsessive, that unhinged? Or did they have to be like that before, apparently normal until something pushed them over the edge? She had thought some more about the situation and now, as she pulled deeply on her cigarette, she pursued what she had decided was the ideal solution to Kenneth's misgivings.

'I'm not going to schlepp around while you turn into the Prisoner of Zenda. So what do we do about it? We disguise you, that's what, and then we can go out without anybody recognising you.' And with that, she grabbed the wig off his lap and jammed it on his head. Kenneth squirmed. It felt like a too-tight cap.

Adele stood back surveying him, her eyes still squinting through the smoke, her head on one side.

'Hmm. It needs work.'

She produced a pair of scissors and stepped behind him. He felt a tugging as she lifted the hair in bunches, and he heard the thin snip-snapping of the scissors. Then he felt the pull of a comb and hunched his shoulders instinctively – but the wig was too jammed on to come off.

'Keep still,' she muttered, and long wisps of hair fell around his face and on to his lap. Soon it stopped being unpleasant and Kenneth became caught up in the anticipation of what he would look like. A lot of the kids messed around with their hair, having it shaved or teased and gelled and dyed into outrageous protests against conformity, but the idea had never appealed to him. He hated it when Donna had appeared with her bleached hair spikey and splotched with green, but he'd never said anything because she didn't have much else going for her.

Adele moved around into his field of vision brandishing scissors and comb like she'd just been jousting with them. She stepped back and eyed him and instead of the cigarette a smile now trembled on her lips.

'Jeezus! Andy Warhol!'

He didn't know who she meant, but the look on her face excited his curiosity even more. He jumped up, scattering discarded hair all over the place and almost ran to an oval mirror on the wall.

'Wow! Unreal!'

A stranger stared back at him. The hair helped, of course, all blonde and short and jagged. But it was the face, too. He hadn't taken a good look at himself for days, but the benefits of regular meals and a leisurely lifestyle were already apparent.

His face had filled out. He had a healthy colour and the feral shiftiness had gone from his eyes, making them seem wider, more open. He had been aware he'd put on a little weight because all his new pants fitted more snugly around his waist. Now, the wig emphasised the changes in his face.

Adele bustled up behind him, pleased at his reaction. She had a stick of cream-coloured make-up.

'This is not a good match, but we have to do something about the eyebrows, they're too dark. Hold still.'

He stood there, watching the look of extreme concentration on her face as she carefully followed the arch of his brows with the stick, then used the pad of her middle finger to smooth in the touches of lightener.

'There,' she said.

He took another look in the mirror, and sure enough the lightened brows made his reflection even more of a stranger.

'Oh my, do you look cute, kiddo!' Adele burbled with delight. 'You're gonna have to beat the gays off with a stick!'

Kenneth laughed self-consciously, sneaking yet another look at himself in the mirror.

'Yeah, it's turned out great,' Adele continued. 'Why, even your own mother wouldn't recognise you now.'

He felt as though she had stuck a knife in his guts. He glared at her reflection venomously.

'What would *you* know about my mother?' he blurted out.

He saw Adele's reflection backing away from him, palms held out flat as if to ward off a physical assault.

'I'm sorry. So I hit a nerve. How am I to know these things if you won't tell me anything? A conversation with you can be like walking through a minefield!'

He relaxed. It wasn't her fault. And now she was trying to be bright again, trying to make him forget the hurt even though she didn't know what it was all about.

'Well? Are you ready to show yourself to the outside world? We won't go far. Just far enough for you to get your confidence back. And I think with that colouring you should wear the light-blue denim jeans and the shirt that I like, the one with the palm fronds on it.'

He followed her instructions, eager to complete the transformation, then surveyed the overall effect in his bathroom mirror. Adele was right. Nobody would pick him for Kenneth Mitchell in this get-up, not even The Man. And the strange thing was that he felt different inside as well as out. The numbed, heavy feeling he carried around with him seemed to have lifted. It was all mad, this dressing up, and it made him want to laugh. He smiled at the guy in the mirror, sharing secrets and feeling safe.

Adele, in a white pantsuit, was waiting for him at the open doors of the double garage. He saw there were two automobiles inside. One was a Mercedes Benz 250CE coupe, silver grey with a blue interior, early 1970s Kenneth reckoned. The other was a BMW convertible, burgundy with beige leather trim and alloy wheels. This was the first time he had seen them and he went closer, inspecting every detail with the silent reverence of an aficionado.

Adele watched him.

'Like 'em, huh? I usually take the BMW if I'm just doing a little shopping . . .'

Kenneth hardly heard her. He was staring at the Mercedes. Adele shrugged.

'Oh, what the hell, if you've got it why not flaunt it!' And she moved to the Mercedes, pausing as she opened the door on the driver's side. 'Hey, you. Down on the floor in back. You never know who's casing the joint!'

She smiled as if she didn't really mean it, but Kenneth saw there was some sense in what she said. The Man had lost him in Boniface Road. If he were persistent enough, he could still be spending time cruising the area.

Kenneth got in and, after pulling the door shut, went down carefully on his hands and knees. The smell inside the car was like incense, a heady mixture of leather and the spicy perfume he'd noticed Adele always wore. And then he heard the engine purr into life and they moved off. He realised how much he was enjoying the subterfuge. It appealed to the secretive side of his nature, this small conspiracy. It was him and Adele fooling the world, and he liked the idea.

As she turned right into New South Head Road, Adele said she thought it was okay to show himself. He scrambled up and over into the passenger seat.

'Want me to light you a smoke?' he asked, anxious to please and also interested in trying the lighter.

'I never indulge while I'm driving,' she replied, not bothering to explain why. He shrugged and settled back, enjoying the luxury.

The humidity which had plagued Sydney for more than two weeks was gone, and it was a sparkling morning in Double Bay. Kenneth looked around with interest before Adele did a quick turn and plunged them into the semi-darkness of a parking station. His first impression of the village-style shopping centre with its smart boutiques, outdoor cafes and tree-shaded streets, was that although every inch of kerb space seemed taken by closely parked cars, there were few people around. He remarked on this when they emerged from the parking station.

'Yes, well the place is going through a bit of a rough time at the moment, hadn't you heard?'

Kenneth admitted he had never been to Double Bay before.

'You *what*!?' she almost yelled. 'But you hung out at the Cross. That's only minutes from here.'

He could have pointed out, but didn't, that there were even shorter distances between the haves and have nots. In Kings Cross, rich yuppie teenagers shelled out upwards of ten dollars a drink at the trendy dance clubs, while just around the corner kids of twelve were forced to take the same amount for doing blow jobs, just to survive.

Adele seemed to take his unfamiliarity with the place as a signal for her to become a tour guide.

'It's always been a sort of poor man's Rodeo Drive,' she told him, as they strolled past perfumeries, art galleries and patisseries.

And Kenneth laughed, not because he understood what she meant but because it sounded crazy and he didn't have to worry about anything because the disguise had turned him into somebody else.

Along the way, Adele pointed out the vacant shops where retail businesses had gone broke, and the hoardings behind which new hotels were rising in the hope that they would revitalise the area.

'In here,' she said abruptly, and steered him into a menswear shop where the first thing he noticed was a – to him – daggy striped sweatshirt with the notice: 'Hom. Made in France. Reduced to $99.' That put him off immediately. $99! *Reduced*?

'You need some swimwear,' Adele told him in a voice loud enough to be heard by the advancing salesman.

'Swimwear,' she repeated, imperiously to the salesman. 'Trunks. Er . . . what do you call them? Bathers?'

The salesman almost bowed, then went over to a showcase. Kenneth nudged Adele, shaking his head and pulling a face. She'd get ripped off for sure in this place. But Adele gave him a "so-what?" look and shrugged carelessly.

When the salesman returned, displaying a range of imported

bikinis, Kenneth got his own back. He looked at them all and then shook his head.

'I think I liked the K-Mart ones better, Auntie,' he said.

'You ungrateful little bastard!' Adele spluttered when they got outside. 'I'll never be able to show my face in there again! And don't call me Auntie!' But she was laughing, pleasantly outraged by his cheek, touched by his concern that she would be overcharged. As if to demonstrate that money was no object, her next stop was at the salon of an Interior Designer. She showed great interest in a late sixteenth-century Jichimu cabinet priced at $18,000, and the Interior Designer showed a similar interest in Kenneth.

Kenneth wandered away as if he hadn't noticed the proprietor's lascivious glances, then stopped in his tracks. There in front of him was a rickety old Aussie meat safe, just like one he'd seen in a squat, with the original green paint peeling off it, a two-door cupboard with rusted wire panels in which people used to keep their meat not only before the days of refrigerators but even before ice blocks were delivered.

The price tag was $2,100. Kenneth stared at it. This was something quite beyond his comprehension. It had to be a joke. He could understand old things, beautiful things from other countries being expensive, but if this meat safe was anything to go by, he could have made a fortune out of the bits and pieces he'd encountered in squats. He looked over to where Adele was still feigning a connoisseur's interest in the Chinese cabinet.

'Auntie? Take a look at this.'

Adele swept over, followed by the Interior Designer. Kenneth took a good look at him as he fawned over Adele. He had the pasty, bloated look of overindulged middle age, an unsightliness compounded by prominent front teeth and the absence of a chin. Why did they all have to look terrible, the ones who lusted after kids? Kenneth thought. It was if their creepy desires remodelled their features.

Adele was being overbearingly charming. She surveyed the awful meat safe as if it shared the same mystique as the tenth/eleventh century Central Indian architectural sculpture of a young woman which had been casually placed beside it. She grimaced as if in torment, looking back and forth between the Jichimu cabinet and the Aussie meat safe. This gave the Interior Designer an opportunity to give Kenneth what he intended to be a smouldering stare, and Kenneth an opportunity to observe how bloodshot his eyes were.

Finally, Adele asked uncertainly, 'Do you think we could pass them off as a pair?'

The Interior Designer gulped and then nodded vigorously.

'Most certainly – if you wished to make a statement.'

Adele said she'd give the combination some thought, and linked her arm with Kenneth's. 'Come along, nephew. Time for your harpsichord lessons,' she said and headed for the door.

Outside, Adele's grip on his arm increased and she began to run, laughter bubbling out, until they reached one of the many arcades. She pushed him round the corner and collapsed.

'You're catching on, kiddo,' she marvelled, her face flushed from suppressing laughter. 'This is fun, huh?'

And it was. A game. Kenneth was playing at being a rich kid, but with none of a rich kid's false values. He knew crap when he saw it, and so did Adele. They were a team.

With arms still linked, they continued jauntily on their way. The names crowded in on him, names of shops that were obviously successful because they were still there. Foreign names. Glitzy names, some of which he recognised, some he didn't. Papoucci, Sprit, Jamale, LaCoste, Yvette's, Franco di Roma. It was like he was in some foreign country. Oh sure, they had ethnic names in the Cross but mostly they were on signs over fast food joints and combined with an English word just to make the customers feel comfortable. Royal Thai. Mandarin's Kitchen. Espagnole Home Cooking. Mama Gianetti's Tucker Box. And, of course, they all had prominently displayed menus written in Japanese, just to mix things up even more.

Adele pulled on his arm and jerked him out of his thoughts.

'Let's do something about lunch,' she said and headed for a gourmet sandwich bar. Kenneth would have settled for a Big Mac or a Pluto Pup, but when he suggested this to her, she hooted.

'A Double Bay Pluto Pup? That's a contradiction in terms. It's like saying "a sophisticated New Zealander"! Forget it!'

They ended up sitting in the shade of the willows growing on the nature reserve at the quiet end of Knox Street. On the way, they had passed yet another outdoor cafe, where a couple of ancient but elegant women were sipping coffee under a Perrier umbrella. Adele gave them a casual wave in passing, and they had inclined their pastel-tinted ashen coiffures.

Kenneth remembered this as they spread themselves and their food on the grass.

'Have you got many ma—?' He started to say "mates" but

amended it to 'friends, around here?'

Adele was unwrapping the thick, juicy sandwiches she had bought. She handed him one.

'That's smoked salmon,' she said. 'Enjoy.'

He took a tentative bite and found he liked it. Adele pointed to the other sandwiches.

'We also have bacon, lettuce and tomato, commonly known as BLT which to us Americans is as popular as your Vegemite . . . there's duck liver pâté, and – oh yes, this one's chicken and asparagus.' She paused to select a sandwich for herself then looked across at him before she took a bite. 'I'm determined not to have you turn into a no-anchovies type,' she said.

'Huh?' was all he could manage with his mouth full.

She took a bite out of her BLT, chewed it and swallowed before she replied.

'A no-anchovies type can be a check-out chick at the supermarket, or a Mr Australia. You see 'em and you know 'em. When they call for takeaway pizza they always, but most definitely *always* stipulate "No anchovies". And you know why? Because their taste buds have been numbed, rendered non-adventurous by years and years of bland junk food. And it becomes a fair indication of their bland, non-adventurous lives. If you don't cultivate the salty bite of anchovies, then you'll have no appetite at all for all the exciting flavours of life.'

She reached out and touched Kenneth's wrist, just as he was reaching for another sandwich.

'Taste, kiddo. Experiment. That way you'll turn out right.'

He pulled his wrist away with a BLT in his hand. 'Thanks for the lecture. Now what about *my* question?'

She gave him a puzzled look. 'What question?'

He threw the sandwich down and swivelled to face away from her.

'You see? You don't even hear what I say to you! All you care about is what *you're* saying. Why don't you just put a Bandaid over my mouth and be done with it?'

'Oh my God, I did it again. Kapow! Another mine just blew up in my face. I'm sorry.'

Her voice came over low and filled with regret.

He inclined his head in her direction, but looked up at the sky instead of at her. 'I wanted to know something, but you just went on with what you wanted to say.'

'A thousand pardons. What did you want to know?'

He liked bringing her to heel. It made him feel wanted, the pleading, apologetic tone in her voice. He reckoned it didn't do her any harm, either, to be put in her place now and again. He waited a moment or two before he spoke.

'I just wanted to know if you've got any friends.'

'Friends? In *this* town?' Her voice climbed high with derision. 'Oh – you mean like the two vultures back there?'

They hadn't appeared as vultures to Kenneth, more like some kind of exotic flamingos resting idly in the shade. Adele was breaking open a container of soy milk.

'Sure, they flocked around when Lambert and me first hit Sydney. They were all over us like flies on a turd. Invitations to this, tickets to that, see you at the races, let's do lunch, oh it was a positive peachy-creamy whirl! Then, when Lambert took off, I got me a good long look at the cliquey, elitist crowd that passes for high society in this burg, and you know something? I didn't like what I saw. Half the pictures you see in the social pages should be in the Police Gazette. If they're not pretentious and boring, they're crooks.'

She took a gulp of soy milk. It left a white moustache on her top lip which she licked off reflectively.

'As for those two Bollinger broads you saw back there, one of them was once found in bed screwing her stepson. Now she's trying to marry him off to a titled member of the British aristocracy who also happens to be a dyke. Nice people, huh?' She offered him the half-finished container of soy milk.

Kenneth shook his head. 'You don't have *anybody*, then?'

'Oh sure. They're not all bad. I have a few chums, but they tend to be people who don't glory in their own publicity. As for the others . . . well, when they roll their eyes at the mere mention of Mrs Lambert Hatherley, as I'm sure they do, and say "she's not PLU" – that's People Like Us – I take it as a compliment.' Her voice softened. 'Just as *you* should when I tell you I think you're turning out to be something real special.'

She reached out and patted the back of his hand and he did not pull it away.

11

It was the first of several similar outings, each more fun than the last, each strengthening the camaraderie that was growing between them.

'Let's pretend we're tourists doing Sydney like we've never been here before,' Adele suggested. 'It's always the same. When you live in a place, you never really take the trouble to see it.'

Kenneth agreed. He had lived in Sydney for all of his short life and he had seen very little of it, but for reasons quite different than those meant by Adele. And so they tipped over the cornucopia that is Sydney and out tumbled the plethora of visual and sensual delights that await those who care to experience them.

Sometimes they used the Mercedes and sometimes the BMW, but the ritual was always the same. Kenneth would hide in the car until they were clear of Boniface Road. It was a game that wasn't a game. Some primitive instinct deep inside him constantly reminded him that the threat remained, that somewhere out there The Man's hate still smouldered.

'Oh come on,' Adele chided. 'If he felt *that* badly about it, he'd be suing the television network for invasion of privacy and God knows what else, not trying to take it out on you.'

'And have it plastered all over the newspapers what they showed him doing? Pig's arse!' Kenneth replied. 'Besides, anything legal costs a fortune, even I know that.'

Adele shut up and played along. She should have known better than to try and dismiss deep-seated fears.

Fortunately, once they were clear of Point Piper, Kenneth's trust in his disguise took over and his misgivings faded. There seemed so much to see and do.

They wandered around the city's green open spaces from the Domain to Hyde Park to the Botanic Gardens. They took a ferry to Manly and ate fish and chips on the beach. They did a tour of the Opera House and joined the Sunday crowds to watch a Surf

Lifesaving Carnival at Bondi. They lunched amongst the Colony's earliest buildings in the historic Rocks area and took tea on top of Sydney Tower. And everywhere, in those closing days of summer, they noticed the multiplicity of races, both tourists and residents, which over the past forty years had revolutionised the look and the feel of Australia.

Adele and Kenneth would arrive home from their exploits and collapse with cold drinks in the morning room to watch the various twilight moods of the Harbour, from the tender rose pink of lightly given promises to the misty purple of darkly realised dreams. Occasionally, he would spend the evening alone while Adele changed and went out again to a gallery opening or a dinner party. But before she did, she would always prepare a meal for him or make sure there was enough for him to help himself.

To Kenneth, Adele was becoming mother, playmate and platonic girlfriend. And it seemed to him that to Adele, he was someone to care for, someone to push around if necessary, but basically someone who was there.

On days they didn't go out, Kenneth would tend the pool and swim in it, and make himself useful doing various odd jobs around the place. Whatever the chore was, he worked at it with a steady concentration, enjoying the sensation of being constructive.

He was careful not to encroach on the territory of duties assigned to Jorge and Rina, and Mr Fitzgibbon the gardener, but there were plenty of other things that needed fixing. It was as if Adele had gone around with blinkers on, or – like a lot of people who basically live alone – maybe she just hadn't cared. There were loose handles on drawers and cupboards, and a kitchen shelf that was in danger of collapsing. He cured a dripping tap with a new washer and a squeaky bedroom door with some machine oil. He mixed paste and glued down wallpaper which had been loosened by dampness. He replaced blown-out light bulbs, tacked down corners of curling carpet, and strengthened a screen door that was hanging off its hinges. The only thing which defied his efforts was a squeak in the kitchen door. He drenched the hinges with oil but the squeak persisted. He reckoned the door would have to be rehung eventually, but it was a job that was too big for him to manage on his own.

'Where'd you learn to do all this stuff?' Adele asked.

Kenneth shrugged. It seemed to come naturally to him, working with his hands, knowing what to do.

She looked a little worried, however, when he found some paint and gave a fresh coat to a dingy length of trellis along one side of the house without consulting her first.

'That's Mr Fitzgibbon's territory,' she said. 'He might resent it.'

The next day, they were under the umbrella on the back terrace when Mr Fitzgibbon appeared round the side of the house and walked towards them. Adele groaned.

'Uh-oh,' she muttered out of the side of her mouth. 'As someone was heard to remark at Elvis Presley's cremation, "Now the fat's *really* in the fire!" '

But they were pleasantly surprised.

'If the lad's got any paint left, there's another bit of trellis needs touching up round the other side,' he said gruffly, then continued on to prune some bushes by the pool. Kenneth gave Adele a sly nudge, and they both grinned like naughty kids behind teacher's back.

12

As the days grew happier and the evenings more placid with unspoken rapport, the nights – as far as Kenneth was concerned – deteriorated into times of nervy insomnia or turbulent dreams. He couldn't understand why. It seemed as if all his personal demons had not been banished by the relaxed security he felt during the day, they had merely gone into hiding until silence and darkness set the scene for them to emerge at night.

There was no reason for him not to sleep peacefully. The days kept him pleasantly occupied with jaunts or jobs. The food was good and the evenings were generally spent watching TV, which was as effective a preparation as any for a sound night's sleep, especially with the (carefully monitored) couple of glasses of white wine Adele allowed him. That was a joke, really, and he had to laugh to himself. 'Allowing' a couple of glasses of wine to someone who'd tried grass, speed, coke, you name it, was like doling out aspirin to a crack addict. But she meant well, and he couldn't knock her for it, and anyway he could always help himself to more later on when she'd tottered off to bed after several generous nightcaps.

He would get into bed drowsily remembering something Adele had said. Maybe they'd been watching television and this movie had come on. Adele would give it five minutes, then banish it with a wave of her cigarette.

'Enough. Change the channel, kiddo. No movie in which the women wear miniskirts is any good. If the men are in Nehru jackets and have sideburns, that's a double no-no. And if the soundtrack music is played by a tinny modern jazz group, it's a triple turkey. Except for *The Sound of Music* there wasn't one decent motion picture came out of the sixties.'

He would stretch out between the sheets, letting her comments amuse him again even if he didn't understand half of what she said. She had this tough way of delivering her opinions which was funny in itself.

117

He would lie there, enjoying an almost-instant replay of the evening's comments, ready for sleep.

Half an hour later, he'd be up, jumpily wide awake, prowling the shadowy ground floor rooms of the mansion, peering through windows, looking for ghouls who in turn were prowling the dark kingdom of night, hunting for the young. Sometimes, he would stare at the expanse where the Harbour was during the day, now a black velvet void scattered with a few low-grade diamonds. Sometimes he would sit there until the cold grey light came to reveal the water as a hard metal floor, indicating nothing of the more familiar scarlet and yellows of sunrise which might follow later.

That was if he was lucky.

If he was unlucky, he might have fallen asleep and swum unsuccessfully against the riptide of memory which swept him back to The Gap, and the occasion when he'd decided he didn't want to live any longer.

He hadn't liked the idea of slashing his wrists. Hanging was something jailed aborigines seemed to have cornered the market in, and an overdose wasn't that much of a sure thing – you could just end up in Casualty having your stomach pumped while some trainee nurse badgered you on why you did it.

No. If he was going out, he'd do it in style. And it had to be a sure thing.

He'd done a break-and-enter in Paddo and scored a VCR. Nice of the manufacturers to make them so slim and weightless and easy to carry. Almost as if they wanted them to get pinched. Anyway, it was in, grab the VCR, and out. He didn't haggle with the fence. He got $25 for it, and that's all he wanted because $25 was more than enough to buy half a bottle of vodka and the taxi fare to Watson's Bay.

And here he was again, crawling under the fence and sitting there on the edge of The Gap, gulping down the vodka with a hot wind whipping at him and telling himself that this way was the best. If he'd tried to shoot himself with a gun, he would've missed. This way was the sure way.

It was at this point that things started to go wrong. He'd been too scared to do it in real life. He'd stood there, swaying on the brink and looking down at the frothy waves hitting the rocks hundreds of feet below, listing all the reasons why he should jump, flogging himself with every painful memory he could rake up, and he couldn't do it. He had crawled back under the fence and staggered off and passed out in somebody's front garden.

But not in the dream.

Too scared, right. Turned away from the edge of the cliff, right. But then he saw somebody on the other side of the fence.

The Man. All ready to grab him and do terrible things to him.

Anything was better than that.

He backed away. And when he turned, he was already tottering on the edge. Up went his arms as the ground crumbled under his feet, and then with the sight of The Man crawling under the fence and coming at him, he began to lose his balance.

Kenneth's outflung arms closed around The Man's body, but it was too late to regain his balance. The Man tried to pull away, no longer the aggressor but the victim, yelling obscenities as locked together they went over the edge, falling . . . falling . . .

Kenneth jerked awake just as the rocks rose up to smash him. Every muscle was tensed. Sweat oozed from his pores.

Adele grabbed him, heaved him up away from the rocks and held him close, cradling him back and forth.

'Okay, already. You were dreaming. It's okay.'

The muscles finally relaxed and Adele stopped rocking. She held him at arm's length, staring at him.

'I heard you yelling, kiddo. Way upstairs. Boy, that sure must have been some Nightmare on Elm Street. Freddie come to get you? Huh?'

He had to grin. She had such a funny way of putting things. And now she was holding him close again, and the rocking resumed, and it came to him that she didn't even care if his sweat soaked into her nightgown, and that made her protectiveness even more precious. Within minutes, he felt at peace.

13

Across the Harbour, way out on the Upper North Shore (a misleading title for a belt of wealthy suburbs nowhere near a seashore), Doris Lytton-Scott was also experiencing a feeling of peace. It was the only kind of peace she knew, the kind that came from knowing with an infinite sense of superiority, that all problems had been solved and all opposition trampled underfoot.

The night air was cool and refreshing, a sign that autumn was not too far away, and as she turned into Cavendish Close the scent of late-flowering shrubs welcomed her. Cavendish Close was a cul-de-sac of twelve houses set in spacious grounds, each screened by perimeters of small trees and box hedges. The native eucalypts growing on each side of the roadway and the absence of fences gave the area a bucolic tranquillity which suited her mood.

Her evening at the Lakeside Bridge Club had turned into an unexpected triumph. Amy Tremlow, her long-time partner, had been laid low by a virus. Doris, much to her displeasure, had been unavoidably coupled with a new member, a woman of Asian origin called Ursula Tsu. She was extremely elegant and seemed quite charming, but Doris was accustomed to Amy Tremlow who, although inclined to be slow and a little fussy, was at least familiar. Doris also disapproved of the Asians buying up every piece of Australia they could lay their hands on, and didn't see why she had to play bridge with them into the bargain.

After a few icily polite words, Doris had resigned herself to a ghastly evening. It was such a nuisance. She looked forward to her bridge night so much, particularly now when it provided an escape from Joan and that fractious infant. It was just like Amy to contract a virus at this most inconvenient of times.

Then something rather splendid had happened. As they collected cups of coffee to take with them to their table, Doris found an unexpected rapport growing with this Ursula Tsu. Each recounted

120

the highs and lows of past games, and they were still talking right up until the cards were dealt.

They had bid to a Grand Slam. There were two aces missing, but Doris had felt a positive surge of confidence in her new partner. Almost as if they had discussed it all verbally, they took a chance.

The opposition players doubled because each of them had one of the missing aces. Ursula, to Doris's astonishment, redoubled and they had made the contract because Ursula was void in one suit and Doris in another. Playing duplicate, they doubled, redoubled and made it to 2,940 points – a club record!

There had been quite a little celebration afterwards, and Doris had graciously agreed to partner Ursula on *all* future occasions. Amy Tremlow and her stupid virus could occupy themselves elsewhere from now on.

There had been the usual offers of a lift home, including one from Ursula Tsu whose husband, a Hong Kong financier of some description, had apparently just purchased a mansion not far from Cavendish Close. However, Doris preferred the fifteen minute walk as was her practice, particularly after the evening's excitement. It appeared things were working out for her very nicely on all fronts at the moment, and the solitude would give her the opportunity of enjoying her various little triumphs in peace.

'Be careful, darling,' Madge Ashton had called as Doris left. 'We don't want you done in by The Slasher!' The caution had been echoed by two of the other old dears.

Doris smiled to herself.

The Slasher was some deranged idiot who was making a practice of attacking young girls up and down the North Shore. His five or so victims had been nastily cut about the arms and legs with something sharp before their screams had frightened him off. Doris had no fears for herself in that regard. Although she paid a great deal of attention to her appearance and her grooming was always impeccable, she was under no delusions that she could be mistaken for a young girl. In fact, The Slasher was probably such a coward he chose his victims for that very reason – their youth and inexperience. Doris was five feet ten inches tall, and in her handbag she had an extremely piercing police whistle and a pressure spray of mace. She felt perfectly secure. And she was halfway along the Close already.

As she passed by the Kitson's, she caught the heavy perfume of their flowering moraya bushes, and visualised their charming meadow-style garden on the other side of the hedge. Shasta daisies, campanula, foxgloves and phlox grew in attractive profusion around the small deciduous trees they had cultivated. Even so, Doris reflected, she much preferred the more formal arrangement of her own garden with its potted trees by the ivy-covered retaining wall, its dwarf conifers and its stone paths around neat banks of azaleas.

It occurred to her that she must try and spend more time in the garden. She wasn't too sure that the new young man was doing all that was expected of him, and she didn't want to discover too late that the place was overrun with caterpillars or rust.

There hadn't been much time for anything, lately, what with Joan and the baby to cope with. Still, they had their first appointment with the divorce lawyer the following day. Tony Hythe was really a most suitable choice. He had an excellent reputation and he had done wonders for Gillian Carpenter in her rather messy marriage break-up.

Once proceedings were under way, perhaps Joan would realise there was no point in mooning around, and she might even be persuaded to take up her career again. She would have no excuse for staying at home once Doris offered to look after the child. Of course, Doris would not *personally* take on the burdensome chores of child care. She would hire a nanny for those duties. Doris would merely supervise, ensuring that some degree of discipline would result in the baby losing its tendency to whimper, sob or howl twenty-four hours a day. Perhaps then it would begin to develop independently from its overindulgent mother.

Similarly, Joan could no doubt be guided back to being her former self. Allan Steinbeck had actually done them all a favour by exhibiting his sexual perversions for all the world to see. No. That wasn't quite true. The revelation had happened in such a way that a scandal might have ensued in the resulting divorce action. If he had chosen to fight the case, his disgusting exploits would have had to be used in evidence against him.

As it was, she had solved the problem neatly and without a fuss. With no job, he would have neither the means nor the will to engage in lengthy litigation. He would be too busy attempting to survive. Joan would ask for no alimony, no child support, just her freedom. Both mother and daughter had the means to meet any expenses, thanks to the late Clive Lytton-Scott whose eminence in the legal profession had enabled him to leave his loved ones more than comfortably well off.

There were only four street lights in Cavendish Close, two on each side. Doris had just passed the second one on her side.

The end of the cul-de-sac was a long, shallow curve in which was set two gateways. The one on the right led to Doris's home, 'Hazeldene Lodge', that on the left to her neighbours, Freddo and Paula Guilatti. He owned an upmarket Italian restaurant which had gained the favour of radio talk-back hosts and disc jockeys and had therefore become famous regardless of the quality of its food. She imported slinky European fashions and sold them from her boutique in the Queen Victoria Building to overweight socialites whose figures would have been better served by Hawaiian mu-mu's.

The Guilattis had installed an ornate lantern over their gates which Doris had always thought vulgar, only one step up from a neon sign. But at least it had provided illumination for this dark end of Cavendish Close.

Tonight, for some reason, the lamp was not on.

This, combined with the shadows cast by the enormous Moreton Bay Fig which grew in the roadway between the two sets of gates, made journey's end for Doris appear far more gloomy than usual. Surfacing from the comfort of her thoughts, it was as if she were walking into a cavern.

Her step faltered for a moment, then she continued on.

Her hand was on the gate when something flashed in the corner of her eye. She turned, and the distant street lights seemed to be reflected on a shiny surface which detached itself from the immense trunk of the Moreton Bay Fig. It rippled towards her, speedily, a sheet of oily reflection confounding her senses at the crucial moment when she should have turned and run.

Instead, she stood there transfixed as a gleaming tentacle thrust out and she felt something slice down the right side of her face, from above the eyebrow down across the eye and cheek to the corner of her mouth. It was swift and it was strangely painless, but she was immediately aware of the path of the wound and the blood flowing into her mouth.

She raised her right hand protectively to cover her face, her precious face, but another blow came and now she felt pain, real electric pain as her hand flopped helplessly.

She reeled and started to fall from the force of another ragged stab under her left cheekbone and her body cringed at the physical mutilation it knew was happening.

The police whistle.

The mace spray.

Her protection. Her strength. Gone, all gone. She wasn't even aware of whether she still had her bag.

She tried to scream, but the sound gurgled out through half-swallowed blood. It was all so quick. You never thought of it happening this quickly. You always assumed you'd have time to think.

Another blow to the side of her head. And then although she didn't know it, she was on the ground, a crumpled heap in a pool of her own blood.

She had really not lost consciousness because of concussion. She had fainted from the shock of the attack and from the knowledge that her flesh, her life, was being ripped open and savaged.

Doris opened her eye. It was the left eye, the one closest to the ground. She appeared to have no control over the right one. The side of her face rested stickily on the soil surrounding the base of the Moreton Bay Fig. She knew she had to get help, but she didn't know how she would do it.

She tried to move her right arm, but the pain from her wrist was so excruciating she stopped immediately. She tried to yell, but all that came out was a gurgle.

Blood spilled out over her chin. It seemed her legs had ceased to exist. Her left arm was still mobile. She moved her fingers. She could feel them moving. That was an achievement.

As she looked across the surface of the ground with her left eye, she focussed on something curved and light-coloured lying there, perhaps growing there. A mushroom. It seemed to glow in the light of the distant street lamps.

She swung her left arm out and was able to grasp it. That was another achievement. If she could do that, then she could do more. She was still alive. Her attacker had gone. She was injured, but she was still alive.

Her fingers curled over the soft shell and yes, it was a mushroom. She could tell from the touch. She brought her hand up to her face, anxious to concentrate on the norm because that would preserve her sanity, and then she could progress to thinking about how best to summon help.

With her hand close up to her eye, she uncurled her fingers. The force of her screams cleared her throat of the blood which had collected there. The force of her screams was fully justified.

She was looking at her own ear.

PART III

'Often a noble face hides filthy ways'

EURIPIDES
Electra. 413BC

1

'You're carrying a lot of hurt inside of you. It has to get out somehow.'

For the third time, Adele had been roused by Kenneth's cries in the night. This time, he was being bashed by his dad. It went on and on never stopping. He was in a corner, all hunched up, trying to shield himself but to no avail. He had found himself cringing for real when Adele wakened him. Now, they were drinking hot chocolate in the kitchen.

'I've never had dreams like this before,' he told her.

Her eyes searched his for reasons.

'I'm no psychologist, but maybe you didn't have them before because everything in your life was bad. Now there's some good, some contrast and that's highlighting all the hurt you've suffered.'

'I haven't slept much for years,' Kenneth said. 'You don't when you're on the streets. Maybe that's another reason.' He tried to force a grin. 'I didn't have time for nightmares, before.'

Adele sipped her hot chocolate then put her cup down. 'All this hurt, it seems to be fighting to get out. Why not just . . . let it out? Talk about it.'

Kenneth was silent. He didn't want to talk about it. He never had and he wasn't used to confiding in someone. He couldn't. Not even with Adele.

'Kids have always run away from home,' she persisted gently. 'It happens.'

'Yeh,' he grunted. 'They run away to join a circus, don't they? That's what happens in story books. But they run for different reasons these days. And a lot of them don't even run away. They're booted out.'

'Were you . . . booted out?'

He shook his head. 'Nah. But I wasn't given much of a choice.'

'Was it your father?'

Kenneth didn't say a word.

127

After a minute or two, Adele continued on as if she hadn't noticed he'd ignored her question.

'You'd never believe it, but I had a very strict upbringing,' she said. 'Nothing physical. No beatings. But there were house rules for everything and by golly I had to obey them. When I was your age, my folks always insisted I be home by nine.'

Kenneth looked at her. 'These days, they'd just be thankful if you came home at all.'

'Was it your father, kiddo? Was it?'

He banged his cup on the tabletop. Hot chocolate slopped everywhere. He got to his feet, glaring at her.

'Give it a rest, will you? I'm going back to bed!'

She matched his rancour. 'Well don't expect any more help from me, buster, if you won't help yourself! You can scream your head off for all I care from now on. I'm gonna wear ear plugs!'

He stopped halfway to the door of his bedroom. Without turning, he knew Adele was taking the cups and rinsing them at the sink. He heard water shooting from the tap with an angry force. Then he turned and watched her walk over and put the cups into the dishwasher.

'Yeh. It was my dad.'

She went back to the sink and picked up a Wettex. She stood there, letting her impatience with him subside. Then she took the cloth over to the table where she proceeded to wipe up the mess.

'And the rest?'

He hesitated.

She went back to the sink and threw in the sopping Wettex. 'Well, come on. Tell me about it, for God's sake!'

He sat down at the table again, feeling strange.

'It's nothing out of the ordinary,' he grumbled. 'Same thing happens to lots of kids.'

She sat down facing him. 'So we're not gonna get *Gone with the Wind*. Big deal. I'll settle for less.' She waited for him to start, and when he didn't she nudged him along. 'Your father. What was he like?'

'He was a pig. A drunken pig,' he muttered unemotionally. 'Leeanne got most of the shit.'

'Leeanne?'

'My sister. Older sister. She must have only been about nine when he started abusing her.'

'How?'

Kenneth's face was ugly. 'Having sex with her. Threatening to

128

kill her if she told mum. Well, she *did* tell mum after about four years, only mum didn't believe her. Or was too scared to.

'So then Leeanne took off. We didn't hear from her for about two years, then she sent a postcard. She was working as a kitchen hand at a logging camp in Tassie. What she didn't tell us was she was on smack. Heroin. We only found out when the call came through that she'd died from an overdose. Sixteen, she was. *He* wouldn't even fork out the money to bring her body back. The loggers took up a collection and buried her there.'

Kenneth was silent. Adele lit a cigarette and waited. After a while, he continued.

'He'd always been a boozer, dad, but after that he seemed to get worse. One night he came home and he was pissed out of his mind. He must have been planning to kick on all night, but when he looked there was only a whisky bottle with about half an inch in the bottom. He drank that, then blamed mum for not having any more in. She called him a drunken swine, so he just swung the empty bottle and cracked her on the skull with it.'

Kenneth's head tilted and he looked upwards with an unfocussed stare at a point where the kitchen wall met the ceiling.

'Funny. Mum just dropped to the floor. It was so quick. But all I could think of was why the bottle didn't smash, like they did in the movies.

'Dad said to leave her and he wouldn't let me go near her, but as soon as he'd passed out I ran and told the neighbours and they called an ambulance. The hospital put in a few stitches, then sent her home. She was never the same after that. Vague. Off the planet.

'She wouldn't bring charges against him, but she left him. Went off to Woolongong 'cause a girlfriend of hers from way back lived there, and she took me with her. Well, that didn't work out. The friend had gone bush, and we didn't know anybody else, and mum couldn't get work. We stuck it out for a few weeks then we came back to Sydney and she tried to make another go of it with dad.'

'She must have been a glutton for punishment.'

Kenneth shook his head. 'I told you she'd gone strange. Anyway, they still fought like cat and dog and he was as bad as ever. Mum kept passing out. She wouldn't go to the doctor, though.'

Again he lapsed into silence. It hadn't been bad up to now, the talking, in fact it had come easier than he'd expected. But now he was up to the worst bit. Maybe he could leave it out. Adele would never know. Or would she?

He glanced at her through his lashes. She was waiting expectantly, beating time with the end of her cigarette on the edge of the ashtray. No. She'd spot it if he tried to detour. She wasn't stupid.

He coughed, making a business of clearing his throat.

'Want something else to drink? A Pepsi?' Adele was quick to ask. He shook his head and continued with his story.

'This particular arvo, I got home from school and found her lying on the bed. But she wouldn't wake up and talk to me. She looked as pale as the sheet she was lying on. I didn't know she was dead. I was cuddling her and she didn't move. All I knew was that she felt real cold, so I was trying to warm her.'

He didn't start bawling, he hadn't done that for years, but his voice choked up and he had to stop.

Adele was hurriedly lighting another cigarette.

'You don't have to go on if it's too difficult,' she said. 'I think I've got the picture.'

'No you haven't, damn you!' he burst out. 'You wanted to hear it, so you have to listen!'

Adele shut up after that. Kenneth found that shouting at her had helped him and although he lowered his voice, the anger was still there to give him the strength to go on.

'I think I was about nine, then. Just a kid. But that didn't stop him from taking it out on me. He started belting me, beating me up for no reason, bashing me and threatening me with worse if I told anyone. That was what I was dreaming about, earlier on. It got so bad that what I did was go out and get into trouble. I didn't care what I did . . . knocking off cars, joy riding, doing some vandalism at schools and welfare centres. And then I got caught, which is maybe what I wanted all along, and they sent me to an institution which was fine, 'cause I couldn't handle things at home any more.'

He had calmed down again. He got up and went over to the refrigerator and took up her offer of a Pepsi.

'I learned a lot at Minda. That's what's wrong with the system, you know? They stick young lads in there with all the more experienced, older kids and instead of getting rehabilitated or whatever, you come out worse than ever. Anyway, when I was released I skipped parole and headed for the Cross. End of story. See? I told you it wasn't much. There's kids with far worse experiences than mine.'

Adele stubbed out the butt of her cigarette. She looked at the smouldering debris in the ashtray, her forehead crumpled.

'I tell you, kiddo, that'll do me.' Her eyes darted up at him. 'Now I understand things a little better. To be honest, I still don't trust you. Not completely. Not yet. And these sudden tantrums you fly into, those are scary too. But now I can figure out why you're like that. And it helps. How about you? Has it helped you, telling me all this?'

He took a swig from the Pepsi bottle, his eyes glazed. It was if he hadn't heard a word she'd said.

'Apart from surviving from day to day,' he murmured quietly, almost to himself, 'the one thing that really bugs you when you're out there on the streets is thinking about other kids at home with a family. It breaks you up. And you feel ashamed of yourself when you see kids jumping on the school bus, or going home from school and running into their houses, or with their parents on some kind of outing . . .'

His voice trailed off. He stood there by the refrigerator with the half-finished bottle of Pepsi in his hand, staring into some other dimension which excluded all of his surroundings and Adele with them.

2

'The theory that psychotic pressures can develop in apparently normal people is hardly new,' the psychologist said. She gazed owlishly at the camera through large, perfectly round spectacles. Her fair hair was a mass of tight little curls and she had a tiny, permanently pursed mouth. She looked like everybody's idea of a kindergarten teacher and her name was Eleanor Misto.

She continued.

'So you see, in seeking to identify The Slasher, we may not necessarily be looking for someone who is visibly disturbed. In his own mind, he may see these attacks as fully justified. He could be retaliating for a real or imagined slight. For instance, a young girl might have repulsed his advances at a particularly vulnerable time.'

Grant Olsen, anchorman of *Upfront*, leaned forward intently in his chair.

'But this latest victim wasn't a young girl. She was a mature woman.'

Eleanor Misto smiled. 'Ah yes. That is why I'm using words like "could be" and "might". Like the police, I'm working in the dark. One can only judge from the evidence and speculate about the rest.'

Allan Steinbeck, eating lasagne in his family home from a plate balanced on his lap in front of the television set, felt inclined to speculate about The Slasher, too. It would be fascinating to know what his reaction was to this latest crime. Would he be flattered? Or would he be angry that the seriousness of the attack tended to overshadow his own meagre exploits?

Allan's attention reverted back to the screen.

'You see,' Eleanor Misto was saying, 'the behavioural patterns of an unbalanced mind can be unbelievably complex or, in contrast, extremely simple. In this case, the assailant appeared to be adhering rigidly to a set routine. Every one of the earlier attacks was

132

repetitious in every detail, not the least the minor nature of the injuries inflicted.'

'Yes, but—'

'Just a moment, I haven't finished what I was saying.' Eleanor Misto did not care to be interrupted either by patients or a television anchorman. 'I was about to deal with the fact that in this latest instance there has been an alarming escalation in the violence of the attack. It's most disturbing. It could mean the climax of his current spate of attacks, in which case there won't be any more for years, if ever. Conversely – and I hesitate to say it, but I must – he could be widening the scope and the intensity of his activities, in which case the nature of his mental state must be deteriorating alarmingly.'

'There is another theory . . .' Grant Olsen began tentatively, as if expecting to be cut off again. He was right.

'That this current attack is not the work of The Slasher?' The psychologist was amused. 'Yes, I'd heard that. But it's stretching coincidence a *little* far, isn't it, to assume there are *two* Slashers running up and down the North Shore?'

'What about it being a copy cat crime?'

'But it wasn't, was it?' Her eyes seemed to grow larger and more penetrating behind the lens of her spectacles. 'It was different, therefore *not* a copy. It was an extension of what he had done before.'

Allan almost applauded. Go, Eleanor, go! She was definitely on his team.

Now, Grant Olsen was asking her about the pressures which could cause someone to behave like this. She considered the question a moment.

'Yes, well one could write an entire textbook on that, because there are so many theories about so many negative influences. Abnormal childhood, restrictive home life . . .'

Allan scraped up the last of the lasagne, shaking his head gleefully. That poor bloody Slasher. He must be wondering what the hell was going on. His confusion was probably making him crazier than ever!

Abnormal childhood. Restrictive home life.

Allan savoured the last mouthful and washed it down with red wine. At least he didn't have those sort of complications in his background.

His childhood couldn't have been happier. There was only himself and Lillian, but they were as close as close can be, which is why he'd always called her Lillian and not Mother. They were more like brother and sister, everybody said so. Lillian had scraped and saved to be both mother and father. It was due to her efforts that he'd been able to go to university, and that made his devotion to her more intense. He grew up deprived of status but endowed with a will to succeed. He made no close friends. Lillian was enough. He placed her above all else. He vowed she would never be left alone and uncared for, even though she told him constantly that she didn't mind deprivation if it were an investment in his future, just as she would manage to bear the loneliness when the time came for him to leave the nest.

They were inseparable until the day she died and it took him three years to recover fully from her passing. Everything he had achieved since was a tribute to her memory. If there were more mothers like his adored Lillian, he affirmed as he poured himself another glass of wine, the world would be a much better place.

He realised that Eleanor Misto had taken her psychotic disorders and disappeared. Grant Olsen, looking relieved at her departure, was now promoting an upcoming review of Australia's tourist industry.

Allan picked up the remote control and snapped the screen blank. Just as he did so, the telephone rang.

It was Joan.

Her speech was halting and oddly formal, her voice heavy with grief.

'Thank you for calling. Your message was on the answering machine. I just got back from the hospital.'

Allan assumed a tone of sympathetic gravity. 'How is she?'

Joan began to whimper. 'Oh Allan. It's . . . it's all so horrible. Her face. Ninety-four stitches.'

There was a pause while she sniffled then blew her nose. She tried to pull herself together. 'The microsurgeons acted quickly and managed to – to restore her ear. But they can't say yet whether the hearing will be impaired permanently. Her hand . . . well, all the tendons were severed. She'll never be able to use it properly again.'

It was music to Allan's ears, and he congratulated himself on delivering the masterstroke of allowing the woman to live in suffering for the rest of her days. Doris Lytton-Scott had always been inordinately proud of her appearance. Even if, in time, she resorted to plastic surgery to improve her hideous looks, it would probably

mean years of agonisingly painful operations. And then there was
her hand. A clever touch, that. There would be no more show-off
dexterity with the playing cards at her precious evenings of bridge,
that was certain.

'Allan?'

He realised he'd been off in his own thoughts. 'I'm sorry,' he
said. 'I'm shattered. Doris and I didn't get on all that well, as you
know, but I wouldn't wish this on anyone. Do the police have any
clues?'

He waited with bated breath. She took a long time to answer.
Then he heard her sniffle and realised she'd been crying again.

'No. No clues. He's done it six times now, and they still have no
lead.'

Five times, dear, he wanted to correct her. 'I suppose they've
been asking lots of questions,' he said.

'They've been very thoughtful actually, not bothering me unless
it's absolutely necessary. Anyway, I can't help them much. I know
so little. I was getting worried because she was late home, and
walked down to the gate. That's when I heard her . . . and found
her. Oh Allan, I'll never forget it – never!'

She began to sob in earnest. Allan drank some wine and waited.
When she showed signs of regaining control, he broached the crucial
issue.

'Joan? Did they ask why you were staying with your mother?
What I mean is, did you tell them about us?'

'Oh no, of course not. Our private life has nothing to do with
them.'

He suppressed his relief. 'It's just that . . . well, our separation
would be just more fodder for the scandalmongers, and—'

'That's exactly the reason I haven't mentioned it. I told them I
was staying with mother to give her some time with her grandchild.
Which reminds me. I'd better go along to the Kitson's. They've
been looking after the baby all day.'

'Take care now,' he said.

Joan seemed to want to linger on the phone.

'How are you?' she inquired.

'Well of course, I've left Horne-Maynard's.' Thanks to your
fucking mother, he added silently. 'I'll be looking for another job
shortly. In the meantime, I'm just trying to get my life in order.'

'We were to see the solicitor today,' Joan said. 'About the divorce. Needless to say, the appointment was cancelled. I won't be

rushing into anything. Not the way things are with mother.'

My God, he thought incredulously. She wants to come back to me.

'You take it easy,' he murmured with feeling.

'You too.' Pause. 'Allan? Perhaps I could come around to the house and—'

'No, darling. I don't think that's a very good idea.' He had his own special reasons why she shouldn't see him right now. 'Everything's fine here. The cleaner still comes, so the housework's taken care of.' Lie. He'd sacked the cleaner, because he didn't want *her* around, either. 'I'm . . . I'm sorry about what I did. It's a weakness and I'm only human, but I think we need some more time apart to make our peace with each other.'

It was all rubbish but it seemed to work. He wanted her on his side at present, harbouring hopes of a reconciliation. That way, there would be no talk of the problems between them which could lead the police in his direction.

He finally got rid of her with a few more gentle platitudes, and was then able to laugh out loud. He didn't want her back and he didn't care about the baby. They'd be a hindrance once he had accomplished his current goals and was free to move on.

Every day he became more amazed at his own resourcefulness. There was the brilliant idea of tagging his revenge on Doris to the series of Slasher attacks. There was the black plastic raincoat which sheltered him from her blood. All he'd had to do was hose it down, then shove it into a Charity Clothing bin. He'd kept the cutthroat razor because it would come in handy at a later date. Any accusations the boy might be persuaded to make could now link Allan with the murder in the squat. Therefore, he might even use the razor to cut out the boy's tongue. Then, even if he lived, prying investigative reporters wouldn't find him such a dangerously damaging blabbermouth. Yes, the tongue. Blabbermouth into blubbermouth.

Still laughing out loud, he poured himself another glass of wine and allowed new ideas and schemes to burst like fireworks in his brain.

3

The morning after Kenneth had told her all about himself, Adele moved him into one of the upstairs bedrooms. She reasoned they shouldn't be on different floors all night while Kenneth's sleep was disturbed.

She helped him gather his belongings together, but he was surprised when they got up there to find she'd had Rina prepare one of the bedrooms facing the front. For some reason, he'd taken it for granted that he'd be in the other big one overlooking the Harbour, the one next to hers, the one formerly occupied by her husband. However, he didn't say anything. The room he'd moved to was fifty times better than the one off the kitchen downstairs and a million times better than anywhere else he'd slept in his life.

'Even though Rina does the rooms, I'd like you to keep this place tidy as a matter of courtesy,' Adele told him as they went in.

'I did the other one, didn't I?'

'So you did and I'm sorry I even brought the matter up. Just be careful of this, though,' she said, indicating a large green and blue vase on a stand by the door. 'It's genuine Ming.'

It could have been genuine Tupperware for all Kenneth knew, but he resented Adele's continuing apprehension about him. After all, he hadn't done anything wrong yet and didn't intend to.

'I'm sorry you don't trust me,' he finally said, as they stashed his clothes into drawers and cupboards.

Adele looked at him helplessly.

'What do you expect, kiddo? You suddenly appear in the middle of the night being chased by some pervert. You've been living by your wits on the wrong side of the law for years. Should I give you the keys to the safe and change my will? Come on. It takes time. We're doing all right, you and me, aren't we? Up to now?'

Kenneth nodded, frowning. 'Every street kid isn't going to mug you or steal from you, you know. They're not professional crims.

137

Crooks do it for a living. Street kids do it just to live. There's a difference.'

'Granted,' Adele said, picking up a handful of socks, 'but either way, owners get separated from their belongings for whatever the reason, so a gal's got every right to be careful.'

'Is this what you call being careful?' he asked, gesturing to himself and the room.

'You levelled with me last night and told me things you'd never told anyone else. I don't think you'd do that if you intended to bop me on the head and run off with the family jewels.'

Kenneth grinned, and Adele looked at him.

'Maybe, as time goes on, we can work out what you're going to do with your life. You seem to have a natural talent for fixing things. That's a start.' She pushed the last drawer shut. 'You've got to have some ambition, though. I hate underachievers.'

And Kenneth was relieved to find that there endeth the lesson.

They went on one of their jaunts the next day, to Darling Harbour, the mid-city waterfront complex. For the first time, Kenneth didn't wear the wig. It was hot and tight, and with the confidence he'd gained he felt he didn't need it any more. Just as long as he didn't go near the Cross, everywhere else seemed safe.

They did the Powerhouse Museum, the Aquarium, and the Chinese Garden and then bought takeaway Mexican and ate their tacos in the sun looking across the water at the rest of the city.

When she'd had enough, Adele said she needed to go the bathroom. She hurried off leaving Kenneth to finish the bean salad she didn't have room for. Just as he was cleaning up with a paper napkin, he heard his name called uncertainly.

'Kenneth?'

He turned around and found himself face to face with Sharon Pettifer.

4

The story of how Australia's tourist trade had picked up since the devastating domestic air pilots' strike of 1989–90 had turned out to be a bitch of an assignment for Sharon.

Interviews with the Minister for Tourism and leaders of the industry had been cancelled and switched around at the last minute, information had conflicted depending on the various sources from which it came, and location filming at popular visitor venues had been hot and uncomfortable. In addition, several of the major hotels had refused to comment on the grounds that the strike was long over and done with and it would be negative to dwell upon its aftereffects.

It was with great relief that Sharon had got the feature to a final edit, with her copy written and approved. It had been slotted into a Thursday show. Then, just two days before it was due to go to air, figures had come in from the United States and Japan showing that Australia had slipped drastically from its regained top place as a favoured destination of holiday travellers in both countries.

The figures couldn't be ignored, so the story had to be tagged with an update. Both Sharon and Jim Abrahams agreed that a studio announcement by Grant Olsen at the end of the item would lack punch. The new information should be given as an integral part of the story.

So, it was back to Darling Harbour, a featured location in the filming, where Sharon could reel off the figures against an authentic background – a clip that could be spliced effectively into the completed film.

The set-up took less than fifteen minutes, despite the interest of strolling crowds whose numbers gave the lie to the negative US and Japanese figures. Afterwards, the camera crew went to lunch. Sharon opted for a walk along the terraced promenades.

She stopped in her tracks.

There was something familiar about the boy sitting on a low wall

139

by the water. She studied the profile. It could almost be Terry, but Terry was dead, his brain jellied by the fumes of aeroplane glue. It could almost be Kenneth, too, but this boy looked too healthy. And yet . . . she decided to take a chance. She called out his name.

When he turned, the look he gave her wasn't exactly hostile, in fact it betrayed little emotion at all, but it wasn't exactly friendly either.

'It's me – Sharon Pettifer. From *Upfront*?'

'Oh. Yeh. G'day.'

There was an aloofness about him, the way he held his head and managed to appear as if he were looking down on her, even though he was sitting and she was standing. She took a step closer, feeling oddly at a disadvantage.

'Just been doing a location shoot over there. It's a wonder you didn't see us.' She gave a laugh which sounded forced. 'Everybody else did.'

He didn't say anything.

She noticed he had the sleekness which comes from good food and a healthy lifestyle. His hair was full and glossy. He had gained some weight and it showed in his face. He was tanned and his eyes were bright and clear. The shirt was expensive and the jeans were well cut. No wonder she'd had trouble recognising him.

She tried again.

'Hey. You must really think I'm the pits. They pushed our show on at the last minute without letting me know. I was out of town. I was absolutely furious. I'm sorry I let you down, I didn't mean to. I've been looking for you all over the place.'

'No worries,' he said, shrugging as if it didn't matter.

'No, I mean it. You disappeared and I was concerned. Especially after what happened to Donna.'

That got through to him.

'Donna?' he repeated sharply.

'You didn't know? She was beaten to death. In the squat. I found her.'

Kenneth was shattered, but he wasn't going to let her see it. He gave another uncaring shrug. 'It was bound to happen sooner or later. To her. To any of the kids. You should know that.'

His attitude was beginning to irritate Sharon. She stopped being conciliatory. 'You seem to have landed on your feet,' she observed.

'Better on my feet that on my face,' he replied, getting to his feet as if ready to go.

'You've still got five hundred dollars coming to you.' The words acted like a speed bump. Kenneth paused as Sharon added: 'I can't give it to you now. Should I still leave it with your friend Marieta as we arranged?'

'No.' The last thing he wanted was to have to front up in the Cross. He considered the options. And there was only one. 'Tell you what. Post it to me. Care of "Horizons", Boni—'

'Hang on a minute.' Sharon scrabbled in her bag and brought out a notebook and ballpoint. 'Now.'

Kenneth gave her the address and as she finished scribbling it down he moved towards her, crowding in.

'And don't give that to anyone else, understand? You let me down once, don't do it again.'

For a moment, all the surface changes to his appearance seemed to slide off like a skin and Sharon saw the grubby undernourished young hustler he was before. Then he was gone, pushing through the crowds and out of sight.

She attempted to follow him to see if he joined up with anyone, but a crocodile of rowdy schoolchildren trooping after a guide cut her off. Then one of them recognised her, nudging his mates, and she was surrounded by autograph hunters. She gave in and started to sign her name on paper sun hats and bare arms.

Kenneth found Adele standing at the top of the steps in front of the Harbourside Markets. She came down to meet him.

'My God,' she said incredulously, 'I had to stand in line! Can you believe that?'

He grabbed her arm and started to usher her away but she held back, refusing to hurry.

'Who was that you were talking to?' she inquired casually.

'Oh, nobody.'

'She didn't look like a nobody to me. Nobodies don't go around wearing Marcello Faidiga raw silk suits.'

Kenneth stopped and faced her, his face flushed and angry.

'Look, if you must know, it was the bird from the television. The one who got me to . . . well you know, I told you!'

'After what she did to you, I'm surprised you'd even pass the time of day with her.'

'Well I did! Now let's get out of here. Please?'

'Don't you want to ride the Monorail?'

'No. Let's go home.'

A cloud moved lazily across the sun and the day lost its sparkle. Adele nodded. The way things were going, home seemed like the best bet.

5

When they got back to 'Horizons', Adele went straight to her room without a word. The silence which reigned in the car on the way home had now widened into a gulf between them.

It suited Kenneth just fine.

He scooped a handful of cigarettes from a mother-of-pearl box in the drawing room and shoved them into his shirt pocket along with a folder of book matches with the word "Francesca's" etched in gold on the cover. Then he picked up a bottle of vodka and went outside.

He shunned the back terrace and the pool area because he would be visible to Adele if she chanced to look down from her bedroom. After wandering around aimlessly for a while, he squatted down behind a clump of rhododendron bushes where the lawns dipped away from the side of the house.

The first few drags of smoke made him feel sick and dizzy, but that didn't matter after a couple of gulps of vodka. He wanted to remember Donna. While he couldn't shed tears, there was an awful ache in his chest which had been worsening ever since he'd been told she was dead. The combined effects of nicotine and alcohol were fixing that. Now, he was beginning to feel terrible all over, but at least he was familiar with these symptoms and they were less upsetting than the ache they were counteracting.

Besides, it didn't seem right to mourn Donna feeling clean and healthy. She'd never been either of those things, not since he'd known her. In fact, now he came to think of it, that was why he'd been able to put on such a convincing act of not caring, for Sharon Pettifer's benefit. Donna had been dead all the time, really. Doomed. You knew it was only a matter of time. An accidental overdose, suicide or being done in by somebody. Like he'd said to Sharon, it was bound to happen sooner or later.

But all that didn't really help any, not when it came to the crunch. For a long time, months probably, Donna had been his only friend.

Someone to talk to, someone who showed they cared. She made up for all the bad stuff. It was like that, at first anyway, until the time came when she was so high twenty-four hours a day, she could have been in another dimension as far as any communication was concerned.

He gulped down some more vodka, then jammed the bottle between his knees while he lit another cigarette from the butt of the old one.

His mind went back.

Donna had been a year younger than him, but even allowing for the fact that kids grow up quicker when they're out on their own, it was obvious she was way ahead of him in the brains department. When she got around to confiding in him, not only did she have an intelligent way of expressing herself, she used words he'd never even heard of. She even let him screw her a few times and made it seem like a real act of friendship, the way she was kind and gentle, insisting that he wear a rubber. And when they clung together in desperate intimacy, they could have been lying in a feather bed rather than on a rotten old mattress.

He remembered his first sight of her, shooting up in an alley. It wasn't the efficient way she handled the needle or how defenceless she looked that caught his eye. He was used to all that. It was the words, heavily etched in ballpoint on her arms like tattoos.

'Maladjusted'. 'Disturbed'. 'Worthless'.

Eventually, when they got to know each other better, she told him she didn't live in the past or the present, but in a void of her own creation with whatever drugs she could lay her hands on. That would do until something better came along to wipe everything out completely.

And the words?

Her parents had divorced bitterly and had involved Donna in a tug of war which demonstrated not their love for her, but their extreme acquisitiveness. They fought over her like they fought over the Porsche, the Sydney Nolan, the home gym equipment and the weekender at Palm Beach.

She was made to feel like just another possession.

Abducted by her father.

Returned to her mother, who then fled with her interstate until her father had obtained a court order. And always, each of them poisoning her mind against the other. There was pain, confusion and divided loyalties. She came out of it emotionally screwed up.

When she went back to school, she told him, she couldn't

concentrate. She started to cut classes and score low marks, so they labelled her Learning Disabled. She misbehaved and showed aggression and they upped the diagnosis to genetic problems, categorising her condition as Attention Deficit Disorder – ADD – a neurochemical disfunction.

That was when they put her on the behaviour-management drug, Ritalin.

Kenneth remembered her picking viciously at a scab on her leg as if it were one of her mother's eyes. She observed that in probing around for the reasons why 'dear Donna' was in such a mess, nobody had thought to blame her parents.

'That was when I really gave up on adults,' she said. 'They're the ones who fuck us up in the first place.'

Donna's eyes had narrowed. Her body twitched and she pushed trembling fingers through her spikes of hair.

'Mum. My mum,' she muttered. 'She wanted from me everything shallow that she'd been brought up to value. Nice manners, pleasant disposition, neatness, respectability. Instead, what she got were these,' she laughed, waving the words on her arm, 'and I don't think she can work out why, even now. If she ever bothers to think of me, that is.'

Donna attributed side effects of the Ritalin as being the final blow to her self esteem. She lost what appetite she'd ever had and suffered from deadly bouts of depression. She tired of trying to cope with it all – school, the never-ending carping of her parents, the specialists, the psychiatrists, the lot.

She split.

Her life now totally unstructured, she escaped to the unrestricted anonymity of the Cross and sought and found more effectively obliterating chemicals than the one she'd been prescribed. And to pay for them, the addict of eleven years and ten months became the youngest prostitute on the block.

When Kenneth first met her two years later, she was hovering on the brink of that final descent into mindless oblivion. It seemed to help her a little, their finding the squat, having somewhere to be together, his being around.

She still had her tricks, sometimes four or five blokes a night, and the money still went on drugs but at least she was coherent for part of the time.

It didn't last. The corrosion of her brain was too far advanced, eating away at her senses of 'self' and 'being'. He saw it happening and he could do nothing. And now, one way or another, she had achieved the lasting peace she wanted all along.

Kenneth got to his feet shakily. The bottle tipped up and what was left of the vodka pulsed out on to the grass, soaking several cigarette ends. He swayed, looking around blearily, frowning and blinking as if seeing his surroundings for the first time.

The sun burned low and red over the treetops. The afternoon had passed and he hadn't been conscious of it. Maybe he hadn't been conscious at all. He knew he was pissed, so it was highly likely he'd passed out for a while.

Donna.

He had to do it for her, he had to. It would be a last ritual, saying goodbye forever.

He staggered across the front lawns and out through the gates. Each step he took echoed hollowly in his head as if he were fathoms underwater. He stared doggedly ahead as he reached the bend in Boniface Road and started down the slope. He knew he was taking a chance going back to the Cross, but his fears seemed to have gone, consumed by the burning desire to do right by Donna.

The main road was thick with peak hour traffic. Horns blared and tyres screeched as he weaved his way uncaringly across to the other side. Reaching the safety of the kerb, he turned around and raised his right arm as if hailing a bus.

Bugger the buses. They were the last thing he wanted to stop. On buses you had to buy tickets and even though he was pissed he knew he didn't have any money. Which was good in a way, because anyone who tried to mug him wouldn't get a cent. That made him laugh, and he stood there swaying and giggling to himself, arm raised, with the traffic hurtling past towards the city.

A small white delivery van with the words 'Krantzky's Smallgoods' painted on its side pulled up so tightly he had to stagger back to stop it taking the end off his nose. A young guy in his late teens leaned a long bony face across to the passenger side of the cabin.

'Where you goin', mate?'

'Just up the Cross,' slurred Kenneth, and clambered in before the driver had time to reply.

'Shit, you don't waste much time, do you? For all you know, I could've been turning off at Double Bay or into Paddo,' the guy said, crashing the gears, stepping on the accelerator and worming his way back into the mainstream of the traffic.

'But you're not, are you? Turning off?' Kenneth asked, his stomach heaving at the stale odours of garlic and processed meat.

'Nah,' the driver laughed. He cast a sideways glance at his passenger. 'Been on the piss, have you?'

'Yeh,' Kenneth managed, and let his head droop. It was the last thing he remembered until he became aware of being pushed out of the cabin.

'Okay, mate. You're home,' the young guy said. 'Hoo roo.' And with a screech of tyres he was off, leaving a bewildered Kenneth on the footpath outside the Hyatt.

It still wasn't quite dark. The neon signs glowed with a fresh intensity as if they'd benefited from the day's rest. Later, they would become garish and unsightly to the eye like a tart's make-up when it's been on too long.

Kenneth knew he had to get off the main drag. His head had cleared a little but he was still sluggish and weak at the knees. And now he was here, the fear had returned. He felt like a fly heading straight for the spider's parlour. But there was something he had to do before he started hiding himself.

He set off, mostly keeping his head down but unable to stop himself from glancing around from time to time. The Man could be close, still on the prowl, still looking for him. He tried to hurry but his legs were like rubber and the exertion brought back the dizziness. The smell from the hot dog sellers didn't help. And then he bumped into a black-suited spruiker, charging across the footpath to hustle business for a striptease parlour. The man was built like Rambo and it was like colliding with a brick wall. He thrust Kenneth aside like a bit of newspaper blown against him in a gale, his eyes fixed on the potential customers.

Kenneth staggered across several masterpieces executed in chalk by a bearded pavement artist, and was only dimly aware of the shouted protests because now he could see the greengrocer's shop with the bucket of cellophane-wrapped roses outside the door.

He slowed up and did his best to saunter past, nonchalantly. There was just one guy serving in the shop. Unoccupied. Gazing out the window.

Kenneth stopped. Someone came along and looked at the display of fruit and vegetables. A woman, already carrying a plastic bag of groceries.

Buy. Go in and buy, Kenneth willed her. But she decided not to and continued on her way.

Then a car stopped, double parked, and a girl in shiny leather pants, long hair bouncing, jumped out of the passenger seat. The guy driving kept the engine running as she ran across the pavement and into the shop. She spoke to the greengrocer and they both went over to a pile of avocados and began feeling them for ripeness.

That was all Kenneth needed. He grabbed a bunch of red roses from the bucket and ran.

Further along, he slowed down. Running was attention-getting, and there could be cops around. Before he turned down a passage, he caught sight of several familiar faces. Nobody he really knew, just people he'd seen around. The rest were strangers, the kind that came and went in an evening, the flotsam and jetsam of Kings Cross. Washed in and then out like the sewage at Bondi.

Thereafter, he kept to the side streets and laneways, the secret burrows of the rabbits in residence who preferred to get from place to place without being seen by outsiders.

He reached his destination in a matter of minutes, but was confused to find that the way into MacFarlane Place was barred by a high planking fence. Dusk was syphoning the last vestiges of light from the day but as far as he could make out, the whole area had been fenced off.

He looked up at a large hoarding and was just able to read the large print:

'The Biarritz. On this site will be built a boutique-style five-star hotel of 40 luxury apartments; a conference centre, an international restaurant, bar and coffee shop; a shopping plaza with 25 exclusive retail outlets; and a twin-cinema complex. Completion date to be announced. A project of the Yasujiro Conglomerate.'

Across a lower corner of the hoarding, a graffiti artist had sprayed the words:

'For sale. Going cheap. Australia.'

Kenneth backed a few paces, looking from side to side. He'd risked a lot, a bloody lot, to come back to this place. Now he realised he'd just as soon be with Adele and the safety and security she generated. But he wasn't going to give up. This was for Donna. There had to be a way in.

Sure enough, the vandals had already been at work. Two planks had been torn away, near where the fence joined the blank rear wall of a neighbouring building.

Kenneth squeezed through the gap and paused on the other side to get his bearings. It all looked so different, and the darkness was almost complete.

He picked his way forward over the rubble, then stopped.

The last terraced house, their squat, his and Donna's, was gone. Nothing remained. The entire area had been squashed flat as if by a giant hand and the debris scooped into hillocks, ready for removal.

He swallowed with difficulty. Not even somewhere to remind him of Donna. No special place to put the flowers.

Again he moved forward, but aimlessly now that he'd been robbed of the purpose of his pilgrimage. It was like treading the crust of an alien planet. The pulverised brick and stone glowed luminously in the dark. The hillocks loomed ominously, sentinels of destruction.

Kenneth took one more step forward and the ground crumbled beneath his foot. He yelled and stood stock still. The nightmare had become reality. He was back on the edge of The Gap, and he couldn't move because in front of him was a drop into eternity and behind him The Man was creeping up.

He stood there, gasping, unable to move. Then he realised he was standing on the rim of an enormous rectangle which had been gouged out of the earth. Straining his eyes, he could make out the perimeter of the hole, but its depths were lost in shadow.

He shivered. It was like an open grave, this vast abyss. He had come to pay tribute to a friend who was dead, but he had not expected to be confronted by a burial ground. This was a grave that had not only swallowed up part of the Cross, but was also waiting with a huge, gaping mouth to swallow up anything else that trespassed on its territory. His heart was thudding and his mouth dry. The drunkenness had passed. Now he was just plain scared.

Something moved behind him.

A piece of rubble was disturbed and it rattled against other pieces of rubble.

Then silence.

Kenneth remained absolutely still, afraid to look around.

Then there was a slight scrunch, closer to him.

Drained of the last vestiges of his courage, he sunk to his knees as if attempting to become smaller and therefore invisible. He should never have come here. It was the booze. He'd got charged up and, as usual, it had made him behave like a dickhead.

And now it was too late.

He turned his head just in time to see a large rat scutter past him. It was as big as a cat, but it was a rat, there was no doubt about that. Even in the dark, he could make out the ugly humped curve of its back. Button eyes sparked briefly and the long, thin snout twitched unceasingly. Then it seemed to pour itself over the edge of the excavation and disappeared into the abyss.

Kenneth bent his head over to one side and was violently sick. When he had finished, he scrambled shakily to his feet and made his way back to the fence. He squeezed himself through the gap then walked away from the demolition site.

Up a back street.

Down an alley.

And when he found a darkened doorway with some depth, it beckoned like a bedroom. He kicked away the rotting newspapers and a couple of needles, and lowered himself down into a corner.

Like the van driver had said, he was home. He was asleep within seconds.

6

It was dawn when he awoke. He had a headache and his mouth tasted of garbage but he was alert enough to know that he should split from this place as soon as possible. He realised he'd dropped the flowers on the excavation site in his hurry to get away, but at least they were there. For Donna.

He walked back to Point Piper.

There was some traffic along New South Head Road, just a dribble at this time of the morning, but he could have got a lift if he'd tried. Only he didn't want to try because his confidence had gone. He felt alone and dirty. And threatened. It had only been a rat back there, but there was something else he'd detected. A sense of brooding evil. It wasn't the effects of the vodka and it wasn't his imagination. It didn't have a smell or an abrasive touch. It was like he was tuned in on a powerful radio beam which sent a message of something unfinished craving completion, something that was moving inexorably in his direction.

As he trudged through Double Bay, he caught the irresistible aroma of freshly percolating coffee from a cafe that served early-morning snacks. From the same place drifted the smell of toasting bread.

His hunger was like a sickness. His stomach cramped up and nausea climbed high in his throat. He was reminded that he hadn't eaten since the Mexican food at Darling Harbour the day before. He began to long desperately for food and drink, but he knew it was out of the question. He had no money, and how could you actually 'steal' breakfast? Eat and run? Run? The way he felt, he could hardly walk, let alone run. He gritted his teeth and crossed the intersection at Bellevue Road and Cross Street and started the climb towards Point Piper.

It was full daylight by the time he turned into the gates of 'Horizons'. It was one of those Sydney mornings that had the bright chill of an ultra-modern kitchen before the oven is turned on. Faint traces of mist still clung to hollows in the lawn.

The house looked solid, almost fortress-like. It occurred to him that the burglar system hadn't been switched on, otherwise he would have triggered it into action. It was much too early for Adele to have got up and turned it off. A time clock. Maybe that was the answer, so that it would switch itself on and off automatically. He wondered why something like that hadn't been installed as a matter of course. Then again, Adele would probably forget about *that* too, and be forever setting the alarm off accidentaly and alerting the police every time she went out after dark. It was a stupid, unwieldy system and it should be on its own circuit, too. He must talk to her about it. Like he'd thought before, a person living alone tended to let things slide.

He found a side window open and clambered through it into the music room. Great. She could have been murdered in her bed. They *both* could be murdered in their beds one of these nights, with the lack of security around the place. He made a mental note to see to it that everything was closed and locked and the burglar alarm switched on every night before he went to bed from now on.

He crossed the foyer on tiptoe, even though the rubber soles of his joggers wouldn't have made a sound. He started up the stairs, then paused. He thought he heard the murmur of voices, and yet that wasn't possible. It wasn't one of Jorge and Rina's days and it was too early for them, anyway. As for that old creep Fitzgibbon being upstairs with Adele, well that would be unreal. Or would it? Maybe the two of them had a poke now and again, just for fun. In spite of the way he felt, Kenneth grinned to himself at the idea and continued on up the stairs.

Halfway up, he stopped again. Now, he could hear the voices distinctly. Low, almost whispers, but definitely real.

Could it be that Adele, realising he was gone for the night, had called in someone else for company? The thought brought on unaccustomed pangs of jealousy. He had to know for sure. He crept silently and swiftly up the rest of the stairs and made his way to the doorway of her bedroom.

The door was closed, as it always was. He pressed his ear to it and listened. And became aware that there was just one voice.

Adele's.

'. . . let the words of my mouth and the meditation of my heart be always acceptable in thy sight. Oh Lord, my strength my redeemer, forgive me of my sins I beseech thee and permit me to ascend and be admitted to thy celestial kingdom. Thus done, I will sing unto the lord as long as I shall live; I will sing praise to my God while I have my being.

'Make me a clean heart, O God, and renew a right spirit within me . . .'

Her voice droned on in muted incantation.

Kenneth backed away from the door feeling guilty, as if he'd been peeking at her while she undressed. He crossed to his own bedroom, went in and closed the door quietly behind him.

7

Adele was helping Rina clear out a cupboard in the hall when Kenneth emerged from his room towards midday.

He nodded briefly in their direction and went downstairs. He had managed another four hours sleep since he got home, collapsing onto his bed and pulling the quilt over himself as soon as he walked into the room. On waking, he'd showered and pulled on fresh jeans and a sweatshirt and while he felt a decided improvement, he was still ravenously hungry.

He made straight for the kitchen. His place at the table was set with orange juice, a bowl of cereal and a jug of milk. Coffee was percolating on the stove. He sat down immediatley and realised Adele had followed him in.

'Well,' she said. 'Enjoy your night on the town?'

Her voice was light and bouncy, but the words had the thrust of a sword. She walked over to the hotplate and poured coffee into a mug.

Kenneth had already slopped milk over his cereal and the first heaped spoonful was in his mouth. He moved it around then swallowed.

'I'm surprised you noticed I'd gone. Thought you'd be too busy praying.'

She froze in the act of putting the coffee pot back on the hotplate. She looked at him, caught offguard, her baby-blue eyes wide.

Immediately, Kenneth was sorry he'd said it. Adele was wearing a voluminous housecoat made of a shiny material with wide blue and green stripes. It had a cowl hood which she had up over her head to hide the curlers. The effect was that of a startled possum peeping through the folds of a marquee. He hadn't meant to hurt her, it was just a comeback to the remark she'd made about him being out on the town. Jeeze, if only she knew.

Adele recovered and bristled defensively as she brought the mug of coffee over to the table and put it down by his plate.

'I've gotten a great deal of comfort from my faith over the past few years, I'll have you know.'

Kenneth couldn't help but be incredulous. He'd always found her unpredictable, full of surprises but he never would have picked her for a closet Jesus freak. Not in a million years. Not from the way she drank and swore. *Or* the way she dressed. Right now, for instance, she looked more like a pensioned-off Madam than a Holy Roller.

'There's a religion for everybody, you know,' she continued. 'Even devil worshippers. And now that you've unearthed this fascinating morsel of information about me, perhaps I might persuade you to join me some time.'

'No way, Hosay,' Kenneth grunted.

'That figures,' she said wryly, then let it drop. She noticed he'd wolfed down the cereal. 'You still hungry?'

'I'm starved!'

'Eggs okay?'

Kenneth nodded. She took two eggs from the refrigerator, broke them into a small bowl and whisked them busily.

'The evening's festivities didn't include dinner, then?'

Kenneth didn't say anything. She'd been determined to get at him from the second she'd followed him into the kitchen, so he might as well let it happen. He concentrated on his coffee while she continued.

'That was quite a party you had yourself before you left. Mr Fitzgibbon found the bottle. Had I known you were so keen on outdoor entertaining, I'd have arranged a luau.'

She turned up the heat under a small skillet and dropped in a piece of butter.

'Omelette or scrambled?'

Kenneth shrugged. She poured the eggs into the pan and moved them around. Now that she appeared to have had her say, he broke his silence.

'It wasn't a party. It was more like a . . . what do they call it? A wake.'

'But what form did it take? An all-night mardi gras?'

'Oh shut up, will you?' he growled. 'It wasn't anything like you think.'

'Well how am I to know? Care to talk about it?'

'No.'

She tipped the eggs on to a plate, scraping the pan out, and brought them to the table. 'I forgot toast. Will just bread do?'

He nodded and started to eat, using the spoon he'd used for the cereal. Adele brought back three slices of bread and the butter dish.

'All this started with that girl, didn't it? The one you met at Darling Harbour? What did she say to you?'

'Forget it.'

'Forget it?' She sat down. Suddenly her face was filled with concern. 'Oh kiddo, I was so worried. I didn't know where you'd gone or what condition you were in. I didn't even know if you'd be coming back!'

He looked at her and felt sorry. She wasn't faking. He could tell from her face that his absence had really put her through hell, a hell she'd tried to banish with the prayers he'd heard her saying. Irrelevantly, he found himself wishing she wouldn't plaster the make-up on. It clogged in the creases that appeared when she got emotional and made her look years older.

'It was just . . . just something I had to do,' he said quietly.

He lowered his eyes to the remains of the scrambled eggs. He couldn't bear the sight of that anxious look on her face any longer. He knew she really cared about him but he didn't know how to handle it.

'I'm back and I'm sorry,' he muttered, hoping that would finish it. He resumed eating. His eyes stayed on the food but he knew she was still sitting there, looking at him.

Eventually, she stirred and spoke.

'Like I said the other night, you've got a lot of hurt inside of you. This is all part of it. Not just the nightmares. The restlessness. Not being able to cope. Getting drunk and taking off. You've got to start healing yourself. If you don't you'll never grow. And you have to grow if you really want to survive in this world.'

He kept his head down. 'What can I do?'

She stood up and began to clear away. 'You have to write full stop to the past, to everything that's happened to you up until now. That way, you can go forward without any hang-ups.'

'Easier said than done.'

'I wouldn't say that.'

She dumped the breakfast things on top of the dishwasher and came back to him. She took his hand, pressing it, forcing him to look at her.

'To start with, I think you should make your peace with your father.'

8

Had Adele's suggestion been made at any other time, Kenneth would have laughed in her face and told her to pull the other one. The very idea of fronting up to his father like some wimpy prodigal son shining with love and forgiveness should have struck him as ludicrous. It was the last thing he would ever have thought of doing, rating even lower down the scale of impossibilities than a date with Kylie Minogue.

And yet he offered nothing in the way of opposition. His night out had unnerved him. The outside world now seemed more menacing than when he was out there coping with it full-time. He stared at her dumbly when she made the suggestion. His silence gave her a foothold, and she continued enthusiastically.

'I've been giving a lot of thought to what you told me. About what happened to you at home,' she said. 'How long is it you've been gone now – three years? That's a long time. Has it ever occurred to you that your father might have recriminations? That he might regret what he did?'

Even in his present receptive mood, Kenneth had to react negatively to that.

'My dad? Regret? He tried to laugh and choked on it. 'Didn't you hear what I was telling you? About what he did to my sister? And mum?'

'You don't know for sure he caused your mother's death. As for your sister it was her decision, long after she left home, to do drugs.'

'Yeh, but . . . !' He seemed not to have the energy to go on with the argument and his voice trailed off. He actually found it immensely relieving to have Adele soothe away the pain. And soothe she did.

'You have all that hostility poisoning your system, corroding your mind. And it may not even be necessary. Look, this is not

157

something impossible I'm asking of you. Either way, you're going to benefit.'

Kenneth got to his feet and wandered around the kitchen. It was like he'd thrown down a handful of Serepax, and the tablets were numbing his brain while something inside him was still fighting to get out.

'What do I say to him? "G'day?" "How're you goin'?" You don't know him.' He tried to glare at Adele but lacked the drive.

She smiled understandingly.

'Yes, you say those things. And you might be surprised at the feedback you get. Even if a vestige of feeling remains then it's worth sustaining. If there's nothing, you're no worse off – better, in fact, for knowing. Imagine the satisfaction. The release. You've faced him and you're the strong one because of that. In essence, you've said: "I'm here, and I'm not afraid because I'm doing all right without you." And if you can do that, I promise you that you can turn away and get on with your life without ever looking back again. You'll be cleansed.'

Kenneth didn't so much agree, he capitulated.

He checked the phone book to make sure the address was the same, but Adele advised him not to telephone.

'No. You just turn up there. That'll give you the advantage of surprise. What time of day will he most likely be home?'

Kenneth told her it'd be a lottery because his father worked shifts.

'That's okay,' she said brightly. 'If at first we don't succeed we'll try, try, try again!' She seemed delighted to have a project, something positive with which to occupy herself.

One afternoon later in the week, she made sure he was dressed neatly in some of the less colourful items in his wardrobe, and they set off in the BMW. However, instead of being the gratifying jaunt Adele had anticipated, it turned into a time of mounting unease for her.

The first twinge came when he directed her to Glebe. She'd had it in her mind as a matter of certainty that the Mitchell home would be located in one of the working class suburbs in the city's west. She had envisaged a small weatherboard house, badly in need of painting, set on a neglected, untidy block of land in an anonymous maze of Streets, Avenues, Crescents and Parades each like the other, devoid of any character or style. She would have been only faintly surprised had it turned out she was slightly off-beam and Kenneth's home was actually in some semirural slum on the extreme outer fringes of Sydney, a recently developed area ill-served by sewerage facilities and amenities.

Glebe was a different matter entirely. Only minutes from the city centre, its Victorian-style residences had become much in demand with the affluent and trendy. Its convenient location, historic atmosphere and proximity to Sydney University were added attractions for prospective buyers.

When Adele commented on this to Kenneth, he told her that Glebe wasn't that popular years ago when the Mitchells went to live there. Only with cockroaches. Even so, she was still dismayed that her perception of Kenneth's background could be so wrong.

Progress along Glebe Point Road was slow, and she had time to study the seemingly endless string of ethnic restaurants that lined the thoroughfare. Then, as they approached the next set of traffic lights Kenneth told her to turn left. She did so, and imposing terraces of two and three-storeyed Victorian houses hemmed them in on both sides.

'We turn right at the Indian place on the corner,' Kenneth directed.

The Indian restaurant was called 'Tandoori Tucker' and Adele wasn't sure whether it was the name or the overpowering smell of curry that turned her stomach as they waited for a break in the oncoming traffic.

Kenneth squirmed. 'Jeeze, that smell. Brings it all back.'

'And up, I shouldn't wonder,' observed Adele as she made the turn.

She parked almost immediately in a space outside a red brick block of units which dominated the narrow dead-end street. Directly opposite, behind the Indian restaurant, was a line of four modern townhouses which had wrought iron balconies in a creditable attempt to complement the older homes in the area. The rest of the street was inhabited by semidetached cottages which appeared to have been painstakingly restored. Adele looked for one that was run-down and neglected, a suitable hidey-hole for a drunk on the skids, but she looked in vain.

'You might as well stay parked here,' said Kenneth. 'That's the one right at the end, next to the fence. Harold Park's over the other side. I never slept much *here*, either. If it wasn't the crowds at the Trots, it was the parents yelling at one another.'

Although from where she had parked the car Adele couldn't see much of the house, it appeared to be just as spruce as its neighbours. But there was something else which turned her unease into alarm.

She grabbed Kenneth and tried to stop him from getting out of the car.

'No. We've come at the wrong time. There's trouble. Look – there's a police car parked outside!'

'Nah – that means dad's home.'

Kenneth avoided her hand and jumped out. He slammed the door and spoke through the open window.

'Didn't I tell you? He's a cop. A bent cop.'

9

Sharon was working on some copy at a computer terminal when Jim Abrahams approached her waving a slip of paper like a fan.

'Accounts just sent this down for you,' he said.

Sharon turned from the screen, her eyes vague, her mind still on the story she was preparing.

'Oh. Thanks.'

She reached out, but Jim pulled it away swiftly and looked at it with eyebrows raised, playing a game.

'A cheque for five hundred dollars made out to "Cash". Now at a rough guess, I'd say you'd managed to track down your little pin-up boy.'

'And you'd be absolutely correct,' she responded. 'So – will you take the fifteen thousand you've won already or do you want to stick around and try for the houseful of furniture?'

They teased and played games with each other most of the time these days. It helped them to avoid those embarrassing little moments which might occur in conversation. The use of a word which harked back to their former intimacy. A pause which could develop into an awkward silence. A look which might betray a certain feeling.

Jim went along with it, even though wall-to-wall flippancy wasn't exactly his scene. It seemed the only way of riding out this break in their relationship while still continuing to work together. It wasn't entirely successful, but it was better than snapping at each other.

Sharon usually instigated the banter, just as she'd been the one to end their affair and the one who had always seemed ready for an argument. Now, she seemed more relaxed for going solo. She was working harder than ever and thriving on it. She was calling the tune, of course, so there was no reason for her to be unhappy about the arrangement, because it was what she wanted.

It was harder for Jim. He was older. And this was the second time he'd lost his woman. Probably for the same reasons. There were those that said, he was sure, that his dedication to his job had left his late wife Frances with time on her hands, and that was why she had turned to alcohol. After years of secret drinking, an infected liver finished her off. He hadn't neglected Sharon as much, but then again he wasn't married to her, and they worked together. The affair had been cosily convenient, but it represented a serious commitment from his point of view nevertheless, and he was having a hell of a time getting over it. Constantly hoping that Sharon would come back to him didn't help any. Neither did her presence in the office every day, but he would rather that than never see her at all.

She caught him off-guard and snatched the cheque away from him. The tips of her fingers touched his hand and the contact sent vibes of excitement rippling up his arm. She laughed at her small victory, folding the cheque in exaggerated triumph.

She had pinned up her hair into a topknot. Delicate flaxen wisps had escaped to float on either side of her face, emphasising its pedigree leanness. The arch of her neck, left bare, looked long and swan-like. Jim realised he was breaking the unwritten rules, standing there, looking at her with the appreciation of a lover. Quickly, he brought his thoughts back to the subject of the cheque.

'How did you find him, the boy?' he asked, not really caring.

'Actually, by accident. I ran into him while we were shooting at Darling Harbour the other day.' Her eyes wandered as she thought about it. 'Strange. He'd changed. In appearance, manner, every way.'

'For better or for worse?' Jim asked, then thought: Jesus! Now I'm quoting the marriage ceremony at her!

Sharon didn't notice. He could see she was still enraptured by the subject of the boy.

'Jim? I'm not talking follow-up here, but something odd has happened to Kenneth since I last saw him, and—'

'Aw, come on, Lois Lane.' The first part was a genuine groan, the name was to keep it light. Sharon nodded in agreement.

'You're absolutely right. It's just what Lois Lane would say – "I smell a story".'

'Another kid on the skids? Pardon my yawn, but haven't we been through the relevance or otherwise of this subject once or twice before?'

Sharon made a contemptuous gesture to the words on the computer screen. 'It certainly has more intriguing possibilities than yet another beat-up on beach pollution.'

Careful, Jim warned himself. He moved to lean his backside against the edge of her desk.

'I thought you'd be tickled to death at the opportunity to rub shoulders and anything else that might be naked and erogenous with all those raunchy blond surfers.'

'Yuk!' She elongated the word into an outraged wail. 'According to my observations, one third of them have ear infections; one third have diarrhoea; and the rest are all nursing sprains, bruises and broken bones. Oh, and most of them are so dumb and chauvenistic they'll probably end up as sports commentators!'

That gave them the first genuine laugh of the conversation so far, and allowed Sharon to risk being serious and sincere.

'Jim? Kenneth's lifestyle hasn't deteriorated. It's improved. Somehow, he seems to have dragged himself up, up and away. Now whether that's by fair means or foul, I intend to find out.'

Jim reminded himself that over and above everything else, here and now he was still Executive Producer of this outfit.

'On your own time,' he said.

Sharon looked at him with mock innocence. 'Of course on my own time. During working hours, my heart belongs to the surfies. And *only* to them.' And with a smile that shrieked 'Touché' she turned back to the computer.

10

There was almost a jauntiness in Kenneth's step as he walked along the street away from the car. Usually, Adele was the unpredictable one. This time, he'd put *her* nose out of joint. Or so it seemed, from the expression on her face. No harm was done, it just gave him a buzz, that's all.

He could see from way up at the other end of the street that Number 27 was no longer the dilapidated dwelling he'd left behind. It had been given a fresh paint job to match its neighbour, the brickwork had been cleaned up, and now he was close it was obvious that a lot of effort had been put into the small front garden, too. Maybe it was an omen. Maybe there'd been an improvement all round.

Kenneth paused at the front gate, his confidence ebbing slightly. It was weird being here again, remembering all that had happened within those four walls, the violence and the pain. The despair and death. All of a sudden, it seemed like he was meeting himself running out of the house down the path and out the gate, bruised and battered inside and out, determined never to return. And here he was, finally back again.

He told himself he had nothing to fear. If the old bugger showed any hostility, he'd be off like a shot. On the other hand, if his dad was in any way conciliatory, then he'd try to bury the hatchet like Adele wanted. He didn't see the point of it all, but if Adele reckoned it would be good for him, then he'd do it for her. She'd done more than enough for him.

He went up the path, noting that all the broken and missing mosaic tiles had been replaced. The pattern was complete again, just as it had been when the house was built at the turn of the century.

The front door had been given a coat of varnish. The two rectangular leadlight panels were identical twins again, the one on the right being a recent substitute for its predecessor which had been

164

smashed by his dad's forehead one rabid night when keys had been lost and drunken savagery was the solution.

Kenneth raised his knuckles to knock on the door, then noticed a new bell-push to one side. He ignored it, and gave three loud knocks in between the glass panels.

He waited. The cane chair had gone from the verandah, the one with the sagging seat his mum used to flop into with her knitting and a cup of tea on warm nights. So had the pot plants on the rickety three-tiered stand which, despite her efforts at cultivation, had straggled greyly in a blighted attempt at survival. There were three ginger jars there now, lumpily grouped together with parlour palms growing in them. Judging from their stunted growth and brownish tips, history was about to repeat itself. This side of the street got no sun, that was the problem. Everything died.

Footsteps clacked along the hall towards the front door. That was different, too. The carpet must have been taken up. Not before time. It was so trodden down and frayed, that—

The door opened abruptly. Not fully, just wide enough to convey suspicion of unwanted callers by the person on the other side.

Kenneth looked up and immediately registered two impressions about the woman staring at him from the aperture she controlled, one hand on the edge of the door, the other presumably on the lock. His first impression was of eyes that were slate-grey and totally without any sparkle or gleam of life. His second was the thin lips, strong enough to crack macadamia nuts.

'Yes?'

As if in some ill-advised attempt to compensate for the lifeless grey eyes, the eyebrows had been plucked to a thin, painful line and the crepey hoods below them smeared with green frosting. Those lips, what there were of them, were crayoned in scarlet. The rest of the face was square-jawed, the skin pallid and spongy, giving the impression that if you poked it with your finger, the hole would stay.

'I wanted to see Stan Mitchell,' Kenneth ventured with a cockiness he didn't feel.

'And who might you be?'

'I'm Kenneth Mitchell. His son.'

The woman tried to slam the door shut, but Kenneth already had his foot there. The force of her action made him wince, but he didn't try to pull it out.

She glared at him. He had time to reckon that she must be wearing a cheap wig. Nobody had blue-black hair except Orientals, and an Oriental she wasn't. And anyway, Orientals had a reputation for courtesy, something she'd obviously never heard of.

As if she realised that amputation was the only alternative and regrettably didn't have the instruments, she pulled back the door, releasing his foot.

'You'd better come in, I suppose.'

'Thanks,' he said and sauntered past her.

The hallway was now a chequerboard of black and white tiles. All the paper had been stripped off the walls, which had been painted cream. The house even smelled different.

Once inside, he paused to let her pass him and lead the way. She was quite tall, but the baggy sweater and stretch jeans she was wearing did nothing for her ballooning hips and thighs.

She led him straight down to the kitchen at the back. That, too, had been remodelled, but Kenneth hadn't time to register much. His father was sitting at the kitchen table eating baked beans on toast.

Stan Mitchell looked up. His long narrow face didn't move a muscle. He was a lean, sinewy man, leaner now than Kenneth remembered. The crew cut was showing a lot of grey. He looked older but trimmer, and the underlying potency of his toughness was undiminished.

'I don't believe it,' he said without emotion. 'You know who this is, Val?'

Val leaned back against the refrigerator. 'He told me.'

Unconcernedly, Stan Mitchell resumed shovelling baked beans into his mouth.

Kenneth cleared his throat. 'I just called in to see how you're going.'

Mitchell swallowed the food then ran his tongue up around his back teeth. 'Took your time, didn't you? Thought we'd seen the last of you.'

Kenneth laughed uncomfortably. 'No way. So, how're things?'

'Things are fine. For starters, I'm off the grog and on the wagon. Haven't touched a drop in two years. Waste of money. These days, I put my dough to better use.'

'Yeh,' Kenneth said. 'The house looks really excellent.' He glanced at Val. 'You two married, then?'

Val folded her arms. 'Nosy little sod, isn't he?'

'He's lookin' good on it, though,' Mitchell said, pushing his chair away from the table. He leaned back, tilting the chair, stretching out his long legs, surveying Kenneth with deep-set eyes. 'So what're you into, son? Dope? Prostitution?'

The 'son' made Kenneth careless. He grinned cheekily. 'I was going to ask you the same thing.'

Mitchell tensed up, bending his legs and slapping the chair back on all fours. He leaned forward looking for all the world like a spider ready to jump.

But before he could do or say anything, the fly-wire screen door squealed and a girl came in from the garden. She was about Kenneth's age, but her long, straight honey-coloured hair and frilly pinafore dress made her look younger, like the drawings he remembered of Alice in Wonderland. Her features were small and pretty, but her face had an unnatural pallor and shadows had nested under her eyes.

'Oh!'

She seemed to withdraw into herself, her eyes darting apprehensively from Mitchell to Kenneth and back again.

Mitchell untensed immediately. He smiled at the girl affectionately as he got up.

'We've got a visitor, darl. No worries.'

She held up an empty plastic tumbler. 'I just came in for some more—'

'Milk? Sure.' He turned, his tone taking on the hard edge of command. 'Val? More milk for the kid.'

Val jumped to it and took a carton of milk from the refrigerator. As she poured some into the girl's tumbler, Mitchell took the three steps it needed for him to join them. Without moving an inch, the girl seemed to draw away from him as his arm went around her shoulder. He looked across at Kenneth.

'You see, son, we're a happy little family here.'

Val finished pouring and took the carton back to the refrigerator. Mitchell gave the girl's shoulder a squeeze. The tumbler wobbled.

'Off you go, petal. Your dad's got some talking to do. Won't be long.'

Without another glance at the room, the girl turned quickly and went out into the back garden.

Mitchell's hardness snapped back in unison with the screen door. He looked at Val and inclined his head towards the door into the hallway. She picked up a packet of Benson and Hedges and a disposable lighter from near the sink and walked past Kenneth into the hallway. A few moments later he heard a door slam at the front of the house.

Kenneth stood there, almost mesmerised by his father, not

knowing what to say. He'd seen enough. It was time to go.

Mitchell moved towards him.

'Like I said, we're a happy little family here. We don't want no trouble, and no outsiders. Understand?'

'I'd better split,' said Kenneth, shuffling back. 'I've got someone waiting.'

Mitchell covered the distance between them in a flash. He grabbed Kenneth's shirt and bunched it up under his chin, almost lifting the boy off the floor.

'Understand?' he repeated, shouting the word with deafening force.

'Yeh. Yeh, I understand.'

'Then piss off and don't come back!'

Mitchell gave him a shove that sent Kenneth through the doorway and into the hall. Kenneth staggered and almost fell. He regained his balance and continued on to the front door. Only when he had his hand on the catch did he feel safe enough to deliver a parting shot. He turned and yelled at his father who had remained down at the other end of the hall.

'Yeh, dad. I understand *everything*. Nothing's changed, has it?'

Then, as Mitchell started towards him, Kenneth pulled down the catch.

Nothing happened.

Frantically, Kenneth jiggled the catch and pulled at the door. He glanced behind him.

His father was halfway along the hall.

He pulled at the door again but it wouldn't budge. That bloody woman must have put on the deadlock. Fuck! He tried the catch again, but it was too late.

Mitchell grabbed a handful of his hair and pulled him off balance. Kenneth's back arched with the pain as he felt himself being tugged around to face his father. He blinked away the tears brought on by the tearing at his scalp and saw Mitchell's deep-set eyes boring into him.

'I know what you're thinking, you filthy-minded little bastard!' the man growled.

Still pulling Kenneth's head back by the hair, he delivered two swift slaps to the boy's face, one with the flat of his leathery palm, the other a backhander. The force of the blows almost knocked Kenneth's head off his shoulders, or so it seemed. The side of his nose bore the brunt of the backhander and his nostrils were immediately swamped with blood. Almost unconscious, Kenneth knew from experience there was more to come. There would be no more talk now, just the usual brutality.

He took the full force of his father's fist in the abdomen. The breath was punched out of him leaving a void of unbearable agony. His immediate reaction would have been to double up, but Mitchell was still holding his head up by the hair, so Kenneth's legs came up off the floor, folding against his stomach. Yelling and screaming was out of the question, as was pleading for mercy. You needed breath for those things and there was none left inside him.

Suspended by the hair, with his legs bent and off the ground, there was only one way he could retaliate. He kicked out and caught Mitchell in the testicles.

The man let him drop and cannoned back against the wall with a yell.

Gasping for air, Kenneth tried to crawl away. But where was away? His sense of direction, his very reason was being obliterated by a cacophony of pain . . . a cacophony augmented when his father's foot slammed into his side and then into the small of his back. Struggling to get to his feet, he became dimly aware that Mitchell was opening the front door.

There was fresh air and light, and he turned to it as a flower to the sun. He had to get out. If he didn't, he would die.

The glare from the open door dazzled him. It was the threshold to his salvation.

But Stan Mitchell had not finished with his son.

As Kenneth reeled drunkenly to the open door, Mitchell again pulled back the boy's head by the hair. The edge of his other hand sliced down in a chopping blow to Kenneth's throat.

Kenneth gave a choking gurgle and sagged towards the floor. But before he collapsed completely, Mitchell's foot caught him in the backside and booted him out. Arms flailing, he careered across the porch, down the steps and landed face downwards on the mosaic-tiled path. In his last conscious moment, he heard the front door slam behind him.

11

Adele checked her watch. Kenneth had been gone for over an hour. They must be having quite a get-together in there.

At least it was a good sign. If Kenneth had had anything less than a friendly reception, he would have been out of the house quick-smart, he'd made that very clear to her. As it was, the length of his visit indicated that a degree of amiability had been achieved. And that was important, very important. She wanted Kenneth to be on good terms with his father for his own peace of mind.

Adele also had an ulterior motive. It was important to her, too, to have Mr Mitchell on their side, even though he sounded like an A-grade, card-carrying shit. She didn't want to explain why to Kenneth at this early stage, but it could mean a lot in the future.

Even so, an hour was about forty minutes too long to be sitting around in a stationary car. She was getting very restless. And she could still smell that goddamn curry.

She reached for another cigarette then decided against it. She'd already had two, whereas normally she never smoked in the car on the principle that it turned the interior into a stinking mobile ashtray.

On an impulse, she slid the key from the ignition, opened the door and got out. She stretched herself and looked along the street. There was nobody in sight. The only movement came from the slightly swaying *callistemon*, popularly known as bottle brush, which were growing at intervals along the edge of the footpath. They needed Mr Fitzgibbon's firm hand. They were overgrown, with branches that flopped untidily down to the ground.

She locked the car door, deciding to stroll down in the direction of the Mitchell house. At least it would pass the time. She might even encounter Kenneth on his way out. If not, Adele had no desire to intrude. There was time enough for her to meet his father at a later date. If Kenneth had not emerged by the time she reached the dead end, she would return to the car.

Up ahead, she saw two legs protruding from under one of the bottle brush bushes. Some drunk or derelict had obviously crawled into its shade. Adele slowed down, debating whether or not to cross to the other side of the street. She didn't fancy any close encounters of the disagreeable kind, and she knew only too well the dangers of being accosted in this town, even in broad daylight.

As she pondered, slowing down her walk, it suddenly occurred to her that there was something familiar about those legs.

The pants.

They were sky-blue cotton drill, exactly the same as the ones Kenneth was wearing today.

And then she broke into a run, fearful of the truth even before it really hit her, dreading yet knowing what she would find. And now she saw the smears of blood leading back to the open gate of the Mitchell house.

Reaching the bush, she dropped to her knees, clawing at the profusion of long, slender leaves, her whimpers of panic becoming pitying wails as she saw Kenneth's bruised and swollen face, the blood still welling from his nose, the purplish marks spreading across his throat, the contorted body.

'Oh my God, what has he done to you!'

Kenneth tried to sit up under the umbrella of branches. Adele pulled herself closer and enfolded him in her arms, taking his weight.

'It's my fault, it's all my fault. I should never have insisted you come here.'

She sobbed as she held him, her grief at his condition mingling with unendurable guilt.

'I wanted everything right between you. You're a minor. We'd need his approval if ever I wanted to be legally responsible for you. Oh, God forgive me, God forgive me!'

Somehow, she managed to get him back to the car and into the passenger seat. Their progress had been slow. Kenneth could barely walk and had to lean on Adele for support every step of the way. Her grief had now been supplanted by a dogged determination to get him away from here and to the casualty ward of the nearest hospital. But when she mentioned this as she started the engine, he grabbed her arm so violently, shaking his head painfully, staring at her with such a pathetic entreaty in his bloodshot eyes, that she agreed to take him straight home instead.

It occurred to her as she drove that treatment at a hospital would entail a statement about what had happened. Until she knew what

171

had gone on between Kenneth and his father, it might be better to avoid that kind of commitment. Kenneth hadn't exactly led a blameless life. His father was a policeman, and a crooked one at that, according to Kenneth. Perhaps the less official scrutiny at this stage, the better.

Neither of them spoke on the drive back to Point Piper. It seemed painful for Kenneth to draw breath, let alone speak. He slumped there, staunching his bloody nose with a wad of tissues. Adele concentrated on getting them home as fast as possible, given that she had to cope with the increasing traffic of the late afternoon peak hour.

Fortunately, Jorge and Rina were still at the house when they got back. Jorge carried Kenneth inside and upstairs as Adele briefly recounted how the boy had saved her from a mugging. She had Rina run a hot bath, then helped Jorge carefully undress him.

Kenneth groaned and cringed as his clothes were gently stripped off him. Adele steeled herself for a closer inspection of his injuries and saw for the first time additional bruises on his body where the boy had been kicked. Again, she felt herself close to hysterics, but fought to sublimate her emotions and appear calm and in control.

Jorge carried Kenneth into the en suite and lowered him gently into the hot bath. They left him there to soak, while Adele and Rina collected cracked ice from the kitchen and bar refrigerators and wrapped it in damp towels.

After Adele got rid of the couple, thrusting a bottle of Dom Perignon at them with profuse thanks for their assistance and assuring them that she was perfectly capable of managing the rest on her own, she took two of the ice packs upstairs and carefully rested them on each side of Kenneth's face, overlapping them across his nose. Relaxing in the hot bath appeared to be having a good effect on him, but Adele worried that he might lose consciousness and slip underwater. For the next two hours she kept vigil, letting in more hot water when necessary and replacing the ice packs on his face.

In between times, she wept.

Quietly and alone.

For Kenneth's vulnerability, for her own stupidity, and for the callousness of the world in general. She desperately wanted a drink but didn't have one because she had the responsibility of looking after an injured boy. She craved cigarettes, but was afraid to leave his bedroom while he was in the bath, and she didn't want lingering smoke to irritate his injured throat. This was her penance, the start

– and only the start – of what she knew would be an agonising period of guilt. She was to blame for this completely. For once in her life, she had been a silly, misguided do-gooder who had brought suffering to the one person in her life she had actually grown to care for.

Mid evening, she helped him out of the bath, wrapped him in a huge Turkish towel, and got him over to the bed.

She found some liniment in the medicine cabinet. She warmed it in the microwave, then took it upstairs and gently massaged it into the bruised parts of Kenneth's body. There was no embarrassment about his nakedness. Relieving the pain was more important.

With extreme care, she smoothed some of the oil into the swollen ridge across his throat. It appeared to be the most sensitive of his injuries. He had difficulty in swallowing, and when he tried to speak, it was in a painfully hoarse whisper.

Adele said she was going to bring in a doctor.

'No! I'll be all right!' The words struggled out of him, while he threshed in ferocious opposition.

Giving in, Adele tried another treatment on his throat. Hot towels, cold compresses. She kept this up for an hour. Then she combined honey and lemon juice and sat there to make sure he sipped the lot.

Something seemed to work. Possibly it was the result of her efforts, maybe it was the painkillers she crushed up in the last of the honey and lemon juice mixture. His breathing became easier and he got drowsy. Soon he was asleep.

Exhausted, Adele dragged herself to her own bedroom, leaving both doors wide open and setting her bedside alarm for two hours ahead.

The alarm was unnecessary. Sleep was out of the question. Even though her body cried out for it, her mind was tormented by relentless pinpricks of recrimination.

12

Sometime during the night, Kenneth woke up. His body burned with the aching activity of the healing process. That figured, he thought drowsily. Activity generated heat. Now where did *that* come from?

Science class.

Just as his mind was retreating back into sleep, he was conscious of movement beside him. He registered immediately that Adele had slipped into his bed. One of her arms burrowed below the back of his neck with great delicacy and he felt himself cradled and incredibly comforted by the soft and scented cushion of her body.

He slept.

13

For the next few days, Adele devoted herself totally to caring for Kenneth. She applied ice packs to the bruising, hot and cold compresses to his throat, and insisted that he stay in bed.

She had no arguments from Kenneth. Apart from the battering to his body, he was weakened emotionally and psychologically by the savagery of his father's attack. Knowing that it was because of his own foolishness didn't help any. He should have just kept his mouth shut and got out of there. Instead, he couldn't resist the parting shot and had paid for it.

Adele's constant moaning that it was all her fault added to his misery until he could stand it no more.

'Stop it!' he croaked. 'Wasn't your fault. Mine. I bad-mouthed him. That's why he trashed me.'

This had the effect of transforming Adele's chagrin into anger.

'Nothing you could have said to him warranted that kind of punishment. The man's a monster. The whole thing should be reported. He should be up on an assault charge!'

Kenneth eyed her wearily.

'Forget it.'

At least it shut her up on that particular subject.

They also reached common ground on the liniment. The smell of it made them both nauseous, so she switched to massaging him with warm Tea Tree Oil, which had the pleasant scent of the outdoors rather than the stink of a locker room.

Adele was no expert at massage, but her gentle caresses aided by the silky lubrication of the oil had a soothing effect which seemed to be dispersing the soreness and pain from the trouble spots.

Once, Kenneth was acutely embarrassed to find himself getting an erection. Fortunately, he was lying face downwards at the time and was able to conceal his condition. He tried to concentrate his mind on other things so desperately that droplets of sweat began to form on his forehead and run down his nose to be absorbed by the pillow. The sweat must have appeared elsewhere too, because Adele stopped working on the bruise in the small of his back.

'Are you getting too hot?' she inquired.

'You could say that.'

The sheer dismay of having her notice his discomfort had the desired effect. The hardness ebbed away. After that, if he began to feel sexy he immediately switched his thoughts to Andy of Zapperama. This was as effective as employing visions of vomit as an appetite depressant.

Adele even cancelled the weekly appointment she had with her beautician, to stay with him. The beautician, she told him, was a Hungarian expatriate called Madame Lupescu, who ministered to her exclusive clientele quite illegally from an apartment in the upper reaches of Bellevue Hill and 'did wonders for the skin'. Kenneth wondered how Madam Lupescu could ever find it under all the layers of make-up Adele usually plastered on.

But as a result of Adele's efforts, the lurid colouring of the various bruises quickly showed signs of fading and the swellings subsided. He remained stiff and sore, but painkillers at night helped him sleep. They were not strong enough, however, to prevent him from drifting up to some surface plateau of awareness during the night.

It was because of this he knew that Adele continued to slip into his bed an hour or two after she had switched off his light and retired to her own room. He found it extremely comforting to have her snuggle up to him, contributing a maternal warmth and softness to the small hours he had never experienced before.

In the mornings he would awaken to find she had gone. There was nothing to indicate she had ever been there except the lingering hint of her fragrance.

This nightly ritual was never mentioned by either of them. It was an unspoken culmination of their relationship, a silent declaration of mutual dependency, an innocent acceptance of fondness and sharing at the most intimate level.

Unspoken did not mean silent. Sometimes, he would become aware of her voice whispering softly in the darkness. Was she talking him to sleep, using the words for the soporific effect of a bedtime story? Was she talking *herself* to sleep? Or was she, in fact, talking *in* her sleep? He would never know. He was just conscious of the tranquil flow of softly spoken words. He would listen for a while, then succumb to their palliative effect and go back to sleep.

Always, the subject was Kelly Green. Adele must have been really rapt in her, Kenneth thought, but was not alarmed. It was harmless. A minor eccentricity compared to some he had encountered.

The words rippled out of the darkness like a stream from its source, endlessly flowing, mostly in monotone, all with the secretive hush of information being imparted in the strictest of confidence.

'. . . why yes, I'm always being asked what she was like as a person. And all I can do to describe her is to say she was a beautiful mass of contradictions. Scared to death one minute, unbelievably cruel the next. Warm, impulsive, shy. Desired by every red-blooded male who ever bought a movie theatre ticket, yet lonely in a crowd, ever searching for some kind of fulfillment. Naive as Rebecca of Sunnybrook Farm, as foul-mouthed as a longshoreman . . .'

And another night:

'. . . snapping at Marilyn's heels all through the late fifties. All she needed was one dramatic breakthrough, it didn't have to be *Hedda Gabler*, just a musical with some depth of character to give her a chance to show she wasn't just an animated centrefold. She had it all over Marilyn in many ways . . . she was reliable, she was punctual and she always walked on the set word-perfect. Of course, she was younger, too . . .'

She referred to Kelly occasionally in day-to-day conversation, but never with the extreme intensity of the nights. Kenneth classed her fixation on the dead movie queen as just another kink, like her religion. She never deliberately shoved *that* down your throat, either. Just said her prayers behind closed doors and left it at that.

Nothing seemed to be too much trouble for Adele if it contributed towards Kenneth's recovery. She had Jorge carry up a portable TV set and went out and bought home an assortment of video games. Because Kenneth had difficulty in swallowing, she fed him nourishing soups, whipped potatoes, scrambled eggs and blender drinks made from milk, fruit, eggs and ice cream.

The damage to his throat was the most persistent of his injuries. The bruising was a satanic rainbow of yellow through purple to black. It hurt when he swallowed and tried to speak and his voice remained a hoarse croak. Elsewhere, he was still sore, but he found on his trips to the bathroom that if he were careful he could move almost normally. Eventually, when Adele saw he was becoming too restless to be confined to bed any longer, she helped him dress and assisted him downstairs.

It was a fine, bright day with the refreshing coolness of an early autumn. Kenneth said he'd like to be outdoors for a while. Adele insisted on looping a warm scarf around his throat, then installed him under the umbrella on the back terrace. She said she'd be back with some freshly squeezed orange juice, but was gone much longer than he expected.

Eventually, she carried out a jug of orange juice and two glasses, apologising for the delay.

'That Holly Zimmerman phoned. Remember – the one I had living here for a time that drove me crazy? She goes through these phases. The constant one is that even though she must be pushing sixty, she's still trying to look like Sandra Dee. Let's face it, even Sandra Dee can't look like Sandra Dee any more so what hope has Holly got?'

Adele poured the orange juice, handed him a glass then sat down. 'I've been through the lot with her. The health kick where she threw down so many vitamin pills she rattled. The Shirley MacLaine bit, when she tried to make out she was in communication with the hereafter. Now, she's into Positive Thinking. Mind over Matter. Which would be fine, except she doesn't *have* a mind!'

She let out a guffaw of laughter and slapped Kenneth's arm when she saw he was grinning, too. After a while she quietened down. They sat in easy silence until Adele observed that by the time Kenneth was up to swimming, the weather would be too chilly and the water cold.

'What about . . . solar heating?' Kenneth managed.

'Wouldn't that mean they'd have to tear everything up to put in pipes?' She considered the prospect dubiously. 'No. No, I couldn't abide all that mess. Not now Mr Fitzgibbon has everything looking so pretty.'

'No mess. Easy.'

'Well . . . we'll see,' she said uncertainly. She poured herself another half glass of orange juice and carried it back into the house.

Kenneth lay back and dozed for about half an hour. Then he had a visitor.

14

Adele spiked her orange juice with vodka and drank it while she puréed cooked vegetables with chicken stock to make a rich soup for Kenneth's dinner.

That done, she decided to go up to her bedroom and give the Good Lord thanks for Kenneth's speedy recovery. She added just a splash more vodka to her empty glass, swished it around to incorporate the orange bits clinging to the sides, and disposed of it quickly.

The doorbell rang just as she was crossing the foyer. She stopped abruptly, as if someone had hit her own personal pause button.

All the usual recriminations crashed into her mind.

Jesus Christ, why haven't I had the gates put on remote control with an intercom like the neighbours? And why haven't I even bothered to put one of those spy lenses in the door so's I can at least see who's standing outside? All these years! I'm a klutz! I'll see to it all tomorrow, but in the meantime, who's this?

Somebody selling something? Like religion? Jehovah's Witnesses? Seventh Day Adventists? Religion she was stocked up on, she didn't need any more.

The doorbell rang again.

Adele didn't move. It couldn't be a social caller. Anyone belonging to her small circle of friends would have telephoned first.

Puzzled, she started towards the front door, just as the bell rang for the third time.

Such insistence. And impatience.

Adele pulled open the front door and recognised the girl standing there immediately. It was 'the bird from the television' as Kenneth had called her after the encounter at Darling Harbour, the lady who had coerced him into playing the sprat that was used to catch the mackerel. The bait. She had used Kenneth as just a piece of flesh, and was therefore as corrupt as the rest of the maurauders who cruised the Cross like sharks.

179

Adele had resented her from a distance, and the feeling intensified close up, particularly as she again presented a picture of casual
elegance in a Lacroix-inspired ensemble teaming a cotton and rayon
floral top with spotted georgette culottes.

Adele almost slammed the door in her face. Instead, she drew
herself up, tensing for an unavoidable fracas.

'Yes?'

'I've called to see Kenneth Mitchell.'

'I'm sorry, you can't. It's inconvenient.'

'What do you mean, inconvenient?'

'If you don't know the meaning of the word, don't ask me. Go
look it up in a dictionary.'

Yeah, now Adele remembered her, even from before Darling
Harbour. She was one of those investigative TV reporters who
usually fell into two categories. There were the smouldering types
who seduced innocent victims into their high-rating webs before
striking, and their more strident sisters often found mangling their
vowels on the ABC and not averse to standover tactics or leaping
fences in order to corner their prey.

This one belonged to neither category. She recalled that the lady
on her doorstep was probably the most lethal of them all, adopting
the 'Hey, mate let's be buddies' approach, then allowing them to
convict themselves (or paying gullible kids to help her do the job!)
Adele tended to classify people in terms of movie lookalikes. This
one was a tall rangy blonde and Adele was immediately reminded
of Louise Albritton, a remarkably polished actress whose career
was tragically confined to B-pictures in the nineteen forties. She
flipped through others of similar type in her mind. Candice Bergen?
Too robust. Eva Marie Saint? Too fragile. Grace Kelly? Well . . .
possibly – before she became Mrs Ranier. The visitor belonged to
the same family as them all, with Katherine Hepburn's bone structure thrown in. But probably this one had none of their finer
qualities. Except, perhaps for their persistence.

'I know I'm intruding, but it really is important. I have something
for him and I'd like to deliver it personally.'

Adele continued not to mince matters.

'Why don't you leave it till another day? Like, when I've hired
some security guards.'

Sharon chose to treat Adele's rudeness as humour. She retaliated
with a big smile which revealed a gallery of perfect teeth.

'I'm Sharon Pettifer. From *Upfront*? I have a cheque for
Kenneth, and I'd *so* much like to say hello to him, Mrs . . . ?'

'Hatherley.'

Sharon knew that already. She had checked the electoral rolls for the area on the way over. However, she was not prepared for this feisty American woman in the heavy make-up and dated gear. Still, Sharon had no doubts she could handle her. She maintained the smile to indicate that the woman's recalcitrant attitude was having no effect whatsoever, sending signals loud and clear that she had no intention of withdrawing gracefully, and if she did not get to see Kenneth on this visit then she would be back.

Evidently, the signals were received and understood. With a mask-like stare which was the very antithesis of a welcome, the woman stepped back and admitted her.

The opulence of the residence did not surprise Sharon.

Understated – and overstated – luxury was par for the course in this neck of the woods.

What did surprise – no, shock – her, was Kenneth's condition. As the boy struggled to sit up in the recliner under the umbrella, Sharon gasped. His face bore evidence of heavy blows. His nose was painfully swollen, and both cheeks were blotched mauvish-grey.

'Oh no! What happened to you?'

Sharon was conscious of the woman standing by like a prison wardress.

'He got into a fight. Boys do, you know. But he's recovering and it won't happen again, I'll make sure of that.' Her voice softened as she switched to Kenneth. 'You need anything, kiddo?'

He shook his head. She looked back at Sharon.

'You got ten minutes. I'm not laying down the law, it's just that Kenneth needs rest and quiet, and you seem to have a distinct habit of upsetting him in one way or another.'

And with that, she turned and walked across the terrace towards the house.

Sharon turned to Kenneth with a conspiratorial smile. 'Why do I get the impression she hates my guts?'

'Adele's beaut!' he lashed back aggressively.

Oh, it was like that, was it? *Adele.* Sharon could see she would have to be careful how she referred to *Adele* in future, if she wanted to ingratiate herself with the boy. He was obviously besotted with the woman.

'You sound awful. Did you get hit in the throat, too?'

Kenneth nodded.

'Have you seen a doctor? I mean, something serious could be

181

wrong. The larynx is a very delicate instrument.'

Kenneth shook his head. 'Don't need doctors. Adele's looking after me. Almost better now.'

Sharon shook her head disbelievingly, but decided not to pursue the matter with him. She reached into her bag and took out the cheque.

'Here,' she said, handing it to him. 'With my belated thanks, and again my apologies for letting you down.'

'You shoulda posted it.'

'I wanted to see you again. You've no idea how rotten I felt, not being able to warn you that the show was going to air. Did you . . . were there any repercussions?'

Kenneth's gesture took in the house, the pool and the grounds.

'Yeh. All this. So you needn't worry. Not bad, eh? Better than a refuge or a squat.'

Sharon nodded. 'Have you . . . known Mrs Hatherley long?'

Kenneth grinned. 'No use trying to pump me. I'm not talking.'

She preferred the grin and the knock-back to surly aggression and felt she had made a little progress. She smiled back.

'I guess questions come second nature to me, even *off* the job.' She paused, fastening the clip on her bag and then looked across at him. 'This may sound corny, but I'd like us to be friends.'

His head tilted back slightly. 'Why?'

There it was again, the haughtiness which she had found so disconcerting at Darling Harbour. Uncharacteristically, she floundered. 'For one thing, you remind me of someone who—' Her voice trailed off. She couldn't bring herself to mention her dead brother. Instead, her brain clicked over and she smiled brightly. 'You can never put into words why you want to be friends with someone, not really, any more than you can say why you don't.'

'Garbage,' he replied scornfully. 'There's always reasons.'

Which was precisely what she wanted him to say. Now, he would feel better for having corrected her.

'You're absolutely right, you know. So I guess it just boils down to the fact that I like you. I find myself caring what happens to you. Do you find that so hard to accept?'

He thought about it. 'A bit,' he said.

At last Sharon knew she was getting somewhere.

15

Adele watched them talking from the windows of the morning room, standing back so that she would not be seen should either of them glance towards the house.

Although she knew about the money owing to Kenneth, she was intensely curious as to what was being said between them. She hated leaving them alone together, but knew beyond doubt that it was the right thing for her to do. She didn't want to alienate Kenneth by crowding him, and she certainly didn't want to give the impression to the Pettifer girl that she was some kind of duenna.

Sharon had evidently taken notice of what Adele said about keeping it to ten minutes, because she checked her watch a couple of times and after the third time said something with yet another of those big fake smiles and made ready to leave.

Adele was waiting at the corner of the house by the time Sharon moved away from Kenneth. She had no intention of letting the girl into the house again, not even to walk through to the front door. She waved curtly, and when Sharon joined her she indicated the path bordered by cool and tropical Philodendrons interplanted with hardy native ferns.

'We can go this way,' Adele told her.

'Thank you,' Sharon replied.

They walked in awkward silence until Sharon spoke again.

'These are beautiful grounds.'

Adele nodded, but didn't reply. She had no intention of indulging in small talk. And neither, for that matter, had Sharon judging from her next remark.

'You've taken Kenneth in, then?' It was more an observation than a query.

Adele paused, her hand on the latch of the door in an ivy-covered retaining wall which gave entry to the front lawns. She gave Sharon a forthright look.

'I've given him a home, if that's what you mean, Miss Pettifer.

And before you draw any hasty conclusions I should point out that this is not just the idle whim of a wealthy woman.'

'Oh, I had no intention—'

'Surely, gathering information by digging into people's lives, then being judgemental is your stock in trade, isn't it, Miss Pettifer?'

Sharon managed a tight little smile.

'I'd like to believe my career as an investigative journalist was governed by a more laudable scenario than that.'

'Good. Then you'll understand that assuming responsibility for someone like Kenneth is no part-time job. It has to be full-time, which means being there when you're needed because problems can arise any hour of the day or night. It means offering stability, not the short-term shelter given in a rehabilitation centre or a refuge where there's a residency limit of weeks, but long term stability. That's the way I see it, anyhow.'

And having got that off her chest, she pulled open the door.

'Shall we?'

As they walked to the front of the house, Adele indicated a freshly painted lattice screen.

'That's Kenneth's handiwork. I don't have lists posted up on the walls, Miss Pettifer, no work schedules. Anything Kenneth does, he does voluntarily. And I must say,' she added with a certain amount of pride, 'he has made himself very useful.'

They turned the corner of the house and Adele gestured to the drive leading down to the front gates.

'There you go. Nice of you to call.'

Sharon seethed with indignation. She was not used to being treated this way, lectured to as if she knew nothing of the problems involved in rehabilitating homeless youngsters, then dismissed like some menial. Wherever she went she was treated with respect. She was recognised. Interviewees with nothing to hide were friendly and cooperative. Those fearful of her probing were on guard but at the least civil. This woman was being condescending and she would pay for it.

Summoning up one of her loveliest smiles, Sharon fired the only shot in her artillery.

'Mrs Hatherley, being as concerned as you are with Kenneth's welfare, I'm surprised you haven't sought medical treatment for that throat of his. His voice is practically inaudible.'

'I would have done so immediately, but Kenneth insisted. No doctors.'

'So you went along with it. I do understand. There's such a fine line between caring and indulgence, isn't there? But I do feel, in this case, he should be persuaded to have some sort of examination, don't you?'

Adele gritted her teeth. 'We'll see.'

'Good,' Sharon said, recharging her smile. 'Bye.'

Adele stood there and watched her until she left through the gates. Then before she returned to the terrace, she went back into the house and with shaking hands poured herself a slug of vodka. She felt angry and vaguely threatened by Sharon Pettifer's visit. She shuddered as the liquor went down, but it helped calm her.

Immediately she joined Kenneth he held out the cheque.

'Keep this for me, will you?'

Adele took it. 'We'll have to open you a bank account. Then you can use it whenever you like.'

'I've been thinking,' he said. 'About heating the pool. You were probably right. Not worth the bother. Don't think I'd go for swimming in winter, anyway.'

He obviously had nothing to say about the visitor. Adele didn't know whether to be pleased or sorry. She would have given an arm to know what had been said between them. On the other hand, if he didn't think it was important enough to talk about, that was a good sign. She tried to get him to follow through on the subject of the pool.

'I don't mind the expense, you know, if—'

'Nah. Imagine getting out of warm water into the freezing cold. Really gross.' He thought for a while. 'Tell you what, though. I reckon we should get a pool cover. Keep it clean for next spring.'

Next spring. Adele could have hugged him. It was the first time she had ever heard him refer to the future in any way positively. And now, here was a plan, and it indicated permanency, and it more than happily dispelled the unpleasant aftertaste of Sharon Pettifer's visit.

16

When Sharon got back to the studio, she went straight to the office of Margaret Fong, who had the reputation of being the network's brightest researcher in current affairs. A third-generation Chinese-Australian, Margaret was a petite dynamo of efficiency with an unflappable disposition and a sunny smile.

'This is a personal favour, sweetie,' Sharon told her, 'but you owe me – remember?'

'I sure do,' Margaret replied. At Margaret's request, Sharon had given her support to several charity fund-raising activities organised by the Chinese community – attending a banquet, drawing a raffle and so on.

Sharon took a pen from a bunch of them in a glass on Margaret's desk and started to write on a scribble pad. She spoke as she wrote down a name and address.

'I want the works on this woman. Everything there is to know about her.' And she tore off the top sheet of the pad and handed it over.

17

Kenneth offered no objection when Adele suggested they seek a medical opinion on the condition of his throat. Although he would only admit it to himself, he was getting sick and tired of trying to communicate in weak, husky whispers.

Adele, on the other hand, thought his voice had improved. The mark on his throat was definitely fading. However, she didn't like Sharon Pettifer's implication that she was neglecting to do what was best for Kenneth. She rang her doctor for advice and he referred her to an Ear, Nose and Throat specialist in Maquarie Street.

She made such a sob story out of a poor defenceless child being attacked by muggers that after initially saying there was a three-week delay in appointments, the specialist's receptionist capitulated to Adele's dramatic entreaties and managed to fit them in the following day.

The diagnosis was good. After the examination, the ENT man told them that the direct and violent blow to the larynx had caused internal bruising to the vocal cords and surrounding tissues, but no permanent damage. No special treatment was required. Kenneth was told to rest his voice and nature would do the rest.

Consequently, they were in good spirits when they emerged into the sunlight of Maquarie Street. Adele spotted a coffee shop and they celebrated with creamy cappucino and hunks of Black Forest cake.

'You sure you can manage that, kiddo?' Adele asked anxiously as he dug his fork into the cake. Kenneth grinned. Could he!

On the way home, they detoured by way of the Blue Lagoon Company which had installed the pool at 'Horizons'. After listening to the advice of a salesman and looking at several photographs of different types of pool cover, they decided on a transparent plastic blanket, custom-made to their pool size and shape. Delivery and installation was promised, on Adele's formidable insistence, within a week.

'It's not *that* urgent,' Kenneth told her as they headed back to Point Piper.

'I don't expect to be kept waiting for anything, once it's been ordered and paid for,' Adele replied firmly. 'Let 'em jump to it, for a change. There's not enough of that customer power in this country!'

When they arrived home, Kenneth went upstairs to change his clothes and Adele hurriedly looked up a number under 'Television' in the telephone directory. Quickly, she dialled the number she'd found and asked to speak to Miss Sharon Pettifer.

Adele drummed her fingers impatiently. If the damned girl didn't come to the telephone soon, she would have to hang up and try again from her bedroom later. This was a call she didn't want Kenneth to know about.

After an interminable delay there was a decisive click and Sharon Pettifer said 'Hello.'

Adele kept it brief, businesslike and to the point. She told Sharon about the consultation and the diagnosis and added off-handedly: 'I just thought you'd care to know.'

'That's very thoughtful of you, Mrs Hatherley,' Sharon replied cordially. 'I'm sure there'll be a big improvement the next time I see Kenneth.'

'Yes, well I don't know when that will be. I'm taking him up to the Gold Coast for several weeks to help him recouperate. I really don't know when we'll be back.'

'Oh.'

Sharon appeared to be thrown off-balance by this information. She repeated her thanks for the call and rang off.

And that takes care of you Miss Nosy Parker, Adele thought as she went to fix herself a drink.

When Kenneth came down, he found her buzzing around the kitchen busily, humming melodies which seemed on the brink of bursting into lyrics, as she prepared to heat the soup she had made earlier.

'Er . . . I don't want to mess up your plans, but I think I could manage something chewy,' he said.

She looked at him, eyes wide with interest, smoothing her hands down over the impossibly-frilled orange apron cut in the shape of a heart, its pink surface decorated with a gaudy combination of roses and pineapples.

'Okay then. We can still start with this soup, but maybe we can follow it with a little cold chicken and salad. And if you can manage all that, maybe tomorrow night we can send out for pizzas!'

He nodded, grinning. It gave him a kick when she responded to his needs with enthusiasm. Involuntarily, he started towards her, his arms out, wanting to show his appreciation.

Adele accepted him, enfolded him and hugged him close.

'You're so good to me,' he managed to choke out. His emotions were making the soreness in his throat worse. Everything seemed to be swelling up in that area and to add to it all he found himself having to blink back tears, which was totally unreal because he never cried and anyway he didn't feel sad he felt happy.

Her hands patted his back.

'Oh, I have my ulterior motives with this Mother Teresa act,' she said. 'I figure if I can get you into a good mood, I can con you into trying backgammon again.'

'Aw no, I'm useless!' His voice cracked drily with the effort of his protest.

'Not at all,' she argued. 'You show promise.' She pushed him away. 'Now why don't you go and get the board out, while I fix the food. And if you chicken out, then I sentence you to watch the Late Late Movie!'

18

The daily production meetings for *Upfront* were usually intense but orderly, with the occasional injoke for light relief and an overlay of good-natured camaraderie which was characteristic of a finely balanced team dedicated to the task of making the nightly show as stimulating as possible.

Generally, there were few real bones of contention from the dozen or so staff members present. As a rule, the attendance was made up of three or four investigative reporters, depending on who was available and not out on a job, anchorman Grant Olsen, the technical director and his assistant, a researcher or two, a film editor, and Jim Abrahams and his secretary who took notes.

Lately, there'd been a change. Whenever Sharon was there the meeting dragged on, the atmosphere became edgy and usually it was because of her. She seemed to be becoming more stridently assertive, questioning policy decisions and the relevance of story subjects, criticising methods of approach and style, and coming up with suggestions which would have been better put in memos.

This morning, she had wasted a great deal of time arguing about what she saw as the increasing use of the show as a political soapbox.

'I think the viewing public is entitled to know what its elected representatives are doing and thinking,' Jim finally interrupted, hoping to cut her off.

Sharon smiled at him. While her manner might be irritating, she was always cordial, something which was inclined to aggravate even more. 'But they do tend to go on incessantly,' she stressed.

Jim gave her a direct look. 'I think we're all guilty of that at times – some of us more than others.'

The skin stretched over her cheekbones flushed pinkly, but she made no reply. There was a short prickly silence, then Jim moved on to the planned line-up for that evening's show. Sharon didn't speak for the rest of the meeting.

When it broke up, Grant Olsen moved past Jim and winked.

'Good on you,' he muttered.

Sharon hung back until everyone else had gone. Jim expected her to do this and was ready for her. The games were over.

'That wasn't very nice,' she said, an edge of truculence glinting dangerously beneath the frills of her charm.

'It wasn't meant to be,' Jim replied. 'Production meetings aren't intended as a platform for your overassertiveness, any more than the show's a soapbox for politicians. You objected to the idea of one while indulging in the other. Both are equally boring and out of place.'

Sharon stood there, tight-lipped. Jim gathered his notes from the conference table, then looked at her.

'I can understand your not wanting to be seen as teacher's pet,' he said, 'but you can't be captain of the ship, either. There's only one captain and that's me. You're stepping out of line and you're doing it a lot.'

Sharon bristled. 'So much for dedication and enthusiasm.'

'Oh no,' Jim replied, shaking his head. 'You're being supremely overconfident, and that's a different matter. You air your opinions loud and long as if you're running the show. The fact that you've shown me the bedroom door doesn't give you the right to muscle in on my job, *or* treat me like shit.'

'I didn't realise you were so insecure.'

'I'm not. Otherwise I wouldn't be telling you to pull your head in.'

She gave a bitter smile. 'It's finally got through to you that it's really over between us, so now you're taking it out on me.'

'I'm not, dammit!' He threw the papers back on the table. His eyes searched hers for an explanation. 'Sharon, what's happening to you? What's giving you this . . . arrogance?'

'Arrogance?' She looked from side to side as if she'd find the reason for his accusations somewhere in the conference room. 'Jim, I'm not your little girl any more. I'm a grown woman, capable of standing on my own two feet. I'm good at my job, and if I feel like speaking out on some professional issue then I will. I respect you, but I'm no longer in awe of you.'

'Is it finding that boy? Did the worry about his disappearance weigh so heavily on you that now you've found him, the relief's gone to your head?'

'Relief?' Sharon was incredulous. 'I don't get any peace of mind from his current situation.'

'But you said he was living in luxury in Point Piper,' said Jim puzzled.

'Yes. With this strange American woman. I haven't seen so much make-up on one face since Tammy Bakker. And she's got him there, all to herself. You know what some Americans can be like. All gung-ho and bluster on the surface, but monomaniacal and stitched-up underneath. She looks just that type. It's unhealthy – just as unhealthy in its way as the boy's former existence in the Cross.'

'She's given him a home, hasn't she?'

'Well, yes but—'

'Would you be prepared to do that?'

'That's not the point—'

'Then what *is* the point? Why are you so concerned about a kid who's obviously better off now than he was before—'

'I don't know how we got on to this subject! But if you must know, having become involved in his life by accident, I'm concerned about him. I work on *Upfront* and I'm concerned about that, too. That's why I speak up. If I'm concerned, if I'm involved, then I'm committed. That's the way I am.'

Committed? Obsessed would be a better description, Jim thought. He wondered why he'd never noticed this trait in her before. It was so glaring all of a sudden.

Again he gathered up his notes. He felt weary. He'd had enough. He started for the door and when he reached it he paused.

'If you have any gripes, Sharon, come to me. Don't air them in front of everybody else, particularly if it means holding up the meetings.' He pulled open the door and turned back to her. 'And for God's sake, try to loosen up a little.'

He waited for her to walk through the doorway, but she stood there. The corners of her mouth twitched with amusement.

'I think I get your drift, Jim. And I want you to know I'm getting that aspect of my life beautifully back on the rails.'

He felt his throat tighten and knew that he had walked right into the trap which had been waiting for him, serrated jaws gaping, all through this confrontation. With a monumental effort, he tried to make the best of it.

'I knew you'd fall for one of those blond surfies. Didn't I say so?'

Now, Sharon was smiling, not only with a delicious sense of satisfaction that Jim finally knew she had someone else, but at the unconscious humour in his remark. With his dark good looks, nobody could look less like a callow blond surfie than Adam Shaw. But she wasn't going to tell Jim that. Let him wonder.

19

At precisely eight o'clock that evening, Sharon walked into Bellini's Brasserie.

She had left the studio early in order to give herself plenty of time for the leisurely grooming she felt the evening warranted. And now that Jim knew she was going out with another man, even though he had no idea who it was, she felt the extra frisson of excitement which usually occurred on a first date. And even though she'd been out with Adam twice before, it *was* a first date – the first one Jim knew about.

He knew about it because she had mentioned it when she checked with him about leaving early. There had been no need for her to check with Jim, she came and went more or less as she pleased, work permitting, but she wanted the opportunity. After their confrontation, she had worked hard for the rest of the day collating all the available data on a cruelty to animals story into a tentative shooting format, and had passed it over to him as she left.

Jim delved straight into it, and appeared not to notice when she made her excuses about not being able to stick around for the show that night because of 'a dinner engagement'. But *she* knew that *he* knew, and he was probably thinking about her right now as the chatter and the aromas of the Brasserie engulfed her with the cosy familiarity of a family kitchen.

Her leisurely preparations had paid off. She felt softly elegant in a superbly cut pants suit in sage wool which complemented her tall slenderness. She had casually draped a long white Isadora Duncan scarf around her neck so that the twin lengths fell below her waist, back and front. Huge tortoiseshell earings peeped from the sleek, smooth fall of her freshly washed hair. Her make-up was discreet but effective, thanks to many long consultations with Gwenda Bright, the veteran make-up lady at the studio who had taught her how to emphasise the gift of distinguished bone structure, while disguising the gauntness which sometimes accompanied it.

Most of the small tables were occupied by couples and foursomes and several people nodded or waved as Bruno, the maitre d', made his way towards her. She registered several members of the rent-a-crowd set who, on the odd night of the week they were forced actually to pay for their own meal, still chased the limelight even if they could only afford an entrée.

Milo van Allen, obese, unwashed and dressed in the inevitable shabby floral shift rose up and tried to embrace her, looking for all the world like an animated overstuffed chintz sofa. Sharon managed to hold the woman and the stench of body odour at bay simultaneously. It was said of Milo, a publicist, that you could ring her at any hour of the day or night and never run the risk of getting her out of the shower. It was also rumoured – understandably – that she was successful at her job only because executives agreed to whatever package she was pushing just to get her out of their office quickly.

Bruno interrupted with a slight bow that addressed only Sharon and effectively dismissed Milo. 'Miss Pettifer, it's good to see you again.'

Sharon smiled. 'I'm joining a friend. Mr Shaw. Is he here yet?'

'In the bar. If you'd like to go directly to your table, I'd be happy to tell him you're here.'

'No, I think I'll have a drink first. Give us twenty minutes will you, Bruno?'

'Certainly.' Bruno moved aside, allowing her to go through to the small, intimate bar.

Sharon paused at the entrance to allow her eyes to grow accustomed to the subdued lighting. She saw him immediately, sitting at the bar slightly in profile to her, his dark, almost black hair gleaming, the heavy moustache curling around the corner of his mouth. She walked over to him.

'Hello, Adam.'

Allan Steinbeck turned around, smiling.

'Sharon,' he said. 'You look sensational.'

20

Adele's visit to Madame Lupescu every Thursday afternoon was a ritual she had observed for years. She had tremendous faith in the Hungarian beautician's skills. There was also the lure of lotions and unguents made to secret formulae which the old lady was rumoured to have discovered long ago in the Caucasus region where the peasants lived to ages well over the century mark. The fact that by the time they reached this great age, their epidermal layers had the texture of crocodile skin was immaterial to Madame Lupescu's exclusive coterie of clients, probably because none of them had ever taken the trouble to find out. The stories of longevity combined with magical formulae were sufficient to conjure up hopeful dreams of everlasting youth among the Eastern Suburbs matrons who revered Madame Lupescu almost as much as they did their plastic surgeons.

Adele had never submitted to the surgeon's knife, and therefore gave full credit for the preservation of her looks to Madame Lupescu and those countless Thursday afternoons of pampering facials. Consequently, having missed one precious session the previous week because of Kenneth's condition, she had no intention of delaying her departure to keep this week's appointment even though – just as she was about to leave – the pool cover was delivered by two men ready to install it.

'Keep an eye on them, kiddo. See that they do a good job,' she told Kenneth, and was on her way.

The installation involved nothing more than the drilling of a dozen holes in the paving around the pool, into which would be slotted unobtrusive metal pins. To these would be secured loops of plastic rope from the pool cover to keep it moored in place.

Kenneth soon got bored with watching them.

The past few days had brought an acceleration in his recovery. With Adele's help and the resilience of youth, his body had mended itself. Even his voice was almost back to normal, although his throat

195

still hurt a little when he swallowed. His energy had returned and he was no longer content to sit around. When Adele had asked him to supervise this job, he had been busy with one of his own – carefully taking a rickety piano stool apart and scraping the joints clean of old glue ready for reassembly. He longed to get back to it and hoped the pool men wouldn't take all afternoon.

An agenda of Technical College courses had arrived in the mail that morning in response to a telephone call by Adele, and Kenneth wanted to have another look at the list when he'd finished working on the piano stool. There were some really interesting subjects under manual trades, but secretly Kenneth was attracted to the introductory computer courses. The trouble was he didn't think he was educated enough for them. Still, if he were quick enough to master video games, he reckoned he should be able to manage computers.

Lost in thought, his gaze had wandered from the pool and now a figure appearing round the side of the house caused him quickly to refocus.

He saw to his surprise it was Sharon Pettifer.

'Hi,' she yelled warmly. 'I just happened to be up this way and thought I'd drop in these get-well presents. How are you feeling?'

'I'm okay,' he replied. He felt oddly uncomfortable at the sight of her. His first thought was of Adele. She'd blow her stack if she knew the TV reporter was visiting behind her back.

'Your voice sounds much better.' Sharon was pulling several compact discs from a plastic bag with the name of a leading record store on it. 'I have no idea of your taste in music, so I got a mixture. There's some heavy metal stuff, Guns and Roses, Poison, Bon Jovi, Madonna . . . you should find *something* you like.' She surmised, correctly as it happened, that any record collection of Adele's wouldn't go past Glenn Miller and Sinatra and that Kenneth would be thirsting for the sounds of his own generation.

'You needn't have bothered,' said Kenneth.

Sharon shrugged, squatting down on the grass. He noticed her dress was crisp and cottony. The long, full skirt had lots of pleats. It looked expensive, but she didn't seem to mind lolling around in it.

'You alone?' she asked.

'Except for them,' replied Kenneth, indicating the workmen.

He wasn't telling Sharon anything she didn't know.

It wasn't by chance her visit coincided with Adele's absence. Margaret Fong's meticulous research had turned up many interest-

196

ing facts about Mrs Adele Ventura Hatherley, even trivial details like her regular patronage of the legendary Madame Lupescu. All Sharon had to do was telephone the beautician, pretending to check on Adele's behalf the date and time of her next appointment.

The old woman had been puzzled, to say the least. Surely Mrs Hatherley had not forgotten her regular Thursday afternoon appointment? Sharon had murmured something about a misunderstanding, and rang off. It was all she needed to know.

Kenneth was looking intently at the CDs. He didn't know what to say and it gave him something to do. Maybe she'd go in a minute.

But Sharon showed no signs of leaving. She brought her knees up and wrapped her arms around them, turning her face up to the sun.

'Does Mrs Hatherley ever hear from her husband?'

The question was unexpected and it caught him off-guard. 'Not that I know of,' he replied, trying to sound unconcerned. 'What's it to you?'

'Oh, I just wondered.' Her tone was casual. 'I gather it really rocked the social scene when they turned up in Sydney together several years ago. You know what a gold digger is? Someone who's after someone else's money. That's what they called her.'

Despite himself, Kenneth was curious. 'Where'd you hear that crap?'

'Oh, I did some checking on her. Amazing what you find in old newspaper files. And there are always people ready to gossip about old times. All sorts of little stories come out.'

'Yeh, I can imagine.' His tone was disparaging. 'Why'd you bother?'

Sharon shrugged, her face still tilted to the sun, her eyes closed. 'Just interested. I'd never heard of her until I brought around your cheque last week. I wondered what sort of woman you'd got yourself mixed up with.'

That did it. Kenneth's temper flared.

'I'm not *mixed up* with her! She's my friend. And anyway, you've got it all wrong. You've been fed a whole heap of shit!'

Sharon's head inclined towards him, her eyes opening but not quite fully. 'Oh?'

'Yeh. They met in Tahiti or somewhere. But he was the one that was broke.'

'Then how could he afford to pay off the mortgages on this place? According to reliable sources, he went overseas to arrange foreign investment and having done that, he—'

'Adele was the only foreign investment he rustled up. She had the money. Plenty enough for two, so she told me. And she bought this place back for him!'

He realised he was shouting at her and the workmen were looking around. He swallowed with difficulty. His throat was hurting again.

'It's not the story that circulated at the time.' Sharon's voice was low, her tone reasonable. 'And besides, if *she* held the purse strings, why would he leave? Why would he walk away from the kind of life he was used to but couldn't afford? It doesn't make sense. And another thing, where would *she* get that kind of money?'

Kenneth was desperate to vindicate Adele and get rid of this bitch.

'Didn't you find out about *that*, too?' he sneered. 'How she got rich?'

'No,' said Sharon, sounding intrigued.

So Kenneth told her. Everything.

21

Adele arrived home suffering an anxiety attack. She had the feeling that unsteady ground was threatening to send her giddily off-balance. It was a sensation she had experienced once or twice before in California when imperceptible earth tremors had preceded major seismic disturbances.

She garaged the car and went into the house. Kenneth was nowhere to be seen. From the morning room, she saw that the pool cover was in place and the workmen had gone.

She began to tear the wrapping off a pot of night cream Madame Lupescu had recommended for the stubborn frown lines between her eyebrows.

'Kenneth?'

There was no reply. He was probably in his room.

The feeling that something was wrong wouldn't go away.

Madame Lupescu had been impossible, that was it. The woman had babbled on in her incomprehensible accent about needlessly checking appointments, and Adele had decided that the old lady was hopelessly confused and blaming her for somebody else's actions. The touch of her fingertips on Adele's face and neck was less feathery than usual as she became more and more emphatic in her admonitions about time-wasting telephone calls. Not exactly the soothing treatment Adele was used to. The woman was getting more and more irascible in her old age. Perhaps she was going senile. Oh God, not Alzheimer's! If she retreated into some kind of twilight world, all her beauty secrets would go with her, and *then* where would they all be?

In the kitchen, Adele was surprised to see the pieces of piano stool still lying on sheets of newspaper much the same as they'd been when she went out. Even if Kenneth had been unable to finish the job, it was unlike him not to clear away. She had found him to be a tidy boy, particularly with things he cared about.

Putting the pot of cream on the table, she screwed up the

wrapping paper and went to throw it in the kitchen tidy. She stared. On top of the rubbish already in there were several highly coloured . . . tiles? She reached in and pulled them out and saw them not to be tiles but compact discs in their covers.

She looked at the titles and frowned. Not her property, definitely not from her collection, in fact she had never seen them before nor would want to again, judging from the titles and the artists.

Still holding them, she hurried through the house and upstairs.

'Kenneth? Where are you, for Chrissakes?'

She rapped her knuckles on the door of his bedroom and went straight in. Kenneth was lying on his bed, fully clothed, his hands clasped behind his head.

'Why didn't you answer?' she demanded, then brandished the records. 'Do these belong to you? Where did they come from?'

Kenneth looked at her sideways, then back to the ceiling. 'You're as big a sticky-beak as *she* is!'

'She? Who's *she*?'

'Sharon Pettifer. She brought 'em.'

'You mean she was here again? At the house?'

The sheer force with which Adele spat out the questions made Kenneth turn and look at her again. He saw rage sparking in her eyes.

'Don't go on about it,' he pleaded. 'I got rid of her, didn't I?'

Adele didn't seem to hear him. 'That pushy bitch. And after I'd told her—'

'Told her what?'

'Nothing.' Now, Adele's anger had simmered down to hostility which seemed directed at Kenneth, as if he were to blame for Sharon's visit. 'What did she want?'

'Just to give me them. Get-well presents, she called 'em. Well, she gave 'em to me and then I got rid of her – for good!'

That seemed to mollify Adele. She tossed the compact discs on the bed.

'Here. It seems a waste, just to dump them. You may play them if you wish.'

She wanted the satisfaction of having him reject them again, but was doomed to disappointment.

'Yeh, reckon you're right,' he agreed. 'I'll play 'em later.'

200

22

Kenneth showered and changed his clothes, taking his time about it. He wanted to give Adele plenty of opportunity to simmer down before he went downstairs.

All ready to go, he decided it was still too early to show himself. Better to wait until she'd had a couple of pre-dinner drinks. No matter what her mood previously, the early evening cocktails always seemed to have a good effect, at least to begin with.

Desultorily, he glanced again at the covers of the CDs, then switched on the TV set which had been installed in his bedroom while he was recuperating. He flicked from channel to channel but got nothing but cartoons and ancient sitcoms. He switched it off then wandered around, ending up at the window.

To his surprise, he saw a woman striding purposefully up the drive. Outside the gates, he could just make out a parked car with someone in the driver's seat. First Sharon, now this woman. *Two* visitors to 'Horizons' in one day wasn't just unusual in his experience, it was a major event.

The woman appeared to be in her sixties. She was unattractively scrawny and her grey hair was combed in a smooth pageboy style which was too youthful and quite at odds with her hawk-like features. She was wearing a cream linen suit, flat-heeled shoes, wore gloves and carried a handbag. She mounted the terrace, then passed from Kenneth's sight as she approached the front door.

Quickly, he moved across the room and went out of the door. Just as he reached the top of the stairs he heard Adele's heels clacking across the foyer and peeped around the corner as she pulled open the front door, glass in hand.

'Why, Edith. What a surprise. What are you doing here?'

She stepped back to admit the woman. From the tone of her voice, Kenneth could tell that Adele was still not in the best of tempers. There was no welcoming inflection in her voice, no warmth.

201

The woman came in, arms tight at her sides, gloved hands grasping the handbag tensely.

'I've been to rather a long luncheon at Eliza's. Friends are giving me a lift home. I asked them to drop me off for a moment. They're waiting.'

Adele's hand dropped from the doorknob immediately, leaving the door wide open. It was if she expected – hoped? – that Edith would dart out again any second. Instead, the woman took several steps towards the centre of the foyer, looking up and around. Kenneth drew back out of sight and heard her say: 'It's amazing how all the memories flood back. I still can't imagine how you can live in this enormous house, all alone. It was meant for families.'

'Big as it is, it would still be too small for the two of us, Edith, so if this visit is intended as some kind of conciliatory approach to—'

'Oh no!'

The woman's determined rejection of Adele's implication rang out loud and clear. It also indicated that she had turned in another direction. Kenneth risked a peep around the corner. Adele was taking a swig from the glass she held. The woman now had her back turned to the staircase. He saw that the back of her jacket was a mass of creases. She'd been right. It must have been a very long luncheon.

'Don't tell me the monthly cheque hasn't arrived?' Adele sounded more bad tempered than ever. 'I warned the bank that if it ever happened again I'd—'

'My being here has nothing to do with the cheque. It arrived on time. It's just that . . .' The woman broke off, wringing her gloved hands, taking a step to the side and back again. 'You're so abrupt with me on the telephone, Adele. It's so difficult to talk with you.'

There was another pause, during which Adele emptied her glass, standing there, waiting, making no attempt to put the woman at ease. Edith began again.

'I just called in on an impulse. It's been weeks since we spoke.' Her voice became tremulous. 'Have you heard from Lambert?'

'If I had, I would have called you. You know that.'

'It's just that . . . it's been so long. Almost two years.'

'You're telling me?' Adele asked belligerently. 'Don't you think I'm not reminded of it every single day?'

'It's not like him to be out of touch all this time. He used to take off by himself before, but he'd always send a postcard, he'd always come back. And I do miss him.'

The woman's pleading petulance was in keeping with her silly pageboy hairdo. Adele snorted.

'You fought like alley cats, the two of you, so don't give me that – not unless you miss the bites and the scratches,' she replied. 'You have to face facts like I do. Your brother was worthless. Wherever he is, I hope it takes a week's rowing up crocodile-infested rivers to get there. *Who*ever he's with, I hope she's dumb enough to indulge him till Hell freezes over. Face it, Edith, we're both better off without him.'

The woman's voice rang out. 'Then why do you think of him every single day?'

'I'm counting them,' Adele replied, 'until I can divorce him for desertion or have him declared legally dead.'

The woman abruptly twisted her head around in anguish, away from Adele, and Kenneth drew back again for fear being seen. He heard her mumble something about not keeping her friends waiting, the clatter of footsteps, and then the front door slammed. Adele's heels clacked over to the drawing room.

Kenneth decided to go back to his bedroom for a while longer.

23

Sharon faxed requests for information on a fifties singer named Adele Ventura to the network's affiliated newsgathering bureaux in New York and Los Angeles, suggesting cross-indexation with the popular music industry and the life of motion picture star Kelly Green.

Then she settled down over some paperwork at her desk, but try as she may she could not concentrate. Always, her mind reverted to the incredible stories the woman had been feeding Kenneth. Or was the reality the fact that *she* was feeding off *him*, nourishing her vanity on a diet of self-conceit based on high-flying Mafia connections and long-dead sex goddesses?

No wonder Kenneth had changed. His remoteness, the flashes of arrogance, the antagonism bred of defensiveness where his friendship with Adele was concerned, all of these capricious moods were obviously induced by a woman whose boasts were dominating his life.

Sharon was no psychologist, but she was willing to bet the woman's fantasies – and they *had* to be fantasies – would in time stunt Kenneth's development. Given the harshness of his immediate past, the opportunity to retreat to a gossamer world of glamorous lies would be tempting, particularly when the storyteller was such a mendacious mother-figure.

Some fresh air was necessary in that pretentious little set-up. Take the 'Gee!' out of glitter and it became litter. Kenneth had to be shown that. He had to realise he'd exchanged one sick environment for another. And one boy's journey through those sort of influences would make fascinating copy, no matter what Jim might think.

Sharon found she had been moving her ballpoint pen back and forth, back and forth in the same place, making a messy doodle consisting of one thick line which had now torn the surface of the page. She quickly scanned the typescript, found it unimportant, so consigned it to the wastepaper basket.

As she did, she saw Jim Abrahams chatting to one of the other reporters across the room. Immediately, she slumped over her desk, leaning on her elbows with one hand shielding her eyes to give the impression she was immersed in her work. She had no desire to talk to him and hoped her pose would dissuade him from coming over. She knew that if they spoke, she wouldn't be able to stop herself from blurting out the substance of what Kenneth had told her. Far better to wait until her enquiries were complete.

She relaxed. Jim wouldn't come over, anyway. He'd been keeping his distance since learning there was another man on the scene. She hadn't meant to be cruel. It was the only way to clear the air between them. Besides which, it had given her a great deal of satisfaction.

She smiled to herself. Adam had come along at exactly the right moment in her life. *And* in the most mundane of circumstances. Any other time, being confronted with a flat tyre would have meant a call to the NRMA followed by a boring half-hour wait until they arrived. But Adam just happened to be there. And had insisted on changing the tyre himself, which he accomplished expertly in a matter of minutes.

It was only when she offered him a cloth to wipe his hands that his eyes – such light, transparent eyes for one whose colouring was dark – his eyes had narrowed, and he questioned almost to himself if they had met before.

Funnily enough, she was thinking the same thing.

Then, suddenly it had hit him. He laughed, slapping his forehead, but from then on his was not the hackneyed coin-in-the-slot recognition she was used to. Instead, he complimented her earnestly on just one of her coverages, the recent survey of the Australian travel industry. It had interested him particularly because, as a travel agent in Adelaide who specialised in tours to North Queensland and the Outback, his business had been hit so hard by the pilots' dispute and the resultant slump in domestic flights that he'd eventually been forced to call it quits. He'd come to Sydney to make a fresh start. He told her he'd had enough of the travel business, but fortunately – being a widower and alone, with enough of a private income to keep him going – he could afford to take his time before deciding what to do with the rest of his life.

All this came as she stood there, car keys in her hand, ready to get into the car and drive away after thanking him for his kindness.

And yet she lingered.

The dark brown hair and the Zapata moustache made a fascinating contrast to his fair skin and translucently pale eyes. Distinctive rather than good-looking. Different. And there was a restlessness about him, a velocity of manner which was compelling. She felt pinned against the car by the sheer force of his conversation, but it was not unpleasant.

She found herself offering a reward.

'You must let me buy you a drink some time,' she said.

He appeared disinclined to accept. 'I just did you a good turn.' He started to back away, shaking his head and smiling. 'It's enough that you can drive away on four good tyres.'

That made him even more attractive. She'd been bored witless by men who fawned on her, not just Jim Abrahams but the studio types, the so-called on-camera spunks who had about as much depth as magazine covers; the businessmen whose wives didn't understand them (yes, they were *still* pushing a ploy she'd first encountered in novels she'd read at school!); the young career achievers who saw her as nothing more than a desirable accessory to their Armani wardrobe.

This one didn't fall into any of those categories. Not yet, anyway. He wasn't exactly Mel Gibson or Tom Cruise either, but what girl would want an actor, anyway? Some guy who wore make-up ten hours a day and played dress-ups *had* to have problems. She rummaged in her bag and found one of her cards. She held it out.

'Think about it.'

He had taken the card and she had driven away. Busy on her next assignment which took her on a depressing round of Sydney's polluted beaches, the encounter had receded to the status of a pleasant memory.

Then he called.

She invented a dinner date so that she could give him an hour over cocktails at Raphael's. If he bored her, she had the escape hatch of going on somewhere else. If he didn't, she could agree to another meeting.

Raphael's was one of those places which seemed peculiar to Sydney, and yet was probably a phenomenon that occurred in all big cities where frenetic night stalkers desperately sought new habitats, patronised them for a while, then moved on somewhere else leaving the original venue bereft. The only answer was for the venue continually to change, even if the change was only from bankrupt former owners to eager new ones.

No, that was not quite correct. There were always other changes.

206

There had to be. The name. A change of theme. Bare-breasted waitresses one week, yashmak'd houris the next. Sometimes a room for illegal gambling, sometimes an alcove for coke sniffers and pill poppers, sometimes just an old-fashioned pick-up bar for singles.

Sharon pondered on the subject as she sat at the bar, sipping a glass of white wine. Adam Shaw was late and she was not amused.

She glanced around. The first time she had come here was four years before when it had been The Elephant Room. She'd been a starry-eyed newcomer and it had all seemed wonderful. Now she looked at it and the stars had gone from her eyes, no longer getting in the way of tacky decor which had been resprayed, refurbished and recycled half a dozen times since and still looked tacky. It just went to prove that money, whether it came from drug syndicates, illegal gambling or the bulging wallets of government-favoured speculators, still couldn't make a silk hearse out of a sow's bier.

Still no Adam Shaw. She resisted the urge to leave and went through the names. The Elephant Room. Accelerator's. Benji's Bar.

Next? It had to be . . . yes, The Dunny. That lasted all of two weeks. The Dad and Dave image didn't go down too well with the yuppies who were all trying to be Gordon Gekkoes in *Wall Street* at the time. How could they reconcile 'Greed is Good' with free Damper nibbles, waitresses in cork-fringed Akubras, and Slim Dusty muzak? It had to go.

And now, after metamorphosing via yet another reopening of empty razzmatazz, it was Raphael's, all pseudo Italian with badly-done freizes of St Mark's Square, a few menacing colonnades and bunches of plastic grapes cascading limply around the bar.

'I'm sorry I'm late. I had to look all over to find it, but it *had* to be this one.'

She turned and he was standing there holding out a single flower. It was a long and slender pale yellow orchid of the utmost delicacy.

'It's a native of Fiji, and you can only get them at this time of year,' Adam continued. He looked from her to the orchid and back again, smiling. 'If you were a flower, you'd be this one.'

Incredibly, Sharon felt herself grow moist. She wasn't used to this kind of treatment and it was kindling all kinds of warm and pleasurable reactions. His gesture of bringing the flower could have been mawkish. It was tender and romantic. His reference to its resemblance to her could have appeared just so much crap. It was touching. And yet despite the gentleness of his approach, she knew instinctively that he was far stronger than she. And it was the certainty of that hidden strength which excited her.

As she ordered him a drink and made small talk about the orchid, her mind went back to something once said to her by Darlene French, the successful, chic and assured editor of the popular women's magazine *Addenda*.

'This is in the strictest confidence, and if you ever quote me I'll deny it,' Darlene had said, 'but what I really crave is a man with the guts to tell me to sit down and shut up! And there are many women who feel exactly as I do.'

At the time, Sharon thought it obscene, a capitulation to the worst kind of sexism. But now she understood what Darlene meant. She had no doubt that Adam Shaw was perfectly capable of ordering her to sit down and shut up, and a hell of a lot more too. And for him, she'd do it. All of it.

That evening, she'd had to leave him on the pretext of the fictitious dinner engagement, but not before she had arranged to meet him for a meal the following night. And after that they had made a third date for dinner at Bellini's Brasserie.

Sharon sat at her desk, head down over words she could not see, reliving the encounters with Adam all over again. There was an intense urgency about the man that aroused her, an urgency that seemed unstoppable. It conjured up interesting speculation about his prowess as a lover. And that was something she had resolved to check out very soon.

24

Hardly a word was exchanged between Kenneth and Adele during dinner. She ate sparsely and drank a lot of wine. Kenneth concentrated on his food to avoid looking at her. Afterwards, he sprawled by the sound system in the drawing room and played the compact discs with, he assumed, Adele's consent if not her approval.

He was so swamped by the grating, crashing beat of Heavy Metal that he failed to notice her displeasure. She would sweep into the room, always with a glass in her hand, her face pained at the deafening noise, move around as if willing him to notice her, then sweep out when he didn't.

It was only in a peaceful interval between records that she came in again and he realised she was drinking heavily and still outraged at Sharon's visit.

'Don't you just hate people like her with those flared nostrils?' she asked of nobody in particular. 'All that exposed skin in each hole? She must spend all her spare time tweezing out the hairs!'

Kenneth just continued to select the next disc.

'And the nerve of that bimbo, with her poking and prying. What does she think we do in here, you and I – full contact Lambada?'

He looked up at her innocently. 'Who are you talking about? Sharon or the other woman?'

'That bitch from television,' came the reply. Then Adele cocked an eyebrow and regarded him, sucking in her cheeks. 'You don't miss much. I thought you were in your room when Edith called.'

'Neither of you was whispering.'

'Well, just for the record, she's Lambert's sister, the only other remnant of the Hatherley clan.'

'And you look after her with a cheque every month. That's nice of you.'

'My, you *do* have big ears, don't you? She's no great chum of mine but I feel a certain responsibility towards her, yes. I don't know why.'

Adele seemed anxious to get off the subject. 'But talking of chums, I've invited a bunch over for dinner, Friday night. You'll like 'em, I think. They're the only people I can stand in this town – and needless to say, Holly Zimmerman is *not* invited! You won't have to do anything. I'm keeping Rina and Jorge back.'

Kenneth nodded and started the music again. Adele pulled a face and left.

He didn't know she was back until some time later, when her wrath was now directed at the music.

'Am I really hearing this?' she yelled in his ear. ' "Too Drunk to Fuck"? What kind of "romantic ballad" is that? Huh?'

Kenneth just shrugged, hoping she'd go away. But now, he noticed, she was carrying the decanter as well as her glass. Swaying, she splashed more liquor from one to the other. Then she went over and snapped down the sound.

'Hey!' Kenneth protested.

She stood there, her face flushed, her eyes popping. 'Those aren't lyrics, they're stab wounds!' she yelled as if the music were still at full volume. 'And maybe it's the lacerations that're causing those yelps of pain that pass for singing!' Her head wobbled up proudly. 'In my day, we had voices, not video clips!'

Kenneth went on the attack.

'Yeh. In your day! That's why you can't handle this stuff. You come from a different generation. Kids like their own music, not something the oldies grooved on. It must have been the same with you. Just because your folks liked the – the minuet, I bet you didn't, did you?'

'The minuet?!' Adele bellowed. It broke through her rancour. She was roaring drunk and her laughter was loud and uninhibited. 'Jesus Christ, how old do you think I am?'

Her laughter went on and on, but Kenneth wasn't impressed. He'd meant it seriously. Finally, she flopped into one of the armchairs.

'God, you fracture me, kiddo. You are fun-nee. Which brings us back to the subject. Have you ever seen anybody actually *smile* in a video clip? I don't mean sneer, or grimace, or grin as they slice someone's foot off, but really and truly smile from happiness. Come on – tell me!'

Kenneth thought. 'Yeh!' he said triumphantly. 'BeeBee Tenterfield smiles all the time.' BeeBee Tenterfield was the current Queen of the Bubblegum Set.

Adele drew herself up imperiously.

'Smile is all she *can* do without suffering a talent haemorrhage. She certainly can't sing. She couldn't hit a note with a machine gun. And as for the so-called dancing . . . fortunately, she's limber enough to skip. So she skips – and gets a standing ovation. Anyone would think she was walking on fucking water!'

Adele took a drink. Kenneth fell back on the carpet.

'Have you finished?' he asked wearily.

'Once upon a time,' Adele mused as if she hadn't heard him, 'the magic was Fred Astaire dancing on the ceiling. Now, there's no magic – just a con job to convince us that some tarted-up jock or jocked-up tart is an entertainer. Fine for the twelve-year-olds. What would *they* know, anyway, except how to shoot up or put a condom on a banana?'

Kenneth was getting really angry. He could understand Adele's dislike of Sharon. He couldn't hack her either, with her pushiness and her sly insinuations. But he'd had enough of all this criticism of his kind of music and its people. He propped himself up on his elbows and stuck his head out belligerently.

'If you're such an expert, why don't you do something about it, instead of just raving on?'

She blinked and glared back at him.

'What do you mean?'

'You're supposed to be a singer, aren't you?' he flung at her.

'Ask me later, the jury's still out!' she yelled back.

'Don't try to wriggle out of it. Show 'em how it's done, if you're so crash hot. Sing up or shut up!'

It was as though he was looking at her through ripple glass, because she actually undulated as an idea squirmed snake-like from her head, down through her body. She squinted at him, suddenly more shrewd than drunk.

'You know, kiddo,' she said, 'I think you just might have something there.'

211

25

Sharon felt as if she were clinging to the underside of an out-of-control truck which was careering downhill on a deeply rutted track towards an ammunition dump.

She could do nothing. She had been powerless from the moment Adam had slid into bed from out of the dark and overwhelmed her with brutal physicality. Immediately, his mouth was roaming over her body, and the urgency she had detected in his manner was affirmed in the restless pressure of his lips. She felt them pursed and hungry at her breasts but as soon as the nipples stiffened his lips moved on, questing down the concave curve of her stomach and down further, probing relentlessly until she wanted to scream 'Go on . . . go on!'

He had her arms pinioned. She played no part in this fast-forward foreplay, other than to respond automatically with her body. Now his tongue was exploring inside her and she began to writhe as much as she was able, confined as she was by the strength of his grip. She began to moan, to squeal.

This was outrageous. Impossible. Before, from Jim, from others, she'd had tenderness, a gradual leading hand-in-hand to a plateau of mutual satisfaction. It had been leisurely, comfortable, reassuring. Not like this.

She began to struggle against him, to protest, but his mouth sped upwards and closed over hers, cutting off her cries. She tasted her own juices on his tongue, but hardly had time to register this before he entered her with the hard precision of a steel-shafted deadlock.

And now the tantalising, maddening friction drove everything else from her mind. She squeezed her eyes shut. She held on to him. He was a truck. She was hanging on. The track was rutted and she was bouncing crazily. She knew they were heading for that damned ammunition dump. It was inevitable. She dreaded it and yet there was this awful craving, but there was nothing she could do except hang on as they went crazily downhill. Down . . . down . . .

The explosion shook her like nothing else had done in her life. The paradisiacal shudders she experienced seemed to be sending bits of her careering around the room. Finally, as they died down, she found the breath to giggle weakly. She thought dizzily that had she been connected to the Richter Scale, she would have registered more than a disturbance from the San Andreas Fault.

'You're laughing,' he said. 'Wasn't it good for you?'

'Totally fantastic,' she breathed.

Good, Allan thought. He needed Sharon as an emotional captive, because through her he would find the boy.

PART IV

'Finish, good lady; the bright day is done,
And we are for the dark.'

WILLIAM SHAKESPEARE,
Antony and Cleopatra

1

He relished standing in front of the full length cheval mirror because it was Adam Shaw who looked back at him and only he knew it was really Allan Steinbeck inside.

He had taken immense care in perfecting his disguise. He had even dyed the hairs on his arms, on his chest and around his pubic zone because right from the start he knew without doubt that he and Sharon would be spending a considerable time naked. He hadn't bothered about the hair on his legs. If she had time to notice those he deserved to fail because he wouldn't be doing his job properly. But there was no way he would fail. That was an integral part of the plan, to conquer her physically and like everything else he had achieved it faultlessly.

He smiled, noticing how the dark moustache made his teeth appear whiter. How she had squealed and squirmed in ecstasy the previous night, not knowing that the force of his passion was powered by an impatient will to succeed rather than any amorous attraction.

Motives apart, his sex drive was always in top gear. Ever since puberty, his appetite had been keen and his performance efficient as several of his schoolmates could have testified, had they not been too ashamed to speak out. At university, his prowess was renowned and it was said of him that if it moved he'd screw it.

Joan had kept him satisfied until the baby came along. It was her withdrawal which had forced him to look elsewhere. It was all her fault. That was why he had no recriminations about consigning her to his past. Her *and* the baby. They were both encumbrances he could well do without from now on.

She had telephoned several times, ostensibly to tell him of her mother's condition, but in reality attempting to achieve a reconciliation, something he had no desire to pursue. For him, the only joy in her calls was derived from the mournful bulletins about the continued suffering of the still-hospitalised Doris Lytton-Scott.

217

What a masterstroke that had been. The police were still hunting for The Slasher, who seemed to have put his activities on hold – probably from the shock of being credited with an attack far more violent and horrifying than any he had actually perpetrated.

Allan selected a tie and went back to the mirror.

Joan.

How easy it had been to keep her away. For her to see him now would be out of the question. There'd always been the chance, of course, that she would come back to the house unexpectedly but he had made her promise not to do that. An enforced separation would be good for them both at this difficult time, he had told her, and would most certainly benefit them when they made a new start. When, not if.

His confidence in their future made her eager to cooperate. She appeared to have forgiven, even forgotten the reason for their estrangement but Allan told himself it wasn't for love of him. He was merely the father of her child, and it was for the baby's benefit only that she wanted the restoration of their family unit. The pathetic fool.

His contempt for Joan made him tie the knot too tightly. He pulled the knot apart and started again. He was as meticulous about his appearance as he was in formulating his plans. Once he had achieved what he had set out to do, Allan Steinbeck *and* Adam Shaw would disappear forever. There would be a third incarnation of his being, but preferably one which did not involve the nuisance of a dye. This third incarnation would soar free because the slate would be wiped clean. His enemies would be gone, consigned to variations of the kind of Hell now inhabited by his mother-in law, with the slut Donna as her hideous handmaiden. He would suffer no anguish. He would entertain no doubts. He would have no regrets.

Satisfied with his second attempt, he settled the knot snugly between the peaks of his collar.

He smoothed the palm of one hand along the side of his head. Pity the dye was such a bother. He rather liked himself with dark hair. He enjoyed seeing a stranger in the mirror, particularly such a dangerously intriguing stranger. He stepped back, the better to see the man framed full-length.

And felt a ripple of excitement.

Sharon would be waiting. But she had waited for him before. Keeping her waiting was a manifestation of his superiority. The fact that she was still there when he arrived and swallowed the most transparent of excuses indicated her submissiveness. That was another thing he had learned. People accepted lies, and the more blatant and highly coloured, the more they were convinced they were hearing the truth. Snatch a flower from an arrangement in a hotel foyer then spin a yarn about searching for this one, unique, exotic bloom and it would be believed and not only believed but cherished.

So let Sharon wait. He'd think of some florid way of apologising for his tardiness. It would be another test of his skill, another opportunity to flex his power. Besides, being made to wait focussed her attention on him right from the word go. He wouldn't need a spotlight. Nobody who was late ever did.

In the meantime, Adam Shaw was giving him provocative glances from the mirror, Adam Shaw who appeared so unfamiliar yet was irrevocably joined to Allan Steinbeck by the same initials just as skin, flesh and blood coalesced Siamese twins.

Allan moved closer. His left hand reached out to touch Adam Shaw's cheek. In perfect unison, Adam Shaw's right hand did the same, and Allan leaned closer so that contact would be made.

Two identical pairs of eyes remained locked meaningfully. Then the eyes moved downwards. Slowly. And up again. And down again, dreamily taking in every exciting detail of the two bodies, one on each side of the glass.

And shortly, the free hands – Allan's right and Adam's left – were fumbling urgently down below.

2

Adele had been right. Kenneth took an immediate liking to her friends, after the initial discomfort of being introduced as the son of 'darling Reuben and Rita Mitchell of Melbourne' who'd asked her to look after him while they were overseas.

The dinner guests accepted him without question. Obviously they'd never heard of 'darling Reuben and Rita', and it was equally obvious that they didn't give a damn.

They were a well-heeled, freewheeling, colourful lot. Like Adele, they were outgoing, shared a raunchy sense of humour and had very definite opinions on everything, which they were not reluctant to make known. Suddenly, the house was filled with loud voices and laughter and Kenneth found they were so busy enjoying themselves all he had to do to fit in was sit there and keep quiet. It didn't matter. He couldn't compete and didn't want to. It was fascinating enough just to observe them.

The first to arrive was a skinny bird with stylishly androgynous looks and the enormous eyes of a night creature suddenly plunged into daylight. In a black leotard and a chunky knitted top, she was introduced as Quandra, one of Sydney's top dress designers but she was quick to point out she wouldn't be seen *dead* in the spangled creations demanded by her tasteless clientele. Her high-pitched giggle was infectious, and Kenneth found himself grinning even when he couldn't follow what she was talking about.

Then came Claude and Natalie Monserrat, full of earthy Gallic humour, who apparently were importers of French champagne. They had given a lift to a ravishingly buxom opera singer called Clio whom Kenneth had seen being outrageous on TV chat shows. She clutched a miniature dachshund to her bosom.

'Why don't you get that thing dipped in bronze and wear it on a charm bracelet?' Adele commented.

'Darling, he's no trouble. You know I always take him everywhere.'

'Yeah,' replied Adele warningly. 'But if he pees on the carpet like last time, you're *both* out!' Then she introduced Kenneth. Clio tossed a mass of raven curls and looked at him, eyes smouldering.

'Stick around, darling. I *may* have you for dessert!'

'You keep your cotton-pickin' hands off of him and stick to your lousy baritones,' Adele said with a violent nudge that almost had the tiny dog disappearing down the singer's cleavage. They lapsed into bellowing laughter.

Others were arriving. They included an amiable American couple from the US Consulate, two hunky footballers called Wayne and Matt who appeared to be on together, and a very fat, jolly man called Fred who owned a liquor store in Rose Bay and whose wife, Muriel, had once been a showgirl.

Jorge, in black pants and a white jacket looking exotic with his golden moonface, moved amongst the guests dispensing champagne cocktails. Rina, also in black, served trays of canapés.

In the kitchen, two caterers who had been busy since mid-afternoon were putting the finishing touches to dinner.

Adele, in a long silk paisley shirt over matching wide leg pants, sparkled like the jewels at her wrist and throat. Kenneth wondered why she didn't socialise more often. She seemed to be having the time of her life, and every now and then she would smile and wink at him just to let him know he wasn't forgotten.

A discussion on the comparative merits of opera houses around the world was dominated by Clio.

'Compared to La Scala, the Sydney Opera House is like an upmarket Pizza Hut,' she declaimed over a chorus of dissent. 'Lousy accoustics. No class. It stinks!'

Fred, the liquor store man, pulled a face. 'And not only the Opera House!'

Clio paused, sniffing. Then she looked down at the dog she had placed at her feet.

'Placido? Is that you?' She looked around and spread her arms helplessly. 'I apologise, darlings. To put it delicately, Placido's been tampering with the atmosphere. Adele – is there anywhere we can put him for a while? Some place warm and cosy?'

'How about the microwave?' Adele replied, and everybody laughed.

At that moment, Jorge showed in a young man with a cloud of black, wispy hair wearing a black velvet suit, a black and white polka dot shirt and a silver tie. He was very tall, pale and thin and

221

with his large thick-lensed glasses he resembled nothing more nor less than a giant stick insect.

Adele immediately swept to his side and linked her arm possessively with his.

'Sweetie. I was beginning to think you weren't going to make it.' Standing on tiptoe, she kissed him on the cheek, then turned. 'Everybody – this is Carl O'Callaghan.'

Kenneth felt a twinge of jealousy which was exacerbated when they moved in to dinner and with a great deal of ceremony Adele assigned him to sit 'as the man of the house' at the foot of the table, the furthest distance from her, while placing Carl on her immediate right.

Kenneth knew Adele was trying to make him feel important, but he would have much rather been close to her. Fortunately, he had Quandra on his left and Fred on his right, so he didn't have to worry about awkward silences. Not only did they keep the conversation going, but they actually tried to include him in it. He didn't expect that kind of consideration from a trendy kook and a jolly redneck, but they kept looking at him while they were talking and waited for him to smile or nod or – in the case of Fred's dirty jokes – laugh, and actually asked for his opinion a couple of times. He appreciated their efforts.

Sydney Rock oysters on the shell were the first course. Kenneth stared at them. It was obvious to his neighbours that he hadn't tried oysters before.

'Eat 'em up, Kenneth,' Quandra urged. 'They'll do wonders for your love life. They're an aphrodisiac.'

'Yair,' Fred cut in, 'if you don't swallow 'em quick, your neck goes stiff!'

Quandra giggled. Kenneth's hand went up to his throat. His preoccupation with the lingering soreness there made him miss the point of Fred's joke.

'It's been stiff for days, and still throbs a bit,' he said.

Fred and Quandra thought that terribly funny. Quandra shrieked and Fred roared. Kenneth wasn't quite sure why, but knew that inadvertently he must have said something amusing. He grinned as if he knew what it was all about and glanced up the table to check if Adele had noticed how well he was keeping her guests amused. But what he saw was enough to wipe the grin off his face. Her head was inclined to Carl O'Callaghan, and they were deep in whispered confidences.

They continued to devote themselves to each other for the remainder of the meal. Kenneth's irritation increased and then he got mad at himself for even caring. What did it matter, anyway? She'd never even mentioned the guy before, so he couldn't be *that* important to her. Kenneth must have been scowling, because Quandra remarked on it. Before he could make an excuse, Rina was between them pouring coffee and then Jorge brought liqueurs.

Adele tapped her glass with a spoon and everybody stopped talking.

'Listen, everybody. I have an announcement.' She paused, and then with great significance she went on: 'I have decided to make a comeback!'

There was an uneasy silence. Then Clio spoke up.

'From where?' she drawled and everybody laughed, but uncomfortably so.

Adele looked at her and there was a warning glint in her eye.

'What I mean is, I intend resuming my career.'

'As a singer?' Muriel, the ex-showgirl, asked. 'Heavens, love, I thought you'd given all that away years ago.'

Adele smiled. 'If you don't change your mind once in a while, you'll end up losing it.' She took a sip of her brandy. 'Oh, I don't mean a gig at the Entertainment Centre, or a concert tour of Europe. Just a record.' She tossed it off casually.

'A record?' chorused at least three of the guests.

She patted the stick insect's hand. 'And Carl, here, is going to be my producer.'

Suddenly, it all clicked in Kenneth's mind. For the past few days, Adele had been in a state of high excitement. She had spent hours on the telephone in the study and had made several trips into town. Kenneth thought it all had to do with arrangements for the dinner party, the invitations, hiring of caterers, ordering food, and whatever else was entailed. She hadn't said anything to him and he hadn't asked. Now he knew better.

Adele was still explaining.

'. . . but naturally, I didn't even attempt an approach to one of the big record companies. We all know what *they* want. A product they can merchandise and market, preferably under eighteen with the mental capabilities of a retarded racoon and a tight ass. A fashion statement, with the tear in the left knee of the jeans, not the right, the left – that's real meaningful, you see. Talent is the *least* consideration.'

223

She waved her empty brandy balloon at Jorge, and while he was pouring her a refill she gave Carl's hand another pat and its owner a warm smile.

'Fortunately, I found Carl, and already he's taught me so much. The business has changed a lot since my day. The producer is also the entrepreneur. He brings together the performer, the record company and the distributor and ties up the deal. It's his concept. He does the arrangements and all the hiring and firing. Clever boy, huh?'

There was more. A lot more.

Kenneth tried to switch off. Adele, stimulated by alcohol and with a captive audience for her revelations, continued on about how wonderful her association with Carl was and how successful she hoped the outcome would be.

People were beginning to get restless. Cups and glasses were drained then fiddled with. Cigarettes were lit and extinguished just for something to do.

It was Carl himself who brought Adele's exposition of the record industry to a close simply by leaning towards her and quietly asking for directions to the bathroom. Immediately, the other guests began to talk amongst themselves, rising from the table and moving around. Then someone suggested charades, and Adele became occupied with distributing pencils and paper.

Kenneth didn't want any more involvement. He felt sick. He'd goaded Adele. 'Show 'em how it's done,' he'd jeered. And now she was going to make a fool of herself, just because of him. Who'd buy a record with her on it? Not kids – and they bought most of the records these days. Oldies? Even *they* wouldn't know who she was, either.

Like Carl, he too felt the urge to go to the bathroom. He avoided the one under the staircase because that was the one for guests. Instead, he made for the other ground floor bathroom along by the study.

He walked in and found Carl on his knees, sniffing a line of coke from the closed lid of the lavatory seat.

'Oh . . . sorry. I didn't know . . .'

Carl didn't even look up. Kenneth backed out and hurried back to the foyer. Clio was just about to go into the bathroom under the staircase. When she saw Kenneth, she changed her mind and came towards him. She clasped him by the shoulders and fixed him with a worried stare.

'You've got to dissuade her from this madness, darling,' she said intensely in a low voice. 'She's obviously very fond of you, maybe she'll listen to you. She certainly wouldn't take notice of any of us.' Her grip on his shoulders remained tight. She seemed genuinely distressed. 'It's always the same. She makes these . . . misjudgements from time to time and it usually ends up in disaster, because she won't *listen*. The last was having that dreadful Zimmerman creature living here. I mean, anyone could see they were chalk and cheese.'

Kenneth was overwhelmed by the closeness of the woman. Her heavy perfume hung like a fog around them. Her breasts, the largest he'd ever seen, were almost out of the top of her dress. Her face, close up, was vivid in its overripe colouring. All this, coupled with the intensity of her manner and the knowledge that he was the cause of this anguish, became too much for him. Or maybe it was just the oysters. Either way, the nausea he had experienced at the dinner table was coming back.

Fortunately, Clio released him and straightened up. She smiled. 'I'd better get into the bathroom, otherwise I'll do it on the carpet and have to blame it on Placido like last time.' The smile faded. 'Remember what I said, darling. Try, won't you? None of us want her hurt.' And then she was gone.

Later, after the other guests had left, Adele took Carl O'Callaghan along to the music room 'to discuss a concept for the album and the choice of my material,' as she explained to Kenneth.

In the kitchen, the caterers and Jorge and Rina were clearing up.

Kenneth waited until they'd gone then took a can of beer from the refrigerator. He pulled the ring tab and let the icy liquid soothe his throat. Then he made his way back to the drawing room and opened a couple of the windows to clear the air of cigarette smoke. He went to turn on the burglar alarm but remembered Carl O'Callaghan was still in the house.

As if on cue, raised voices came from the music room. It sounded like they were having a real bust-up, which indicated that maybe Carl wouldn't be staying all that long. At least it signalled an end to all that lovey-dovey stuff, but unfortunately he had a feeling it would take a lot more than a disagreement with her producer to dissuade Adele from going ahead with her feather-brained scheme.

3

'I've always been rather singleminded,' Sharon said reflectively. 'I suppose I get it from my hard-working parents. They had a delicatessen at Coogee near the beach and kept it open seven days a week.' Then her mood turned grim as she thought of them, so busy they hadn't noticed their only son was slowly killing himself. And she hadn't been there to notice it, either.

They were lying in darkness on the bed, the sheets thrown off to cool and dry their damp bodies. It had taken Sharon a full fifteen minutes to recover from their love-making. As her breathing returned to normal, Allan had asked her to tell him more about herself.

Up on one elbow, he was lightly touching each of her nipples in turn, caressing them with a circular motion. Idly, he vizualised pinching one of them between his thumb and forefinger, exerting tremendous pressure to squeeze the information he wanted from her like toothpaste from a tube. And there would be an end to this tedium. But with this lady, that kind of treatment wouldn't work. It had to be done with subtle coaxing.

'I loved school, but I didn't fancy being an academic,' Sharon continued, dragging her thoughts away from Terry. 'I desperately wanted to be a ballet dancer but it was obvious I was going to be too tall, even as a child. So then I switched my ambition to being an opera singer.' She laughed to herself. 'I guess I wanted to be in the spotlight one way or another. Well, that didn't work out either because I didn't have the voice for it.'

Allan gave a sympathetic murmur.

She continued. 'Then I decided I was going to be the intrepid girl reporter. So actually, I ended up doing what obviously I was best suited to, because English was always my best subject. And then when this television opportunity came along, the part of me that wanted to be in the spotlight was satisfied, too. I was very green and very scared at first but as I said, I'm very single-minded

226

and I made the most of the opportunity.'

'You certainly did.' Allan transferred his caresses to her stomach, or where her stomach should have been. There was no womanly bulge, just an empty hollow. 'Your family must be proud of you.'

'There's only mum and dad,' she said shortly, wanting an end to the subject, 'and I don't see much of them any more. How about you?'

He drew his hand away from the empty hollow with distaste and casually settled on his back, one arm behind his head. 'There's no one. I'm all alone.'

'Not any more,' she whispered. She waited a few moments, then said: 'You told me you were a widower . . . but don't you have parents? Family?'

'None,' he replied. 'There was only ever my mother.'

He paused for an instant and it became an eternity of memories filled with Lillian. He experienced again the pleasures and the pain of their utter devotion to one another and, unaccountably, for the first time in years, he remembered the one person who had tried to come between them.

Mildred had been Lillian's elder sister who, upon being widowed, had been invited to stay. It wasn't the same with her in the house. Lillian squandered time on her; sat and talked for hours with her over cups of tea; went on shopping expeditions with her and did all sorts of things that a nine-year-old boy could have no part in. He felt threatened by the hateful creature and knew with a dreadful certainty that she would eventually monopolise his mother completely, forcing him out.

Mildred had grown frail in her bereavement, and it had not taken much guile or strength for him to tiptoe behind her and push her downstairs. Her neck had snapped like a dry twig and the tragic accident, as it was called, brought mother and son even closer together.

'You loved her very much, didn't you?' Now Sharon was up on an elbow, leaning over him. 'Your mother, I mean.'

She kissed him softly on the cheek.

'You know, Adam, you can be so intense at times it's scary. You make my brand of single-mindedness seem positively easy-going.' Her lips brushed his face again. 'What do you want?' she asked.

'A new life,' he answered truthfully.

Sharon settled back again. 'That's understandable. Losing your business as you did. I guess it explains a lot of your intensity, too. The forcefulness, the drive you have to get on with things. Even

227

when you're sad, like just now, you—'

'You were supposed to be telling me about yourself,' he interrupted, trying to keep his voice tender. The bitch was actually trying to psycholanalyse him. This was *his* game, he asserted furiously, *his* headhunt!

'I think I just about covered everything,' she replied, rubbing her leg against his.

'Oh, I'm sure there's a lot more. How do you separate yourself, the real you, from your job? Where does the reporter stop and the human being take over?' He stretched his lips over his teeth so that a smile would sound in his words. 'I'd find it hard not to get involved. Some of the difficult situations you have to deal with. Do you ever want to . . . hang in there? Help?'

He felt her tense a little.

'Funny you should say that. Yes, it's hard at times. Particularly when you suspect that just by intruding for the sake of a story you may have worsened a situation.'

'Does it happen often?'

'No. But it did recently. And yes, I *am* hanging in there, trying to help a little. Trouble is, I don't know whether I'm doing it for the sake of the person involved, or just for the sake of a follow-up story. A bit of both, I suppose.'

He waited, afraid to speak. He knew what she was talking about. It had been easier than he thought. She was going to tell him about the boy. Expectation prickled through his body. Fantastic. Quite fantastic.

'My God,' Sharon said. 'You're ready to go again.'

His penis had regained its length and stiffened against her leg.

'Finish what you were saying.'

She laughed. 'Are you kidding? Besides, I hate talking about work in bed.' She'd had enough of that with Jim Abrahams, and not enough of this.

Not in bed, eh? Well, that was something he'd learned. He swallowed the bitterness of his disappointment and decided that in the meantime he'd make her suffer for the delay.

'Let's try something . . . unusual this time, shall we?' he suggested.

4

The next morning, Kenneth found Adele checking the kitchen. She was too absorbed in her inspection to look at him, but just waved him to the table where his breakfast was set out.

'Not a mark, a splash or a stain anywhere,' she said with satisfaction. 'Those caterers were good. I'll use them again.' She brought over his coffee and gave him her full attention. 'Enjoy yourself last night?'

He ignored the question. 'Why didn't you tell me about the record?'

'I wanted it to be a surprise,' she said, her eyes wide and blue.

'A shock, you mean.'

She shrugged and went back to her own cup of coffee where she'd left it on the bench.

'You suggested it.'

'Don't blame me!' He started to eat his cereal, then banged down the spoon. 'You must be off your skull. I don't want to be nasty, but who's gonna buy an album with you on it?'

'It's worth a try. It gives me another reason for living.' She raised her coffee cup, then lowered it again as something else occurred to her. 'Besides, there are such things as cult phenomena, you know.'

'Come again?'

'Cult phen-om-en-a,' she repeated, breaking it up into syllables, 'are movies or records or anything out of the mainstream that because of a certain quality of performance succeed with a discerning section of the public. Carl seems to think an album of mine could fall into that category and catch on.'

'Oh he does, does he? Then what was all the arguing about last night? I got sick of hearing it and went to bed.'

She began rinsing her cup under the tap. 'That wasn't an argument, it was an airing of artistic points of view.' She paused, then turned, giving in. 'Okay, so it was an argument. We'd decided the album should have a positive attitude, nothing bluesy or depressing, very commercial but with a nostalgic quality. So I'd gotten a list of possibilities – some standard evergreens, a couple of Beatle numbers, two or three lightweights with cute lyrics and a few of sentimental value. Well, he didn't dig any of them. Most of them he'd never even heard of! Then he started coming up with titles *I'd* never heard of!'

She grabbed a dishtowel and dried the coffee cup energetically.

'When he started to talk Andrew Lloyd Webber, I told him: "Look sonny, I'm neither Mary Magdalene, a mangey cat, nor some freak in a mask, so forget it!" '

Kenneth brightened. 'Then it's all off?'

Adele shook her head. 'We compromised. Some of his suggestions, some of mine. That's the bottom line in any business, kiddo. Compromise.' She hung her cup on a vacant hook with the rest of the set. 'Now he's gone away to fix the arrangements. Clever boy, that one.' She started for the door. 'Put your breakfast things in the dishwasher when you've finished.'

'Why didn't you do the same with your cup?' he asked truculently.

She stopped, her hand at the door.

'Because washing it and drying it helped keep my hands off of you! Oh kiddo, you can be so aggravating! Now look, I am going to the music room to rehearse – and that's where it's at from now on. I don't want to be disturbed, not for anything. You'll just have to amuse yourself.'

'I'll work out how much money you're gonna make.'

'I won't be making a cent, wise guy. Any proceeds from this album will go to the Children's Hospital, I've already stipulated that. Satisfied, Mister Smartypants?'

She swept out, knowing that as an exit line it couldn't be topped.

True to her word, she spent most of the next few days at the piano in the music room. Kenneth heard her tinkling away for hours, and was sorry he'd mended the piano stool with such strong adhesive. If it had collapsed under her, maybe it would have wrecked her enthusiasm.

Her voice was rich and pleasant and he could detect the stages of improvement the more she used it. In addition, she had confidence and style, even he could recognise that. But Adele and her songs belonged to the day before yesterday, there was no getting away from it. And while the oldies might be willing to pay money for nostalgia from a big-name singer who they remembered from their youth, the fact remained that nobody knew Adele and cult or no cult, nothing could alter that.

Kenneth kept busy completing a couple of jobs around the house, and fortunately for him the autumn weather took a sudden turn for the better. The temperature rose, giving Sydney what the TV weather men referred to in their constipated vocabulary as an Indian summer, and he was able to resume swimming again.

He untied the cords securing the pool cover and folded it back just far enough at the deep end to give him room for a dip. He was too canny to remove it permanently. He knew the heat wouldn't last for more than a few days, so he left the cover floating each night, ready to be secured again if he got up one morning to find frost on the grass. In the meantime, swimming gave him a reason to be out of the house and out of earshot of Adele's rehearsals.

One afternoon, he was just about to go into his bedroom for a shower after a swim, when the door opposite opened and Rina came out. He stopped and stared at her. Lambert's bedroom was always kept locked. He knew because he'd tried the door several times.

'What're you doing in there, Rina?' he asked.

'I clean. Once a month. The room is kept the same, but it must be cleaned.'

He noticed she was carrying a fawn and green tweed jacket. She held it up and poked her index finger through a large moth hole.

'You see? I go to tell Mrs Hatherley. Something must be done. The clothes should be given to charity, or a stronger um . . . um . . . um . . . repellent must be used. It is such a waste. And if nothing is done, these moths will spread to her room. And yours.'

Kenneth reached out and took the jacket from her.

'Yeh, well you can hear how busy she is at her singing, and she doesn't want to be disturbed. I'll tell her what you said tonight.'

Rina nodded and moved back to the bedroom door, key in hand.

'You can leave that, Rina. I'll put this back, then get it out to show her, later on.'

The girl nodded and flashed him one of her pretty smiles. Then she went off towards the stairs.

Kenneth stood there until she had turned the corner, then went into the room.

He stood on the threshold and looked around. It was identical in size to Adele's with the same magnificent view out over the Harbour. He noticed a connecting door between this bedroom and

231

Adele's. He also saw that the furnishings in here were heavier, more masculine. There was a gloomy mahogany four-poster bed, the kind they featured in horror movies, and there were tallboys, sideboards and cupboards in matching wood. A wall of mahogany panelling consisted, on closer inspection, of sliding doors which – when he opened them – revealed enough expensively-cut suits, jackets and trousers on padded wooden hangers to stock an exclusive menswear shop. And there were shelves upon shelves of shoes. Black, brown, grey, white, leather, suede, patent, canvas, slip-ons, lace-ups and boots.

He pulled open the side drawers, each one a trove of personal luxury. Neatly-folded socks made of silk or wool; linen handkerchiefs each monogrammed with the initials 'L.H.'; underwear and dozens of shirts either white or discreetly patterned.

He frowned and stepped back.

Everything around him was still, as if the room were holding its breath, waiting for his next move.

From below, Adele's singing voice drifted up with surprising clarity, given the distance:

> 'I would gladly give the sun to you
> If the sun were only mine
> I would gladly give the earth to you
> And the stars that shine . . .'

On an impulse, Kenneth moved closer again and began feeling in the pockets of the casual jackets that hung there, sliding the hangers along as he finished with one, pulling the next one into its place.

Every pocket was empty.

Then he started on the suit jackets. He moved swiftly from habit as if expecting to be caught at it, even though he was doing nothing wrong.

With only two more suits to go, his fingers encountered something hard as he pulled a jacket of light grey worsted towards him. Quickly, he slid his hand into the inside breast pocket and felt a cold, metallic rectangle. He pulled out a gold cigarette case.

He pressed the catch and it flew open to reveal four Sobranies on one side, secured by a gold clip, and an inscription on the other in flamboyant script.

'To Lambert. Everything I have is yours. Adele.'

And then he became aware that down below, as if synchronised by fate, Adele was singing:

> 'Everything I have is yours,
> My life . . . my all . . .'

5

Kenneth passed on Rina's warning about the moths when Adele emerged from the music room around cocktail time, but she was in no mood for domestic trifles. Apparently, Carl O'Callaghan had called her during the afternoon to say the orchestrations were ready and he'd booked a studio for the following day to start putting down some tracks.

Adele was almost trembling with excitement as she poured herself a large vodka.

'It's positively amazing. Have you any idea how long it usually takes to do an orchestration? And this boy has done a dozen in less than three days. He's a workaholic, obviously. I'll probably need to make some changes as we go along, he's not heard my phrasing yet, but even so it's quite an achievement.'

The ice rattled in her glass. She took a long drink then looked at Kenneth.

'Want to come with me, tomorrow? For luck?'

The invitation was genuine, he could tell. She'd hated his resistance to the record and now she was asking for his support. He nodded.

'Sure. I'll even hold your hand, if you like.'

She feigned cold superiority. 'That won't be necessary, buster!' But she followed it up with a smile that had relief in it.

Kenneth noticed she limited herself to the one drink before dinner and ate lightly. Then she left him to clear the dishes, and bustled upstairs.

Later in the evening, she reappeared in a voluminous terry-towelling dressing gown, a towel wrapped turban-style around her head and a thick layer of cold cream on her face.

'Don't look too closely, I'm not fit to be seen,' she said, waving her hands. 'I just want a nightcap to sip in bed. I'm having an early night.'

The next morning, he didn't see her until it was almost time to leave for the recording studio. He'd awakened to the odd sounds of her vocal exercises, breakfasted alone, and then proceeded to get himself ready. He was in the foyer, waiting as she came down the stairs.

There was something different about her, he noticed it immediately. It wasn't that her hair was suspiciously redder than it had been the day before, or that her face reflected a restful night and extra care in the application of make-up. It wasn't even her clothes, although the deliberately casual outfit of loosely-cut wide pants in acid green with a matching three quarter length jacket and white cotton sweater was especially flattering.

An aura of importance seemed to emanate from her. There was a kind of pride in the way she held herself, a grace in the way she descended the stairs. As she drew closer, he saw how her eyes shone and the happiness in her smile.

'All ready to go? Good.'

She handed him the leather portfolio of sheet music she was carrying. Just before they went out of the front door, she took his hand and squeezed it. Her voice was low and dynamic.

'This could be the start of something big, kiddo. Not just for me. For you, too. Now that you're well again, we'll have to start thinking about *your* future, too – what *you're* going to do with your life.'

And then they were on their way.

6

A boy in a grubby sweater and torn jeans took them along to the control booth. He wasn't much older than Kenneth and told them his name was Warren.

Kenneth's preconception of recording studios gleamed in his mind with glass and chrome and high-tech design. Reality, as usual, had been a total let-down. For a start, the studio was in a dingy building which had the sad, terminal look of the condemned. An arthritic lift took them to the third floor.

'I thought it'd be like . . . well, like a TV studio, a place in its own grounds, with a car park and . . .' Kenneth stopped searching for words when he saw Adele's tightly compressed lips and realised he wasn't making things any better.

On the other side of a glass-panelled door with a nasty crack in it, the reception area was dismal, deserted and needed a clean. Warren, when he appeared, seemed perfectly matched to the decor.

In the control booth, Carl O'Callaghan hovered over a massive control panel looking more than ever like a giant praying mantis. He had on a black T-shirt with a phosphorescent bolt of lightning across the front and his black jeans were so tight they made his thin legs look eleven feet long. He advanced on Adele with his similarly long, thin arms outstretched and embraced her. It looked so weird to Kenneth, he half expected the record producer to start spinning a cocoon around her.

After a few pleasantries, Carl turned back to the control panel. Adele made a sign to Kenneth, who had been completely ignored until now, to sit down on a sagging sofa covered in peeling orange vinyl. Then, as if to pass the time, she moved to the sloping sheet of glass which was the wall behind the control panel. Cupping a hand to the glass surface, she peered into the semi darkness on the other side. She shrugged and turned to Carl.

'When do we go to the main studio?'

He peered at her through his bottle-glass spectacles.

236

'What main studio?' he asked. 'This is where we work.'

Adele looked puzzled. 'Here? I don't understand.' She pointed through the glass wall. 'You couldn't cram a trio in there, let alone an orchestra.'

He continued to peer at her.

'Orchestra?'

'The musicians. My backing.'

'Oh.'

Carl leaned over and patted a flat box like a video cassette recorder. 'It's all in here – the digital sampler.'

Adele shook her head slowly. 'I still don't understand.'

'Where've you been, lady? I mean, I know it's been a few years since you did any recording, but I didn't realise you went back to wax cylinders.'

Carl spluttered a laugh and for the first time looked in Kenneth's direction as if expecting him to join in. Kenneth didn't. Even from where he was sitting, he could see the white specks clinging to Carl's nostrils and he knew it wasn't dandruff.

Adele turned frosty.

'That's not funny, Carl. I want some explanations. All this is new to me, and I need to know what I'm getting for the money I've laid out.'

Kenneth's ears pricked up. It was the first time he'd heard about money changing hands. He'd assumed the performer was paid to make a record, not the reverse.

Carl, sensing trouble, backed down.

'Cool it, Adele. It's just that I'm so used to doing it this way, I forget people ever did it any other way. And it's not just me, so don't get any ideas that I'm some kind of electronic freak. This is how the entire industry works now. Shit, you'd have to be Linda Rondstadt or Streisand to walk into a studio full of musicians these days.'

'So tell me.'

'There are outfits that just collect sounds. They hire a string section, let's say, and they ask the violins to play middle C and they record that digitally – not on tape, but on a digital disc in a sampler, which is a form of remembering, but it remembers digitally so that the sound quality is perfect and lifelike. And then they go up, usually twice per octave . . . the C and the G and the C and the G. Drums are done the same way. They get a drummer and pay him to hit a snare drum, his kick drum, his tom toms, his cymbals, and then sample them all. You can do it with guitars . . .

237

all the woodwinds – but they're the weakest because, like, the saxophone is so expressive, the way it growls and bends notes—'

'Just like the human voice,' Adele observed drily.

'Oh, we don't put you in there,' Carl reassured her.

'Thank Christ for that!'

'Let me tell you. The producer – that's me – goes along and from this library he picks his favourite sounds. He buys them, takes them home and puts them into his digital sampler.' Again he patted the flat black box. 'That's what I've done. That's what I have in here. And using the computer, I've built up the basic accompaniment for your numbers and that's what you're going to be singing to. We layer your voice in, then later we get the other musicians coming in one by one and we layer them in too.'

Adele blinked, her face tense.

'So I'm just one of the layers, huh?'

Carl spread his hands. 'Loosen up. This way we save a hell of a lot on the budget. You'll get used to it. And think of the quality. If you cut a big orchestra live, mistakes that can never be corrected get through. Now, it's definitely one musician at a time. Sychronisation all the way. Every contribution just perfect.'

Adele still looked far from convinced, but she was weakening.

'Let me hear what you've got, then.'

'Sure,' said Carl eagerly and began flicking switches. 'You see? When linked to the sampler, this computer is a little recording studio within itself. We can set tempo, alter keys . . .'

Kenneth felt a nudge. Warren inclined his head towards the door. Kenneth got up and followed him out.

A kettle was already boiling in the cubbyhole that served as a kitchen.

'Coffee?' Warren asked.

Kenneth nodded.

Warren spooned instant coffee into two chipped mugs then filled them with boiling water. 'They'll be at it for hours like that. It gets totally boring.' He produced a cold meat pie out of a brown paper bag and mimed breaking it in two. 'Want to go halves?'

Kenneth shook his head and helped himself to milk and sugar. Warren started wolfing the pie down. He was already overweight, bulging out of his jeans. A food junkie, Kenneth thought. It seemed like everybody was a junkie of some sort.

'Does that kind of thing go on all the time?'

'Nah,' replied Warren, swallowing the last of the pie and licking the dribbles from his fingers. 'Not often. Only when you get the old timers in. Can't hack it, y'see. He's got another one of 'em slotted in at the moment, too. Madge Lamb. Heard of her?'

Kenneth shook his head.

'Used to be a big stage star in the forties and fifties in musical comedies,' Warren told him. 'Must be pushing seventy, now. Been retired for years. But she just had a heart-lung transplant, so she's back in the news. They're gonna shove her into a revival of some crappy old show at the Theatre Royal, so Carl grabbed her while she's hot. Suppose we'll have to go through all this with her, too.'

He took a packet of biscuits from a cupboard and when Kenneth refused one he proceeded to eat six or seven. Kenneth finished his coffee.

Warren rinsed the mugs under the cold water tap, wiped them against his jeans, then put them on a battered tin tray.

'Better take them some, I suppose. What's she have in hers?'

'Just plain black.'

Warren made the coffee and emptied the rest of the biscuits on to a saucer.

When they got back to the control booth, Kenneth saw that Adele was now on the other side of the glass wall, standing at a microphone with headphones on. A percussion/bass guitar track was playing loudly, almost drowning out Adele's efforts to sing. Kenneth took the mug of black coffee from the tray, waiting for the right moment to take it in to her.

The right moment arrived quickly. Suddenly, Adele broke off and snatched the headphones from her ears. She waved them, angrily shaking her head. Carl stopped the backing track.

'Do I have to have these cans?' she yelled, glaring through the glass. 'I'm getting this disembodied voice through them and it's me. I'm hearing myself as well as the backing and it's distracting. I can't gauge anything.'

'You'll get used to it, Adele.'

'You keep *saying* that, but I'm not. Look, why can't I have a little loudspeaker in here. You can feed the backing through that. Then I'll be able to hear my own voice clearer as I sing, without having the sound of the backing *and* me all mixed up and deafening me through these damned cans.'

'Oh, we don't do that any more because we can't get the separation.'

'But what about *me*? What about how I *feel*? How do I get the quality in my voice to sell the fucking song?'

Kenneth left the control booth and went next door into the

studio. It was painted black and was even more claustrophobic than it appeared through the glass wall. Carl's voice was coming in, soothingly reiterating the reasons why it had to be done this way. He held out the mug of coffee to Adele. She darted a look at him, her eyes like slits.

'Thanks, kiddo.'

He nodded, managing a grin, then left.

There was no lunch break and the arguments continued incessantly. Adele refused any more coffee and sipped water. Kenneth retreated to the kitchen with Warren three more times. Twice Warren rolled joints which Kenneth was glad to share with him. He hated to see Adele under this kind of pressure, and found himself caring about her as he had cared for only two other people, his mother and Leeanne. The dope helped, but not much.

By three o'clock, Adele had laid down eight tracks of one song and six of another. Exhausted, she suggested they call it a day.

7

Adele drove home with vicious precision. She remained tensely silent except for one remark while they were caught by traffic lights.

'And to think I called that bozo a genius,' she muttered grimly. 'If he's a genius, Elvis ate Pritikin!'

Immediately they got back to 'Horizons', Kenneth poured her a stiff drink and made her sit down. She offered no objection. She drooped limply.

He went upstairs and ran her a hot bath. When he came back, she had finished her drink. In just a few hours she had aged twenty years. Strain had etched deep wrinkles in which stale make-up clogged. Her eyes were puffy and her mouth sagged at the corners. He watched her drag herself upstairs and remembered the woman who had descended those very same stairs with such magical presence that morning.

After a while, he realised how hungry he was and decided to do something about dinner. He looked in the refrigerator and found some cold cuts of ham and salami, a tub of potato salad and another of bean sprouts. He assembled these at one end of the dining room table, together with some fresh tomatoes, sliced bread and butter and pickles. He set out plates, knives and forks, and opened a cold bottle of white wine. He took a swig from the neck of the bottle, then sat down and waited.

Presently, Adele came downstairs in a floaty negligee. The soaking had done her good. She seemed calmer and less drained, but there was a frail quality about her which disturbed him. He'd seen her feisty and arrogant, sarcastic and funny. He had felt the lash of her tongue when she was angry, witnessed her strength in many forms, but never any weakness. Not like this.

'You've been busy,' she remarked quietly, looking at the spread. She sat down.

He poured her a glass of wine and felt good. 'You look after me, don't you? Now it's my turn.'

She sipped at the wine, but ate little. She watched Kenneth eating for a while then sighed.

'Oh Lord, where are you? I've prayed to you so hard for this to turn out right.'

Kenneth looked at her. 'Stuff Carl and his record,' he said. 'Don't go on. It's not worth it.'

'I can't walk away from it. Not me. Not now. But you can do something for me to make it easier. Don't come with me tomorrow, kiddo.'

He bristled. 'I'm coming. I'm not letting you go on your own.'

'I'd rather, believe me,' she said with conviction.

8

Allan stood in the living room of Sharon Pettifer's apartment and looked around him. There wasn't a drawer he hadn't gone through, a book he hadn't shaken, a cupboard he hadn't inspected and a letter he hadn't read. There was a pad of personal telephone numbers, but no address book. She must have that with her. Or perhaps she kept an address book at the office. And that would put it out of bounds. Security at the television studio was strict, he'd established that. A stranger without authority would not get past the front gate, let alone be allowed to wander through the building.

Those were the big obstacles. The studio and Sharon's job.

Had she been a typist working regular hours in an office, she would have been easy to shadow. He could have tracked down the boy merely by following her to one of their meetings. And he was sure, by now, that there was some contact between them, which increased his fears about what she might be coercing the boy to do next. A new panel game – 'Spot the Paedophile'? Or even worse – 'Spot the Murderer'? Although Allan had a new appearance, it wouldn't stand up to investigation, not while his roots remained embedded in Allan Steinbeck's soil. The trouble was one could never be sure of Sharon's movements at any time of the day because of her job.

Sharon's job. That was the reason he was here, alone in her apartment this evening. Without warning, she'd had to fly up north to cover a corruption scandal in a coastal holiday resort. Two days wasted when he could have been worming vital information out of her.

Sharon had insisted on giving him the key to her apartment. He'd had to convince her he felt terribly uncomfortable where he was staying, as an excuse not to take her back there for the night. Although he had no feelings left for Joan, it offended his sense of propriety to share the bed they'd used with another woman. And Lillian would not have approved, either.

243

'If you'd feel more comfortable at my place, you're quite welcome to stay there while I'm gone,' Sharon had said.

And so he'd had plenty of time to search the apartment, and although he'd found no clue to the boy's whereabouts, it had given him something constructive to do. And at least it had proved what he suspected all along. Sharon probably kept the address he wanted in her head.

He must persuade her to divulge it naturally, even though he longed with his entire being to torture her until she screamed it out. But he was afraid that once he started, his passion for revenge would make it impossible for him to stop. He knew the extent of his power and what he was capable of, and he didn't want to kill her like the girl in the Kings Cross squat before she told him what he wanted to know.

There was no other way.

There had never been alternatives in his life. He did not know the meaning of alternatives, any more than he recognised the existence of compromise and compassion. There was only what had to be done. The removal of the boy, and in the process Sharon, was the only means of clearing his path to a new life, just as getting rid of Aunt Mildred had been the only way of reinstating himself as the sole focal point of Lillian's affections.

The clarity of his intentions almost overwhelmed him in its simplicity. To surmount every obstacle required so little effort, provided one leapt over them in the most direct, uncomplicated fashion. Obviously, it was a wondrous formula for living shared by only a small coterie of superior beings. Otherwise, there wouldn't be so much confusion in the world.

But there were degrees of simplicity. Sharon's apartment, for instance, was simplistic to the point of sterility, like the girl herself. The walls were a pale beige, the furniture a mixture of Scandinavian and modular. Light-toned wood and soft white leather. A set in a TV studio. No personality and little warmth.

His mouth curled in a mischievous little smile. If she liked white so much, perhaps some white heat would jolly the place up. He visualised smoke-blackened walls, the polished wood reduced to ash and the divans and chairs bubbling and steaming and finally becoming charred hulks reeking of burnt animal hide. What a transformation it would be, and all from the striking of a match. It would be like the transformation his sexual domination caused in Sharon, the spitting and the spluttering of her, the writhing and the sweating as if she were a strip of pork skin thrown on an open fire.

It opened up a whole new train of thought for him. What a poetic twist it would be if both were engulfed in one gigantic funeral pyre. Sharon and her apartment. It was a notion to be considered seriously, but only put into practice after she had told him what he wanted to know.

The telephone's ring penetrated his fancies with the jagged thrust of a saw-knife.

He winced at the intrusion and hesitated, debating whether or not to answer it.

It continued to ring long after a casual caller would have hung up. Sharon, he thought. It had to be Sharon.

He picked up the receiver.

'Hello darling,' she breathed from far away. 'How are you?'

'I'm fine. Missing you, but otherwise fine.'

'It took you a long time to answer.'

'To tell you the truth, I'd dozed off on the divan. I'm so comfortable here. It's like home.'

'Oh, I disturbed you. I'm sorry. Was there enough food in the fridge? Enough to drink?'

'There's enough of everything except you. When are you coming back?'

'That's why I rang, to tell you I'm flying back tomorrow morning. I'll be at the studio all day, but I'll be with you in the evening. Oh, and don't forget Friday's party, will you?'

'I can hardly wait. Hurry.'

Yes, I can hardly wait, he repeated to himself a little later as he stretched out in Sharon's bed, ready for sleep.

9

After a lot of argument, Adele got her way. Kenneth agreed to stay home the following day.

'The bottom line is I don't want all that unpleasantness going on in front of someone I care a whole lot about,' she admitted finally.

And that did it. Kenneth nodded reluctantly and muttered okay.

She came over and kissed him lightly on the cheek, then went wearily off to bed. He sat there for a while, thinking, then got up and cleared the remains of the makeshift dinner back to the kitchen.

Adele had restricted herself to one glass of wine and the bottle was still over half full. Kenneth took it with him to the drawing room and finished it off while watching an old Clint Eastwood movie on television.

It was after eleven by the time that everybody in the movie except Clint had expired in a bloodbath. Kenneth got up sleepily, leaving the empty bottle in his chair, and turned the television off. Then, as he did most nights now, he went over to the digital panel behind the window curtains and pressed the numbered code sequence which activated the burglar alarm.

All the lights went out.

That bloody rotten circuit breaker, he cursed to himself. The weeks had gone by and just because it hadn't acted up again since that first night, nothing had been done about it. Right! First thing in the morning, he'd be on to the electrician.

He was feeling too tipsy and too tired to bother about resetting the circuit breaker. One night wouldn't matter. And he could find his way upstairs in the dark.

He had just got undressed and into his pyjamas when he heard a sound from across the hall. At first, he thought it was Adele praying again, but after listening for a few moments he realised she was sobbing.

He left his room, went across the hall and quietly opened the door of Adele's bedroom. She must have heard him or perhaps sensed his presence because the sobbing ceased immediately. Kenneth made his way over to the bed, then clambered on to it and lay on top of the bedspread.

'Now you go to sleep, y'hear?'

He felt her nod in the dark then he snuggled against her, feeling the warmth of her beneath the bedclothes and putting one arm across the mound of her body.

He lay there listening to the distant lapping of water in the Harbour. Gradually, it was obliterated by the sound of Adele's breathing. It became loud and steady as she lapsed into sleep and when she began softly to snore he slid carefully off the bed and went back to his own room.

10

'Don't worry, kiddo. If that bastard O'Callaghan says anything out of line today, he'll be talking through an empty neck!'

Adele was back in a fighting mood the next morning, and a good night's sleep seemed to have done her a power of good. Nothing was mentioned of Kenneth's visit to her bedroom. She had either forgotten or preferred not to mention it, just as her nocturnal visits to him when he was recovering from his father's attack had never been discussed.

Kenneth caught her filling a hip flask from the vodka decanter after breakfast, but backed out of the room before she saw him. Despite her show of bravado he could see she was tense and nervy and he conceded that she'd probably need a nip or two to help her through the day.

Before she left, he told her about the circuit overload the previous night and asked about an electrician. She told him the number was on a list of tradesmen fixed to the inside of the pantry door.

Kenneth walked with her to the garage and gave her a big hug before she got into the BMW. Mr Fitzgibbon was just arriving, and when he saw them he pulled open the gates.

'And that's another thing,' Kenneth said, leaning through the car window. 'Those gates should be electronic. All this running backwards and forwards pulling 'em open and shut all the time, it's really spack.'

'Spack?'

'It's a buzz word for stupid.' He thought for a moment. 'Or it *was*. They change from day to day. I've been out of it for weeks, so it's probably ancient by now.'

Adele leaned towards him. 'Do you mind? Being out of it?'

'You kidding?' He grinned incredulously as if she were crazy.

Adele rested back in her seat and turned on the ignition. 'Just so's I know. You talk to the electrician about everything, huh? Bye.'

248

He waved as she headed the car down the drive and stood there with his arm up until she turned into Boniface Road.

There had been a heavy dew overnight. The grass, the leaves all glistened like telltales with the evidence of it. But the sun was already warming things up, cruising in a cloudless sky, lower than its summer altitude but still coming on hot and strong. Kenneth knew it was going to be another day for swimming.

Great. But business first.

He looked up the electrician's number on the list in the pantry, but when he called it he got an answering service. He left his number on the recording then kicked his heels around the house in the mistaken belief that the electrician might call back straight away.

When Jorge and Rina arrived, he felt safe in leaving the house for a swim. He almost skipped across the terrace. The flat stones felt cold and damp to his bare feet. But when he heaved back the pool cover half way over itself and felt the water, it was warm and pleasant. The cover not only kept out the leaves, it stored heat.

After about an hour of making like a dolphin, he heaved himself out and sat, arms clasped around knees to dry out, face turned up to the sun and stuff all the crap about skin cancer. Who wanted to live forever, anyway? To Adele's age and a bit further on, maybe, but no more. Who'd want to be a hundred in a wheelchair? Besides, there was too much aggro in the world, too much pain. You could take just so much, but there was a limit. Look at the shit Adele must be going through right at this very minute. At her time of life. And for what?

The electrician returned his call most conveniently, just as he went back to the house. Kenneth told him about the circuit breaker going off.

'That security system should be on a separate circuit,' he declared authoritatively into the phone. 'There must be some overload problem in the house, so it's gotta be fixed.'

'That'll mean rewiring,' the electrician told him. 'It'll cost you.'

'Just get here and do it,' Kenneth replied. 'Oh, and we want the gates made electronic.'

'Jeezus mate, you're looking at money.'

'Listen, just get here,' Kenneth said. 'You're talking payment when you haven't even sized up the job yet!'

There was silence from the other end, but Kenneth didn't notice it. He'd realised he was talking like Adele, and what's more he liked the feeling.

'It'll have to be Monday,' the electrician said.

That stopped Kenneth in his tracks. He'd thought he was going great. 'What about today?'

'I've got commitments, mate. Monday morning, that's the best I can do.'

'Okay. Monday morning.'

Kenneth slapped the phone down. Now he had something to do. It was a question of security.

He remembered seeing a length of chain in the pool shed. After he'd changed from his bathers into jeans and a sweatshirt, he went out and got it. In the garage, he rummaged through shelves of old nails and forgotten tools that looked like rusting bones. Amongst them he found a stout padlock with a key in it.

He took the chain and the padlock down to the gates. They were still open. He heaved them together, then looped the chain around the two inner uprights and attached the padlock. Everything fitted. Excellent, he thought. That would do until the electrician came to fix things.

He unlooped the chain and gathered it together with the padlock, then pulled the gates open ready for Adele to drive through when she got back. He was halfway up the drive when Rina came out on to the front terrace.

'Mr Kenneth? Somebody want you on the phone.'

He started to run.

'Mrs Hatherley?' he called. Adele came first to his mind. She needed him, perhaps. She was in trouble. Carl-fucking-O'Callaghan had pushed her to the edge and—

'No, not Mrs Hatherley.'

The electrician. Maybe he *could* come today. Kenneth was almost to the steps, trailing the chain, clutching the padlock and thinking that now they wouldn't be necessary.

But it wasn't the electrician.

'It's a lady,' Rina said as he passed her on his way inside.

11

Sharon and her cameraman arrived back in Sydney mid-morning with three explosive interviews providing evidence of Council malpractice in regard to property developers and land deals around Barrier Bay, plus enough film coverage to illustrate the resort's monstrous rate of growth over the past ten years.

Jim Abrahams was nowhere around when she arrived at the *Upfront* offices, in fact apart from a couple of secretaries answering phones and typing copy, the entire production unit seemed to have dispersed and disappeared after that morning's conference.

She was glad nobody was around. It gave her the opportunity to sit at her desk in peace and map out the presentation of the material she had collected over the past two days. She also made a list of the contentious points involved for the network's solicitors to examine. Having refused breakfast on the plane, she felt the first pangs of hunger just as she finished her deskwork. Although it was still a little early for lunch, she decided to brave the studio canteen for a snack.

The place was almost empty when she got there, but by the time she had finished her salad sandwich and was on her second cup of coffee, more people had begun to drift in . . . floor crew, recognisable on-camera faces, office staff and some rubber-necking members of the public, there for the taping of an audience participation show. Then she saw Jim Abrahams walk in. The angst she had felt after their last confrontation had dissipated. He'd handed her another hot assignment. And she had a lover. She could afford to be generous. She waved to him, and when he'd got his meal he came over to join her.

As he unloaded his tray, Sharon looked at the plate.

'Pie and chips? Oh Jim, that stuff 'll kill you.'

'Tell me something that won't these days,' he said with a wry grin. 'How was the jaunt?'

'Great. I've already worked out the approach, it's on my desk. Where were you?'

'They're assembling montage segments showing the network's twenty-five years on air for the party tomorrow night, so I've been helping out. You're coming, aren't you?'

It was the twenty-fifth anniversary of the network's debut and a big celebration had been organised in the main studio.

'Oh yes, I'll be there.'

Jim showered his chips with salt, then pulled the skin off a blister pack of tomato sauce. Sharon shook her head helplessly and made ready to go. She really couldn't handle watching him eat such rubbish. However, his next words stopped her.

'Still sniping at your young boyfriend's benefactress, I hear.'

'You hear?'

'Yes. Margaret Fong happened to mention she'd done a bit of research for you on the subject.'

'Oh?' said Sharon, with an arch smile. 'And did she mention it before or after?'

'Before or after what?'

Now Sharon's smile broadened. 'You know,' she implied, playfully. For the past week, the buzz around the office was that Jim and Margaret Fong had become a discreet item. Sharon was glad. Now she had Adam, she was happy that Jim had found someone else too, particularly as it was a girl like Margaret Fong who, as a successor, was hardly dazzling enough to put Sharon's nose out of joint.

Jim gave her a look and let the implication pass. He speared some chips on his fork.

'What do you think of the latest on the woman, the faxes from the States? Not exactly a pretty story, but I don't know why you're even bothering—'

'Faxes? What faxes?' she interrupted sharply.

'They came through while you were away. They're in your tray.'

Sharon jumped up. 'I didn't look. I was thinking about Barrier Bay. Jim, excuse me – I was just about to go, anyway.' And she hurried off.

12

With great reluctance, Kenneth agreed to meet Sharon at a coffee shop in Double Bay because there was such determination in her voice. He knew that if he just hung up in her ear, she'd probably front up at the house and he didn't want Adele arriving home and finding her there or even discovering that she'd been there. Adele would be tired and upset after another session with O'Callaghan, and Sharon would be the last straw.

He'd suggested that Sharon tell him what she wanted over the phone, but she refused to talk to him at length and said she had to come over to Double Bay anyway, to pick up a dress.

Just before two o'clock he telephoned for a taxi. It was the first time he'd ventured out on his own since the night he returned to the Cross. As he sauntered down to the gates to wait for the cab, he realised he'd lost most of his fear. Even when he saw a limousine cruising along Boniface Road, it meant nothing to him. Like most slowly cruising cars these days, it contained nothing more threatening than Japanese investors looking for houses to buy, even those that were not for sale.

When he got to the coffee shop his first impression was that she hadn't arrived, but then he saw her sitting at a table at the back in a corner. As he slouched over, he took in how upright she sat, hair all gleaming gold and loosely tied back, the suede jacket over a mannish white shirt. He saw the sparkle in her eyes and the flush in her cheeks, and thought how less thin and bony she looked this time. Actually, she looked good. Pity she was such bad news.

'Come and sit down,' she said with a big wide smile, turning simultaneously to wave in a waitress hovering nearby.

'I don't want nothing,' Kenneth muttered.

'Then just bring me a large, fresh orange juice,' she told the waitress. That done, she gave him her full attention.

'Well Kenneth, you're looking great. How's the throat?'

'Okay.'

253

She suddenly seemed at a loss as to what to say next. *Stop sniffing glue, Terry! Stay away from that freak, Kenneth!* She picked up a paper sachet of sugar from a bowl in the middle of the table and turned it over and over in her hands.

He watched her, not moving, enjoying the sensation of making her feel uncomfortable.

Presently, the waitress brought a glass of orange juice. Sharon accepted it with a fleeting smile, then asked him: 'Are you sure you won't have something?'

'I told you, didn't I?'

She took a sip of the orange juice and made a face.

'Watered-down concentrate. It says "fresh" on the menu.'

He smiled perversely. 'You'll have to do one of your exposures on it, won't you? The Great Juice Rip-Off.'

She regarded him with a frown.

'I get such negativity from you. Why do you dislike me so much? I've only ever tried to be your friend.'

'Like feeding me bullshit about Adele? That your idea of being a friend?'

'I don't like to see you being used.'

'You used me, didn't you?'

'Not like she's using you. When you left Kings Cross and went to her, you just exchanged one kind of predator for another. She's using you to fabricate the illusions she wants to believe in. She's feeding you lies, drawing you into her own little fantasy world and I can't just stand by and let that happen, no matter how much it rubs you the wrong way.'

Her voice had become shrill and a couple at a nearby table were casting glances. Sharon didn't notice them. She was too busy fumbling in the large leather handbag she had lifted on to her lap. She brought out two sheets of paper and held them up.

'These are faxes from the United States. I asked our contacts there to check her out.' She separated one sheet from the other. 'Our New York Bureau couldn't find anything. But the people in Los Angeles managed to dig up one item from the files. Only one, but it's significant – a newspaper report from the early sixties.' She looked at the second sheet. 'It says that while employed as a maid to "Love Goddess" Kelly Green, sometime singer Adele Ventura was accused of stealing a valuable emerald ring from the star. Miss Green said the ring had been a gift from her fiancé, the fabulously wealthy Sheik, Prince Mahmoud Hassan, ruler of the oil-rich Arab principate of Doubani. Ventura was arrested and interrogated by

Beverly Hills detectives, but the charge was later withdrawn.'

Sharon lowered the page and looked at him intensely.

'You see? She didn't dub Kelly Green's singing voice. She was nothing more than a servant – and a thieving servant at that. So much for the tale she told you.'

She folded the pages and stuffed them into her bag, then put the bag back down by her feet. She straightened up, reached for the glass of orange juice, then remembered she didn't like it. She pulled her hand away.

Kenneth stared at her.

'So what d'you think I should do?' he asked her levelly. 'Tell her she told me lies and walk out on her? Is that what you want? So what do I do then? Go back to the Cross?' He shook his head. 'I don't understand you. You say you want to be my friend, but—'

'There are alternatives,' Sharon interrupted. 'You have all your life before you.' She paused, then continued brightly. 'I could get you a job at the studio. They like young people, young people who can be trained. It wouldn't be much at first, but it could be the start of a career.'

'Me?' Kenneth asked incredulously. 'Work in television and get as screwed up as you?'

He saw her face redden.

'You're jealous of her, aren't you?' he went on. 'You're jealous of Adele, because in your mind you'd adopted me as your responsibility, your own little Save the Children project, but instead you found me with her and that didn't suit you, did it?'

She was trying to be rational, to reassert herself.

'That's not true, Kenneth.'

He stood up, scraping his chair back on the tiled floor with such a shove that it fell over. He looked down at her with narrowed eyes.

'I'm only a kid, but I can see through you. You may get a kick out of helping people you think are inferior to you, but if they start going up in the world and you had nothing to do with it, you can't stand it. You need to be Miss High and Mighty so much, don't you, and you'll put the boot in anything that gets in your way.'

The waitress approached hesitantly.

'Would you like the check?'

'Give it to her,' said Kenneth pointing at Sharon. 'But I wouldn't count on her paying it. She thinks your orange juice is shit!'

And he swung around and made his way noisily through the tables to the door.

13

When he got home, Kenneth wandered around the grounds for a while trying to get his thoughts in order. If there was one set of lies, there could be more.

As soon as the sun crept behind the trees, a chilly greyness made him shiver. He went inside just as Jorge and Rina were leaving. On an impulse, he asked Rina for the key to the locked bedroom saying Mrs Hatherley had asked him to sort out some of the clothing ready to be collected by a charity. She brought out several keys on different rings, liberated one and gave it to him. Then they left.

He went upstairs, unlocked the bedroom door and went inside.

Half an hour later, he came out, locked the door and crossed to his own room. Now, it was almost dark. He didn't switch on the light, but flopped on to his bed and pulled the quilt up over himself. He curled into the foetal position and tried to sleep, but he found it impossible. Too many worrying thoughts were at loose in his brain.

Time passed. Then he heard the car coming up the drive. A few minutes later, the front door banged as Adele came into the house. He didn't move. He heard her calling his name but he stayed where he was. If only he could be by himself forever. Just him, no one else. That was the only way a person could be safe.

She knocked at his door.

'Kenneth?'

'Yeh?' He knew she would come in anyway, she always did, so there was no point in not answering. There was no way of avoiding it. She'd have to unwind. She'd have to talk.

He pushed himself up as she came across the room and switched on the bedside lamp. She had a large drink in one hand and a cigarette in the other and she looked awful, twice as bad as the previous afternoon. She seemed to have shrunk in her clothes. Her face was pale and haggard and her hair was stuck up as if she'd pushed nervous fingers through it too many times. She was blinking a lot as if her eyes had grit in them.

Wearily, she sat down on the edge of the bed. He knew it was opening the floodgates, but he had to ask the question.

'How did it go?'

She took a drink and drooped hopelessly.

'Well for starters, you can forget about spontaneity. There's no place for that any more. Time was when a group of musicians got together there'd be moments when exciting things would happen. Peaks of performance. But those moments no longer exist because everybody does their bit separately. He had me putting down so many tracks for each number I lost my feel for pitch and phrasing.

'Then he says: "The first two lines of verse one on track seven are good. We'll follow them with the second two lines from track four. Then the chorus from track one . . ." Jesus, it's like he's putting together a jigsaw puzzle.'

She made the obligatory pause to take a gulp from her drink and inhale some smoke. Kenneth put in another question.

'But doesn't that mean it'll turn out good? The pick of the best?'

She shook her head. 'What you end up with is like a poor print of a marvellous oil painting. No life, no texture. No emotion. It's a mechanical rendition without reality, something that can never be duplicated live. I realise now why so many recording stars don't do many concerts, except the ones who are drowned out by continually screaming kids. They don't sound as good as they do on the disc, never will. Some of them even just mime to their records and call that a live performance.'

She looked around for an ashtray but there wasn't one. She got up and went into the bathroom. Kenneth heard the hiss as she dropped the butt into the toilet bowl. Then she flushed it away.

He wished she'd go. She was making him feel worse with her jumpiness and the pathetic quality of her complaints. There was nothing he could do about her situation. She was living in the past, out of her depth. Refusing to face that was doing terrible things to her.

She started talking again, even before she came back into the room.

'Every time I'd try to "sell" a lyric, he'd pull me back.' She mimicked. ' "No sweetie, hold it in, you're *performing*" – as if "performing" were a dirty word. He wants me to blend into the background. Like Muzak. It's as if too much emotion scares people. The world has forgotten what performers do, what entertainers are all about. Let's face it, there aren't too many around any more.

Sammy Davis has gone . . . who's left?'

She was wandering aimlessly around the room with jerky steps, sipping her drink and groping for answers.

'I may not have done any work for a while, but I'm not exactly a novice. I made records. I duetted with Buddy Clark and Guy Mitchell, did some backing for Frankie Laine . . .'

He couldn't help himself. 'And the Kelly Green stuff, too.'

She shot him an impatient glance.

'That was a different scene altogether. I'm talking about making bona fide records. In those days, you'd walk into a studio that was booked for a three-hour session. There'd be the orchestra, the vocal group plus everyone else. You'd hear the arrangement which you'd worked out beforehand, they'd balance the sound, then you'd have the rest of the three hours to get two sides down. And when you walked out of there, often before time was up, you had a finished performance on disc. Not any more. Today, the Carl O'Callaghans are the stars, the producers who flick the switches, who can drop in a note or a word from another track if they're not happy with the way it is. And if there's still some of the singer's heart left in, they can cut it out in the final mix.'

It was giving Kenneth a headache, this intensity of frayed nerves, all the pointless ranting. He couldn't bring himself to sympathise with her any more. This was something she'd got herself into and could easily get herself out of if she weren't so bloody stubborn.

Fortunately, she had finished her drink and was not prepared to carry on without a refill. She looked at the empty glass then reluctantly made for the door.

'I'll be back,' she said. Kenneth panicked and thought of locking himself in the bathroom. He didn't want to hear any more. But then, as she went out of the door, she stopped and asked: 'Did you call the electrician?'

'Yeh, but he can't come till Monday.' He saw how he could make his escape. 'That reminds me. I'm going to padlock the gates every night till he comes.' He got up off the bed. 'You're not going out again tonight, are you?'

'I can hardly make it up and down the stairs,' she said. 'And I won't be going out tomorrow, either.' Her tone became mocking. 'Mister O'Callaghan has given me the day off. He has the rest of the musicians going in – one by one, of course – to add their parts to the basic accompaniment.'

She handed him the empty glass.

'Be a pal and bring me another one when you come back upstairs.

Save me a journey. Make it quick and make it strong.'

The evening had turned bitterly cold and he broke into a run down the drive to get the job over quickly. He pulled the gates together and secured them with the chain and padlock. A full moon hung low and heavy, regarding him like the one malevolent eye of a Cyclops. Its luminosity shed light over the grounds, but in consequence the shadows were darker and filled with menace. He lost no time in getting back to the house.

He not only took the drink up to her room, but the vodka bottle as well, along with a segment of her favourite camembert and some crackers on a plate, hoping that with food and drink in her room she mightn't bother venturing downstairs later on.

He needn't have worried. She was in her bathroom filling the tub when he went in. Quickly, he put the food and drink on one of the bedside tables and left. He fixed himself some sandwiches in the kitchen and watched television for the rest of the evening. Adele made no further appearance. Later, when he went to bed, he paused outside her door and heard the whispered entreaties of her prayers.

14

The Italian Restaurant in Surry Hills was uninspiring, even clichéd at first sight, with its chequered tablecloths and candles in Chianti bottles, but it had an excellent reputation for food.

Allan noticed Sharon was unusually quiet. Her assignment had worked out fine, she had told him, and there was nothing lacking in the way she embraced him after their separation. But he detected a moroseness in between the bursts of conversation, something to suggest that her mind kept flitting elsewhere to a place or subject she found unpleasant.

Like most Italian restaurants of its type, there was more noise coming from the kitchen than from the diners. There was a particularly loud crash as something heavy and metallic fell to the floor. This was followed by an explosion of voices, each attempting to top the rest with ever-increasing levels of stridency.

Sharon looked at him with a rueful smile. The noise had brought her back.

'You're not eating,' he took the opportunity to point out.

He'd watched her shoving the superb Fettucine alla Romana around on her plate for the past five minutes. However, she'd finished two glasses of red wine in the process, which was unusual because as a rule she drank sparingly.

'I'm sorry,' she smiled at him, 'it really is delicious. Could I have some more wine?'

He poured the wine. With luck, it would loosen her tongue.

'Darling, is there something wrong?' he asked. 'I keep feeling I'm dining alone.'

She bit her lip and hunched her shoulders in an attempt at cuteness he found repellant. But at least she drank some more of the wine he'd poured and now she was making an attempt to eat her dish of pasta.

He made a show of snapping his finger and thumb. 'I know! It's that "difficult situation" you mentioned the other night, isn't it?'

He'd decided to dive in, to take advantage. 'Come on, tell me about it. There's nothing like getting a problem out into the open.'

She looked at him, a forkful of pasta poised in midair.

'I can't give you full marks for perception because it's probably so obvious. Yes, you're right. It's the "difficult situation".' Maddeningly, she pushed the pasta into her mouth and he had to wait until she'd chewed and swallowed it.

She took another drink of wine, and then out it came. She started to talk on the one subject he was interested in, the one reason they were here together, the one reason why he'd been screwing her, and it all started to ooze out so easily.

'It's a *rotten* situation, to put it bluntly. I've been so concerned about this kid, this boy. He's one of many lost souls, but you can't help them all, you just try to do your best with the individual.'

Another gulp of wine. Good. He must order a second bottle with the veal. She had actually said 'This boy'. She had put his target into words for the first time. The barricades had crumbled. Now she must lead him through.

Sharon pouted.

'There's nothing worse than to have your own goodwill pushed back in your face. I mean, it's no big deal to me. I just want him to have a decent chance in life.'

'Of course,' Allan murmured encouragingly. His pulse was racing. He wanted to reach over and throttle the rest of it out of her.

'I had to go over to Double Bay anyway today, to pick up this outfit. And you haven't even mentioned it.'

The outfit consisted of a collarless double-breasted jacket in dark-brown linen, over a matching pleated skirt.

'I love it,' he told her, 'but then you have such good taste I love everything you wear. Or maybe that body just makes the clothes look good. Go on.'

The words tumbled out, but all he was registering was Double Bay. That proved it. The boy was still hiding out near where he'd disappeared.

She accepted his compliment with a smile and dug her fork into the pasta. 'Well, I was going over there so I decided to kill two birds with one stone. Unfortunately, the reverse happened. There was just one bird – me. And the stone was very rough and very painful.'

She ate some more. He waited until she laid her fork down on the plate. She reached for her glass and drained it.

'I intend to get rather tipsy tonight, darling, so you'd better watch out.' She beamed up as if a fabulous idea had occurred to her. 'Tell you what – let's go back to *your* place.'

He tried to desist.

'Oh Sharon, you know how I hate the place. I'm house-minding for friends of friends. It's not like a hotel room which is anonymous and therefore acceptable. This place is imbued with the lifestyle of strangers. It's not for us, believe me. I've told you so many times how uncomfortable I feel there. I don't want that feeling translated into our relationship.'

'Methinks the gentleman doth protest too much,' Sharon replied archly, raising her glass. She realised it was empty, then seemed to undergo a change of mood. She put the glass down. She was swaying a little in her chair, but her gaze was direct. 'I feel like . . . like getting away from everything familiar tonight. And that includes my apartment. *And* this . . . this problem.'

'There's only one way to solve that – and that's to get it off your chest,' Allan insisted.

'I will, I will,' replied Sharon, her mood changing to one of petulance. Three glasses of wine and she was a lush, Allan thought.

She scowled. 'To have my motives questioned. To have a sincere offer of friendship rejected . . .'

Her arm flew out and almost hit the waiter who had come to clear their plates. Allan ordered another bottle of red wine.

'But no more of that,' she concluded. 'Too depressing. Later, maybe.'

Later *definitely*, Allan decided.

She was swaying a little more when they reached the house, but despite that and a tendency to be kittenish she was still quite lucid. Allan suggested liqueurs and poured her some Drambuie.

She took it, then wandered around making disparaging remarks about the furnishings.

'Don't think much of your friends' tastes, Adam. What's in here? Kitchen? Yuk . . . early House and Gardens.' She took a sip of the Drambuie, showed her approval by licking her lips, then took another sip. 'Where's the bedroom?'

'The master one's through there,' he told her.

She disappeared through the doorway and he didn't follow her because he assumed she wanted to use the bathroom. He sat on the arm of a chair and waited. When she came back, he saw that she had taken off her jacket. She was holding the almost-empty liqueur glass in one hand and fumbling at her bra with the other.

'I need help,' she said.

Allan got up and went to her.

'I think we'll be more comfortable inside,' he said and guided her back into the bedroom. He unhooked the catch on her bra and let it fall. Immediately, she was in his arms, her eyes closed, her open mouth searching for his. He managed to take the glass out of her hand and put it on the bedside table, then crushed her tightly against his body. She felt his erection and began moaning.

'You'll have to learn not to waste your energies on the wrong people,' he said softly in her ear.

The moaning stopped. 'Wha-what?'

'The boy.'

She sighed. 'Oh Adam, not now.'

'Yes,' he insisted firmly. 'Now. I want you to tell me all about him. Clear it out of your mind. That way we'll have a far better time.'

She went completely still in his arms, considering what he'd said. 'Well . . .'

'Come on, darling. It's for the best. And besides, you puzzle me. He doesn't sound as if he needs help. Double Bay's hardly a ghetto for the underprivileged.'

She pulled away from him a little so that she could focus on him while she talked.

'Oh he's not underprivileged. Not any more. Overindulged, more likely. And he's not exactly in Double Bay, either. He's—'

The telephone rang in the living room. Instinctively, they both tensed as if caught out in something nefarious. Allan waited for the ringing to stop, but it didn't.

'Aren't you going to answer it?' Sharon asked in a whisper, as if she suddenly feared they might be overheard.

The ringing went on and on. Allan decided there was nothing for it but to answer the damned thing.

'Won't be a minute,' he said. Firmly, he sat her down on the bed then went out, closing the door behind him.

In the living room, he picked up the receiver.

'Hello?'

Joan's voice was emotional and accusing. 'I've been trying to get you all evening. Where've you been?'

'Out for something to eat,' he replied carefully.

Her voice faltered.

'It's mother. She's . . . she's dead.'

'Oh, I'm so sorry.' He meant it sincerely. He *was* sorry, extremely sorry that the old bitch's suffering was over. 'But I thought she was—'

'Oh yes, she was recovering, in a fashion. They were even allowing her to get up for a few hours . . . in a chair. But they had to keep her away from mirrors.'

She began to cry, then controlled herself.

'She waited until there was no one around, then found her way to a bathroom. There was a mirror there. She must have seen her face, how hid— how hideous it looked. And she threw herself out of the window.'

He resisted the temptation to ask how many floors she fell, but consoled himself with the thought that if Doris Lytton-Scott had to go, at least she went in the utmost torment. Joan's next words, however, took the pleasure out of the moment.

'I need you, Allan. I need you right now, and if not now – and I realise it's quite late for you to come chasing across town – then tomorrow. We've been apart long enough. I can't go through any more of this alone. I can't, I just can't!'

His mind raced. There was no way he could let her see him as Adam Shaw. How could he explain the drastic change in his appearance? Besides, if he were to disappear effectively after accomplishing what he'd set out to do, there must be no link between Allan Steinbeck and Adam Shaw.

'I – I can't. Not tomorrow.'

'*Can't?*' Her voice was shrill. She had sounded ready to break, but now a dangerous note of indignation was giving her strength. 'I'm still your wife. What could be more important than being at my side at a ghastly time like this?'

'I have to fly down to Melbourne tomorrow. I really have to do this. It's a job. The chance of a lifetime. You know what the situation is. I can't afford to miss out on an opportunity like this.'

There was silence at the end of the line. Then she spoke.

'Well, when will you be back? It should only take a day, shouldn't it? Or two at the most?'

'Yes,' he was forced to agree.

'In that case, I'll try to hang on. I know how hard it is to get decent jobs these days. And it might be a good thing for us to make a fresh start in Melbourne, where nobody knows us.' Her voice hardened. 'There's a service for mother on Sunday, and you *must* be here for that. You *must!*'

It was Thursday night, which gave him two full days. Two days. That's all he had left. When he didn't turn up, she'd come after him. He had to be gone by then.

'I'll be there, I promise. Now try to get a good night's sleep and I'll try to call you tomorrow from Melbourne.'

He hung up to stop her quibbling further. It was a relief just not to hear her voice. He turned.

Sharon was standing across the room. She had her linen jacket clutched in front of her and there was a perplexed expression on her face.

'Bad news?'

Quickly, Allan tried to review everything he'd said. He had not called Joan by name, nor had he used any form of endearment. No, he'd been careful not to, in case Sharon had overheard something from the bedroom. But he had not counted on her actually coming out and listening in. He should have known. She made her living poking her nose into other people's business.

He dropped his eyes and made a play of looking sad while he fabricated a story. Sharon waited.

'An acquaintance of mine, a colleague in travel, actually, here in Sydney . . . his business folded, too. But unlike me, he didn't have other assets. He couldn't face the debts. He's taken his own life.'

'Oh. I'm sorry.' Sharon seemed to have sobered up remarkably quickly. She frowned. 'But what was all that about Melbourne?'

He hesitated, then went on. 'I'm ashamed to say I was fibbing. That was his wife. Having gone through that scene myself, business collapsing, all that sort of thing – and that coming soon after losing my own wife – I'm not the best person to give her support. I don't think I'm up to it. There's a service on Sunday. I'll pay my respects then, when I've become a little more used to the idea that he's gone.'

'Would you like me to come with you?' she asked sympathetically.

Allan almost laughed in her face. That would really shock Joan! A husband who was unrecognisable with a tall, blonde mistress on his arm! That would give the late, unlamented Doris a send-off to end all send-offs! And thinking of services, it occurred to him that if all went well, Sharon would be starring in one of her own very shortly.

He shook his head gravely.

Sharon began struggling back into her jacket. He hadn't noticed she was already wearing her bra.

'What are you doing?'

She gave him a wan smile. 'I think we'd better call it a night, don't you?' She looked around with a slight shudder. 'This place is really getting to me. It has a feeling of desolation about it.' She nodded in the direction of the telephone. 'And after tragic news like that. . .'

'Well, let's go back to your apartment, then.' They'd been interrupted at a crucial moment, and he wanted to retrieve it.

Sharon shook her head and picked up her bag from the chair she'd thrown it in when they'd arrived.

'I'd rather not.'

'At least let me drive you. You had quite a bit to drink.'

'No, I'm fine now.' There was an edge of irritation to her voice. 'Adam, please. Let's face the fact that the evening wasn't one of our best and try again tomorrow night. It's the party, remember? Give me a ring at the office in the morning.'

He had to let her go. But he certainly *would* try again the following night. And he would succeed no matter what, because now he was running out of time.

15

For most of the following morning, Adele paced up and down restlessly, her face a mask of discontent. Kenneth did his best to keep out of her way. At times, she would shut herself in the music room. After some scales, she would begin to sing, accompanying herself on the piano, but after only a few bars something would displease her and she would crash her hands down on the keys in a succession of discords.

Then she would reappear again, making coffee and prowling from room to room.

Kenneth spent as much time outside as he could, even going into the pool despite the fact that some of the previous night's chilliness had resisted the sun's efforts to warm the day. He realised the Indian summer was coming to an end and he would not be able to swim for very much longer. It didn't matter. His days at 'Horizons' were numbered anyway. He knew too much ever to feel secure there again. His trust in Adele had been destroyed.

'You'll have to fix your own lunch,' she told him, coming out onto the terrace. 'I can't concentrate on anything. I can't switch off. I keep wondering what's going on there, at the recording studio.'

Kenneth noticed the way she twitched, her hands never still. The daily make-up job hadn't helped. Her face looked hard and strained.

It was no use, he couldn't shrug her off. He couldn't be cold to her, not while she was like this.

'How much bread did you put into it?' he asked softly.

Her head went on one side and she looked past him, as if she couldn't allow her eyes to meet his.

'Ten thousand dollars.'

'You paid him ten thousand bucks? Just to be treated like shit?'

'I didn't know that came with the deal. I looked on it as an investment. For charity, as well as my own ego. I told you any profits will go to treating sick kids. Anyway, the money doesn't matter. I want that album to be a personal statement. One that says Adele

267

Ventura can still deliver. I don't care if one person buys it or a million. Just as long as I prove it to myself.' She managed a sad smile. 'Although the chances of that get smaller all the time, the way O'Callaghan's screwing around. That's what's tearing me apart.'

She looked down to where her foot was tracing invisible patterns on the paving stones. 'I know it's difficult for you to understand, kiddo. It's like I was born on a soapbox but no one's ever really listened to me, not once in my life. I've always been one step behind somebody else. In my career, singing for Kelly. In Acapulco, living with Joe. Never Number One. That's why I'm praying "Maybe this time. Just this once." '

He wanted to move closer and touch her, to say something that might reassure her, but he did nothing and remained silent.

Then her hands flew up in a gesture of impatience.

'Wait a minute! Wait one cotton-pickin' minute! What the hell am I doing here? I'm paying for this clambake, I should be there. At the studio. *He* won't like it, but at least I'll get the feel of what the musicians are doing – and maybe I'll get to make a few suggestions myself!'

She hurried into the house. He stayed outdoors until hunger forced him to the kitchen to forage for some lunch. While he was opening a can of baked beans he heard the front door slam and then one of the cars moving off.

She hadn't even bothered to say goodbye.

Her restlessness seemed to have communicated itself to him and once he'd eaten the beans and drank a bottle of Pepsi, the rest of the day stretched like a freeway, endless and boring in front of him.

Wracking his brain in search of something to do, he felt a sudden urge to play video games, not the toys Adele had bought him while he was recuperating, but the real thing, the big gutsy machines with the menacing sound effects, programmed to blow your mind if you weren't skilful enough to show 'em who was boss.

He went over to the canister on the shelf above the microwave where Adele kept a supply of what she called 'fun money'. He'd taken fifteen dollars for taxi fares the day before, but he'd noticed there was quite a deal more in there. He counted what was left. Fifty-two dollars and seventy-seven cents. He reckoned fifty dollars ought to be enough, so he folded up the notes and stuffed the wad in the pocket of his jeans and put the small change back in the canister. Before yesterday he'd never taken anything from the house. Now, he didn't care.

16

The young constable walked up the drive to Allan Steinbeck's house and rang the doorbell.

He waited, whistling soundlessly to himself, but nobody came. He rang the doorbell again, then strolled across to the garage. The door was down and locked, but there was a window in the side. He looked through it and saw that the garage was empty. He glanced at the front of the house again then walked back to the gate.

It was his good luck there was nobody home. Now, he reckoned, he'd be able to dodge the query altogether. It was probably a dead-end, anyway. Some car – a white Volvo the informant thought, but couldn't be sure – had side-swiped two or three parked cars up the Cross in Victoria Street, weeks before. The informant had also remembered the first four digits of the car's registration number, which wasn't bad considering he'd just had his motor cycle pinched at practically the same time.

The Motor Registry had cooperated and come up with a long list of possible variations based on the given first four digits. So far, this had resulted in a lot of time-consuming and abortive checks around the city and suburbs. By a process of elimination, the computer had now indexed the registration number of one A. Steinbeck of this address, with the significant information that the Steinbeck car was, indeed, a white Volvo.

The young constable went through the gate and closed it carefully. This wasn't exactly the type of crime-busting job he'd envisaged on joining the Force, but if his luck held out – and with the next four days off-duty – this small-time chore would have be assigned to one of the other blokes, or conveniently forgotten about altogether.

In the house, Allan waited unmoving until the policeman drove off.

It was probably nothing important. Had it been a serious matter, there would have been two of them. Still, any contact with the law was to be avoided at this crucial stage. Adam Shaw still had things to do before he was consigned to oblivion.

17

The Hoyts Entertainment Centre in George Street was bursting at the seams with kids. Lines of them were queuing for tickets to the afternoon sessions, others were mobbing the milk bar counters, always on the move even when standing in line, always talking or yelling or pushing or whooping. Some were just wandering around, stuffing their faces with hot popcorn or Baskin Robbins ice cream or lollies or all three.

Either they were all on school holiday or the truancy rate had gone through the roof. Kenneth wouldn't know. He'd lost track of everyday things like school holidays years before.

A gang of youths with hairstyles ranging from totally shaved to rainbow mops pushed their way through, swaggering and swearing. In a corner, three girls of around twelve sat on the floor, puffing away at cigarettes in a fog of their own exhalations. A wild-looking boy, dirty and skeletal, staggered out of a gents toilet obviously having a bad trip. He almost fell over a lost child standing in his path and bawling, then collapsed against one of the pillars, clinging to it and starting to bawl like a baby himself. Two ushers came and dragged him off.

It all had as much to do with the screening of motion pictures as an airline terminal or a football stadium but that didn't occur to Kenneth. He hadn't experienced a scene like this for weeks. It gave him a comforting feeling, being alone and anonymous amongst young people his own age, all doing their own thing. And there was so much noise. The huge cavern vibrated with chatter. A large bank of television screens belched screeching sound effects and fortissimo dialogue from its patchwork quilt of images. And from way over at the back came the rumble of electronic burps, a capella of liquid bleeps and bloops punctuated by the crash of a space machine or the explosion of a neutron missile.

Stopping only to change paper money for a handful of coins, Kenneth made for this sonic playground like a junkie headed for

270

the needle exchange. He waited impatiently until a machine became available. It was a 'Ninja Warriors', not one of his favourites but good enough to start on.

He didn't do well. A kid vacated the next-door machine, a '1942' and he moved to that, shoving a coin in immediately, the quicker to establish occupancy. The kid's score – 152,770 – remained on the screen to taunt him. He managed 138,220. His reactions were sluggish, his scores dismal. He persisted. The more he played, the more his wits sharpened, the more nimble his finger on the button.

And when he proved his supremacy over one machine, he moved to another, a 'Double Dragon' or a 'Crime City', sometimes having to wait a while until it was free but now not minding the wait because he used the time to familiarise himself with the tactics it used to defeat the kid in front.

Adele and her problems were gone from his mind. It was as though his stay at 'Horizons' had never happened. The games required total concentration, and their value as an escape from reality was proved once again.

He needed more coins. He took the remaining notes from his jeans and counted them, reminding himself that he must keep enough money in reserve to pay for the taxi. Taxi? Where to? Oh . . . *there*. He was wearing jeans and a T-shirt, exactly what he had worn when he became part of Adele's household. There was no need to go back. No need at all.

A boy with shaved arcs over his ears and an arm around a girl sporting a faceful of spots shoved in beside him.

'You finished?' the boy inquired.

Kenneth nodded and stepped back. The couple moved in to take his place, the girl licking a paddlepop.

Definitely a no-anchovies type, Kenneth thought with an involuntary grin. Adele. That was one of her— He booted the connection from his mind and moved off to get some more coins.

He found himself caught behind a group of oldies. One of them, a big man with a Middle European accent, was saying: 'All this shaving of the heads. The Nazis did that to the Jews and the homosexuals. The French did it to collaborators. And in the old days, the treatment for children with lice was to shave off their hair. Always, shorn heads have been a symbol of hopelessness, degradation or disease. Do you think that by adopting this ugliness, the young people of today are trying to tell us something?'

Kenneth realised the group wasn't moving. They were part of an intermission crowd from one of the ground floor cinemas, sipping the last of their coffee from polystyrene beakers. He sidled around them.

And froze.

With the passing of time into late afternoon, the crowd had got older. But they still kept on the move and as he pushed his way around the coffee-drinking group a clear path was made before him in way that reminded him of a long ago Bible class about the parting of the Red Sea. For an instant, it was just like that before people backed or stepped into the briefly vacant space.

But in that instant, he had caught sight of The Man. Right at the end of the undulating human tunnel, he was facing the other direction, but turning around as if looking for someone. Kenneth?

It wasn't The Man as Kenneth remembered him, and yet in some strange way it was. The dark, glossy hair and the moustache weren't familiar, but there was something about the body and a resemblance in the profile which caused him to stop in his tracks. His confidence fled, the feelings of security dragging behind it like the entrails of a wounded animal.

A bell rang stridently. He backed and turned. He felt trapped and he gulped convulsively. Whether it was The Man or it wasn't, he sensed danger. He had to get away.

The Middle European man and his companions were moving towards the entrance to Cinema One. Other patrons were also converging on the doors. A solitary usher stood waiting to be shown their ticket halves.

The bell stopped. Kenneth allowed himself to be moved forward by the gentle flow of adults. He kept to the side away from the usher. Shuffling along, he aligned himself beside the group who were still discussing modern youth, sheltered from behind a formidably well-upholstered couple.

He slid inside with such ease, he could have been oiled.

The lights in the cinema were already dimming. He climbed the steps to the very back row and settled down in the middle of it. There was nobody up there and he was in a good position to see if The Man had followed him. People were still coming in, but most of them were returning to seats in the front and middle sections of the small, steeply raked auditorium. As the lights dimmed further, it became more difficult for Kenneth to see their faces. However, nobody climbed to the very back rows except a boy and girl who were more interested in themselves than their surroundings. They took seats two rows down from Kenneth and immediately began to kiss one another with a devouring passion.

Kenneth relaxed. He felt reasonably safe. He'd had a scare, but he'd reacted sensibly and with speed. Fast action for self-survival was nothing new to him. But the nebulous cause of his evasive behaviour still puzzled him. The man he had caught sight of in the foyer was, on reflection, very different to The Man. Different appearance, different colouring. Was he being paranoid or had, in fact, some sixth sense triggered danger signals?

Kenneth sat down lower in his seat and shut conjecture from his mind. He was on his own, he was in the dark, there was nobody to hassle him and he was about to see a show for free. Things could be a whole lot worse.

It wasn't all perfect. The feature started and it didn't take him more than a few minutes to realise it wasn't his kind of movie. All talk and no action. Boring. However, this place was his sanctuary and he wasn't about to leave it so soon. He forced himself to concentrate on the screen with the result that he nodded off to sleep and snoozed sporadically for most of the movie's length.

When he woke up, his neck had a crick in it and his legs were cramped from being pushed against the back of the seat in front.

He looked around.

The couple in front were still trying to eat one another and there were no newcomers to the rows in his vicinity. Up on the screen, the characters were still ear-bashing one another. It appeared they were all against this rich old bird who'd ruined their lives by her interference. Kenneth felt they deserved it for being so boring.

He turned sideways and arched his back. He stretched out his legs, flexed his arms and yawned. When he glanced at the screen again, the old bird was having her say.

'You don't know what it's like being a woman on her own,' she sobbed, tears spilling down her raddled cheeks. 'You can't imagine how it feels, getting old with no son or daughter, no family. There's just this terrible emptiness. Nothing . . . nobody.'

He sat up and took notice. The old bird had become Adele and it was as though Adele was saying the words. It hit him forcibly how much they applied to her situation and had provided the motivation for her kindness to him and for the gratitude she expressed when he'd done something for her.

He shifted his body around uneasily in the seat with a vague feeling of guilt. He'd been hard and ungrateful even to think of leaving her with no one. She needed him, as he needed her. Who cared what she'd done in the past? What did it matter if she'd told him lies to bump herself up a bit? There were worse things. Nobody was perfect. And he was the *last* person to be finding fault with other people.

Suddenly, he had a tremendous longing to be back with her. The feeling overwhelmed him with its urgency. He got up and left the cinema. Emerging into the foyer, he kept close to the wall, making for the main entrance, his eyes automatically darting around for signs of danger.

Darkness had come with early evening, along with a marked deterioration in the weather. Rain was drizzling down and he was momentarily dazzled by the bright lights of George Street, reflected garishly in the gleaming pavements. He was reminded of the night The Man had come to Kings Cross to get him, and it intensified his eagerness to return home to Adele.

Taxis were in short supply because of the rain, and there were a number of people huddled under umbrellas at the kerb outside the cinema complex. It took only minutes for his impatience to get the better of him. He jumped his turn and nimbly leapt into a cab while the next in line were busy shaking down their umbrella.

'You're in a bleedin' hurry, son,' the driver said with a grin. He was an elderly type, not far from retirement by the grey and weary look of him, and he probably had grandchildren Kenneth's age.

'Just heard me grandad's crook,' Kenneth replied, playing along with the image. He gave the address and sure enough, inspired by a certain empathy with this concerned grandchild, the driver had him at the gates of 'Horizons' in twenty minutes.

Kenneth paid him and jogged up the drive. Through the mist of rain he could see several lights on in the house.

She was home.

He ran across the terrace eagerly.

'Adele?' he shouted in the foyer, brushing the rain off himself.

He found her in the drawing room, huddled in one of the large armchairs with the pent-up energy of a cornered animal about to spring. Her hand clutched the inevitable glass of vodka like a claw, the whiteness of the knuckles gleaming in the lamplight. Her eyesockets were black pits, her mouth hard with anger.

'I needed you, you little prick,' she growled at him. 'I needed you desperately. Where the hell have you been?'

18

Anders Solvig had a thatch of blond hair and a clipped moustache of a darker, sandier hue which skirted the corners of his mouth and became a perfectly shaped van Dyke beard. His parents were Scandinavian migrants who had brought him from Europe to Australia as a child in the 1960s. They were now dead. Anders, who possessed a keen talent for business, was now contemplating a completely fresh start. He had a plane ticket to Darwin, but Darwin would not provide the drastic change of scene he was looking for. He regarded the place as merely a stepping stone. His sights were set on South-East Asia, Indonesia perhaps, where the turmoil of unrest would make it comparatively easy for a man with his superior capabilities and financial means, a man of charming ruthlessness and no scruples, to gain a foothold.

Anders Solvig had no passport as yet. Perfectly formed and with an identity all his own, he was still wandering around the back roads and alleyways of Allan Steinbeck's imagination. But when he emerged, Darwin would be a most suitable place for him to establish tangible evidence of his existence. The flow of Asian refugees and illegal immigrants into the top end of Australia by sea and air had nourished, so he had heard, a thriving cottage industry there in forged passports and faked identification papers.

Allan smiled to himself at the prospect. He was sitting in a comfortable armchair in the foyer of the television station where Sharon was employed. The security guard at the barrier had waved him in, having received word from Sharon that she was expecting a guest for tonight's network anniversary party. Now, Allan was waiting for her to put in an appearance. His smile came from the satisfaction of knowing that everything was in place. His plans were meticulously in order.

The blond wig he had bought in the city earlier in the day would cover Adam Shaw's dark brown hair. Off would come the moustache, to be replaced by a shorter one and a beard in Allan's own natural colouring. The stubble of the first few days would be quite in keeping with Darwin's informality, and the new lightweight gear he had already packed for the tropical climate would further aid his transition from dark, brooding city-bred Adam Shaw to sunburned Nordic type, Anders Solvig.

Allan marvelled again at this gift he had to transform himself and concluded that it must have been developing in him over the quiet years. He had quickly grown to treasure this moving on, each new character connected to its predecessor only by an umbilical cord of initials which, for some reason, he was reluctant to abandon. The bridge he crossed from one to another was becoming easier to negotiate each time he approached it. The procedures were growing more routine and familiar, the safeguards merely a matter of formula.

He had achieved so much that day. The investments bought with Joan's money had been cashed in earlier, at the same time as he had milked their joint bank accounts. Today there had been purchases to make, a plane ticket to buy. The only time he had diverged from his program was when he felt impelled to go into the cinema complex. The pavement, the steps and the foyer inside had been crowded with young people. The thought had come to him out of the blue. What if *he* were there, the boy he was searching for? It had been a whim, an indulgence at best, and of course he had not seen the boy.

He shrugged to himself. Such coincidences didn't happen, just as on a larger scale a life based on chance would not amount to much. It was all a matter of certainty. There had to be goals. And goals were attained by the skilled manipulation of events and people according to the ritual of carefully made plans. He had always worked hard in terms of study, long hours and dedication. And all that it had got him was the kind of contempt dished out by Doris Lytton-Scott and the people at Horne-Maynard's. There was more to it, he had discovered. There had to be an uncompromising intensity, an ability to transcend morality and a freer use of the power to dispose of anyone who got in his way.

Anders Solvig would be good at all that, even better than Adam Shaw. And there would be others. A whole dynasty of creations, growing ever more efficient.

Allan stood up, smiling as Sharon appeared from a corridor and approached him. She was wearing a loose, flowing gown threaded with silver, ready for the party. There were others in the foyer, guests coming in from outside and mingling with friends on the staff who were waiting to welcome them. He heard greetings exchanged and little cries of pleasure. He took Sharon in his arms and kissed her as if they were alone and in love.

19

'What's happened? What's the matter with you?'

Kenneth stood there panting, conscious of the rainwater trickling from his hair down the back of his neck.

Adele drank unsteadily, spilling some of the liquor down her chin. She was still huddled tensely in the chair as if an attack of cramp were drawing her into herself.

'Happened? I'll tell you what happened. That son of a bitch O'Callaghan cheated on me. He never intended for me to make a record. He just spent my money on backings and expenses for somebody else!'

'Huh?'

'He didn't expect me today. I – I walked in and . . .' Her voice began to tremble. She took another drink and swallowed defiantly. 'He had *her* there, singing to my arrangements. My arrangements! Some old crone called Madge Lamb. She's gonna make the record, not me. He said *my* voice just wasn't working out, the stinking bastard!'

'He can't do that, can he?' Kenneth was struggling to take it all in.

'No?' She struggled up and stood in front of him, head jutting out, a tightly wound spring of hostility. 'Well he sure as hell's having a damned good try!' And then she swung around and marched over to refill her glass.

'You can dob him in,' Kenneth said, floundering for some way to placate her. 'You can tell the cops.'

'Yeah. I could call in the CIA too, for all the good it'd do me!' She slopped vodka into her glass and suddenly went limp, moaning. 'Oh dear God. I needed that record so badly.'

'What about if you sue him?'

She turned.

'*Sue* him?' Her voice was a hard screech. 'Have you any idea of the cost of litigation these days? Or the years you have to wait to get a civil action into court? And what about the humiliation? I've

277

had about as much as I can take right now, without having the whole thing plastered over the newspapers!'

'Okay then, don't do anything. Let him rip you off. But don't take it out on me!'

Kenneth had had enough. He could understand the hurt and the anger she was feeling, but he wasn't about to be the target for her invective. She'd been living on her nerves for days and now something had snapped and she was teetering between self-pity and unmanageable rage. And well on the way to being pissed out of her skull into the bargain. And for what? Some stupid record that nobody would buy anyway. Ten thousand dollars. Thrown away. He thought of the food it would buy for the kids he knew were starving up at the Cross, the kind of comfort some of them would never know. Adele and her tantrums became petty and unimportant. He turned to leave the room.

'Where are you going?' she yelled. 'Or more important, where have you been?'

He stopped and turned back to face her, slowly. He wasn't about to try and match her fury. He kept it cool and low.

'Does it matter? I mean, with all this other stuff you're going on about, does it really matter? I came back, didn't I?'

'Probably to see what *else* you can steal,' she said, weaving across the room, the glass to her lips.

'Steal?'

She pounced.

'Don't think I'm so upset I haven't seen how much money is gone from the kitchen. In your own two-bit way, you're as much a crook as O'Callaghan!'

'Me? I've never taken anything from here except what you're just talking about. And I reckoned I'd earned some pocket money for all the jobs I've done.'

Now he was as angry as she was. He'd tried to be scrupulous in the way he behaved and all he was getting was accusations. 'What does it matter to you, anyway? You throw away ten thousand bucks, then give me heaps for taking a few stinking dollars. Take it out of that cheque you banked for me. Fifty today for playing video games, fifteen yesterday for taxis.'

'Taxis? Yesterday?' She was like a retriever, nosing her way along the trail of something she automatically assumed was suspect. 'You never told me you went out yesterday. Where did you go? And for what?'

'For the truth!' he yelled at her. 'To get away from your lies and find some reality!'

'Lies?' In an instant she had gone quiet. Still.

'You didn't do any singing for Kelly Green,' he sneered. 'You were her maid. A fucking servant!'

'Where did you hear this? Who told you—?'

'What does it matter? It's true, isn't it? And you call *me* a thief? What about the ring you pinched from her?'

'It was that bitch from television, wasn't it? She's been filling your mind with this poison. Why does she want to turn you against me? I've done nothing to her.'

'Never mind that. It's true, isn't it?'

Adele moved this way and that way as if trying to find a way out of her own personal maze. Then she stood still, facing him. When she spoke, her voice was deceptively level. Kenneth stared at her unwaveringly, determined not to be conned.

'It's partly true. What you heard. It's not something I'm proud of, but it didn't happen the way it seems.' She paused, going back in time.

'I ghosted Kelly's singing, like I told you. And we became friends.'

She smiled.

'It was like our own little secret society with just two members. Us, and the voice we shared. Then she got restless, sick and tired of the empty musicals they kept pushing her into, even though musicals were going out of style. She wanted to do what Munroe was doing, get into straight comedy and drama, but they wouldn't hear of it. So she went on suspension, refused to work. That affected me, too, so she took me into her home. I wasn't a maid like they said. I was more a secretary-companion. I did everything for her and was glad to, just to tide myself over the bad times.'

Her tone soured. 'Then she met Moody, which is what everybody called Mahmoud, the Arab Prince. He was just a filthy-rich jet-set playboy, but he was handsome and charming and he swept Kelly right off her feet just at a time when she felt she wanted out from Hollywood. I told her she was wasting herself on him, throwing away everything she'd worked to achieve. She wouldn't listen. She told me she was determined to marry him and go off to live in some Godforsaken palace in the middle of a desert.'

Adele was losing the calm she'd had at the beginning of her story. She began to move around feverishly.

'I told her to look at Rita Hayworth. That gal did the same – married Aly Khan, tried to resume her career when they divorced, but was never the same again. Kelly didn't hear a word I was saying. It was . . . it was like she was bewitched. I got so angry at the waste, I took the ring. It was a stupid thing to do, but I did it because I was in a fury. To get back at me, she reported it to the cops. Then I gave it back and we made up and she dropped the charges.'

Her voice dropped and she stopped moving.

'Thank God we made up when we did. Just one week later, they were flying to Arizona in his private jet to meet Kelly's folks and crashed into a mountain. They were both killed.'

Kenneth saw the glint of tears in her eyes, but the intensity of the flood of words and information bewildered him. He just stood and stared, damp and starting to shiver, wondering why the hell it should matter anyhow.

The lack of response from him roused Adele from her sad reverie. Blinking back tears, she weaved around him, drunkenly taunting.

'Well? Satisfied?'

'Oh, forget it.'

He turned and began to walk out. Adele lurched quickly and put herself between him and the way to the foyer. She waved her arms, vodka slopping everywhere.

'Okay, okay, you don't have to believe any of it if you don't want to. So I *wasn't* her voice, just a little groupie who worked for her. And on the side, a nothing piano bar singer, working my way around the traps. Got stranded in Acapulco on a gig that fell through and met Zampini. There. Like that version better? Huh?'

She swayed, eyes popping, awaiting his reaction and when none came it irritated her even more.

'Well? Do I comply more with *Miss Pettifer's* low opinion of me now? Does that cut me down to size?'

Kenneth was not capable of a reply. He was more confused than ever. He felt cold and clammy and he started to shiver. The physical took over from the tangle in his mind. He moved forward, circling to avoid touching her. He left her standing there and went upstairs.

20

'There are three essentials for a party in the television industry,'
Sharon told Allan as they approached the big double doors with
'Studio A' painted across them. 'The venue has to be enormous to
cope with all the inflated egos. The music must be loud enough to
drown out the insincerity. And the lighting has to be tricksy, to
mask the desperation that otherwise might show in the faces.'

They pushed through the double doors and immediately Allan
saw that the three essentials were in evidence. He was conscious
of the immensity of the studio, even though 'flats' – pieces of
scenery from old sets – had been used to close in the party area.
The music *was* loud, and fought against an amplified soundtrack
coming from several large monitor screens showing retrospective
video clips. The lighting was subdued, but its intimacy was continually pierced by laser-like flashes and the dappled reflections of a
rotating mirror ball suspended in the cavernous void above.

They were faced with a wall of people, all brandishing glasses
and all talking at once. The frenzied chatter threatened even to
overpower the music in terms of decibels and when Sharon spoke
again she had to raise her voice considerably to be heard.

'You'll see them all tonight. Not just who's who but who's
through. That's the nature of the beast, unfortunately. You'll notice
a majority of young people. They're technical and floor crew,
mostly. Maturity and experience don't count for much any more.
Young people come cheaper, and they're prepared to work long
hours and inconvenient shifts.'

'You seem very cynical about this business you're in,' Allan
observed.

Sharon shrugged and pointed to the nearest monitor screen
featuring a segment from a nineteen-seventies quiz show. The com-
pere had sideburns down to his chin, and was wearing a psychedelic
shirt and flared pants. A group of people standing nearby had
interrupted their conversation and were hooting derisively at him.

'See what I mean? One day top of the ratings, next day the pits. They could be laughing at me like that in a few years.'

Allan put his arm around her shoulders. 'Somehow, I don't think they will be.' He paused, the more to enjoy his private little joke, then said: 'How long do we have to put up with this, anyway?'

Sharon looked at him. 'Half an hour at most. Then we split. All right?'

That was what he wanted to hear. She had taken him upstairs before coming in here, to show him the *Upfront* offices. She had even pointed out her desk. She had shown him their viewing room, comfortably furnished with several armchairs and a monitor system, and the cutting room where their film was edited. On the way down to Studio A she had indicated several other production offices, but Allan was more occupied committing their route to memory, as was his practice in unfamiliar places. There had been nothing that resembled an address book on her desk. Possibly it could be in one of the drawers. In any event, if they were not staying he would have no opportunity to go back up there and look. He fingered the slim smooth shell of the cut-throat razor in his pocket. If they were not staying, a look at an address book would not be necessary, anyway.

Several people came up to Sharon, kissed the air around her face and shrieked platitudes. She introduced Allan as 'my fellah, Adam' and looped her arm through his possessively. They all smiled brightly, but their eyes were coldly analytical, particularly those of the women. He could imagine the gossip. 'Who's *he*?' 'Where did she find *him*?' But he didn't mind being seen with Sharon. Adam Shaw was destined for oblivion soon, and if it came to the point of asking, these people would merely be describing someone who didn't exist. A wraith.

Despite the crowds, obtaining a drink was easy. Long trestle tables were spaced at regular intervals, set with glasses and staffed by efficient waiters who were offering red and white wine and beer. Further along, three of the tables had been arranged into a U-shape and guests were already helping themselves to hot roast meats carved on the bone, salads and French bread.

Having armed themselves with glasses of white wine, Sharon and Allan decided to give the food a miss. They moved on, edging through the other guests. More people greeted Sharon as they passed, but Allan became aware that she seemed to be on the lookout for someone in particular.

Her grip on his arm tightened. She pulled him off in another direction, and moments later they were face to face with a dark, thickset man whom Sharon introduced as Jim Abrahams, her chief. Allan shook hands and felt the man's eyes upon him. He knew he was being summed up, but not in the cold analytical fashion he'd experienced previously. Jim Abrahams was friendly, perhaps a little too polite, and his scrutiny was filled with interest. A rival for Sharon's affections, perhaps? Yes – but out to show he wasn't exactly bereft of female company. Rather obviously, Allan thought, Jim put his arm around an attractive Chinese girl standing next to him and introduced her as Margaret Fong, a co-worker on *Upfront*.

Sharon seemed to blossom all of a sudden, like a flower exposed to the sun. She became more animated, laughed a lot, clutched at Allan's arm tightly and lost no opportunity to make eye contact with him. Obviously, she was out to prove something, too. What children they were, she and this Jim Abrahams, changing partners and then making out they didn't care.

Already Allan was bored. The noise was getting to him and the conversation was uninteresting. Meanwhile, precious time was being wasted. His attention wandered and he found himself watching a newsreel of some boat people, refugees from Cambodia, on the nearest monitor screen.

Ever attentive, Sharon followed his gaze. 'Isn't that terrible?' she commented.

Jim and Margaret turned their heads to watch, too.

'It's a miracle they ever got here,' Jim said. 'Look at that tub, it's so low in the water. If you know anything about boats—'

'I'm afraid I don't,' Allan said. Another boring subject was rearing its head and he didn't want to get involved.

'That boat reminds me of a woman I know,' Sharon said, winking at Jim and Margaret, then clutching Allan closer and explaining to him: 'Actually, she's more of a tramp steamer with a cargo of worn-out fantasies.'

Allan put his mouth close to her ear. 'And does she have a young stowaway in one of her lifeboats?'

Sharon exaggerated her amazement. 'How perceptive of you, darling!'

At that moment, a rather ugly, plumpish girl wearing too much make-up and a lot of plastic beads elbowed her way in and grabbed Sharon by the arm.

'Pickie-time, sweetie,' she drawled. 'Pickies for publicity. Come with me, it'll only take a minute.'

'Oh Jackie,' Sharon protested, 'I don't want to be in the Sunday papers with my mouth open amongst all those facelifts and fashion failures!'

Jim and Margaret laughed. Jackie shook her head and tightened her grip.

'No – this is for *TV Week*! Can't say no to *TV Week*, darling, can we? Just one shot, I promise, with Grant Olsen and that gorgeous spunk, Pietro Scali.'

Sharon threw a helpless glance at Allan. 'I'll be right back,' she managed, before she was pulled away into the crowd.

Margaret looked at Jim. 'I suppose she meant Adele Ventura,' she said.

'Who?' Allan inquired with a smile.

'The tramp steamer she was talking about.'

'Oh.'

Allan experienced a sudden jab of excitement. Adele Ventura. Now he even had a name to go on. Everything was coming together, just as it should.

When his mind clicked back, Jim had gone to get more drinks. The Chinese girl had turned to talk to a neighbouring group of people. Allan didn't mind having a few moments alone with his thoughts before Sharon returned. It gave him an opportunity to savour the joys to come.

21

The one publicity shot stipulated by Jackie expanded into four, featuring various clichéd party poses. The last one had Sharon sitting down on a fold-up chair they'd dragged in from somewhere, with Grant Olsen and Pietro Scali crouched behind her, peeping over her shoulders. As soon as they were done, the photographer and Jackie disappeared into the crowd. Grant and Pietro smiled at Sharon then moved off to rejoin their own groups.

Sharon remained seated on the chair, thankful to be off her feet for a minute or two. She leaned her head against the side of the TV monitor next to her and closed her eyes. She'd had a tough day and had worked right up until it was time to get ready for the party. Changing at the studio meant she'd had no opportunity for even a brief rest before they'd rung her from the desk to tell her that Adam had arrived.

The music stopped. She found it a welcome respite. Just a few seconds more, and then—

She heard her own voice coming from inside the cabinet. Craning her neck to look around the corner of the monitor without getting up, she saw herself on the screen. Now *that* was a photo opportunity missed. She, Grant and Pietro looking at her on the . . . no. A bit too narcissistic, perhaps. She put her head back against the side of the cabinet and closed her eyes. Trust Jim to include her street kids feature in the retrospective round-up. It had been a damned good segment, even though it had caused such dissension between them.

Enough of this malingering, she thought. She must get back to Adam.

Adam?

She opened her eyes, but although she could hear his voice, he was nowhere to be seen. And then she realised where the voice was coming from, and she quickly got up from the chair and looked at the screen and saw the boy Kenneth being picked up by the man, except that the man—

285

It couldn't be Adam. It looked nothing like him. But the man on the screen had Adam's voice. She dropped to her knees, sticking a hand over one ear to block out the party noises, and pressed the other ear up against the monitor. She heard the man's last few persuasively suggestive words to Kenneth, and then there was a cut in the taped collage and a cute girl singer with ribbons in her hair who had since grown up to be an international superstar was doing a number on a 1960s teenage pop show.

Sharon sagged back on her heels and stared at the girl on the screen but not seeing her, perplexed at what she had heard and oblivious to the people around her.

The amplified music started up again and heavy metal rock began formidably to do battle with the voices of the guests.

Sharon pushed herself up, but one of her heels caught in the hem of her dress and caused her to overbalance on to the floor. It was an embarrassing and ungainly sprawl, and she struggled to free her heel which was pulling at her dress and stopping her from getting to her feet. Just then, a self-styled TV critic who had managed to stay around for years more by licking arses than by the quality of his work, paused in the act of sailing by.

'Sharon Pettifer pissed?' he proclaimed in a loud voice to his faded wife who ran a sandwich shop. 'Whatever next?' He passed on, not even attempting to help her up. But in gazing back at Sharon in a superior fashion, he collided with the chair she had vacated and tumbled over it, flat on his face.

Sharon scrambled up, taking advantage of the ensuing debacle to lose herself in the crowd. Her heart was thudding. She felt strangely light-headed and she was appalled to find she was blinking back scalding tears, though whether it was because of the vocal/visual conundrum she had been faced with or the nastiness of the TV critic she was unable to discern. All she knew was that she had to get away from the crowd, and quickly.

Keeping her head down, she pushed and edged her way through to one of the towering flats which marked the perimeter of the party. She slipped behind it and found herself in darkness. The sudden seclusion helped her get a hold on herself. She stood there and took several deep breaths, then dabbed at her eyes with the edge of a loose sleeve.

Adam would be waiting for her, but it had been only a matter of minutes since she left him. There was something she must do. She started to walk, hurriedly following the studio wall, and eventually came to a metal staircase which led to the control room with its big glass window.

She ran up the stairs and pushed open the door at the top. There was just one person in there. She'd seen him around the studio a lot. Ben? Ken? Oh God, names were so important, especially when you needed to use people. He was a big, hulking guy. Good-natured. Always ready for a joke . . . Len! That was it. Len.

'Just popped up to say g'day, Len,' she began matily. 'You're doing a fantastic job.'

'Aw, thanks Sharon.' He felt himself flush with pleasure. He'd heard she was an uptight, standoffish cow but here she was, taking the trouble to be friendly and even remembering his name.

'This compilation tape is especially good,' she continued, nodding at the screens above the control panel.

'Yair, well I didn't have anythink to do with that,' he admitted. 'I'm just playing it.'

'I'd love to have another look at it. In fact, several of us would,' she said, giving the impression that a select group were going to adjourn for a private viewing. 'How long before it finishes?'

'Right after Olivia's number here,' he replied, indicating the pretty young singer on the monitors, 'but I gotta tell you the next one – the blooper tape with everybody's mistakes on it – is much better. Gawd, the filthy fuckin' language, you wouldn't believe it!'

'Perhaps we'll get to that one later, Len. Oh look – it's finished.'

He took the videotape out of the machine and replaced it with the blooper tape. He moved towards another machine.

'What are you doing?' she asked.

'Gonna rewind it for you,' he answered.

'Oh don't bother.' She darted forward and took it from him together with its case. She didn't want it rewound to the beginning, just to the next to the last item. It would be quicker if she did that herself.

'Thanks a lot, Len.'

At the bottom of the stairs, hugging the tape to her body, she encountered a waiter heaving a carton of wines towards the party.

'Listen,' she said authoritatively. 'I'm Sharon Pettifer of *Upfront*. I want you to take one of those bottles up there to the guy in the control room – with a glass of course – as soon as you can. Okay?'

The waiter recognised her and got the message.

She hurried on, following the towering walls of Studio A until she saw an exit sign. On the other side of the flats, the party was in full swing as if nothing had happened. But something had happened to Sharon. She couldn't fully comprehend just what, but she had to find out.

She pushed the exit door open and went through, finding herself in a scene dock where pieces of sets and a vast assortment of furniture were stored. Studio A was where the network's phenomenally-successful soap opera was done, so Sharon had to edge her way through all the unsightly icons of suburbia as envisaged by campy set decorators whose depiction of the real world was governed by minuscule budgets and their own contempt. She stumbled around leatherette lounge suites in garish colours, avoided woodgrain veneer coffee tables in odd shapes, and passed a myriad hymns to bad taste in the form of laminex dining settings, quilted vinyl cocktail bars, bedroom suites inspired by galleons and gondolas, piles of lurid carpets and nasty light fittings, cheap and mass-produced like the scripts and the players.

At the other end, she emerged into a corridor she recognised and ran up a flight of stairs around the corner from Wardrobe. She paused for a moment at the top, out of breath, then she set off again, her feet sinking into thick carpeting as she passed suites occupied by the network's executives.

On and on she hurried, her mind crowded with uncertainty. What she suspected was impossible. And yet if it were true, the implications were monstrous. She was a trained observer, but her vision had been glazed by desire. That was one explanation. Another was that she was completely wrong, and the similarity in voices was nothing but a technical distortion. Either way, she had to know.

The carpeting gave way to vinyl tiles and she was back in familiar territory. Just a little further along was the *Upfront* production unit's offices.

She had seen no one. The entire floor had been deserted in favour of the party, and this was to her advantage. She couldn't face anyone, and certainly she couldn't go back and face Adam, not until she had solved this puzzle.

As she reached the viewing room she looked over her shoulder, back along the corridor. It was empty. She went inside the room, closed the door carefully behind her and switched on one of the table lamps. She crossed to the monitor equipment and switched on the viewing system. The screen stirred with an expectant luminosity as she took the videotape out of its case and slid it into the deck. She picked up the remote control and pressed 'Rewind'. The fast backtracking images faded up on the screen and she purposely let the street kids excerpt rush by. She stopped the tape during the preceding clip, an ancient black and white panel game, and let it begin to run forward at normal speed.

Her mouth was unbearably dry. Knowing she had time to spare, she went over to a cupboard where the *Upfront* staff kept a secret stash of liquor to help them relax after particularly stressful times. She found some scotch and some brandy. She poured some of the brandy into a glass and drank a little. The liquor burned her throat as it went down, but it helped. She turned quickly as she heard herself speaking: 'At first, this seems like a glittering road to adventure. Too late, kids find it's a one-way street with no going back . . .'

She rushed over and turned up the sound. And stood back, waiting. And then it came up, the shot of the boy and the man in front of the El Alamein fountain. She heard the man's voice and she listened closely, concentrating with an intensity that was almost painful.

It was Adam's voice, there was no doubt in her mind. She ran the section back and replayed it. No doubt at all. Again, she replayed the same section, then freezed frame at the point where the slowly zooming camera had the two faces in close-up. She squatted down, near to the screen.

It was incredible. The resemblance was suddenly so easy to spot. Take away Adam's dark colouring and the moustache and you had the same eyes, the same cheekbones, the same nose, the same mouth.

Sharon got to her feet slowly and turned from the frozen faces on the screen. She flopped down in an armchair.

She couldn't blame herself for not spotting the resemblance before. She hadn't seen this tape for weeks, and even then this man had been just another fleeting image amongst many. There had been no reason, ever, for her to connect him to Adam Shaw . . . *her* Adam. Or were the indications there and she'd missed them? She remembered the insistent drive with which he approached their relationship, as if it were a journey with a destination to be reached in a hurry. She had assumed that destination was bed, but even after they'd started sleeping together his insistence had continued . . . an insistence on her telling him about Kenneth. Yes. She recalled now how the subject had kept coming back in conversation. . .

Behind her, the door opened noiselessly.

Sharon squeezed her eyes shut and pressed a finger and thumb against the lids. The problem was, what to do now? She could go to the police, but what had Adam done? Charming a girl into bed wasn't a crime. And whatever his plans for Kenneth when he tracked the boy down, criminal intent had to be proved. He wanted to find the boy, of that much she was certain. And for that reason he had courted her. No. *Conned* her. She pressed against her eyelids with greater force and cringed with humiliation. What a fool she'd been. What an easy mark.

Out of nowhere Donna, the girl in the squat, came to mind. Donna, the girl who'd been murdered for no apparent reason, the girl who had shared her squalid shelter with Kenneth and might therefore be assumed to know where he was hiding out. Sharon herself had even suggested this as a motive, but no one had listened.

Donna, another easy mark.

Sharon shivered and opened her eyes. And then every nerve in her body jumped as the freeze-frame timer expired and the images jerked back to life. The crackle of the soundtrack, magnified by the turned-up volume control, sounded like a raging forest fire after the long silence, and Adam's voice boomed out its vile suggestions to Kenneth in yet another intolerable replay.

She rose swiftly and went to turn off the equipment. The screen went dark, the tape clicked to a halt and there was silence except for the screams of conjecture in her head.

She straightened up, looking at the wall, trying to make some sense out of the situation.

Jim. She had to go downstairs, back to the party, find Jim and tell him what she'd found out. He was safe, secure. Dependable. He'd know what to do. He hadn't wanted to listen to her on this subject before, but now he'd have to. She wouldn't tell him about the sex, no one would ever know about that. Her story would be that she suspected Adam Shaw from the beginning and had led him on.

She began to turn, but before she could complete the movement a hand was clapped over her mouth and she was pulled back with enormous force, back against someone who had her pinned by another arm around her waist.

'It's always fun catching up on old movies, isn't it?' Adam's voice breathed in her ear. 'But there's a time and place for everything.'

She tried to struggle, recalling the special she'd hosted on defence tactics for women, full of clever little karate chops and lethal kicks to the testicles and elbow jabs and fingers thrust into eyesockets and realised she'd been so busy saying the words she hadn't absorbed any of the lessons.

He held her tighter.

'I missed you. I asked around. Then somebody joked that the last place they'd seen you was on the monitors, talking about kids at the Cross. That's when I started to get concerned.'

His grip on her began to shift.

'I'm going to remove my hand from your mouth. But I'd advise against your making any noise because there's nobody on this floor to hear you. Apart from that, you'll feel a pressure against your cheek. That'll be the blade of an old-fashioned cutthroat razor. If you make any movement at all, I'll use it in quite a new-fashioned way.'

Sharon remained stiffly against Adam's body, afraid of shifting an inch. But when his hand went from her mouth, she was unable to prevent herself from sagging forward, gasping for breath. Instantly, his forearm went under her chin, securing her by the neck. Then his other arm released her waist and she felt something pressing against her cheek, biting into the skin.

'There,' his voice came softly from behind. 'Now we can talk.'

He waited until her gasping had stopped.

'I'll be very brief. You must know what I want. The whereabouts of the boy. He's with a woman, isn't he? Adele Ventura, I believe her name is. The address, please.'

'No—' she started hoarsely, then squealed as she felt the blade slice with a twinge into the epidermal layers of her skin. Then deeper, so that it stung.

She shook her head in an attempt to distance her face from the blade, but he took it for another refusal. With a grunt of exasperation, he wielded the blade deftly across her forehead and down the other cheek. Sharon let out a whimper that was a mixture of outrage and horror. He was cutting up her face. Her face! She could feel the blood running free, forming droplets at her chin, and then it was in her eyes, blinding her. She began to wriggle in panic, the cuts on her face now smarting unbearably. Her stomach contracted and her body shuddered as waves of nausea and fear engulfed her.

Adam let the knife drop and swung her around. His fingers went around her throat, slipping greasily on the blood. He anchored his thumbs against her windpipe and pressed. Sharon's frightened eyes, shedding pinkish tears, popped out at him from a blood-streaked mask.

'You're going to tell me sooner or later, you know,' he whispered. 'Why not save yourself further pain?' And his thumbs increased the pressure on her windpipe.

He felt a gurgle of sound rising up and eased away his thumbs. Her entire head trembled in a spasm of concentration.

'Th – thirty-five . . . Boniface Road . . . Point Piper.' Every word took an effort and she could barely breathe, let alone make herself audible, but it was vital to her survival that he got the information he wanted. She swallowed painfully. 'It's . . . it's a house called "Horizons".'

'Ah, Boniface Road.' In contrast, Adam's voice was a caress. 'Yes, I was there that first night. If only I'd persisted in my search I might have saved us all a lot of trouble.'

And with that, his hands became like a vice around her throat and remained so despite her ineffectual struggles against him until she gave one last splutter and stopped breathing. He let her lifeless body slip to the floor.

22

When Kenneth reached his bedroom, he went straight through into the en suite and turned on the bath taps. Water gushed out, and by the time he'd jammed the plug in, steam was rising. He peeled off his damp clothes. He was still cold and shivering and the idea of a hot bath was appealing. Usually, he took showers but this time he needed not only to submerge himself in the warmth but the time to think that a prolonged soak would afford him.

Even as he lay back in the water, the bath so full that he was almost floating, his mind was made up. It was time for him to move on. He wasn't so thin-skinned that he couldn't stand the verbal abuse Adele had hurled at him. He'd had worse than that. But it was the fact that it *came* from Adele. The way she'd turned on him meant he could never trust her again. He'd been stupid to drop his defences in the first place. It went against everything he'd learned over the years. Never trust anyone, no matter what. Whatever you do, do it for yourself. Then you've only yourself to blame and if you want to take it out on yourself then you can. Block out or black out, it's your own choice.

She'd made such a big deal about caring for him and being his friend. And all it took for her to turn with fangs bared was a bit of personal strife that she'd brought on herself and which had nothing to do with him.

Give up on adults. That's what every street kid he'd ever met had said. Give up on them because they're the ones that cause all the problems, everything from lowering your self esteem to wars. He'd been slack to forget that. The easy living hadn't been hard to take, but the cost had been having to swallow a lot of lies, keeping quiet when a true friendship meant being able to speak your mind, and being dumb enough to believe it might go on long enough for there to be a future.

Despite the relaxing qualities of the warm water, he felt a familiar dull ache spreading downwards from his chest. He remembered it from a few other times. It was his feelings dying. Given a day or two, there'd be nothing. Just the numbness that would make it all bearable.

He slid down under the water, squeezing his eyes shut tightly and holding his breath. This would be a good place to stay forever. It was warm and dark and secret. If only he didn't have to breathe. He held his breath for as long as he could, then broke the surface, gasping and spluttering.

He settled back again, resting the back of his head against the rim of the bathtub. Leaving somewhere was usually easy. Where to go was the problem. Even if you went thousands and thousands of miles, like to Perth, you wouldn't really be getting away from everything. He'd heard that even in Perth, more kids committed suicide than died in car accidents. And what was the national rate somebody had been spouting about on TV? One in seven Australian kids did themselves in. A rate that had doubled over the past twenty years.

Something had to be wrong, but figures were bullshit, anyway. There was only one important statistic that counted and that was yourself. Even then, you always ended up on somebody's list. Best dressed. Unemployed. Dead.

He knew there was only one place for him to go. The Cross. Another bit of human wreckage dumped back on the garbage tip after a failed attempt at recycling.

Typical.

They spent millions working out how to recycle paper and glass bottles and drink cans, but if you were a person there wasn't much hope of a fresh start. He pondered on it, then decided that as far as he was concerned, maybe the recycling wouldn't be a *complete* failure if he did something about it. Okay, so he'd have to go back to the Cross, but he didn't have to stay there forever. Maybe this time, he could work things more to his advantage. He'd already sidestepped a few of the lethal options like doing drugs till they killed him, not having safe sex and doing so many break and enters that on the law of averages he'd be bound to get caught. He'd avoided these pitfalls and he'd starved at times, but it had been worth it.

Even these last few weeks had been worth it, now he came to think about it, because he realised that something of Adele's feisty attitude to life had rubbed off on him. He'd sunk into the bathwater with thoughts of oblivion but he'd come up to the surface again, so maybe that was an omen.

He smacked a hand violently on to the surface of the water and sent splashes in all directions. Some of the water hit his face and he was almost successful in convincing himself that the smarting in his eyes was caused by the suds. The numbness was slow in coming. He needed it, he needed it badly, because he wasn't adjusted yet to the new scene, no matter how optimistically he tried to look at it. The numbness was important. It enabled you to break away without looking back, and it was the only means of getting from day to day . . .

He heard the door to his bedroom open and then close very quietly.

Shit. And he hadn't even thought to lock the bathroom door.

'Hang on,' he shouted, and stood up in the water. He didn't want her coming in here. He climbed out of the bath and slopped over the floor. He'd forgotten to place a towel close enough to grab and his angry splash at the water had left pools on the tiles.

He pulled one of the big, crispy towels off the rack by the door and mopped at his body.

She hadn't bothered to answer him. Or didn't want to. Or was too drunk to.

He wrapped the towel around his middle.

When he opened the bathroom door, the light shafted across the darkness of the bedroom.

'Adele?' he said, peering into the shadows. 'Don't play games.'

23

Allan squatted and wiped his hands on the skirt of Sharon's dress, on one of the few patches which wasn't already disfigured by splotches of blood. Then he went over to the intercom telephone in the viewing room, consulted the dialling code and rang down to Reception. When the girl answered, he asked her to order him a taxi and gave her the name 'Stratton'. Arnold Stratton might one day succeed Anders Solvig, if it became necessary.

He took the videotape out of the machine, put it in its case and without a final glance at Sharon's body, he went out into the corridor, closing the door of the viewing room behind him.

On the way down, he found a washroom where he rinsed his hands. Then he rinsed the blade of the razor, wiped it carefully, folded it back into its case and put it into his pocket. Sharon's blood had flowed freely from her face in a spectacular fashion, but his clothes had escaped all of it, except for a nasty stain on the sleeve of the hand which held the razor. He took his jacket off and sponged the sleeve with wet paper towels as best he could, then used dry paper towels to remove the excess moisture from the material. He put the paper towels down one of the toilets and flushed them away. He put his jacket on again and found he could hide the damp part by positioning his arm against his body.

Somebody had discarded a folded newspaper in one of the bins. He took it out and refolded it around the videotape. He made sure there were no pink stains on the washbasin, then left.

The receptionist in the foyer was giggling with two drunken party guests who had brought her a glass of wine and a chunk of bread with a slice of roast beef on it. None of them paid any attention to Allan as he passed by. He crossed directly to the main entrance and as he passed through the doors he was just in time to see the barrier arm at the security gate being lifted to admit a taxi. He walked out to meet it, identified himself as 'Stratton' and told the driver he wanted to go to Central Railway Station.

It was a nuisance having to rely on taxis but in another way there were advantages, such as using them to lay false trails. He was glad he'd sold the Volvo to a dealer up the Parramatta Road. He had a feeling, from the way the young policeman had looked into the empty garage, that the Volvo was the reason for his visit. The cash from the sale had been added to the rest of his funds, all neatly packed under Anders Solvig's new clothes in one of his suitcases.

At Central, he paid the driver and walked off towards the station, dropping the folded newspaper with the videotape inside it into the first garbage bin he passed. He glanced back and saw the taxi he'd vacated was already moving off with another fare. He walked back to the rank, got into another taxi and told the driver to take him to Point Piper.

He settled in the back seat and felt a warm glow of satisfaction as the taxi negotiated the city traffic and began to nose its way along Oxford Street. Sharon had been so quick to divulge the boy's whereabouts he wondered whether he shouldn't have just bailed her up and threatened her right at the beginning. But at that stage it had seemed impractical. His approach to her seemed to warrant a certain finesse, and he had enjoyed being the manipulator in the subtle game of cat-and-mouse. Besides, the delay had enabled him to finalise all the preparations for his departure and regeneration in a faraway place.

He had the driver drop him on the main road and walked the rest of the way to Boniface Road. Everything was proceeding according to plan. The rain of the early evening had passed over. The night sky was clear and for the second night in succession an incandescent full moon reigned, a heavenly clone of its daytime partner.

He began counting the numbers as he walked along the deserted road, and it was only when he saw the gates of Number 35 that he realised luck was against him. He stopped, desolated and remembered the blinding lights as he walked up the drive of this house that first, fateful evening. Then he moved against a tree and stood in the shadow of its boughs looking at the gates. Somehow, in his mood of optimism, it had never occurred to him that Number 35 would be this particular house. It appeared to be the most accessible in the street and yet of the ones he had reconnoitred the evening he had pursued the boy, only this one had such a demonstratively showy external security system. He had no way of knowing then as now, if the security system was in operation and without that knowledge he could not risk entering the property. All the exhilaration he had felt gave way to deadening frustration. He had progressed so far, meticulously covering every eventuality, only to be confronted by this seemingly insurmountable obstacle. To give the boy and his protector prior warning was out of the question. He couldn't risk going through those gates.

He leaned back against the tree and attempted to clear his mind. There must be an answer.

24

Adele moved out of the shadows by the door, into the shaft of light coming from the bathroom. She switched on the bedside lamp and stood there, looking at him.

The first thing Kenneth noticed was that she hadn't a glass in her hand. And in the interim she appeared to have sobered up a little. She was certainly striving for more control of herself. Her upright stance, the stiff angle at which she was holding her chin spoke of assertiveness. Only her eyes screamed panic.

'I wondered what you were doing. You've been gone so long.'

Kenneth didn't speak. That was his defence. If he didn't say anything, she would. And every time she spoke she put herself at a disadvantage.

'I've ordered takeaway pizza. You'd better get ready to eat.'

Her voice had the take-it-or-leave-it challenge in its tone which he remembered from the very first night he came here. But now there was a tremor in it.

They stood there, facing one another, Kenneth still in the bathroom doorway wearing just the towel around his middle, Adele in the navy jump suit with fake leopard collar and belt she'd worn to the recording studio. Like her, it had a creased and crumpled look. She began to pluck at the belt with nervous fingers.

'Well?' she demanded. 'Are you going to stand there all evening? Why don't you say something?'

Kenneth cleared his throat. 'The next time I go downstairs'll be tomorrow morning. And that'll be to get out of here. For good.'

She bristled. 'Oh stop behaving like a spoiled brat!'

'If I am, it's because you've made me one,' he replied.

'Look, buster, I had a shattering experience today. The shock of finding out I'd been taken for a ride was devastating. So I don't want any more crap from you.'

'Then leave me alone.'

She glared at him, twitching, for a few moments. Then she went over to the door. Kenneth assumed with relief that she was going. Instead, she just went into the hall and brought in a drink she'd left on a side table out there, no doubt to create a good impression when she first came in. She took an enormous gulp and stood there, legs apart to keep her balanced, as if sizing up for a fist fight.

'Now listen to me, Kenneth. You get dressed. You come down-stairs. And you start being pleasant.'

'Get stuffed.'

She took another gulp. 'Okay, okay, so I may have said a few things you didn't like. Put it down to my state of mind. My God, haven't I been through enough?'

'Yeh. Until next time. Then you'd turn on me again. No way. I don't trust you any more.'

Her eyes flashed dangerously. The neat vodka was getting to her, topping her up.

'Then get the hell out of here. Go back to Kings Cross. Live the kind of life you were living there and you'll never see thirty.'

'Maybe I don't want to see thirty.'

'Tell me that when you're twenty-nine and a half! Go on – go! Why wait until tomorrow? Go right now and see if I care!'

'If that's the way you want it.' Kenneth shrugged and moved to the chest of drawers. 'I'll just be taking one shirt and one pair of jeans. What I came with.'

'Oh you needn't be so scrupulously honest all of a sudden,' she jeered. 'Take the lot. The whole damned lot!'

Kenneth turned deliberately.

'Your husband didn't, did he?'

She froze.

'What?'

'Lambert. He didn't take *anything* with him. He left his suits and his underwear . . . all his clothes. Not to mention the cigarette case you gave him.'

He saw her face turning grey, but he had to go on with it. There was something in him that made him want to get back at her, and now he couldn't stop.

He nodded his head towards the door and the bedrooms across the hall. 'His passport's in there, too. And all his credit cards. You should've got rid of them, you know. Evidence. Where'd you put him, Adele? Because he never left. He's still around here, some-where, isn't he?'

Still she didn't move or speak. Now, he was doing all the talking and it was giving him strength, paying her back for wrecking his confidence in her and spoiling everything.

'You did him in, didn't you.' It was a statement rather than a question. 'For his money.'

'I told you. He didn't have a cent. I was the one with the money.' The voice came out of her, but it was like the computerised voice of a robot.

She tossed aside her empty glass hopelessly and it hit the leg of the bedside table but miraculously it didn't break. It rolled on the carpet. She watched it, then her head jerked back to Kenneth and the chin was high again.

'I'm not ashamed of what I did. He used me and my money and then when he had what he wanted, when I'd saved this place for him and he'd regained his social status, he told me he was going to divorce me and if I didn't settle the house and an income on him he'd fake terrible evidence against my character. It wasn't his threats that got to me. It was his total rejection of me as a person, someone who'd loved him enough to help him get back where he felt he belonged.'

She walked over to the bed and wearily lowered herself down on the edge.

'He always carried his gun around. Part of his boyish charm. I used it on him and for once in my life the timing was just right. The pool excavation was all ready for the cement. And that's where I put him. They poured the cement two days later.'

There was a long silence. Kenneth turned to the drawer he'd opened and took out a pair of underpants. Adele's back was towards him, bent and shrunken like a blow-up doll with a leak. He let the towel drop and pulled on the underpants.

She heard him moving and turned her head. He took a T-shirt out of another drawer, pulled it on, then went over to the built-ins and took out a pair of jeans. He looked over at her.

'Like I said, just what I came with.'

She screwed up her face incredulously. 'You're not *still* going? I thought . . . . I thought that once you knew everything, you'd—'

'You're safe,' he interrupted. 'I won't tell on you. He treated you like shit and he got what he deserved. I'm not like him. I don't want anything from you.'

He started to pull on the jeans.

Adele got up from the bed.

'You're not leaving this house tonight,' she said resolutely. 'I won't let you.'

Kenneth, bent over with one leg in the jeans and one leg out, looked up at her. 'What're you gonna do? Shoot me too?'

'Oh you mean little bastard!' she burst out. It was as if one last spark of her old feistiness had survived and his defiance had fanned it into a flame. She marched over to the door, one hand thrust in her pocket. 'We'll see how you feel in the morning!'

She went out, pulling the door shut and immediately Kenneth heard a key turning in the lock. He finished pulling on the jeans, then threw himself on the bed. It appeared he had no choice in the matter.

25

Allan smashed a fist into the trunk of the tree which cloaked his torment in its shadows. He didn't feel a thing and therefore it provided no counterirritant to the agonies of frustration that were torturing him. He had to face the piercing certainty that the boy had triumphed again, merely by existing. First there had been the trap of the hidden camera and concealed microphone. Now there was the trap of a security system which the woman had said, he now remembered, was wired to the local Police Station. And each time the boy was there. The tempting bait to entice him towards destruction.

Sharon was gone, now the boy had to be eliminated. Only then would Allen feel completely safe. He had done too much, come too far to accept defeat. And yet there seemed no alternative to defeat. To make matters worse, no further delay was possible.

Joan was poised to come looking for him if he didn't turn up at her mother's funeral. And now there was Sharon's body in the viewing room where it would most certainly be discovered the following day.

At a pinch, he could hang around until morning, and take his chances in broad daylight when the alarm would be turned off. But he was booked on the first flight out to Adelaide, and thence on to Alice Springs and Darwin, and he needed the night to transform himself fully into Anders Solvig.

No. It had to be now. It had to be tonight.

If he couldn't get in, then possibly an urgent telephone call might bring the boy out. But what could that call be about? He knew nothing of the boy except that he must be killed, and he could think of no message that would suffice. Not even if he said the call was being made for Sharon. He'd gathered relations between them were too strained for the boy to take much notice of any summons on her behalf.

He pondered on whether deliberately to trigger off the alarm system, then quickly conceal himself either in the grounds or in the house. But if it brought the police, as it would, they'd inevitably search the property for intruders. The risk was too great.

But still he refused to accept defeat. It was totally unacceptable. If he were to live, the boy must die. That was the bottom line. And if he couldn't live, he would die and take the boy with him.

Headlights turned into Boniface Road. Allan drew in closer to the tree trunk, waiting for the glare to pass.

It didn't. The vehicle approached slowly, then pulled to a stop outside 'Horizons'. Allan skirted around the tree trunk to remain concealed, then carefully peered out. He saw a bizarre little van, with a slanting tower stuck on its roof like some kind of crazy chimney. The garishly painted sides of the van told the story – 'Pisa Pizza. We Tower Above the Rest.' And underneath, a telephone number. Every other available inch of space was occupied by crude cartoons of pizzas hovering like flying saucers over gondolas, tilted glasses of red wine, mandolins and garlands of garlic and tomatoes.

Allan felt stirrings of hope as a short, chubby man jumped out of the driver's seat and went briskly to the back of the van. He opened the doors and reached inside. First, he brought out a chef's hat which he rammed on to his head. Then he lifted out a large thermal bag. He pushed the doors shut, then hurried across to the gates. He leaned against one with his shoulder and pushed, as if following a familiar routine.

Allan held his breath.

The gate eased open with a rusty creaking, and the man stepped through the gap and disappeared along the drive.

Allan almost exploded with exhilaration. Not only had it been demonstrated that the security system was inactive, but avenues of opportunity he had never even contemplated were now open to him.

26

Adele actually found herself humming as she emerged from a refreshing shower and patted herself dry. She was still lightheaded from the vodka, but she was feeling decidedly optimistic. The altercation with Kenneth had far more significance for her than the perfidy of Carl O'Callaghan, and swiftly pushed her original mortification into the background.

She slipped into clean, cool underwear and thought of ways she could get back at Mister Carl O'Callaghan. If that recording studio was his happy hunting ground, then she'd buy it. Rentals by the hour or by the day in the recording industry seemed exorbitant from what she had gathered, therefore owning a studio could prove profitable – particularly when she upped the rates to O'Callaghan. And if he bucked and opted for another studio, she'd buy that too! In fact it suddenly seemed like a marvellous idea to buy all the recording studios she could and have a whole chain of them.

The music business. It was her world. Getting herself a piece of it meant she would be able to improve conditions for the artists, make her studios a welcoming environment for talent.

Talent. Yes, she could *find* new talent and nurture it. If you owned the recording studios, you had to have *some* say, for Chrissakes! One thing was certain. There'd be no more dirty deals like she'd had from O'Callaghan. In fact, this could be a way of squeezing him out of the business.

She selected the swishy blue and green striped taffeta housecoat she loved so much from her wardrobe, then went to her dressing table to apply a touch of make-up.

It was a great idea she'd just had. She smiled helplessly at herself in the mirror. Always the survivor. From the pits to the peaks, and all it took was a few hours of emotional trauma which had probably only shortened her life by a mere four or five years! Big deal. Maybe that would be the way for Kenneth to go, helping her with the recording studios. Being young, he'd be up on all the music

305

trends. With some tuition in business management, in time he could possibly—

She paused, leaning close to the mirror with a lipstick at her mouth.

It really all came back to Kenneth. He wasn't mature enough to see it, but what they'd gone through tonight was unavoidable and probably very necessary. Somebody once said that people were brought closer together by the secrets they shared. She hoped that was true. Because there was little about her now that Kenneth didn't know.

She pressed her lips together to distribute the colour. He wasn't stupid by any means. He would come to realise that people automatically kept things back from strangers, from a sense of caution as well as to make a favourable impression. Inevitably, as intimacy developed with time, it all came out and readjustments had to be made. Well, it *had* all come out . . . well, most of it.

She put out her hand, allowing her forefinger to stray delicately over a small photograph stuck in a corner the mirror. Creased at the edges and slightly faded, it showed a beautiful girl on a beach. Hands on hips, feet dug into the sand, she was wearing shorts and a skimpy top. Her mass of red hair was tousled by the breeze and she was laughing happily at the camera.

'Oh Kelly,' Adele murmured, 'I spent a good part of my life wanting to be you. Now, I just hope I've enough time left to be myself.' She gazed at the photograph for long moments, then carefully she pulled it away from the mirror and after some deliberation, she put it out of sight in the bottom drawer of her dressing table.

As she left her bedroom, she looked across at the locked door of Kenneth's room. Give him time, she told herself. Just give him time to cool off. She desperately wanted to go in there and hug him and tell him that despite her mistakes and her tantrums and drunken rages, he was all that mattered. But although she hesitated outside his door, she forced herself to continue on downstairs. He was an intelligent kid. He'd get over his hurt, and—

The doorbell rang.

Adele reached the bottom of the stairs, crossed the foyer and opened the door.

The man in the jaunty chef's hat smiled at her.

'Mrs Ventura? Your Pisa Pizza order.'

Adele stared at him. 'Where's Orlando tonight?'

'Oh, he's on another run.'

She hesitated. Orlando usually delivered her orders and she never paid him at the door because he was always gallant enough to carry everything through to the kitchen. But she certainly wasn't going to have this new one inside.

'If you'll just wait there, I'll—'

She reached for the thermal bag, but the man waved her aside with a flourish.

'Oh, no it's far too heavy. Allow me.'

He stepped inside and then he faltered, looking back at her. 'The kitchen?'

She was too bemused by his audacity to object.

'This way,' she said, and led him across the foyer, through the drawing room and the dining room and into the kitchen. She kept walking, not stopping until the kitchen table was between them. She watched while he heaved the thermal bag on to the table, unzipped it and began to unload its contents. Then she went to get the canister from the shelf above the microwave oven so that she could pay him. It was only when she looked inside the canister and saw it was empty, apart from some small change, did she remember that Kenneth had cleaned it out. Still holding it, she turned around.

'How much do I owe you? Do you have the check?'

The man paused, then put a plastic bucket of cole slaw on the table.

'I must have left it in the van. Sorry.'

'Well, surely you can tell from my order? A large pizza with everything, cole slaw, bean salad and garlic bread.'

His eyes seemed to glaze over for a moment.

'Er . . . yes. That'll be . . . fifteen dollars and eighty-five cents.'

The bill was twenty-two dollars fifty. They'd told her over the phone when she'd made the order. They always did.

So now she knew. Either this guy was so inexperienced he was going to send Pisa Pizzas bankrupt, or he was a phony. She had registered other things about him. He seemed to move in spasms and his eyes, when his mind wasn't thrown by a simple question about the cost of a pizza order, were feverishly bright.

Was he a junkie?

There were other things. The big stain on the sleeve of his jacket looked like he'd dragged it across one of the pizzas, which didn't do much for her appetite. The knuckles of his right hand were freshly grazed and gleamed with blood. And why would a pizza delivery man – or a junkie for that matter – call her Mrs Ventura?

To staff and tradespeople, she was Mrs Hatherley. When her last name had been Ventura, it was 'Miss'. But never in Australia. Here, she was Mrs Hatherley.

He didn't look like a thug. The suit was made of quality cloth and well cut. He even sported a collar and tie, for God's sake, although the tie was pulled off-centre.

A rapist? Adele's black sense of humour surfaced. With that heavy dark moustache and that pale, intense look, she should be so lucky!

The touch of humour was as brief as the thought, then the unease returned. The only way she could get rid of him was to pay him, but the only way she could pay him was to leave him here and go upstairs for her purse – if she could get as far as the door.

He was pulling a foil-wrapped cylinder of garlic bread out of the bag. He glanced up at her and smiled.

'There's an awful lot here for just one person.'

She smiled back, hoping that the corners of her mouth weren't trembling. 'Oh no,' she asserted. 'I don't make a practice of dining alone. I'll have company.'

She was about to continue, inventing guest rooms full of ravenous friends who were about to descend from upstairs, when he spoke again. And what he said reinforced her fears.

'The boy, I suppose. The boy you have staying here.'

She looked at him sharply. He zipped up the empty bag with an air of finality and casually returned her gaze.

'Somebody mentioned it at the shop. Orlando, probably.' He smiled and indicated the various containers. 'Kids love this kind of stuff, don't they?'

She forced herself to smile. 'Not enough, apparently for him to hurry home. I don't know where he's got to.' She rattled the canister and held it out to show the small change. 'I usually keep enough in this to take care of expenses. I'll have to go upstairs and get my purse.'

To reach the door, she would have to pass him where he was standing at the other end of the table. She veered off by the refrigerator. 'May I offer you something while you're waiting? A Coke? White wine?'

He pulled out a chair. 'No thanks. With your permission, I'm quite happy just to sit.'

She nodded. It made him seem less threatening, his sitting down like that. She walked to the door.

'I won't be a moment,' she said. And went out.

27

Allan got up immediately and took the receiver off the wall phone, just in case she decided to make a call from upstairs. Then he went back to the chair, sat on it, put a foot up to the edge of the kitchen table and tilted the chair on to its two back legs.

The woman was nervous, of course she was, it was understandable with an unfamiliar man in her house. But unfamiliar or not, he had the wholesome image of a pizza delivery man and that must count for something. He had toyed with the idea of killing her immediately. Jamming the thermal bag over her head and smothering her would have been a refreshing change of pace but as usual, his instinctive gift for choosing the correct course had told him to wait. And sure enough, she had proved her worth by volunteering the information that the boy was out but expected back for dinner. That saved him the bother of searching from room to room in this pretentious barn of a place. He still had plenty of time to accomplish what he had set out to do, and what's more he now had some time up his sleeve because he'd be able to drive away in style in that idiotic delivery van.

His methods were becoming those of an entrepreneurial showman, he realised, definitive and polished in skills of manipulation. These days, he continually found himself seething with clever ways of destroying any opposition that blocked his path, and those who did not oppose him but actually helped – like the woman Ventura – were rewarded with a few more precious moments of life before being discarded like used teabags.

Sometimes, when circumstances appeared beyond even his control, the fates usually organised a generous solution for him, as in the case of the fortuitous arrival of the pizza delivery. Again and again it was being proved to him that he was one of the blessed.

He didn't hate people, Allan reassured himself. He just hated to lose control. Of late, there had only been this wretched boy who must be punished for daring to threaten the structure of his life. It

309

could have been any innocent man the boy had enmeshed in his web of deceit, some sex-starved suburban wimp who would have sizzled and melted on the hot-plate of scandal, never to be heard of again. How unfortunate for him that it had been Allan Steinbeck, a sleeping tiger content for the moment with his image of family man and corporate climber and strong enough to retaliate when his very existence was threatened.

Allan leaned back further on the tilted chair so that both legs resting on the tabletop could be stretched and crossed. Fragmented thoughts detached themselves from the melting iceberg of his mind and floated freely in warm currents of memory.

Aunt Maude. Graham MacKenzie. The boy. It wasn't as though he'd had to devote his life to the removal of obstacles. Just now and again. Quietly and efficiently. With a few other scores like Doris Lytton-Scott settled on the side . . .

Graham MacKenzie.

Now why, just at this very satisfying time, would he think of Graham MacKenzie?

Allan smiled and shifted his legs to a more comfortable position. The woman would be scrabbling in some diamante purse by now for the money to pay him. Maybe she was also titivating her hair or smearing on more lipstick. She looked the type. There was something in the way she looked at him that smouldered behind the bars of her caution.

The fragment of memory labelled Graham MacKenzie drifted back, and he realised that the recollection was natural. The circumstances were not at all similar, but Graham MacKenzie had been an enemy, an obstacle, just as much as the teenaged betrayer he was waiting to dispatch.

'There *is* someone else,' Joan had confessed, in an excess of the confrontational truth which had been fashionable at the time. She was everything he wanted, had needed and had searched for since his beloved Lillian had died. Joan Lytton-Scott was a strikingly attractive career girl who appeared strong enough, overly caring enough to be the only one who could possibly rank beside his mother, not replace her – no one could do that – but come close to filling the void she had left in death. But suddenly there was Graham MacKenzie. A rival. And a formidable one because he was from a wealthy family, his father a barrister and an old and respected friend of Joan's parents. Graham was studying law himself, and was a better catch from every point of view.

Fortunately, Graham liked to carouse and he had the fatal flaw of decency, and therefore had responded to the friendly invitation to down a few drinks with his rival. A whole nightful of drinks later, and Graham's demise became nothing more than a front page picture of a huddled carcase, decapitated by a truck on the Pacific Highway. His car was parked nearby, the driver's door wide open. The autopsy showed an excess of alcohol in his bloodstream. 'Death by Misadventure' was a convenient cloak thrown over a drunken larrikin's attempt to take a leak over on the other side of the road.

When the sympathetic headshaking was over, Allan had Joan all to himself. Only too late he found her strength evaporated where her mother was concerned, a definite minus. And Doris Lytton-Scott with her well-bred scorn proved to be an obstacle he'd had to circumvent rather than remove. Joan had defied her mother to marry him. Not that it had been a bother in those early days. Away from her mother, Joan was a satisfying, supportive, vibrant partner who wanted all the sex he could give.

Until the baby came along. And then he'd been shoved to one side and Joan became a weak and whining wretch who cared only for her child . . .

Allan swung his legs off the tabletop, righted the chair and jumped up. He was forgetting – he had things to do.

28

Adele hurried upstairs, out of breath before she was only halfway, her heart thudding and her head resounding in time with a painful rhythm. Stress was interreacting with the liquor she'd had earlier to produce an instant hangover. Another drink might fix that, but there wasn't time, God dammit.

She unlocked the door to Kenneth's bedroom and went in. Kenneth was curled up on the bed, half-asleep. He stirred as she sat beside him, putting her mouth close to his ear, whispering urgently.

'Listen to me—'

'What? What's up?'

'Listen, for Chrissakes. There's a man downstairs. I don't like the look of him. He asked about you—'

Kenneth jerked up, suddenly alert.

'A man? Who is—?'

'Keep your voice down!'

'Who is he?'

'He delivered the pizza, but—'

'What?' Kenneth's tone became incredulous. 'Aw, come on – pull the other one.'

'He's not the regular delivery man. And he's kind of creepy. He knows you're staying here, said someone at the shop told him, but I don't trust him. I thought . . . maybe he could be the man who was after you.'

'What's he like?'

'Well he's very dark, with—'

'No, it's not him,' Kenneth said definitely. He'd overreacted at the Cinema Centre and nearly wet his pants for nothing. He wasn't about to do it again. He looked at Adele with suspicion. 'How many drinks have you had?'

'That has nothing to do with it!' Now she was angry. She clutched at him, her body working overtime. 'I'm scared for you. I'm scared for both of us.'

He pulled away from her. 'You don't fool me,' he grunted. 'This is another one of your games. You're just trying to get me back on your side—'

'I'm not!'

'—so's I'll stay. Well, it's not gonna work. If you're that scared, why don't you pay him and get rid of him?'

Adele leaned closer, frantically. 'There was no money in the kitchen. You took it, remember? But that was good because it gave me the excuse to come up and warn you.'

He glared at her, totally unconvinced.

'Okay, you've warned me. Now leave me alone.'

She shrank back. 'You're impossible! Here I am, half out of my mind with one thing and another, and—'

'Yeh. That's it. You just said it. You're out of your mind.' He hunched over on to his side, his back to her.

She got up off the bed and stood for a second, looking at his back. Her eyes glittered furiously, her hands clenching and unclenching. She exhaled with force, an escaping gust of exasperation, then left the room.

Swiftly, she crossed to her own bedroom. She must hurry, she thought as she went inside and picked up her purse. She had no idea how long she'd been gone, and the one thing she didn't want was that the man should become suspicious. She looked longingly at the telephone beside her bed. There wasn't time. And anyway, who could she ring? If Kenneth wouldn't believe her face to face, how could she convince someone at the other end of a telephone? She hadn't any facts. He hadn't threatened her, he had just made a couple of verbal errors and acted pushy. The rest was pure instinct on her part.

And that's what she would continue to rely on.

She tossed her purse on the bed, unopened. There was no way she would go near that man again.

She left her bedroom and walked along the hall to the top of the staircase. At the top, she looked down, expecting him to be halfway up the stairs, creeping towards her, pale face upturned with that awful chef's hat still tilted at a rakish angle on his head.

The staircase was empty.

The foyer was empty.

313

She gripped the banister rail and took a deep breath.

'Are you there?' she called.

She waited, her eyes fixed on the archway which led to the drawing room.

Silence.

She was beginning to think he hadn't heard her when he suddenly appeared, carrying the empty thermal bag. Still wearing the chef's hat. He looked up at her inquiringly.

Actually, thought Adele, he really was quite attractive. From a distance, that was. Close up, you could see the eyes that crackled like stoked-up furnaces.

'Look, this is awfully embarrassing,' she said in a loud, clear voice and staying exactly where she was. 'I find I'm out of ready cash. But I'm a regular customer. Just tell them at the shop to add it on the next time.'

Her tone was firm enough to negate any attempt at disagreement. And if he started up the stairs towards her, she could be back in her bedroom with the door locked before he reached the top. And if that happened, she would have a viable reason for calling the police.

He stood there for what seemed like an eternity. She waved her hand imperiously in the direction of the front door and forced herself to smile.

'If you wouldn't mind letting yourself out? Goodnight.'

He nodded his head and the chef's hat flopped ridiculously. She saw the flash of his teeth.

'No worries, ma'am. Enjoy your dinner.'

He walked to the front door and let himself out, closing the door behind him. Adele waited for a few seconds then ran down the stairs. Sure that he would burst in again before she got there, she hurried across the foyer, flung herself at the front door and snipped the lock.

Safe.

She rested her back against the door and waited until her breath came easily. Then the practical side of her took over. She went through to the kitchen and turned the wall oven on 'Low'. She took the pizza on its plate out of the container and put it on the middle shelf together with the foil-wrapped garlic bread. She put the containers of salad into the refrigerator and then paused, her hand still on the fridge door.

It might be an idea to ring Pisa Pizza on the pretext of apologising to the manager for not paying the bill, and then find out some

314

details about their new delivery man, sending out very strong vibes that she'd prefer Orlando in future.

She turned to go to the wall phone and stopped.

It had no receiver.

The cradle was empty and a tuft of wire, neatly sliced, showed where the receiver had been severed.

She turned and ran through to the drawing room where there was another telephone. She found another empty cradle and another tuft of cord. She felt her flesh dip to zero. He had removed and taken away with him both telephone receivers. That meant that if she'd tried to call for help from her bedroom it would have been useless. So much for her brilliant escape strategy had he charged upstairs at her.

Her mind raced. She would have to find some way of depressing the cradles to bring back the dialling tone. Otherwise, she wouldn't be able to use the bedroom phone or the one in the study. She could jam something heavy on this horizontal model, but there was still the wall phone in the kitchen. Sticky tape. But where was the roll of sticky tape?

She began to tremble. It was always the same. The roll could be in any one of a dozen places, because she took it up and used it and put it down again and never returned it to its proper place, but she'd better start looking because—

And then she realised there was a better, more certain way of summoning the police. All she had to do was turn on the security system, and if he were still out there prowling around – and he surely wouldn't leave the grounds after going to all this trouble to isolate her – then the alarm would go on and the cop shop would be alerted and those good ol' dependable boys in blue would be around in a few minutes. Well . . . *several* minutes. But at least it would get help under way.

She crossed to the windows and pushed back the heavy curtains and punched the four-number code on the digital pad.

She reeled back. All the lights came on in the grounds and flared through the windows at her with the thrust of flames.

And then, just as suddenly, everything went off, inside and out.

Adele stood in pitch darkness, blinded by the sudden reversal, and just as she had on several other occasions she silently cursed the circuit breaker. If anything had registered at the police station, it was so brief it would have been written off as another default. When did Kenneth say the electrician was coming to put the system on a separate circuit? Monday? This was Friday night – a little too long to wait, she thought bitterly.

She was beginning to discern shapes again. With the passing of the early-evening rain, the full moon had made another appearance, and now that her eyes were becoming accustomed to the gloom she could see the terrace and the lawns bathed in a bluish-white glow, as glacial as her own body temperature. Where moonlight penetrated the house through windows, there were sapphire-bright shafts thrusting through the darkness.

She began to shiver. It wasn't fair. She'd been through enough today and she was reluctant to move in case the mere shift of her body brought more unpleasantness. Kenneth would *have* to come down now and press that damned red button in the fuse box so that they could have light again, and then they could find the sticky tape and fix the phones and—

Faintly but distinctly, she heard the kitchen door creak open.

She knew immediately what had happened. He had unlocked the door when she'd left him alone in the kitchen. After seeing him leave through the front door, her relief had been such that it had not occurred to her to check the kitchen door.

And now he was back in the house.

If Adele had been reluctant to move before, now she was petrified. She listened, leaning against the darkness for some other sound and imagining his progress across the kitchen and into the dining room and then slowly but surely across the drawing room towards her, keeping to the shadows, avoiding the moonlit patches, lithe and menacing, as confident of his direction as a heat-seeking missile.

She stood there fighting panic, knowing that she must stand there no longer. She must defend herself and she must protect Kenneth and there was only one way to do it.

Carefully, keeping the rest of her body still, she slipped her feet, one after the other, out of the high-heeled satin mules she wore around the house. To accomplish what she had in mind, she would have to cross the highly polished floor of the foyer, and barefoot was the only way to do that soundlessly. Then she fumbled at her waist and undid the single clasp of her housecoat. It had to go. Its fullness would impede her progress and the taffeta rustled at the slightest movement. She eased her shoulders out of the garment and being full, it slid off her body easily. She held on to its folds and gently let them subside to the floor. She took a step away and felt unencumbered in nothing but her slip. The freedom gave her a spark of confidence. Strange, but now she was nearer nakedness than before, her shivering stopped.

She took another step to the side, recalling with the certainty of long familiarity the size and position of each piece of furniture. Everything she did must be completely silent, she told herself. Even the passage of air in and out of her mouth must be minimal to avoid the slightest sigh. She glided slowly, one careful step at a time, keeping to the shadows at the edge of the room. Since the creak of the kitchen door she had heard nothing, but that one sound had been enough.

A rectangle of moonlight cut across in front of one of the leather divans. Just before she reached it, she lowered herself down on to her hands and knees and crawled along, hidden from the light by the back of the divan. Now, she only had to cover a few feet to the foyer which, with no natural illumination at all, appeared a blacker than black hole.

She was almost there when a noise came from the dining room. She recognised what it was. He had bumped into one of the chairs and nudged it against the edge of the table. Acting on the assumption that it might have distracted him for a second, she raised herself up and quickly flitted into the absolute gloom of the foyer.

She dashed to the other side, then paused for an instant, listening. Not a sound.

Had he seen her at the window just before the lights went out, or would he assume she had remained upstairs? Either way, with her as a distraction and provided Kenneth remained in his room, the boy would be safe for the moment. She moved off again, out of the foyer and along the corridor and stopped when she got to the music room.

The door was closed. Her hand gripped the knob and turned it slowly and carefully as far as it would go. She pushed against the door and it opened smoothly, but with a protesting squeak she hadn't noticed before. She slipped inside and closed the door just as carefully. This time, there was no squeak.

She looked around and made for the giant bulk of the grand piano, her hands reaching out for its polished surfaces. Steadying herself against the curve of its body, she dipped her hand inside and felt for the hidden shelf which had been revealed to her years ago by the dealer from whom she had bought it.

At first she couldn't locate the shelf. It had been so long. The back of her hand brushed against taut wires and she could feel rather than hear the humming caused by even feather-light contact. Then her groping fingers touched cold metal. She allowed her fingers to trace the shape, the squat butt . . . the concave cylinder . . . the short polished pipe. Once she determined exactly how it lay, her fingers clasped firmly where they were supposed to go, and she brought out the .38 revolver which had been Lambert's plaything until she had used it to kill him.

It was heavier than she remembered, but perhaps hurt and hate had given her extra strength the last time she had held it. She let it lie across the palms of her hands and looked down, unable to see it clearly but hearing again the two shots which silenced Lambert's lacerating taunts and ended his life; feeling again the unexpected jolts up her arm.

The next time, if there were to be a next time, she would grasp it firmly with two hands and stand with her legs planted apart as she had seen cops do on countless television shows . . . that is, if she were given enough warning.

Warning!

It came perfectly cued into her train of thought, the warning murmur of a floorboard out there along the corridor. She began to shiver again, and not just because she was standing there in her slip. Adele knew she could no more face him if he burst through the door, here and now in the claustrophobic confines of the music room, than she could a marauding tiger. Even with the gun in her hands she couldn't face him. She wouldn't even *see* him, for God's sake! She had to get out of here. She had to get out of the house.

She turned and fumbled her way over to the grey rectangles of the french doors. There was a key. It should be in the lock. She found it, twisted it the wrong way, and it jammed. She pushed and pulled until it rattled in the lock setting again, expecting any second to be attacked from behind. The chambers clicked as they slid back. She pressed down the handle on the right-hand door and she hurried out, leaving it open. She didn't care, she just wanted to be free of walls that pressed in and corridors that creaked and a house she loved which had suddenly become a prison.

The paving of the path along the side of the house was harsh against the pampered cushions of her feet but it was a penalty for freedom she willingly accepted. She was out where there was fresh air and space, and room to run. She let herself through the high brushwood gate, a twin of the one on the other side of the house which protected the rear portion of the house and its grounds. She hurried on, towards the front corner of the house, not knowing what she was going to do, not caring for the moment, just relieved to be free.

318

As she reached the corner, she tripped over something across the path and fell to one side on the grassy border. The grass was cold, but the ground was soft and spongy and although she landed face downwards, she knew immediately she wasn't hurt. There was, however, a distinct minus. She had dropped the gun.

She pushed herself up on her knees and desperately scrabbled around with flat palms to locate it. Then the moon peeped at her from behind a scudding cloud, and in its helpful light she saw the revolver lying just out of reach. She dived for it, spreadeagled on the ground. Her hand closed around it. Welcome back, old friend, I thought I'd lost you. She thought the words but panted as if she'd had to squeeze them out audibly. She pushed herself up into a sitting position and tried to overcome her desperate breathing. The pause allowed her to realise just how hard her heart was thumping.

She was in bad shape. She had to get away or she would die. She knew it with absolute certainty. This was still the day she discovered she'd been made a fool of, conned into financing musical arrangements for some musical comedy has-been who'd become a medical miracle. It was the same day that she had revealed everything to Kenneth. And had quarrelled with him. And as a result had been threatened with losing him.

And now this. A madman in the house. The thought spurred her into action. She scrambled to her feet, keeping the hand holding the gun up and away from her body. Her heart was still thumping against her ribs, and now the thudding was echoing painfully at the back of her head again. Automatically, she glanced back to see what she'd tripped over and saw a leg across the path. The body was mostly on the other side of the path. And in the moon's continuing illumination, she saw a chubby face she recognised as Orlando's, the regular pizza delivery man, staring up at her as if with amazement that a huge, darkly glistening extra mouth had been carved under his chin.

She backed. The shivering stopped. Who the *hell* did this guy think he was, taking over her house, terrorising her and murdering an innocent delivery man, yes, who the *hell* did he think he was?

She ran across the lawn in front of the house, looking up to locate the window's of Kenneth's bedroom. Then she yelled.

'Kenneth! Hide yourself! For Chrissake's, hide yourself or get out! There's a madman in the house! Kenneth!'

Her voice sounded strange, muted as if turned into vocal muzak by one of Carl O'Callaghan's modulators. The words hung on the night air like wisps of vapour. But she daren't wait to see if they had any effect. She ran to a clump of rhododendron and hid behind it.

There was no point in making a dash down the drive for the gates. If the intruder chose to follow her, he could outrun her with ease. And even if she made it to the road, what would she do? Go calling on neighbours, barefoot and wearing only her slip, toting a gun and babbling about some guy terrorising her? She could just imagine their faces. Such things didn't happen in Point Piper! By the time they made any sense out of her, even though she might convince them eventually, Kenneth would be dead. And he was her first priority. She must be quick. She had to go back into the house, that was crystal clear to her now. But first, she had to reset that damned circuit-breaker!

29

There was no gradual awakening, no slow surfacing from a bottomless pit with the gradual perception that miraculously she was still alive after facing death. It happened with the abruptness of a thrown switch and Sharon tore through the excruciating membrane of consciousness like a circus animal leaping through a paper hoop. She was suddenly aware of an unbearable buzzing in her head, the sound of a million angry bees. Simultaneously, she felt the pain of her swollen, ravaged face and realised she was fighting to draw breath through air passages seriously dilated by bruising.

Fear gripped her, unaccountable fear because she could not remember how she arrived at this state even though she could still feel the terrifying pressure of thumbs against her windpipe. She began to thresh around on the floor, gulping for air. She was lying on her back now, but nothing seemed to work. Her mind was cloaked in the buzzing noise, her body refused to function, and unless she got more air into her lungs she would suffocate. She tried to make sense of it. Was this some horrible nightmare from which she would wake up with sweat on her brow and a pounding heart?

As she lay there, blinking lids starchy with dried blood, the awful memories began to leak back like the seepage of sludge through imperfect floodgates. Her eyes began to water, flushing the greasy film away, allowing her to bring her surroundings into focus. Was she in the apartment? No. She moved her head and the pain in her stiff, enlarged face throbbed agonisingly. She was able to make out a television set. And chairs.

Images were now conquering the buzzing in her mind. Crowds of people, laughing, talking, drinking. Jim. Loud music. Flashing lights. There was the shame of falling over and having some lousy TV critic sneer down at her . . .

Her eyes focussed on a low table. On it was a glass with amber

321

liquid in it. Brandy. Yes, she'd been drinking some brandy while she watched the videotape—

And now she remembered everything, and all the hurt, all the shame and all the fear came back and materialised into a series of tormented moans. Making the sounds added to the pain in her throat, but there was no way she could stop. Adam. The razor. The cuts. The throttling. The address. The boy. Now her moans became louder with a shocking intensity and reverberated in her head, waging war with the buzzing. She had given Adam Shaw the address. Even now he was probably on his way there. How long had she been unconscious? Maybe he'd already killed Kenneth Mitchell. No. There still had to be a chance, there still might be time.

She struggled on to her stomach and scrabbled her way to the table. The brandy would help, what was left of it. If only she could manage to reach up and close her fingers around the glass . . .

She rested on her left arm, pushing up, biting her lips against pain and dizziness, reaching up and over the edge of the table for the glass. Her flailing fingers made contact, tried to grip, tilted the glass, and then it slipped out of her grasp on to its side. The remains of the brandy flowed over the polished surface of the table towards the edge. Sharon collapsed back on to the floor, but managed more by chance than design to position her upturned face in the path of the drips. The first few missed her mouth and rolled across her cheeks, searing the open wounds. She moved her head, and now a thin stream of the liquor was falling directly into her mouth. She gulped, almost choking, but made herself swallow even though the burning sensation it caused was almost intolerable.

The stream lasted for only a matter of seconds, but Sharon managed to swallow enough to feel it give a kick to her system. She lay back, forcing herself to remain still while the alcohol took effect. The effort of trying to reach for the glass had exhausted her and had increased the variety of her suffering. Only the warmth of the brandy as it reached her veins was giving her the strength to go on.

Again, she slowly raised herself up on one elbow. She felt something roll down her cheek and assumed it was brandy until she saw the fresh drops of blood falling on to the already-stained folds of her dress. Her face. She needed to get help quickly, for her own sake and for the boy's. Otherwise she would bleed to death or choke and the boy would no doubt meet a similar fate. She struggled up further. It mustn't be allowed to end that way. Not Adam Shaw's way. No way.

She swung her free arm and grabbed hold of the cord which led to the telephone on the table. She pulled and brought the cradle and receiver tumbling down on the carpet. She lowered herself down and looked at the numbers on the dialling keyboard. Reception. That would be the only telephone manned in the entire building. The number for Reception was . . .

The buzzing in her head increased. What *was* the number? She made herself concentrate. She knew there was a dialling code on the table, but she also knew she could not raise herself up again. One-eight. Eighteen. That was it. She pointed her index finger and brought it down on the two numbers. Then she burrowed her head along the carpet, bringing it close to the receiver. She waited for what seemed an interminable length of time before the girl on the desk answered.

The girl giggled, said "Reception", then giggled again and muttered: "Stop it! I'm trying to answer the phone. I'm still on duty, you know!" Another giggle. Then: "Hello? Anyone there?"

Sharon managed a deep intake of breath which sent barbs shooting into her neck and down into her chest. The girl was impatient, she wouldn't hang on for long, there were distractions. Sharon knew this was her only chance. She summoned up all her strength to do the hardest thing she had ever attempted in her life. Speak.

30

Kenneth heard Adele calling from the lawns below his bedroom, but it just sounded like more of the same claptrap he'd had to put up with when she'd crept into the bedroom whispering a lot of shit about the pizza deliveryman. She must have sunk a whole bottle of vodka, at least. That was the only reason she'd be raving on like this. Not that he could really blame her. It must have been the pits, finding out what was going on at the recording studio like she did. Even so, it was no excuse for going berserk.

His curiosity got the better of him.

He got up off the bed and went to the window. He felt he had to see if she was cavorting on the front lawns like it sounded she was, because if so, he'd go down, persuade her to come inside, then give her some more booze to knock her out completely. That way, he'd get some peace. And she'd be out to the world until lunchtime tomorrow, by which time he would have left without her having had the opportunity to cause another scene.

He looked out of the window. The lawns were snowy with moonlight. Adele was nowhere to be seen.

He looked from side to side.

No sign of her.

From the vantage point of his window, he could see down the drive to the gates. And although the huge spreading trees along Boniface Road made a gloomy backdrop on the other side of the gates, he could distinguish the chunky white blur of the Pisa Pizza delivery van parked outside, with the distinctive tilted tower pointing up from its roof like a ready-to-go hard-on.

Kenneth turned back into the room. He blinked in the darkness and shook his head. Despite what he'd told her, she'd even tried to turn on the security system and it had gone bananas again. So there were no lights. She would have felt safer, he supposed, had he followed his recent practice of padlocking the front gates, but he'd forgotten what with all the drama. And a good thing, too, because the pizza man wouldn't have been able to get in with Adele's order.

The pizza man.

He paused with one knee on the bed, ready to throw himself down.

Something was wrong.

Shortly after Adele had tried to give him the jitters, he had distinctly heard her getting rid of the pizza man. He'd heard it clearly, because she'd obviously called down to him from this level of the house. He'd heard the front door bang, and then he'd relaxed because once she'd got her bogeyman out of the house, maybe she'd stop acting crazy.

But that seemed a long time ago. The van was still there outside the gates. Those guys were always on the move. It was in and out. Wham, bam, thank you ma'am – but with fast food. They didn't hang around.

Kenneth slowly bounced up and down on his knee.

No matter how tanked she was, Adele had never had the jitters like tonight. She was too tough. It would take something really bad to scare her. And he'd ignored her. What had she called out from down below?

Hide.

And something about someone 'in the house'. And she was outside, calling this . . . warning? . . . up to him.

He took his knee off the bed and moved across the dark room to the door. He put out his hand and grasped the doorknob. Had Adele locked him in after her second visit? No, he remembered distinctly that there'd been no rattle of the key in the lock after she'd gone out.

So if he wasn't locked in, what was holding him back? There was a sourness in his mouth, and his chest felt constricted. He stood there listening and the house listened with him. And heard nothing. But nothing was a lot more sinister than a lot of noise . . . Adele yelling or cursing or falling over furniture, or even a few natural sounds of the evening like the creaks of the house as it settled down for the night, a breeze stirring the branches of the trees, a neighbourhood dog barking.

But there was just this . . . nothing.

He couldn't stand like this forever, getting more and more spooked out, he *had* to make a move one way or another. He tightened his fingers on the doorknob and turned it slowly, not wanting to be the first to break the silence, then he pulled open the door and stepped into the hall.

It was at precisely that moment that all the lights came on and the alarm began its clamour outside.

Kenneth stood motionless, as did the man along the hall at the top of the staircase. In the instant that they registered each other's presence, Kenneth recognised him as the man he'd seen at the movies, the one who had terrified him because even though his appearance had changed Kenneth knew him instinctively to be The Man. And what happened next confirmed it.

'Betrayer!' The Man screamed. It was a battle cry which launched him towards Kenneth, charging along the hall with great strides, except that instead of a sword his raised right hand brandished an open cutthroat razor.

Kenneth backed into the bedroom swiftly and tried to slam the door. But The Man had already flung himself at it, pushing with enormous strength. Kenneth pushed back, but it was obvious he was going to lose the contest. Already, The Man had one arm through the widening space and Kenneth's feet were sliding backwards on the carpet. It had been a lost cause, anyway. Even if he'd managed to close the door, he couldn't lock it without a key.

Still pushing against the door as hard as he could, Kenneth twisted his head around, looking for something to defend himself with. There was nothing within reach, except for the heavy vase on the small side table, just along from the doorway.

It would have to do.

Abruptly, he stopped pushing and stepped back. The Man, unprepared for the sudden lack of resistance, burst into the room off-balance as the door flew open. Even before he turned, Kenneth was gripping the vase by its rim and heaving it up, putting his other hand under the base. By the time The Man faced him, Kenneth was hurling the vase at him with as much force as he could muster.

The vase caught The Man full in the chest, but his arms went around it and he would have kept his balance had he not taken one step back and trodden on the glass Adele had thrown down earlier.

One foot rolled from under him. He dropped the vase and reeled back, both arms jerking up. The long, sharp edge of the razor sliced into his cheek and his screams topped even the crash of the vase as it hit the floor and smashed to smithereens. Kenneth saw the spurt of blood and the glint of polished steel as the razor flew across the room, and then he ran.

Outside the door, he made the mistake of hesitating. Which way to go? To the right and down the back stairs to the kitchen? To the left and down the main staircase to the front door? It was only a fraction of a second, but it robbed him of the precious distance he needed to keep his lead. He ran to the main stairway and started down the stairs, two at a time. Just as he reached the curve, he flashed a glance back and saw The Man leaping at him from the top of the stairs, arms extended as if he were about to fly, his face a ghastly apparition of fresh blood, his eyes afire with hate.

Kenneth kept going, but The Man toppled into him from behind, clutching at his legs and bringing him down. Locked together in struggling confusion, the two of them tumbled down the rest of the stairs, bumping and rolling over, one trying to hang on, the other trying to disentangle himself all the way until they hit the hard floor of the foyer.

Kenneth found himself on top of The Man, who was winded because he had broken the fall for the two of them. The boy wriggled free, pushed himself to his knees and began to crawl away. But then he felt himself grasped by the ankle and pulled with such force that he was twisted on to his back. The Man heaved himself on top of Kenneth, strong fingers going for the boy's throat.

Kenneth tried to struggle, but it was useless. The moment his throat was gripped, the old bruising reacted painfully. Two thumbs pressed down on his windpipe, and now it wasn't the pain, it was not being able to breathe. Blood splashed on his face and he looked up with already-protruding eyes and saw how the slash of the razor had cut deeply from high on the cheekbone to the corner of the mouth, leaving a large flap of flesh hanging bloodily. Then Kenneth's vision blurred and he felt his tongue swelling. The little strength left in him was ebbing away fast.

'This is for daring to tamper with my life,' Allan rasped, but only he knew what he was saying. Severed nerves had robbed his lips of movement. The words came out as blood-soaked gibberish. His head came closer as if to make sure of seeing every exquisite detail of his victim's torment. Kenneth's vision cleared. The sudden proximity of the ghastly wound with blood welling from under the flap of useless cheek and the lips slobbering pink froth added to his nightmarish slide towards death. But the ultimate horror was about to come. The Man's face moved closer and Kenneth knew he was about to be kissed by that hideously ravaged mouth. He summoned up what seemed to be the last vestiges of his strength. His arm bent up and his hand grasped the dangling flap of flesh and he gave it one almighty tug.

It was as if Allan had been plucked off him by an enormous

hand. The pain must have blown off the top of his head. He rose into the air with an ear-shattering howl. Kenneth's fingers slipped away from the slimy hunk of flesh. At the same time, he felt the pressure go from his throat as Allan's hands flew to his own pain-wracked face.

Kenneth sucked in great gulps of air, rolling to one side. Somehow, he managed to scramble to his feet and stagger away into the drawing room breathing in choking gasps, across to the dining room, blundering into furniture and knocking over a lamp. He didn't see Adele as she came into the foyer from the other side of the house or hear her as she shrieked his name.

Allan did, as his hands came away from his head. His face was on fire and the flames were searing into his brain, but he knew the boy was getting away and he had to go after him. The woman was of no importance.

Adele had brought the revolver up into a firing position, but a back-handed swipe from Allan sent her staggering back. She hit the wall with tremendous force and collapsed against it. The gun went off, sending a bullet to bite into the plaster of the ceiling.

Kenneth fumbled at the kitchen door, praying it wouldn't be locked. He heard the sharp report of the gun as he pulled the door open and fell through into the night, but it only served to frighten him even more.

He made for the rear of the house, dizzy and disoriented, registering vaguely that all the floodlights were on and the alarm was still making its noise. That could mean the police had been alerted, but for once all he wanted was for the circuit breaker to bring darkness again so that he could crawl somewhere and hide. If The Man caught up with him now, there would be no escape. His throat was swelling rapidly and little air was getting through to his lungs. His body ached from scores of bruises. His head whirled giddily and he had barely the strength left to put one foot in front of the other.

He turned the corner on to the terrace, tottered across it and fell down the stone steps leading to the swimming pool. As he pushed himself up, the alarm noise cut off abruptly, causing him to look back towards the house.

The Man came around the corner and lumbered on to the terrace with an awesome determination, his face a grisly, gleaming obelisk.

Kenneth made off as best he could around the side of the pool. He would feel safer if he could just put the body of water between himself and The Man. They could circle it indefinitely until help came, or until one of them collapsed. And then it wouldn't matter any more.

By the time he'd made it around to the other side, The Man was coming down the steps. A spasm of unbearable nausea sent Kenneth down on his knees. It sapped the little energy he had left, but even more frightening was the certainty that if he threw up, there was so little passage left in his throat he would choke. He looked up, his legs too weak to function. Already, The Man was on his way around the pool.

'Stop!'

The voice rang out with such authority that Allan paused and looked back. Kenneth turned his head and blinked through a mist of tears.

Adele was at the edge of the terrace, feet apart and standing steady and erect like a ship's figurehead in the eye of a storm. At arm's length, both hands clasped the gun. The singing Cinderella had become Boadicea, barefoot in a crumpled slip.

There was no way of knowing whether it was the triviality of Adele's image that failed to impress Allan, or whether it was just that he did not care any more. He turned away and continued walking around the pool.

Kenneth started to drag himself desperately along the ground towards a rockery.

Adele fired.

The bullet caught Allan in the shoulder and spun him around. He staggered to the tiled rim of the pool, hovered there for a moment looking as if he would fall in, then recovered himself. He paused then continued on his way, rounding the narrow end of the pool.

Kenneth heard Adele call out again. Twisting his head, he saw her running down to the pool. He looked back. Now, Allan was within a few yards of him. Adele shouted yet again, then positioned herself on the other side of the pool. Kenneth closed his eyes, waiting for the gunshot, praying for a direct hit.

There were several audible *clicks*.

Kenneth opened his eyes. Adele was struggling to fire the gun, but nothing was happening except the *clicks*. He turned his eyes, looking up. Allan stood over him, his breath coming in great slobbering gasps, crimson froth bubbling from his mouth. Adele cursed and threw the gun across the pool at him. It sailed harmlessly past, wide of its mark.

Allan reached down, blood spurting from his shoulder, the ghastly flap on one side of his face hanging loose. From the rockery he heaved up a boulder twice the size of a football and raised it above his head, ready to dash it down on Kenneth. The boy looked up. This was it, and they both knew it. Their eyes met for the last time, and the crimson froth on Allan's face elongated as if in a smile. Then he stretched his arms and his body to the maximum. Kenneth focussed on the boulder, up there in the sky like a big, black moon. His insides cringed, his body incapable of movement. In an instant, in a fraction of a second, it would come crashing down on his head.

With a shriek as piercing as the whistle of a steam engine, Adele shot out of the darkness, head down, arms outstretched. She cannoned into Allan, her head hitting him in the stomach. As he overbalanced backwards, still holding the boulder, her arms went around his middle, further propelling him back. They teetered on the edge of the pool, then the weight of the boulder caused Allan to overbalance completely. Locked together, they landed on the silver sheet which was the untethered pool cover.

Their combined weight, plus the weight of the boulder, drew in the sheet to enfold them as they sank beneath the surface of the water, its strings wriggling like the tentacles of a sea creature. Their struggles caused the huge cloud of plastic to bulge and undulate, releasing spurts of pink-coloured ink in the process.

'Adele!'

Kenneth's frantic cry was wrenched from his gut. He struggled to get up, but the effort was too much. Blackness engulfed him and he collapsed back onto the grass. Even then, it seemed he was struggling against unconsciousness, and when he came to, it was with arms and legs threshing and hot tears splashing down his face.

'Oh Jesus, oh God! Adele . . . !'

He coughed up some bile, then crawled to the edge of the pool. The turbulence had subsided. The cocoon of plastic now rested on the bottom of the pool, a great, glistening underwater shroud. A few bubbles lazily drifted up to the surface, then all was still. As Kenneth gazed helplessly, still fighting for breath, the wail of a police siren could be heard coming closer to Point Piper.

PART V

'The art of living is the art of knowing how to believe lies.'

CEASARE PAVESE

1

'I want to go back to work.'

Even the act of talking without moving her lips pulled at the skin of Sharon's face under the dressings. It felt as if someone were pressing a handful of thorns against the flesh. But her gaze was strong and defiant and showed nothing of her discomfort.

Jim Abrahams shifted his bulk uneasily on the hospital chair by her bed.

'Eventually. Sure.'

'They take the stitches out tomorrow. I'm talking about next week.'

Jim shook his head. 'You'll need cosmetic surgery. The specialists told you that.'

'I'm not prepared to wait that long. Oh, I'll have it done, but in the meantime I'm not going to hide my face like some Phantom of the Opera. I want to be the first lady TV reporter who doesn't look like she was embalmed by Estée Lauder.' She thought for a moment. 'In fact eventually, when I *do* have the patch-up job done, you can film the whole thing. Imagine the visuals. Before and after. It'll make quite a story.'

Jim gave his weary now-I've-heard-everything smile. 'You're something else, Sharon.'

Now, her voice mirrored the weariness of his smile. 'Yes. So everyone tells me.'

Jim reached into his briefcase and pulled out a paperback. 'I brought you this just for fun. But if you really insist on going back to work, it can be your first assignment.' He threw it on the bed. Dominating the front covers the title *Ratings* was splashed glaringly across a pair of naked breasts that screamed silicone implants.

Sharon groaned. 'You're not asking me to interview Sophie Davenport? You wouldn't do that to me.'

'It can be your baptism of fire, seeing as you insist on being a martyr,' Jim grinned. 'That's just an advance copy. It hits the stores next week.'

Sharon picked up the novel and examined it gingerly. 'I know. I've heard all about it. A fifth-rate American soapie star writes a Z-grade exposé of the television industry and we all jump through hoops to publicise it. I can just imagine Sophie fluttering those stumpy eyelashes.' Her voice went into a high-pitched whine. ' "You'll just have to guess who the characters are based on", she'll trill.' Sharon reverted back to her own voice. 'As if anyone cared. The characters are based on no-talents as shallow as she is, people you wouldn't want to meet, let alone spend three hundred badly written pages with!'

'I skimmed through it and it's not all bad,' Jim reasoned. 'There's a great description of a blow job.'

'Well, it's like they always say,' Sharon commented drily, 'write about what you know.'

Jim guffawed delightedly. 'Oh, I can see this is going to be quite an interview.'

Sharon allowed herself a smile, even though it hurt. 'And guess who's going to get all the attention? Not Sophie – me! Me and my scars.' Her smile turned bitter. 'The badges of my own stupidity.'

'*And* courage,' Jim added quietly.

Sharon dropped the book and began to pick at the bedcover with her fingers. 'Oh no. If we're talking courage, we're talking Adele Ventura.' She paused, then continued in a low voice. 'What she did . . . well, that's courage.' She shook her head ever so slightly. 'I wish I'd been, oh, I don't know, a little more understanding of her.'

And then she asked the question Jim had been dreading.

'How's the boy?'

Jim hesitated. 'He's disappeared.'

2

Kenneth had fitted the element from an electric kettle with a hole in it to another which had no hole, but no element either. The coil of wire rattled loosely. He decided to risk trying it out, anyway. What the hell. He poured some water from the jug he'd kept handy, then plugged the kettle in, holding his breath. Nothing happened, no flash, no explosion of sparks, just the quiet *rerrrring* from under the surface of the water which meant the element was doing its work.

He sat back on his heels, pleased, and reached for a cigarette. He'd started smoking again, which was bad news, but he reasoned he had to have one prop, one bad habit. He'd start worrying about cancer when he turned forty. He lit up and switched the kettle off. He'd take it over to Ana later. She wouldn't have to boil water in a pan on a single gas ring any more.

He inhaled deeply, looking around his room as if for the first time. It seemed incredible that he'd been here almost a month. At first, the room had been empty except for an old army cot with a threadbare blanket. Now, it was furnished with all sorts of bits and pieces that everybody had pitched in with, day by day, week by week, even though he kept saying he wouldn't be staying long. Nobody seemed to listen. They just kept on carrying stuff in. Junk, mostly, and things to mend, like the rocking horse for little Carlos. Everything had once belonged elsewhere, but ongoing familiarity was making the room and its contents his and his alone.

Almost a month.

He could think about Adele, now, without getting too screwed up. At first, it had been a nightmare. The cops and all their questions, piecing together the late and unlamented Allan Steinbeck's secret life of deception and death from bits of information gathered from all over the place. And then there were the media reporters, even more insistent, buzzing around like a cloud of insects.

'Is it true Adele Ventura altered her will to leave you everything?'

'How long will you be staying on in the mansion? Has the family made any move to get rid of you now she's dead?'

To the first question, Kenneth would growl aggressively: 'She gave me her life. She gave me *my* life. I don't give a fuck about her will, she's already given me enough!'

As for 'the family', it consisted only of Lambert Hatherley's sister Edith, who had made a couple of tentative visits to 'Horizons', regarding him warily as if he were going to steal off with all the furniture. Jorge and Rina and old Fitzgibbon had staunchly assured her that Kenneth had been staying at the house for weeks as Adele's guest, so there wasn't much she could do. Even so, he soon got sick of the questions, upset by the constant reminders of what had happened, and uncomfortable in the house on his own.

Jorge and Rina had sensed he was about to split and had shyly offered him a bed while he decided what to do and where to go next. That did it. Suddenly, he found himself part of a whole community of Central American refugees centred around a Pentecostal Church in the western suburbs. Some like Rina and Jorge had been able to scrape together the deposit on a 'handyman's dream' house, in other words a falling-down ruin from Victorian or Federation times. Others scored a Housing Commission dwelling because of illness or extreme deprivation. All of them, like Kenneth, were on the run from something bad. Nicaragua, El Salvador, Kings Cross, it didn't make any difference. With their friendly natures, they quickly sensed a common bond and infected him with their gritty fight to survive and a rollicking sun-ripened optimism.

He discovered that Rina and Jorge were actually skilled computer operators, prevented from following their careers by lack of English, a situation they were rapidly seeking to correct while they made ends meet with their cleaning chores. They were overjoyed at having Kenneth on hand full-time to practice their English with, and promised that as soon as they could afford their own computer they would teach him all they knew in return. Others sought him out to converse in English, too. Lawyers working as security guards, doctors sweeping factory floors, they all wanted his help with this new language.

Communication bridges were crossed in a mixture of Spanish and English. They began to call him Kenito. Families constantly and happily overlapped so that he never quite knew who belonged where. There were parties at which he developed a taste for tamales, and fried tortillas, and pupusas filled with cheese and minced pork. He was even getting used to the lethal drink they

336

favoured, made from fermented pineapple.

They discovered his aptitude for fixing things. Everyone had arrived in Australia with a bare minimum of belongings. After initial spells in refugee centres, it was up to them to find their own accommodation, but when they did there was nothing to put in the rooms and no money to spend. Household goods and furnishings had to come secondhand from charity organisations or be scavenged from tips. And, needless to say, every piece was broken, rusted, or cracked and now, practically every piece ended up in Kenneth's room awaiting his attention.

Now he came to think of it, no wonder a month had passed so quickly. They had made him feel important, wanted, these people called Ramirez and Rodriguez and Alvarez and they had not given him time to lament about the past. Jorge and Rina and Karina and Salvatore and Nancy and Armando and Roberto and Ana and Francisco and all the children, they had become his friends, his shield. And there was Maria. She alone was worth sticking around for. A girl his own age, she had lustrous black hair, a skin as shiny and golden as honey, and huge dark eyes which told shyly of her interest in him. She really turned him on and, judging by the sly winks and knowing smiles, everyone knew it.

He grinned to himself and wondered what Adele would think of it all. She'd probably make some wisecrack or other, but she'd be happy for him because whatever mistakes she'd made, she always wanted the best for him. That was why she hadn't rushed off and changed her will in his favour. Oh, everyone had their own theories as to why. They hadn't known each other long enough. She didn't know she was going to die. Or – worst of all – she didn't care all that much about him. That one really hurt. But he knew different. He was sure of it. Adele wouldn't have wanted him lumbered with a lot of shit he couldn't handle, stuff involving guardians and trustees and hysterical legal objections from Edith Hatherley. Adele wanted him to make it on his own. She knew he would in the long run. And he knew it, too.

Poor bitch. She was incredible and he'd never forget her and what she'd done for him.

There was a shout from the backyard down below. He stubbed out his cigarette in a chunky ashtray inscribed 'Greetings from the Blue Mountains', heaved himself up off the floor and went to the open window. Francisco had just driven an ancient pick-up truck in through the gates. The back of it was loaded with junk. Leaning over the sill, he could make out a rusty exercise bike, a wreck of

337

a sofa, a rolled-up inner spring, curtain tracks and a couple of lamps, a faded bean bag, some frayed carpeting and . . .

Francisco had seen him and was gesticulating excitedly at something tucked between the inner spring and the bean bag. Kenneth stared down. A computer keyboard? It *couldn't* be . . . could it?

With a wave, Kenneth pushed himself away from the window and hurried downstairs. He had a lot to do.

3

Joan Steinbeck sat absolutely still in the dusk-darkened living room of 'Hazeldene Lodge', the large house in Cavendish Close left to her by her mother, Doris. For the first time in weeks, all was silent. The media hounds had decamped from the front garden. The trashy women's magazines had stopped ringing up to offer exorbitant amounts for her side of the story. At last they had left her in peace.

The house stirred with a series of creaks and Joan suddenly realised she had been lost in unaccustomed solitude for what seemed like hours and probably was. She hurried upstairs.

The nursery was in shadows. She switched on the lamp. The baby blinked and stared at her from the playpen across the room. It struck her once more how much little Allan was starting to resemble his father. The wisp of sandy hair, the pursed, petulant mouth, the look of resentment in the big blue eyes . . .

Resentment. Of course the little pet felt resentment, she thought, and it was fully justified, too.

'Oh my darling, I've left you alone for far too long again. I'm so sorry.'

She started across the room, but stumbled over something. She reached down and picked up the head of a stuffed toy, a grinning bear. Looking up, she saw that the rest of the decapitated animal was with the baby in the playpen. She went over and put the head of the bear on the mantlepiece. It added to an impressive line-up, because there already were the heads of a stuffed cat, a stuffed duck and a stuffed monkey. It had become quite a trick of little Allan's to show his displeasure – and strength – in this destructive fashion.

Joan resolved to pay him much more attention from now on. She squatted down beside the playpen in which the baby was sitting on the floor, holding on to the rails with his tiny hands.

'I'm sorry,' she repeated softly, and extended her fingers through to him. Immediately, he let go of the rail with one of his hands and made a small fist around her little finger. She smiled indulgently, then winced as her finger was bent back. 'Now, now, there's no need to hang on like that. I'm not going to leave you, I promise.' She tried to withdraw her hand, but the baby held on to her finger tightly, still bending it further and further out from her hand.

And then Joan Steinbeck screamed as pain ripped up her arm and she heard the bone of her finger break with a sharp, distinct crack.